YOU HAVE NEVER R̶E̶A̶D̶ GRIPPINGLY HORRIFYING AS *DEADLY MEDICINE* . . . BECAUSE IT'S *TRUE!*

I swear . . . I will follow that method of treatment which I consider to be for the benefit of my patients, and abstain from every voluntary act of mischief and corruption, from whatever is deleterious and wicked; I will give no deadly medicine to anyone . . .

From *The Oath of Hippocrates*

"The ultimate responsibility of anyone in the medical field is to preserve life. And that is why this case is so bizarre, so unique, and so horrifying."

—Nick Rothe, Assistant D.A., Closing arguments, 1984

". . . Poisoned I.V.s, injections, and other life-threatening actions on Jones' part, made all the more reprehensible because they were committed against those unable to tell about it and done to make Jones appear heroic. . . . A chilling veracity . . . The book is striking for the feeling of horrifying powerlessness it provokes as Jones murders again and again."

—*Booklist*

Deadly Medicine

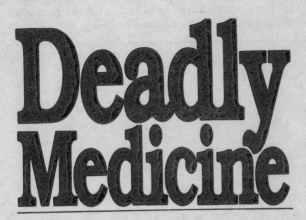

Kelly Moore
Dan Reed

ST. MARTIN'S PAPERBACKS

DEADLY MEDICINE

Copyright © 1988 by Kelly Moore and Dan Reed.

All rights reserved. No part of this book may be used or reproduced in any manner whatsoever without written permission except in the case of brief quotations embodied in critical articles or reviews. For information address St. Martin's Press, 175 Fifth Avenue, New York, N.Y. 10010.

Library of Congress Catalog Card Number: 87-38265

ISBN: 0-312-91579-9

Printed in the United States of America

St. Martin's Press hardcover edition published 1988
First revised St. Martin's Paperbacks edition/October 1989

10 9 8 7 6

To Chelsea McClellan
whom we know only through the memories
of those who loved her, and

To the Investigator
whom it has been our privilege to come to know.

I swear by Apollo, the Physician, and by all the gods and goddesses:

I will follow that method of treatment which, according to my ability and judgment, I consider to be for the benefit of my patients, and abstain from every voluntary act of mischief and corruption, from whatever is deleterious and wicked; I will give no deadly medicine to anyone, even if asked, nor suggest any such counsel; I will, with purity and holiness, pass my life and practice my art.

From The Oath Of Hippocrates

It was the last Friday of summer, 1982. Newspapers reported the funeral plans for Her Serene Highness Princess Grace of Monaco. World leaders focused on Israel's day-old military takeover of West Beirut. Movie theaters advertised *Poltergeist, Tron, Raiders of the Lost Ark,* and *E. T.* Chrysler sidestepped a UAW strike. Pan Am laid off 5,000 employees. The Dodgers won their seventh in a row, 9 to 2 over the Astros. And on that day, at 1:20 P.M., in the small Texas town of Comfort, fifteen-month-old Chelsea Ann McClellan died.

The pathologist who conducted Chelsea's autopsy found no clear cause of death and so concluded that the McClellans' baby had succumbed to "atypical Sudden Infant Death Syndrome," the label of choice for unexplainable deaths in apparently healthy infants. Three weeks later, however, a curious lab report persuaded the local District Attorney that the little blond-haired, blue-eyed girl had, in fact, been murdered.

Chelsea's death touched off a two-year investigation which eventually revealed that the child's killer, licenced by the state to care for her infant patients, instead had been poisoning them with deadly medicines. Department of Public Safety detectives soon discovered the same woman was connected to similar incidents in San Antonio, sixty miles to the south. In all, the deaths of over thirty infants and the near-fatal emergencies of more than sixty others would be attributed to this woman, though she would be convicted of only two crimes.

We first heard of these events one night in March of 1984, over two-and-a-half years later, when an old friend called from San Antonio to say hello. During the conversation, she mentioned a case she was involved with as an Assistant District Attorney, a case that by that time had been in the headlines of every Texas newspaper for over a year.

"But why would anyone want to kill babies?" we asked her.

"Well," she responded after considering for a moment, "I think she liked it."

We met the woman convicted of murdering Chelsea McClellan in December 1984, when we were just beginning our investigation. The woman we spoke with inside the Women's Penitentiary at Gatesville, Texas, surprised us.

She was then in her mid-thirties, plain, heavyset, quiet, with a pair of compelling, pale-grey eyes. Except for the baggy uniform worn by all the inmates of the Women's Penitentiary, she appeared in every way to be a perfectly normal mother of two. With convincing sincerity, she professed her innocence and provided reasonable explanations for the evidence against her. After five hours of conversation, we left the prison wondering how a jury could have found this woman guilty.

Since that meeting, we have communicated with almost everyone involved in this case, from the parents of the infant victims to the doctors and nurses who had been responsible for their lives, from the men who prosecuted and defended the accused to the jurors who sat in judgment. We read and cross-referenced 15,000 pages of documents. We found out more than we ever wanted to about medicine, the course of a criminal investigation, and the twisted thoughts in the mind of a killer.

What follows is a faithful and accurate rendering of the series of events that led to the death of Chelsea McClellan and the conviction of her murderer. It has been compiled from personal interviews, letters, declarations, memoranda, courtroom transcripts, secret grand-jury testimony, official statements, newspaper accounts, and medical records. To protect the innocent and the unwitting, we have changed a few of the participants' names and, in isolated cases, composited characters. To promote clarity, portions of some interviews and other quoted passages have been condensed or refined.

We hope you will discover in these pages, as we did, a true-life allegory about the nature of human evil and the possibility of choice.

Los Angeles, California
June 21, 1988

PART
1

The Addiction

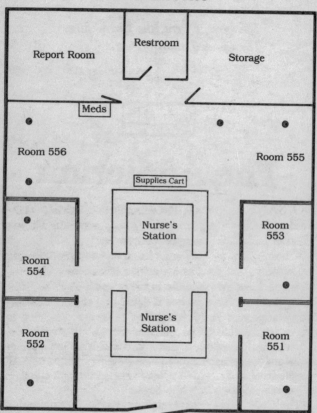

San Antonio's PICU

ONE

The bow is bent, the arrow flies.
The wingèd shaft of fate.

Ira Aldridge, On
William Tell,
Stanza 12

NO SANE MEDICAL PROFESSIONAL LOOKS FOR-
ward to a Code Blue emergency, but many will tell you
what an incredible experience it can be.

A hospital visitor may not even notice a Code Blue call;
the voice on the PA system always maintains a discreet,
calm tone. But every medic in the hospital hears it. They
know that it means a patient is dying of a cardiac or respiratory arrest and needs immediate treatment. The first to
arrive administers CPR. Another wheels in the nearest
"crash cart," a metal cabinet that contains all the medications and tools the doctors might call for. When enough
people have assembled—at least one doctor and a couple
of other medics—the battle begins.

The Code Team does everything medically possible to
save the life of the patient. They fight aggressively, even
brutally, racing against the progressive damage of oxygen
deprivation to vital organs—the kidneys, liver, heart, and
brain. The struggle can last a few minutes or can stretch
up to an hour. The medics surrender only when the Code
Team's leader determines that irreversible injury has oc-

curred and the body is no longer a habitable shell for the person that is slipping away.

A Code Blue demands the very best from its participants: split-second decisions, technical proficiency, absolute concentration, faith in one's skills. From the Code Team's leader, the senior physician present, it also requires a rare kind of courage—the ability to let go when the battle is lost. It is a responsibility that every doctor dreads facing, especially for the first time.

By the end of 1980, Dr. Kathleen Mary Holland had participated in many Codes during her four years of medical school and first eighteen months of a pediatrics residency. She had not yet, however, had to lead one. Each time, a more senior doctor had been present to take charge. Her turn finally came one predawn December morning, two-thirds of the way through a thirty-hour shift.

"Code Blue in the PICU."

The words woke Kathleen instantly; even in sleep some part of her mind was always listening, never quite relaxed. She shoved herself up off the bed in the residents' Call Room and headed down the corridor to the Pediatrics Intensive Care Unit (PICU). As she ran she willed her nerves to quiet, her heart to beat slower. She tried to second-guess which of her patients had gone bad, and why. She also prayed, as always, that a more experienced doctor would show up to run the Code. Without breaking stride, she pushed through the double doors of the PICU and cut toward the knot of medical personnel clustered around the bed in Room 553.

In 1980, Medical Center Hospital's Pediatric Intensive Care Unit filled a room not much bigger than a two-car garage. The six tiny glassed-in cubicles lining the side walls consumed the bulk of the floor space. The central nurses' station, surrounded by two chest-high counters, took up most of the rest. The cubicles housed eight cribs flanked by ranks of machines and monitors webbed together by a tangled network of wires. A dreary, hospital-green colored the Unit, broken only by the bright red of the crash cart standing in a rear corner of the room.

A PICU's patients are the hospital's sickest children. They are almost always drugged and often unconscious. Even so, they are routinely tied down with strips of gauze to prevent any movement that might dislodge a breathing tube, the leads of a monitor, or the fine intravenous needles embedded in an arm, foot, or scalp. The care administered to these tiny patients is exacting, with pharmaceutical dosages calibrated to the ounce of patient weight and all procedures scaled down for miniature organs and immature immune systems. The stakes for the PICU's medics are high—the survival of an infant who hasn't yet had a chance to experience what life has to offer. A Code Blue in a PICU is, therefore, perhaps the most frightening.

Kathleen was, at that time, 33, slightly older than most third-year residents. She had a serious manner coupled with an easy laugh, and carried the extra pounds of a schedule too busy for regular exercise. She wore her straight, dark brown hair short—severe and plain. Her broad, angular features reflected a Slavic heritage; her frank, pragmatic mannerisms spoke of her blue-collar childhood in Albany, New York.

Kathleen had started college late and hadn't finished until she was twenty-four, when she entered a joint Ph.D./M.D. program, preparing for a career in medical research. Shortly before completion of the doctoral program, an unexpected and trivial dispute with her advisor killed her hopes for a Ph.D. With only one year of medical school remaining, she suddenly faced the prospect of becoming a practicing doctor. She chose pediatrics as her specialty "because I found working with children, you didn't have to play the ego-games you do with adults." She then threw herself into the task of learning medicine as a practical science.

The habits of a researcher proved hard to shake. "She

was a lot more methodical than most," a nurse remembers of Kathleen. "She'd spend hours working on something like adjusting the rate and pressure of a respirator, for example, which the other docs just tossed off or left for us nurses." Kathleen tackled every problem with computerlike efficiency, amassing data, assessing the significance, calculating the solution. Some found her manner dry, even plodding, but she was uncontestably thorough. Her background had given her her own peculiar set of weaknesses and strengths; she came to the Code as well-equipped as any second-year resident.

Striding into Room 553, Kathleen joined three nurses and a nervous medical student at work on a four-to-five-month-old infant. A glance at the monitors told Kathleen—the only doctor present—that the patient was in the midst of a full cardiopulmonary arrest.

"I remember the med student was holding a mask attached to an ambu-bag—a manual respirator—over the child's face. A nurse I didn't know stood next to him, sliding a resuscitation board underneath the infant. Jorge Montoya* the Unit's male nurse, was doing external heart massage. And Genene was there, starting an IV. I was glad to see her; from what I knew of her work she seemed like a really good nurse, and she had a reputation for being good in a Code. Tough. You know, aggressive, quick."

"Vitals?" demanded Kathleen, stepping to the crib. Genene looked up and rattled off the statistics.

"I believe the patient was Jorge's," Kathleen recalls, "but Genene had all the information. She was the kind of nurse who always seemed to be on top of things."

The baby was suffering ventricular tachycardia—a rapid, irregular contraction of part of the heart muscle. He had limited cardiac output, fluctuating blood pressure, and

---

*Though all the people in this account are real, and all the events entirely factual, the names of some individuals have been changed to protect their privacy. An asterisk (*) in the text indicates the substitution of a pseudonym for a true name.

no spontaneous respirations. He was motionless, and very blue.

"What's this kid's weight?" demanded Kathleen as she brushed aside the med student with the ambu-bag. She slid a laryngoscope down the baby's throat so she could see to place the plastic endotracheal tube that would ensure a reliable air passage for the duration of the Code. She then attached the ambu-bag to the trache-tube and began to pump, allowing the deliberate rhythms of respirating the child to calm and order her thoughts. Her eyes flitting from monitor to monitor, she watched the baby's moment-by-moment progress.

"It's a difficult experience to describe," says Kathleen. "You're concentrating so hard, everything seems really intense and far away at the same time. And because the stakes are so high, it's easy to lose control. You get this speeded-up feeling and you have to stay on top of that, or your nerves take over and you can't think."

The baby had been admitted with an influenza that had left him severely dehydrated. Kathleen's immediate objective was to coordinate the boy's heart contractions and expand his volume of fluids to bring his blood pressure back up. Kathleen knew that medication was probably the best option to regain cardiac function but had to struggle for a moment to calculate the proper dosages for an infant this small. Her computations completed, she turned to Genene who was waiting with vial and syringe already in hand.

"I specified the amount of lidocaine I wanted—that's what we use to break the looping electrical impulse in the ventricle muscle that's causing the tachycardia. I also probably prepped sodium bicarbonate to counteract the acidity in the blood, and calcium chloride to strengthen the heartbeat."

Genene drew the medications almost as fast as Kathleen called for them from vials the nurse had already selected from the crash cart's shelves. Montoya injected the loaded syringes into the child's IV port.

"Lidocaine in," he called off. "Bicarb going in. Calcium going in."

Seconds melted into minutes as Kathleen waited for the various drugs to take effect. At the two-minute mark, the child's heartbeat was still erratic, his color had barely improved, and his blood pressure was still dependent on chest compressions. The drugs weren't working.

"You don't want to overmedicate the child by repeating the meds too soon, but you've got to keep moving. If something doesn't work, you try it again or go on to something else."

Kathleen was considering her options when the pattern on the cardiac monitor changed.

"We've got V-fib!" Genene reported.

The child's heart was now merely quivering, all of its electrical impulses firing randomly, lacking any coordination. No blood was being pumped.

"Prep for defib," Kathleen ordered.

Focus and duty shifted. The defibrillator was wheeled in and Genene checked to make sure it was grounded, turned on, and charged. She then squeezed two small dabs of silicon lubricant onto the electrode paddles and handed them to the doctor. "Prepped."

"I remember wondering," Kathleen later said of the moment, "'What the hell am I going to do if this doesn't work?'" The doctor took the electrodes and rubbed the pads together, spreading the lubricant evenly. She then positioned the paddles against the boy's torso—one to the right of the upper sternum below the clavicle, the other on the left side near the base of the lung.

"Clear."

The nurses pulled back. Kathleen pressed the trigger button. Ten watts of electric current coursed through the child, contracting every muscle in his body. The jolted heart sputtered into activity—a short sequence of coordinated effort—then faltered.

"Recharging," advised Genene, before Kathleen thought to request it.

Kathleen spread the lubricant for a second try.

"Clear."

Again the infant's heart sputtered, twitching in unsynchronized spasms; again it died out. Kathleen handed the paddles to Genene.

"Resume compressions," she ordered, considering whether the child could tolerate doubling the charge.

"I felt frustrated," Kathleen remembers. "I was doing everything right, by the numbers, and the team was working well together, but the boy wasn't responding."

"Time?" asked a deep, authoritative voice.

"I looked up, and Dr. Robotham, the Director of the PICU, was stepping through the doorway. I was both unnerved and relieved. I thought Robotham would take over."

One of the nurses reported the time—almost half an hour. The baby had been without a spontaneous heartbeat for a long time.

"Your patient's dying, Doctor," the Director commented. "What's your wattage?"

"I'm prepping a double now," Kathleen replied.

"Get on with it."

Kathleen shut the Director from her mind and turned her full attention to the child. "I was running out of time, but I knew the drugs we had pushed were still active, so I hoped the double charge would do it. I looked up to ask for the paddles and found Genene holding them—already prepped."

"Clear."

Once more the infant jumped with the current. All eyes focused on the monitor as jagged blips plunged across the screen.

"Sinus rhythm and holding," offered Montoya, as the monitor's peaks and valleys settled into a recognizable pattern. "Blood pressure rising."

"I watched the pattern a few moments more," Kathleen recalls, "afraid that it would break. Then I realized the baby wasn't going to die. You just can't imagine what that feels like. The relief. The pure joy. The terror you've been holding inside evaporates. You feel— To be in on a save is one of the most incredible experiences there is.''

Kathleen set the paddles aside, grinning her thanks to her team. ''I think we've done it, people.'' For a moment the assembled medics allowed themselves to share the victory.

''I don't remember much of what happened next, I'm sure after that I just took care of the things that needed to be done,'' says Kathleen. ''I probably put the child on a ventilator, and asked Montoya to put some Lanolin on the burns. I would have ordered ABGs—arterial blood gases, a blood test—and found the boy's intern to discuss further treatment.

''You always end up talking about it, reliving it, trying to get rid of the residual tension. I remember the med student congratulated me. I wanted to tell him it wasn't as hard as you think it's going to be, but that's not something you can really tell someone.''

Kathleen stepped out of 553 to the central counter where, as doctor in charge of the Code, she began to write up her account. ''Robotham came up and told me I'd done a good job. That meant a lot to me. I really respected Robotham, still respect him; he was a brilliant physician and a truly decent man. Some of the residents grumbled about him because he could be pretty hard-nosed—he wasn't afraid to embarrass people on rounds. He took medicine seriously. He worked harder than any other attending doctor and I guess he expected the residents to do the same.''

Genene also stepped up to congratulate the young doctor. ''I told her how much I appreciated her work,'' Kathleen says. ''She'd done a good job during that Code and every time I worked with her after that, she handled herself very well.''

A long-term working friendship had begun.

When Kathleen completed the Code's paperwork, she

went back in to check on her patient. Standing at the crib, she looked down at the child whose life she had saved.

"It takes a long time to learn how to be a doctor," Kathleen explains. "When you graduate from med school, you get the title, but just because they call you a doctor doesn't necessarily make you *feel* like a doctor. It takes a while to get your feet under you. Sometimes you feel like you're just playing a part, but then, gradually, that feeling goes away—you gain confidence in what you've learned and in your ability to cope with whatever comes along. I remember thinking that night that I was going to do just fine."

The Investigator

We understand that you aren't happy with the way this case turned out. Why?

Well, I think that we owe the public a tremendous apology for not having done a more complete job. We should've had a definitive, hard-core task force assigned for another year, possibly two. The investigators assigned to this case should have been given free rein, and we weren't. We were handicapped with all kinds of unnecessary protocol. But that's San Antonio. I tell ya, I've spent a career in the military, lived all over the world, and I've never seen *any* place where politics insinuates itself into every aspect of your life more than it does right here in this town. I think somebody decided to wrap things up way too early. I would have felt more comfortable if we had spent some additional time examining, and reexamining, two or three specific deaths, with the object in mind that a firm, knowing decision be made to prosecute or not to prosecute. That wasn't done.

We only got one murder conviction—just one, mind you. Admittedly, the evidence wasn't as strong in many of the other deaths, but in my mind it was very strong in a number of them. We clearly established Joshua Sawyer's death was a murder, and I think we should have moved ahead on that front. I don't accept the almost casual suggestion: "There doesn't seem to be enough."

Now, I'm not an attorney, so I can afford the luxury of not subscribing to their reasoning. But I'm not criticizing just the attorneys. I come down just as hard on investigators because, for us, the ultimate goal—our purpose, if you will—is to find out what happened. To establish the facts. To prove a case one way or the other by pulling together as much evidence as we can, regardless of where it falls into place. I believe very strongly that justice is the name of the game. When we allow anything to get in the way of the pursuit of that goal, we too become wrongdoers.

Did you see that Paul Newman movie *The Verdict?*

Yes.

You remember that woman who'd been driven out of nursing because of the altered document? She took the stand, looked over at the hospital officials, and said: "Who are these people? *Who are these people?*" Remember that? The same thing applies in this case: Who in the hell are these people?

If you're going to put yourself into the position of running a hospital, whether you're the top man or an assistant, you've got certain basic obligations, and those obligations include—first and foremost—taking care of patients. That's what a hospital is all about; that's what that Unit is all about: helping those little ones have as much chance as possible to grow up.

You sound almost bitter.

Bitter? Yeah, I guess I'm bitter. I don't think I can *begin* to articulate my bitterness about the way this whole affair was handled.

[THE SPEAKER PAUSED]

Have either of you any objection if I smoke?

No. Go right ahead.

You're sure? I don't want you nice people going back to California and sayin': "You know those damn Texans, they blow smoke in your face." You're not going to do that, are you?

No, no. We want you to be as comfortable as possible—you're going to be doing most of the talking. We've been told you know as much about this case as anyone.

I probably know more. You see, I'm really the only one who learned about the entire case, the whole nine yards: what-all went on here in San Antonio and what happened later, up in Kerrville. I was the investigator for both ends; the counties worked out some sort of arrangement. I spent almost two years looking into it, pretty much full time, so I'll probably have a lot to say about it, although just what exactly, I don't know. I just want you to know that although most of what I say is pretty well substantiated with hard evidence, some of it is opinion. I'm relatively opinionated, especially when things are meaningful to me—whether those things happen to be extremely good or extremely bad. I just want you to bear in mind that this is my perspective, and some people are going to disagree with me because they perceive things differently. I've been accused of sometimes hearing a different drummer. I choose to listen to the one I hear.

Most people involved haven't been so willing to share their thoughts. Why are you?

For me, the importance of the matter is in . . . I guess the bottom line is your book, okay, and the manner in which you put it forth. You need to get the whole story in there.

It's quite a puzzle. We were hoping you could fill in some of the holes.

I'll certainly try.

TWO

*Man's highest merit always is, as
much as possible,
to rule external circumstances and as
little as possible
to let himself be ruled by them.*

Goethe

IF ONE PLACE CAN BE SAID TO HARBOR THE
soul of Texas, it must be San Antonio. A sprawling,
friendly city built beside a spring-fed river on a branch of
the Chisholm Trail, its deep steel-and-concrete canyons
shade that holiest of Texan shrines: the remnants of the
Mission San Antonio de Valero, known in legend as the
Alamo. In 1836, 192 self-proclaimed "Texicans" chose
to hold the compound against the army of Generalissimo
de Santa Ana, more than 6,000 strong, in order to buy
Sam Houston the time he needed to save the Republic of
Texas. At dawn on March 6, after a lengthy siege, Santa
Ana's troops overran the mission. Every one of the de-
fenders died, but they took over ten times their number
with them. The martyrs of the Alamo embodied the virtues
and vices Texans still like to claim for their own: courage,
tenacity, sheer bullheadedness, strength, grit, fighting
skill, and the willingness to give one's life in defense of
one's ideals.

For most of the century following Houston's triumph
over Santa Ana's army, San Antonio based its commerce

around the needs of the cattleman. Following the First World War, the city increasingly allied itself with the nation's military. By the 1960s, one-third of San Antonio's economy was directly attributable to the five military bases that surround it.

In the 1970s, the city's leaders, in conjunction with state government, began to reshape San Antonio's future. With an eye toward a growing tourist trade, they worked to transform San Antonio into one of the nation's loveliest urban centers. They also took decisive steps to thrust the city into the international spotlight by staking a claim on the wide-open territories of biotechnological research and development. Texas intended to make San Antonio into its own version of California's "Silicon Valley." To that end, state and local government began the tricky task of preparing the facilities and building the reputation necessary to attract the best and the brightest medicine had to offer.

Civic leaders took up the battle. Mayor Henry Cisneros, San Antonio's first mayor of Mexican ancestry, co-opted the exciting promise of biotechnology as part of his platform. Money from all sectors poured into the University of Texas's Health Science Center (UTHSC) and the school's teaching facility—Medical Center Hospital located in the northwest outskirts of town. In little more than a decade, the medical school and hospital upgraded to state-of-the-art equipment and techniques, and the Health Science Center became spotted with faculty members of Nobel Prize stature. At the same time, the city built schools, laid freeways, and expanded the airport in preparation for the waves of foreign invaders—scientists and industrialists from the north—they knew would come.

In a small way, Kathleen Holland participated in this Yankee invasion. Her husband—a librarian at New York's Cornell University at the same time Kathleen was a student there—was lured south by a promising job at the San Antonio Public Library. Kathleen, on the brink of entering a doctoral program in New England, ended up applying to and enrolling in the graduate school in medical research at UTHSC. A year later, her application to the medical school was also accepted. Almost by accident, Kathleen had become a fledgling member of a medical community with a skyrocketing reputation.

In the beginning, Kathleen had dreams of remaining within the competitive world of medical academia. She had made a good start on this goal by pursuing her joint Ph.D./M.D. credentials, the value of which continued to rise as the University of Texas aggressively pursued the best faculty and facilities available. Kathleen felt confident she would be able to carve out a niche for herself like those occupied by the brilliant young men and women who served as both her teachers and as the hospital's physician administrators.

The falling-out with her Ph.D. advisor forced her to change her plans, but by then she was no longer willing to consider leaving Texas. Once she got used to the idea of becoming a practicing physician, she started looking at Texas cities and towns for a place to begin her career. Without knowing it, Kathleen was part of the earliest dividends Texas earned on its investment in San Antonio's medical community—she was one of the many bright, hard working, highly trained young doctors who would, for generations to come, provide quality health care for Texas citizens.

In the early months of 1981, Kathleen narrowed the scope of her search to the Texas Hill Country, a band of rolling hills laced with rivers and dotted with oaks and wild pecans. Stretching in a crescent from Waco in the north to San Antonio in the south and west halfway to El Paso, the hills mark the decline from the high, wide-open plains of northwest Texas to the low-lying delta lands that fan out from the Gulf of Mexico. In the spring, when the blue bonnets brush the Texas Hill Country with their vibrant color, there is nowhere more beautiful.

Kathleen conducted her investigation into the towns of the Hill Country with the kind of methodical thoroughness she had learned during her years of research. She picked out areas that had a substantial population of young childbearing adults who could provide her with a steady clientele. She checked into available hospital facilities and the presence or absence of other pediatricians. She drove hundreds of miles to take a look at the most promising locations—she wanted to find a place she could build a home.

By April, she had settled on a town called Kerrville, about sixty miles to the north and west of San Antonio, off Interstate 10. A retirement community nestled on the banks of the Guadalupe River; the town was growing rapidly and attracting an influx of young people looking to escape the city. The handful of doctors in Kerrville had encouraged her interest, promising her the use of the hospital facilities and spreading the word that a newly trained pediatrician would soon be joining the community.

Kathleen hired a business manager to advise her, signed a lease on an office still under construction, and began the long, slow, painstaking task of pulling together all the money, equipment, and supplies she would need to open her own pediatrics clinic. At that point, she still had almost a year to complete the task as she finished her residency with the Bexar County Hospital District. Even so, she had already begun to worry whether she had left enough time.

Dr. James L. Robotham represented another kind of return on the State of Texas's investment in San Antonio. He was the best that medicine had to offer, a young man with impeccable credentials, unflagging discipline, and real dedication. The plate on his office door named him director of Medical Center's Pediatric Intensive Care Unit. Inside, the plaques on the walls further identified him as the brilliant, compulsive doctor he was: medical school at Johns Hopkins; pediatrics residency through the prestigious Toronto's Hospital for Sick Children; chief resident at Boston City Hospital's Neonatal Intensive Care Unit; three years in an advanced program at Johns Hopkins; and at age 33, a full professor of pediatrics, anesthesiology, and physiology.

Recruiters from Medical Center and UT's Health Science Center first contacted him in 1978. They had a primitive, backwater PICU on their hands and needed a minor miracle to turn the situation around. Although Jim Robotham was young, he had the drive, the knowledge, and the ambition necessary to accomplish that miracle. The medical school and hospital made the best offer they could. The salary, of course, would not be comparable to that paid by private institutions, although the title—PICU Director—did have a certain cachet. The school and hospital promised to do what they could to facilitate Robotham's research in cardiopulmonary and developmental respiratory physiology. They also promised the young doctor complete support in his attempts to create a full, functional, multidisciplinary PICU.

In essence, the university was asking Robotham to leave one of the most respected and well-equipped hospitals in the world—Baltimore's Johns Hopkins, situated within an hour of Washington, D.C. and two hours of New York City—to take the helm of an understaffed, underequipped PICU in the relative cultural wasteland of south-central Texas. The prospect must have been daunting, but the challenge evidently held some appeal: Robotham and his wife decided to make the move. The young doctor and his small family arrived in San Antonio in March 1979.

Robotham's first priority had been to upgrade the PICU's equipment from its then nearly Stone Age 1968 levels. The job turned into a real education in political wrangling, but after a year it was almost completed and represented one of the few battles Robotham had managed to win. Every other objective the PICU Director set for his Unit remained outside his grasp because of the elusive cooperation of different departments within the hospital.

An obvious antagonism between the Surgery Department and Pediatrics had turned the PICU into a kind of no-man's-land. All of Surgery's infant patients were sent to the PICU to recover, placing them in the care of the Pediatrics Department, a situation the surgeons clearly did not enjoy. The surgeons therefore had little incentive to be receptive to the new young Director's instructions or innovations. Robotham had soon learned the frustrating truth: San Antonio was a very political town, and nobody trusted outsiders.

The Director found himself constantly at odds with certain members of the Surgery Department, particularly about the kinds of treatment appropriate for Pediatric patients. Robotham later bitterly reported that a resident once had to summon the Director to stop a surgeon from pulling a Swan-Ganz catheter from a critically-ill child because, the surgeon confessed, "I didn't understand it and it confused me."

"I have watched," Robotham complained to his superiors, "as staff surgeons delayed and delayed a child's shunt revision until the child was in extremis. I have listened to a doctor from Neurosurgery insist that a ventricular catheter cannot be used to lower intracranial pressure when I have successfully done so, consistent with well-established neurosurgical literature." For months, Robotham fought futilely to induce Neurosurgery to institute the regular practice of monitoring intracranial pressure, then finally gave up. Instead, he persuaded the residents to perform the monitoring without first attempting to obtain the consent of the neurosurgical staff.

Robotham had also struggled, largely in vain, to upgrade the educational and medicinal value of the teaching "rounds" conducted each morning in the PICU for the benefit of the medical students and residents. He recruited the generous help of Dr. David Littlefield from the Pharmacology Department, who daily made the effort to provide detailed information about pediatric pharmacology and drug interactions. Dr. Michael Lorring, a pediatric radiologist, also consented to be drafted for morning rounds, providing daily reviews of all X rays taken of the PICU patients during the previous twenty-four hours. Unfortunately, many of the doctors who rotated into the Unit as one of each month's two "pediatric attendings"—the pair of doctors primarily responsible for patient care in the Pediatrics Ward—resented Robotham's efforts to expand the importance of these regular 7:30 A.M. rounds. They were not prepared to make the time commitments Robotham expected, nor toe the lines Robotham drew.

The Director faced equally unpleasant battles with the nursing administrators. From the first, he had wanted to hire a teaching nurse who would be responsible for improving the skills of the PICU nurses. Creation of the position, however, required the consent of the top nursing administrators of both the hospital and the Health Science Center. Since neither side seemed inclined to talk to the other, Robotham served as mediator, making and modifying his proposal first before one party, then before the other. After months of patient lobbying, he finally obtained the go-ahead. He recruited the exceptionally well-qualified RN Shirley Menard for the position, only to have his victory snatched from him at the last minute. When Menard arrived, hospital administrators made her responsible for the education and training of nurses throughout the entire Pediatrics Ward, leaving her little time to focus on the PICU.

Since Robotham was unable to obtain outside help with the problem of educating his Unit's nurses, he undertook to solve the problem himself. He realized that the quality of nursing was one of the primary factors in his patients' survival. The nurses were the ones present twenty-four hours a day. They needed to be able to spot the small changes that could signal a baby's decline or an impending crisis. They needed to identify the problem and know what steps to take until a doctor arrived. Accordingly, the Director was determined to do what he could to broaden his nurses' knowledge of medicine. For the first time in the Unit's history, nurses were invited to join the residents and medical students on morning rounds, and Robotham actively lobbied the Night- and Day-Shift nurses to attend. For the Evening-Shift nurses, whose schedules did not permit them to join morning rounds, Robotham squeezed time from his overloaded schedule for "mock rounds" in the late afternoon. Five days a week, he escorted the nurses from crib to crib, asking them to provide patient summaries and prognoses, answering questions, encouraging them to be aggressive in their concern for patient care.

Throughout 1980 and into 1981, Robotham had a prize pupil on his nightly rounds, a nurse who showed unflagging interest, asked perceptive questions, and consulted medical texts on her own to obtain additional information. Though the Director wasn't aware of it, the other nurses sometimes referred to Genene Jones as Jim Robotham's "pet." It never occurred to him that he favored Genene; he fostered medical talent wherever he found it, and he truly thought of Genene as "the outstanding bedside nurse in the Unit."

The PICU's head nurse, Pat Belko, agreed with Robotham, if only on this single point. She, too, thought that Genene, in a crisis, was one of the Unit's finest nurses, although Belko had had her doubts when Genene first arrived on the floor in October 1978. At the time, Belko had been understandably concerned by the fact that Genene became too emotionally involved with her patients. The very first baby assigned to Genene's care had died, and her orientation nurse had reported to Belko that Genene "just went berserk." The new nurse moved a stool into the child's cubicle and sat staring at the body, sobbing for a good half-hour. Belko had seriously considered transferring Genene out of the Unit but had decided to wait and see. She was glad that she had; in the months that followed, Genene repeatedly impressed Belko with her dedication and drive.

For an LVN, Genene had an excellent understanding of anatomy and physiology and was endlessly curious about symptoms and treatments. One nurse recalls that Jones's ability to read and detect problems in a patient's EKG printout was particularly impressive. So too was her willingness to help other nurses with their patients. If at times she seemed somewhat insistent in her suggestions, she would, far more often than not, later prove to have been correct. She had the rare habit of arriving early for work and often staying late. She also, as everyone acknowledged, had an extraordinary gift with needles. Whenever Dr. Robotham needed an intravenous line started in one of the Unit's small patients, he always called for Genene. The babies' veins were both thin and resilient, and therefore difficult to target. Belko had seen some nurses reduced to tears as they tried, over and over, to penetrate the center of a tiny, wavering vein. Genene never seemed to have a problem. As they said in the Unit, "Genene could start an IV in a friggin' fly."

Because of Genene's obvious talent for medicine, both Belko and the Director had encouraged the nurse to return to school for her RN license, but Genene made it clear that she could not pursue that possibility. She had two small children to raise alone and a full-time job that she cared about passionately.

Genene was then about thirty years old. She was a heavyset 5'4", but not ungraceful in her movements and mannerisms. Her short, light-brown hair framed a long face with a small mouth, a large, irregular nose, and a pair of incongruously prominent grey eyes. Those eyes gave her face such a charismatic vitality that the various imperfections seemed almost unimportant. Her voice was soft, her laughter loud and a little raucous. She had a mannish force about her personality and seemed to emanate a sturdy kind of strength, but in fact, suffered almost continuously from a series of stress-oriented ailments.

Slowly, Dr. Robotham became aware that the combination of single-parent tensions and the pressure of intensive-care nursing was taking its toll on Genene. He spoke to Belko about it, asking her to assign Genene to the least ill patients. That lasted one week. Genene herself insisted that she be reassigned to the most critically ill. "I didn't trust the others," she later explained. "We were understaffed most of the time and many of the 3-11 nurses were GNs (Graduate Nurses), just out of school, and didn't know what to do if a kid went bad. And they do, you know. Go bad."

When Belko gave in to Genene's request, Robotham went over her head to the senior nursing administrator, Virginia Mousseau. He asked the administrator to make some arrangements to enable Genene to work out her personal problems without being forced to give up her job. Evidently, Mousseau felt Robotham was meddling in areas outside his sphere of authority. She referred the matter back to Belko.

By the spring of 1981, Robotham learned that Genene was increasingly the center of problems and controversy in the Unit. Residents complained that she attempted to order them around and tell them what medications to use. Some of the nurses clearly didn't like her and felt she took advantage of Robotham and Belko's interest in her.

In some ways, the problems Genene faced in the Unit mirrored those faced by Robotham. The Texan penchant for political maneuvering and factionalism manifested itself in a strong polarity of opinion about this talented nurse. Belko did her best to discourage the gossiping, and protect Genene from the unproductive hostility directed toward her, but Genene sometimes proved to be her own worst enemy. On one occasion Belko was obliged to place a fairly serious criticism in the nurse's employment records when Genene stopped by the Unit on her evening off to check on a very sick baby she had been caring for for several days. The Night Shift nurse complained to Belko formally about Genene's unorthodox behavior and the obvious "smell of alcohol on Genene's breath." Belko warned her friend not to repeat her mistake.

One nurse in particular—LVN Pat Alberti—set herself against Genene, refusing to share patients with her and routinely double-checking Genene's work. "Some of us thought she was doing things to make the people she didn't like—maybe I should say 'hated'—look bad. Like putting notes in the charts to make a kid look sicker than he really was and make the residents look like they were doing something wrong. It wasn't just me," Pat says simply. "Most of the residents couldn't stand her because, you know, she was so pushy, always trying to boss 'em around. Some of the residents got along with her okay, like Debbie Rasch and Kathy Holland, and that crowd. The rest, she just hated: the little Oriental doc, Liz Richards*. And Houghuis. Larry Houghuis. He wouldn't take any guff from Genene. You know, he was the kind of guy who's always real sure of himself, cocky, even back when he was just a lowly med student. Real handsome, and real funny. Our group loved him, but Genene just hated him. Genene could work up a powerful hatred."

Others saw a different Genene. Jorge Montoya remembers Genene as "a very good, highly experienced nurse." The Evening Shift's Charge Nurse said she "relied on Genenes's expertise a great deal, especially in handling the more serious illnesses." Others spoke of her dedication, her willingness to pick up an extra shift, or even stay late tending a patient past shift-change if she felt the child's stability was tentative. Such behavior was unauthorized, and Genene was written up for it once, but Genene was not the type to let minor administrative rules impede her efforts to care for her patients.

And Genene clearly cared for the infants in her charge. When Genene lost a patient, it was as if she had lost one of her own children. Paul Fulcher, a security guard at Medical Center Hospital, remembers escorting Genene to the morgue on several occasions. "She acted quite a bit differently from the other nurses—who were usually quiet and withdrawn. Genene, on the other hand, would moan and cry and rock the baby in her arms all the way down.''

Christopher Hogeda had spent more than half his ten mouths of life in Medical Center's PICU, suffering from a complex of congenital heart defects. At the beginning of May 1981, Christopher developed hepatitis and an infectious lung disease. The Unit's staff nursed him carefully, trying to keep him alive long enough to correct his problems surgically.

On May 21, shortly before 7:00 in the evening, Christopher slipped into cardiac arrest. Genene Jones, his assigned nurse for that Evening Shift, was the first to arrive. She began CPR.

Dr. Larry Houghuis was covering Pediatrics that night and took over the Code upon arrival. He quickly assessed the child, injected two rounds of cardiotonic drugs, and once resorted to the defibrillator, but the baby showed no signs of recovery.

Jones began to suggest medications. The doctor ignored her. She repeated herself, her voice rising and growing more frantic.

"Shut up!" Houghuis snapped at her, trying to concentrate. The boy was dying; nothing seemed to work.

Genene started in again, insisting that Houghuis administer specific medications. He resolutely refused to acknowledge her existence, asking another nurse to draw up what he felt were the appropriate drugs.

Genene started to hyperventilate, shrilly sucking in air, then lapsed into a full asthma attack. She sagged to the floor, wheezing and gasping, tears rolling down her cheeks. "Get her out of here," Houghuis snarled, still struggling to save the little boy.

Medics hustled in to carry Genene from the cubicle and out of the Unit. Behind them, Houghuis tried one last round of drugs. At 7:32 P.M., defeated, he stepped back and declared Christopher dead.

Four years later, the Investigator commented, "The best I can figure it, Chris Hogeda was the first."

The Investigator

Did you have an opportunity to investigate Genene's background? Or were you at all interested in that?

Yes, we were interested, but there were limitations imposed. We didn't want to go in there and just tear her family apart, but we did want to see if there was anything in her background that might shed some light on what happened later.

Genene grew up in the San Antonio area. She graduated from high school near her home in the northwest sector. She was born in 1950, and just a few hours after birth, she was delivered to Richard and Gladys Jones, her adoptive parents. Richard had, among other things, a billboard and bus-stop advertisement business. He was a big man—six feet, 240 pounds—sort of a freewheeling, jack-of-all-trades kind of guy. In the late fifties or early sixties, he built a supper club out on Fredricksburg Road—the Kit Kat Klub—by all accounts a nice place to eat and maybe do a little dancing.

He also built the family home—took a couple of

large house trailers and kind of built in the center portion between them. It looks like a real nice place, sort of countrylike. Great for bringing up kids: enough room for 'em to breathe, you know, but with the high school—John Marshall—still within walking distance.

Genene was described as being a real cut-up at school, real boisterous. She worked in the library and evidently just loved to push people around verbally. You know: "Do this, do that. Who in the hell do you think you are?" That sort of thing. She was remembered as being above and beyond the norm in the pushiness area. It was kind of a constant thing with her. Anyway, she was going with this guy and he liked her, and I guess she was about eighteen at the time. He was a year or two older and getting ready to go into the navy. So, Genene tells him, "I'm pregnant."

He says, "Okay, I'll marry you." So they get married not long after her father died of cancer. Pretty soon, it's obvious she's not pregnant and he says, "I thought you said you were pregnant."

She says, "I lied to you."

He says, "You didn't have to lie to me; I would've married you anyway. I love you." You know, it was one of those things. I talked with the guy and he appeared very sincere.

They were married for about five years and at first lived in a little cottage behind the mother's place. About 1970, he went into the navy. After boot camp, they moved to Georgia—to some small depot down there—to prepare him for several months' duty on an aircraft carrier in the Mediterranean. When he shipped out, she came back to San Antonio to stay with her mom.

When her husband got back, he was reassigned to Tennessee. They lived there for a while, and the marriage went through its ups and downs for two, three years. Their child was born in Tennessee—a son named David*.

The husband was next assigned to San Diego for several weeks' intensive training in preparation for a tour of duty off the Vietnam coast. While he was away, Genene—without advising him—went back to her mother's again.

In the meantime, her younger brother (also adopted) had blown himself up—apparently by accident—with a homemade explosive device. Kids get involved with this stuff—they put gunpowder in a can, it blows up, and in this case, it caused his death. This was difficult for her to take. From all indications, she was pretty close to her family, and particularly close to her adoptive father. Anyhow, during this rather troubled time she filed for divorce.

Her petition described her husband as a "man of violent and ungovernable temper and passion who had, on several occasions, struck her with great force." I was curious about that, so I asked him if he ever physically abused her. He said he had never struck her. Tell you the truth, I'm not at all certain he has the physical attributes to take on Genene. He's not a large man, and Genene Jones doesn't impress me as the type of person who would take too much crap from anybody. If they'd gone the distance a couple of times, my money would have been on her.

Anyway as a result of Genene's story the court granted an order that barred him from contacting either her or their baby. Two months later, the motion was dismissed because they had reconciled.

Let's see, they moved into a small house on North Broadway then, and Gladys, Genene's mother, financed Genene's enrollment in beauty school. After graduation, she worked for a period of time as a beauty operator or hairstylist or something out at a small shop in Methodist Plaza—right there in the Medical Center Complex. But she didn't stay too long with that. About '76 or '77, she quit her job, divorced her husband, and decided, "I want to be a nurse." Again backed by her mom, she enrolled in LVN school, a one-year program that teaches the basics of nursing. Apparently she did pretty well, and in the meanwhile, she became pregnant again. As best we could tell (without turning over a vast number of rocks), her second child, a beautiful little girl, was fathered by a guy she was close to in LVN school. We have a name and a number, but we weren't interested in pursuing the subject.

In September of '77, two months after her daughter was born, Genene took the state licensing exam for nurses and passed. She was given a position at Methodist Hospital but left after eight months due to a conflict with one of the doctors—he didn't like her attitude and wrote her up for "Improper and unprofessional conduct while on duty." She was asked to resign.

Genene's next job was downtown, in Community Hospital's Obstetrics and Gynecology Ward. After three months there she left to have minor surgery and never went back. In October of '78, she answered an ad for nursing jobs at Medical Center Hospital and, on October 30, spent her first day on the floor of the hospital's Pediatric Intensive Care Unit.

Some interesting events were related by her husband. Genene and her husband evidently didn't have a whole lot of money when they were first married, so Genene took it upon herself to take a couple hundred dollars in money orders from her father-in-law's cash register—he had a small convenience-type store out in the far northwest side of town. Of course he found out, and he was a little upset about it but just said, "You know, you don't have to do this."

Now, this is not a condemnation of her—and I really don't see that it's connected to later events, but it is a bit unusual. I guess what it illustrates is that she did the wrong thing. But this was the only real questionable wrinkle we discovered. Aside from the time she allegedly shot her brother-in-law in the leg when he threatened both Genene and her sister.

I usually don't look for things like this, but when the young man—again, I'm talking about her ex-husband—when he finally decided he was going to talk to me, he seemed to want to tell me everything, I guess. And to a point, he did talk about everything, although he did get hung up in one area. I forget exactly how, or why, or for what purpose . . . we were sitting in a coffee shop hashing this out, and I remember he implied that part of the reason they were divorced was because of something sexual in nature, but he didn't want to explain it. I respected that because I felt he was being straight with me. He hadn't wanted to be interviewed; we had to fish him out of the woodwork. But once I got him to sit down and talk, he was real helpful. I couldn't determine the veracity of all of his statements, but I had the *feel* that he pretty much opened up to me. Anyhow, the point is, it wasn't fun and games; it was a serious discussion. It was serious to him and it was serious to me.

He said that when he heard about the investigation, he was shocked. Of course, he hadn't seen her since the mid-seventies, when they were divorced. He's settled down now, I understand—about to get married again. He's left Genene and that part of his life behind.

I asked him if there was anything he knew about her that now, looking back, might help clarify her later behavior. He said no. He said, "I don't know that Genene had all her marbles back when I knew her, but I wasn't much better. We were just kids."

There's a lot of evidence these days linking child abuse with later criminal acts. Did you find anything to suggest that Genene was abused, or that she ever abused her own children?

We have no indication she physically abused her own children. In fact, she was portrayed as quite loving, although several nurses told us that when she worked in the PICU, the older boy would sometimes call the Unit and ask, "Mommy, when are you coming home?"

The problem was that she was working late afternoon/nights, very often coming in early and staying late. She was always an early bird at work—an hour early was not unusual for her. She wanted to know what was going on. She had an apartment and sometimes she'd leave the kids there alone, sometimes in the care of a babysitter. She evidently wasn't the most attentive of parents, but there's no suggestion that she ever abused her kids in a physical sense.

On the home front, we had information from different sources indicating that she was very close to her adoptive father. He was "Daddy" and was, evidently, just what daddies are all about. We did not conduct a neighborhood inquiry. We did not want to bring that down on the mother, who is a rather ill woman. The father's already dead; I mentioned that. Her other brother, I understand, also died from cancer at a relatively young age. And there was also a sister, but we didn't track her down.

I talked with one of Genene's good friends, a high-school classmate. They had been close, but this girl hadn't had any real contact with Genene since she'd gone into nursing. This woman was just shocked when she found out about all this. When I talked to her, she still couldn't believe that it'd happened. She had nothing but nice things to say about Genene: what a great person she was, what a loving person. And we heard this throughout the investigation, from many people.

James Robotham was one. Early on, about '79, '80, even early '81, Dr. Robotham thought the sun rose and set on Genene. He thought that she was one of the best nurses he'd ever met. He gave her a lot of his attention—teaching, answering questions.

In the fall of '81, when things had started picking up,

Robotham took off on a well-deserved vacation for, I think, a few weeks. You have to bear in mind that by then, the old 3—11 charge nurse, Pam Sturm, had already transferred off the Evening Shift, leaving nothing (besides Jones) but inexperienced graduate nurses running the 3—11. So there was a period of time when things were pretty much in the hands of Genene Jones.

Up to that time, Robotham thought that she was a very talented nurse. Then he started getting information that maybe there was something wrong. When he got back, by the middle part of October or the early part of November, things had deteriorated to a point where Robotham went to Dr. Franks who was, technically, his boss and told him: "We've got a problem."

THREE

But what does eternal damnation matter to him who has found, in a second, infinite pleasure?

Baudelaire, La Chambre Double

IN 1981, THREE NURSES REGULARLY WORKED the 11–7 graveyard shift in the PICU: Charge Nurse Tony Torres*, LVN Suzanna Maldonado, and LVN Pat Alberti. The other men and women standing the long, lonely hours of the Night Shift were agency nurses, or nurses from other shifts, or the Pedi-general ward, filling in when the regulars had the day off or the number of patients warranted. It was Suzanna and Pat who, day in and day out, kept watch over the Unit's babies when the rest of the hospital slept.

Despite clear differences in temperament and background, Pat and Suzanna were good friends. Pat was the aggressive, outspoken one, always entertaining her friend with dry, uncomplimentary assessments of their co-workers and superiors. Five foot four, with short blond hair and a heavy country-Texas accent, Pat was doggedly good-humored and cute in a spunky, adolescent way that still lingers, much faded. Like any intensive-care nurse, she was fiercely dedicated to her patients—one of the few characteristics she shared with Suzanna.

Suzanna Maldonado had a reputation for her quiet nature and good temper. Of Mexican ancestry, she evidenced a good deal more respect for the male-dominated medical hierarchy than Pat Alberti. The level-headed Suzanna became a natural sounding board for Pat's criticisms of the system or the doctors or the nurses or the weather. So, when Pat came to work on the first day of autumn and discovered that two of the Unit's four patients had died during the 3–11 Evening Shift, it was Suzanna she hunted down for a talk.

"It just seemed like too many kids were dying on Genene's shift," Pat remembers, "and that's what I told Suzanna. Time after time, I'd come on and one of the beds would be empty. Suzanna kind of agreed, so we decided to check the Book."

The PICU's Book was a statistical log regarding every child admitted to the Unit. Recorded in columns across a double page were, among other things, each patient's admission date and time, the entering diagnosis, each of the assigned nurses, and the date and time of discharge or death. During a break in their assigned duties, Pat and Suzanna sat down with the big blue Book and began to make notes. Working from the present back into the past, they scanned the entries for information on any PICU patient who had died in the last few months.

José Reyes was the most recent death, one of the two patients who had coded earlier that same night. The four-month-old baby boy had suffered two cardiac arrests in two days. The first occurred on September 20 at 10:50 P.M. The second, fatal arrest hit José at 7:45 P.M., just a few hours before Pat and Suzanna had come on duty. On both occasions, Genene had been the assigned nurse.

Only fifteen minutes before José's death, the Unit had lost another patient: René Cruz, a one-month-old girl. She died of a prolonged, unexplained bleeding episode.

Two-year-old Rosemary Vega had been admitted to the Unit on September 15 after routine surgery to remove a

constriction on an artery. The following day, under Genene's care, she suffered a fatal cardiac arrest.

Mark Oler, aged ten months, had two cardiac arrests on
the Evening Shift, one on September 3 and one on September 4. after the second arrest, he was pronounced dead
at 5:52 P.M. Although the arrests occurred while the baby
was in RN Carla Tieman's care, Jones had assisted with
both Codes.

On August 14 at 8:52 P.M., Patricia Sambrano, four
months old, died after her third cardiac arrest in two days.
All occurred while she was under Genene's care.

Terry Garcia, just three weeks old, spent her entire life
in the PICU. On August 5 she suffered her first cardiac
arrest; on August 6 she suffered her second; on August 7
she began to bleed uncontrollably; on August 11 she arrested and died at 6:15 P.M. Assigned nurse on all occasions: LVN Genene Jones.

On July 3, six-month-old Richard Nelson died after
three cardiac arrests in as many days. Assigned nurse:
LVN Jones. On June 15, José Estrada unexpectedly never
awoke after surgery, but instead arrested and died. He was
under RN Tieman's care, but Genene had been present at
his death.

On June 7, two-month-old Theodore Navarro died after
suffering two cardiac arrests in three days. Assigned nurse:
LVN Jones.

On May 24, five-month-old Feliciano Rodriguez died of
cardiopulmonary arrest at 7:14 P.M. Assigned nurse: LVN
Jones.

On May 21, ten-month-old Christopher Hogeda died of
cardiac arrest at 7:32 P.M. Assigned nurse: LVN Jones.

In five months the Unit had suffered nineteen cardiac
arrests with thirteen fatalities. Jones had been the assigned
nurse for eight of the thirteen deaths; for three others,
Genene had assisted with the final Code Blue.

The pattern was plain, even if its significance was not.
Pat whispered to Suzanna, "What are we going to do?"

Because of the way Medical Center Hospital was run at that time, Suzanna Maldonado and Pat Alberti were two of only a handful of people in the hospital who were in a position to spot this frequent connection between Genene Jones and the Unit's fatalities. None of the residents were likely to notice; their assignments rotated between the four institutions that composed the Bexar County Hospital District. They spent no more than two or three months each year at any one facility, and those were comprised of short rotations of four to six weeks. The frequent change in location was deliberate, intended to expose the young doctors to the widest variety of patients, maximizing their opportunity to cope with and learn about many different kinds of medical problems. "In 1981," Kathleen remembers, "I was assigned Medical Center's Pediatrics Ward three times: six weeks in January and February, four weeks in May, and another six weeks beginning in early September through mid-October."

The attending physicians—faculty members from the Pediatrics Department—also rotated in and out of the Unit. Interspersed with their teaching duties, research projects, and medical practices, they had one-month assignments in Medical Center's Pediatrics Ward once or twice a year. Dr. James Robotham was the only doctor who had any continuing contact with the Unit, and his attention to patient care was greatly diluted by the thousand-and-one frustrating tasks he faced as the Unit's Director.

The nurses, therefore, were the only medical personnel who witnessed the long-term fluctuations in the Unit's survival rates. And of all the nurses, none were so cognizant as Alberti and Maldonado. The Day and Evening Shifts had more frenetic paces: doctors wandered through on rounds or special visits; families came by to encourage their sick babies. Surgeries were performed, and most admissions or discharges made, during the Day and Evening Shifts. Consequently, these shifts had more nurses, more

activity, and more distractions from the long-term rhythms
of the Unit. On many nights, however, only Suzanna and
Pat were there, tending the patients, sharing the mundane
tasks, gossiping together through the quiet hours, watching
life ebb and flow through the PICU.

"We've got to take this to Belko," Suzanna responded
to Alberti's question.

"Well, she ain't gonna believe us. She knows I don't
like Genene. She'll just think we've got it in for her."

"It's all right here in the Book," Suzanna insisted
quietly. "She'll have to believe us."

Suzanna took the list to Pat Belko the next day. "But
she wasn't very interested," Alberti remembers. "She
said she'd look into it, then told Suzanna she wanted us to
stop spreading gossip about Genene. She said—and it was
true, I guess—that Genene always volunteered for the
sickest patients, so it was only natural that more patients
were going to go bad on her.

"But, you know, we just couldn't understand why *all* of
'em were dying on Genene's shift. I mean, why weren't
they dyin' on the Day Shift, or on our shift? Genene was
there every time. It just didn't seem right."

Even though Pat Belko had warned Suzanna against
spreading rumors, the Head Nurse took the matter seriously enough to make an oral report about it. As a result,
Belko and her supervisor, Judy Harris, spent some time
examining the Book, taking notes on admissions and the
overall number of deaths between June and September
1981. Harris remembers that after considering the acuity
of diagnosis for each patient and the continuing increase in
the number of admissions to the Unit, she and Belko concluded that the death rate was not unreasonable.

Neither Belko nor Harris produced any kind of written
memo or report concerning these events, nor did they in-
struct any subordinate to make further inquiries. Harris

also declined to file an official report about the matter with her superior, Director of Nursing, Virginia Mousseau.

After a number of days passed and Pat Alberti and Suzanna Maldonado saw that nothing had come of their complaint, they took their disturbing problem to the Unit's Director, Dr. James Robotham. In the interim, two more patients died. Three-month-old Paul Villareal was admitted to the hospital on September 22 for a low-risk cosmetic operation on his skull. The Pediatrics and Surgery Departments bickered back and forth whether to go forward with the scheduled surgery; Paul had been suffering some upper-respiratory congestion for several days and had had a temperature of 102 degrees on September 19. Pediatrics advised the operation be postponed; Surgery advised Pediatrics to mind their own business.

Paul arrived at the PICU at 11:45 A.M. on September 22, the operation completed. The Day Shift nurse noticed some tachycardia, or an abnormal speeding up of the heartbeat. The Evening-Shift nurse—Genene—reported seizure activity at 7:10 P.M. The following day, again under Genene's care on the Evening Shift, Paul arrested at 6:00 P.M. but recovered after the administration of lidocaine, dopamine, Isoprel, Dilantin, and phenobarbital. The next night, September 24, at 6:00 in the evening, Jones noted on the child's charts that he was "oozing everywhere." For more than an hour, Paul bled, his blood pressure dropping. Finally, at 7:10, he suffered a second cardiac arrest. At 8:30, he was declared dead. Genene sat listlessly in the corner of the Unit, staring at the floor. She was heard to ask, softly, "Why? Why did he have to die?"

One week later, on October 1, three-month-old Placidia Ybarra, admitted to the Unit with suspected congenital heart disease, suffered a fatal cardiac arrest at 10:10 P.M. She, too, had been in Genene's care.

Troubled by the statistics Suzanna and Pat presented him, Robotham informed his superior, Dr. Robert Franks, acting chairman of the Pediatrics Department. Franks instructed Robotham to take a look at the records of all the patients who had died in the Unit during the previous six months to see if he could discover anything unusual. "Let me know what you find." Robotham began the long, tedious task immediately. In the Unit, business continued as usual.

On October 10, José Flores suffered a cardiorespiratory arrest during a CAT scan at a little after 3:00 P.M. A second arrest at 4:39 P.M. killed him. Genene was in attendance for both events.

Beginning October 15, a Down's syndrome baby named Albert Garza developed a daily pattern of bleeding episodes during the 3–11 shift. Dr. Houghuis insisted Jones was overmedicating with a blood-thinning agent called heparin because she didn't know the proper dosage.

"Initially, I was called to the PICU to look at the child because his blood was not clotting," recalls Houghuis. "I was, of course, concerned, and because he had an arterial line (which is normally flushed with heparin), I checked the charts. An appropriate concentration was listed: half a unit per cc.

"I then examined the child and found by the bedside the equipment necessary to start an intravenous line. At that point I asked Nurse Jones if she was using any heparin in her IV flush solutions. She said she was indeed."

"At what concentration?" the doctor asked.

"A lot less than you do."

"And what is that, exactly?"

"One cc heparin to two cc's saline."

Dr. Houghuis stopped cold, unable to believe what he'd just heard. "What did you say?"

"I take one cc heparin and dilute it with two cc's saline, for three cc's total."

Dr. Houghuis was flabbergasted. The correct concentration was one-half unit—*one 2,000th of a cc*—of heparin per cc of saline. Genene had been using 500 units per cc of saline. Dr. Houghuis took a black, felt-tip pen and wrote out the proper formula on the bed sheet. He stood back, expecting some response.

"When I'd finished, she just looked at me with a blank stare for a moment, then walked away."

The next day, October 18, Robotham issued a new directive to PICU nurses concerning the use of heparin: "All injections of the drug must be witnessed." Albert Garza had no more bleeding episodes. For almost two weeks, all went well in the Unit.

On October 31, Halloween, two-month-old Cecilia Berlanga suffered three episodes of cardiorespiratory arrest before she died. Assigned nurse: LVN Jones.

The Investigator

*People we've talked to keep referring to a "diary"
Suzanna Maldonado kept. Can you tell us anything
about this diary?*

It wasn't a diary; it was a list of patients and the dates
and times of their death.

Was it similar to this chart here?

Yes, though this list is a bit more lengthy. Obviously,
when Suzanna approached Belko in the fall of '81,
some of these incidents hadn't yet occurred. This is a
more comprehensive look at the situation.

The key point concerning this chart is that we didn't
have to do any real digging to get at this information.
All of it was contained in what we call the Pedi-Book,
the Floor Book, the Unit Book. At the time of each
kid's admission to the Unit, all that information is
logged in. The symptoms and problem areas are also
logged, as is the diagnosis, the doctor assigned, the
time of admission, the time of reassignment to a less

intense unit or a discharge, the nurses assigned for his
or her care, the child's age, its temperature, weight,
and height—all that is logged into this big, multi-
columned book. "Expiration" has a column of its own.
When the book is opened, everything pertaining to that
kid is right there; left to right, all across the two pages.

DEATHS IN THE PICU
(January 1, 1981, through March 17, 1982)

Patient	Age	Date	Shift	Time	Bed	Assigned Nurse
J. Rodriguez	1 mo	Jan 01	7–3	1135	556-1	RN Johnson
A. Gutierrez	5 mos	Jan 15	11–7	0258	552	RN Maldonado
S. Miller	12 days	Jan 28	11–7	0700	553	RN Torres
D. Trujillo	1 mo	Feb 12	11–7	0050	552	RN Tieman
A. Garza	10 yrs	Feb 23	3–11	1700	551	LVN Jones
M. Santos	3 mos	Mar 21	7–3	0900	553	LVN Canady
M. Carrasco	2 yrs	Apr 16	3–11	1700	555-1	RN Hollenbeck
J. Estrada	2 yrs	May 08	3–11	2037	554	LVN Jones
C. Hogeda	10 mos	May 21	3–11	1932	552	LVN Jones
F. Rodriguez	5 mos	May 29	3–11	1914	551	LVN Jones
T. Navarro[1]	2 mos	Jun 07	7–3	1410	553	LVN Jones
J. Estrada	7 yrs	Jun 15	3–11	1557	551	RN Tieman +
R. Nelson	6 mos	Jul 03	3–11	1850	556-6	LVN Jones
V. Valenzuela	3 wks	Jul 07	3–11	1610	554	RN Peace
S. Gonzalez	7 mos	Aug 04	3–11	1820	555	RN Tieman
T. Garcia	3 wks	Aug 11	3–11	1815		LVN Jones
P. Sombrano	4 mos	Aug 14	3–11	2136	554	LVN Jones
M. Oler	10 mos	Sep 04	3–11	1754	549-2	RN Tieman +
R. Vega	2 yrs	Sep 16	3–11	1952	551	LVN Jones
R. Cruz	1 mo	Sep 21	3–11	1930	555-1	RN Tieman +
J. Reyes	4 mos	Sep 21	3–11	1945	551-1	LVN Jones
P. Villareal	3 mos	Sep 24	3–11	2030	551	LVN Jones
P. Ybarra	3 mos	Oct 01	3–11	2245	553-1	LVN Jones
J. Flores	6 mos	Oct 10	3–11	1734	555-1	LVN Jones
C. Berlanga	2 mos	Oct 31	3–11	2210	554-1	LVN Jones
M. Gonzalez	1 mo	Nov 01	7–3	0645	553-1	RN Maldonado
R. Gutierrez	2 mos	Nov 25	7–3	1402	551-1	RN Johnson
B. Souza	1.5 yrs	Dec 10	3–11	2000	555-2	RN Montoya +

DEATHS IN THE PICU (*cont.*)
(January 1, 1981, through March 17, 1982)

J. Sawyer	1 yr	Dec 12	3–11	2122	551-2	LVN Jones
M. Medina	4 mos	Dec 19	7–3	0925	551-1	RN Sturm
C. Olivarez[2]	4 mos	Dec 20	3–11	1558	553-1	LVN Benkert+
M. Zuniga	1 mo	Dec 21	3–11	1645	555-2	LVN Jones
D. Rios	2 yrs	Dec 22	3–11	2110	553-1	LVN Jones
P. Flores	9 mos	Dec 24	3–11	2035	554-1	LVN Jones
J. Lewis	2 mos	Jan 07	3–11	1730	554-1	RN Montoya
P. Zavala	4 mos	Jan 17	3–11	2150	551-1	LVN Jones
R. Gonzalez	1 mo	Jan 18	11–7	0304	553-1	LVN Alberti
A. Garcia	5 mos	Jan 22	3–11	2135	555-2	LVN Jones
R. Aguirre	6 yrs	Jan 31	3–11	1543	554-1	LVN Elvery+
F. Jimenez	1 mo	Feb 26	3–11	1813	551-1	LVN Jones
V. Williams	9 yrs	Mar 01	7–3	1228	551-1	RN Bailey
D. Noyola	4 mos	Mar 13	3–11	1810	556-1	LVN Benkert+
C. Baker	10 mos	Mar 13	3–11	2140	554-1	LVN Jones

[1] Navarro . . . . Jones was assigned to this patient on the 7–3 this date.

[2] Olivarez . . . . Jones had no patient assigned to her care this date; she signed out at 1743 hours and went home.

+ . . . . Although Jones was not the assigned nurse, she was present for this patient's death.

The information on this chart—an exhibit I prepared for Jones's second trial—is supported by each individual's medical charts which were scrutinized with a fine-toothed comb by some of the finest medical minds in the country, Dr. Murray Pollack of Washington, D.C.'s Hospital for Sick Children chief among them.

Murray is an interesting fellow. He's now the assistant director of the Intensive Care Unit at the Sick Children's Hospital. That man really worked for us. In his younger days, he'd been some kind of activist, I understand, and when we explained the case to him . . . well, he wanted to help. It meant something to him, you know? So he flew down and went through those records for days—hundreds of them. Then he went around and asked the doctors perfect questions—

right on the money—like he'd just handled the kids himself.

Anyway, the basic information is in that Floor Book, and that's Belko's book. She was the one in charge of the nurses in that PICU.

Why do you think Belko was supportive of Genene?

I can't give you a precise answer. I can give you an honest answer and hope that it's correct. Belko was protective of Genene because she thought of Genene as her protégé. She wanted Genene Jones to become an RN. Belko herself had made a very rapid climb up through the nursing ranks. Although she'd been a nurse for a long time at Medical Center Hospital, she'd become a Clinician-3 in charge of Pediatrics in a relatively few short years.

Several years earlier when Belko started, she was connected to the accidental death of a child through overdose. That was investigated by medical authorities from outside the hospital, which is the appropriate way to handle such a situation—it's better than an internal investigation because it brings in some element of independence—and she was absolved of any criminal wrongdoing. But the stigma evidently stayed with her for a while. Whether or not that background influenced her perception of Genene Jones or ongoing activities of a questionable nature in the Pedi-ICU, one can only surmise.

So you think Belko might well have had a predisposition of sorts, to be defensive on behalf of Genene because Belko herself had suffered through a period where she'd been the object of unfair gossip?

Possibly that had something to do with it. Possibly.

FOUR

*For the red blood reigns in the winter's
pale.*

Shakespeare, The
Winter's Tale, *IV. iii*

AT THE BEGINNING OF NOVEMBER, GENENE
Jones took a medical leave of absence. Records indicate
she underwent what was termed "minor abdominal surgery" and was off work for four weeks, from Sunday,
November 9, until Monday, December 7. During that
time, the Unit was quiet; not a single Code Blue, bleed-
out, or unexpected cardiorespiratory arrest occurred.
Though two of the Unit's patients passed away, no one
was surprised—both children had been admitted in the
final stages of a terminal illness.

For most of the staff members, if they noticed the drop
in the number of deaths and emergencies at all, it simply
seemed as if the PICU's run of bad luck had played itself
out. For others, however, like Alberti and Maldonado, the
coincidence of a Code-free month during the period of
Genene's absence had frightening implications.

Dr. Robotham, too, was now uneasy. On December 3,
he had completed his review of every death for the previous six months. His scrutiny of these case histories had

proven disconcertingly inconclusive. He had found no proof of deliberate or negligent wrongdoing; still, he could not account for Genene's frequent connection with the Unit's fatalities. The records he had studied showed that in each case, death had been preceded by symptoms that might foreshadow a sudden fatal decline. For virtually all these deceased patients, death was neither unexpected nor predictable—it was simply the possibility that had occurred.

When the Director of Pediatrics, Dr. Robert Franks, finished reading Robotham's Chart Review, he concluded that it did not substantiate the suggestion of possible nursing misadventure. He sent the report on to the hospital's chief administrator, B. H. Corum, with a note attached criticizing Robotham's spelling.

Within a week—three days after Genene's return, on Thursday, December 10—just after 7:00 P.M., a Code Blue sounded for the first time in thirty-six days.

Early Thursday morning, Bobby Souza's mother had taken her eighteen-month-old son* to Medical Center's Emergency Room. The ER medics admitted Bobby with severe abdominal pain and immediately sent him upstairs to the PICU. During the 3–11 shift, RN Jorge Montoya was assigned to care for the child.

An otherwise healthy youngster, Bobby had picked up a viral infection he had not been able to kick. He was dehydrated and listless but still had enough energy to raise hell when Montoya strapped his small arms so he wouldn't pull out his IV lines. Bobby fell into a peaceful sleep shortly before 6:00 P.M. Although Montoya's dinner break wasn't scheduled for another forty minutes, he asked the shift's head nurse—that night it was Charge Nurse Judy Anderson*—if he could start his break while Bobby slept. Anderson consented. She and Nurse Jones would keep an eye on the resting child.

Forty-five minutes later, Montoya returned early from

his supper. He spotted Genene at the nurses' station and asked her how Bobby was doing.

Genene shrugged. "He was fine last I saw him, but ask Judy; she was just in there."

Rather than interrupt Anderson, Montoya went in to check on the little boy himself. He saw immediately that Bobby had taken a turn for the worse. His skin had blued, he was limp, and his heart monitor showed a fitful pattern. Montoya turned to summon a doctor just as the boy's flatline alarm began to drone.

"I've got a Code in here," he yelled out the door, then whirled back to the bed to begin CPR. Genene rushed in with the crash cart, squeezing in beside Montoya to position an airbag over the baby's face. In another moment, the rest of the Code Team crowded into the cubicle.

For three-quarters of an hour, they fought. Several times Bobby's heart sputtered into activity, only to fail moments later. At 8:00 P.M., the boy was declared dead.

After Bobby's death, Anderson sent Jorge Montoya home. She also called and canceled the temporary nurse who was scheduled to help Pat Alberti and Suzanna Maldonado during the next shift. Two nurses would be enough to take care of the Unit's three remaining patients: an infant male suffering from a severe bronchial infection, the little girl in the cubicle next to him who had just come out of surgery, and an eleven-month-old boy who was comatose, a victim of smoke inhalation. His name was Joshua Sawyer.

Joshua had been admitted to the Unit two days earlier, on Tuesday, December 8, following a fire in his home. Fire fighters had managed to save him from the flames but only after he had inhaled enough hot smoke to coat his seared lungs with a thick layer of soot. When the ambulance delivered him to Medical Center Hospital, his bodily functions had all shut down—he had stopped breathing, his heart had stopped beating, and he had lapsed into a coma.

The Emergency Room personnel put him on straight oxygen and somehow got his heart pumping again. They then transferred him up to the PICU where the specialists transformed him into a human pincushion. Two IVs dripped low doses of Dilantin and phenobarbital into Joshua's bloodstream to alleviate the mild convulsions that periodically shook him. A third IV suffused him with fluids. An intracranial bolt measured the pressure surrounding his traumatized brain. A Swan-Ganz catheter, inserted through a vein in his neck down into his heart, monitored cardiac function. Joshua clearly was in critical condition, but a CAT scan showed his brain was still alive. Doctors were guardedly optimistic.

The prolonged oxygen deprivation undoubtedly had caused some brain damage, but with a child Joshua's age, such damage often proves completely reversible. The brain of an infant, unlike that of an adult, has the capacity to generate new growth. There was a good chance Joshua could bounce back. As the days passed, the boy's nurses watched carefully for any small signs of recovery.

Within 72 hours, Friday, December 11, Joshua's body had cleaned enough soot from his lungs so that he was breathing on his own. His mild seizures had ceased under the Dilantin. The doctors had even reduced the child's medications, considering him vastly improved. Although the pressure in his skull continued to fluctuate, they believed that if the boy just regained consciousness, he might very well recover.

At 7:00 P.M. that Friday evening, Joshua's newly assigned nurse called the resident on duty, Dr. Gonzalez, for assistance when Joshua's heart began to beat with rapid, irregular twitchings. "Genene told me," Gonzalez recalled, "that earlier that day, doctors had been forced to apply the defibrillator and inject Joshua with one full round of cardiotonics before his heart's fluctuations came under control. I suspected that the catheter in Joshua's heart might have shifted slightly, irritating the heart's walls, provoking the attack.'' Delicately, Dr. Gonzalez eased the catheter out a couple of centimeters.

Four hours later, at the end of Genene's first shift with Joshua, Pat Alberti entered the cubicle to find Genene talking earnestly with his parents, Mr. and Mrs. Sawyer.

''I heard her tell them that they shouldn't hold out false hope,'' Alberti remembers. ''She said that Joshua had gone a long time without breathing and that his brain couldn't have survived. She told them that it might have been better if Joshua *had* died, because if he lived, he'd probably have to be institutionalized.

''I couldn't believe it. I'd never heard anything like that in my life. Nurses aren't supposed to say those kinds of things to a patient's family. It's not our job. That's a *doctor's* job. And besides, I thought Joshua was doing pretty well; I thought he was going to make it.

''I almost went in and dragged her out of that room myself, but then I thought maybe I better get someone else to take care of that; at this point Genene and I definitely weren't very friendly. So, I went and found the Night-Shift charge nurse.

''I told her what was happening. I said that after 11:00, Joshua was my patient, and asked her to get Jones out of there.''

At 11:10 P.M., after some prompting, Genene Jones left the Unit, and Alberti went in to check on her patient. What she found infuriated her still further.

''His heart monitor showed a strange pattern, but he didn't appear to be in any distress. His tubes and monitor lines were tangled like spaghetti. There was a half-empty bottle of Plasmanate lying on his medication tray, and I couldn't find any orders for it. There were two replacement bottles of IV solution in there that weren't even the right kind. If I'd have used those bottles without checking, I might have hurt that baby.''

Alberti and the Charge Nurse straightened the room, then spent the better part of a half-hour unraveling, tracing, and marking Joshua's lines. Their careful checking revealed that the monitor's transducer dome (which converts the heart's contractions into electronic signals) was not properly screwed into the back of the console. They corrected its alignment, and Alberti was reassured when a good, steady pattern appeared on the instrument's screen.

"I volunteered to write up an Incident Report," says Alberti. "I figured that Belko and Robotham probably needed a reason to transfer Genene out of the Unit and this seemed pretty good to me. But the charge nurse told me she wasn't going to write anybody up. All she did was put a little note in the log."

Encapsulating the incident, the charge nurse wrote: "Transducer noted to be not plugged in."

Alberti kept close watch on Joshua for the rest of the night. Through the late hours and into the morning, Joshua continued to rest comfortably. At the end of her graveyard shift, Alberti worked up her nerve and then approached the Unit's supervisor, Pat Belko, who had just arrived for the 7–3 shift-change. Alberti complained about the irregularities in Jones's care of Joshua: her conversation with the boy's parents, the disconnected transducer dome, the presence of inappropriate medications, and the unmarked, tangled lines.

"She told me that she was sick and tired of all the gossip and rumors. I guess she figured I was out to 'get' Genene and, you know, she always liked Genene for some reason. Genene was kind of like Belko's 'pet.'"

Like the charge nurse before her, Belko, too, declined to file a report.

Genene resumed charge of Joshua the following afternoon. During the intervening sixteen hours, neither Pat Alberti nor Susan McKinney (the baby's nurse on the 7–3 shift) had experienced any difficulties with Joshua. On the

3–11, however, he again began having problems. In the early evening, Genene noted on Joshua's chart her observation of a Cheyne-Stokes respiration pattern—the breathing rhythms commonly exhibited by dying patients gasping after their last breaths. At 7:50 P.M. she wrote: "Asystole preceded by bradycardia," indicating she had observed a brief cardiac arrest preceded by a slowing in Joshua's heart rate.

Less than thirty minutes later, Joshua's heart stopped altogether. Genene called a Code Blue. The emergency team swung into action, massaging the small chest, administering drugs, trying every trick they knew to shock Joshua's heart into resuming its work.

Joshua pulled through, but his heartbeat was weak, irregular. His attending physicians ordered a blood test to check the level of Dilantin in his bloodstream. The small, controlled dosages he had been receiving were intended to alleviate his coma-induced convulsions, but high concentrations of the drug can sometimes trigger heart failure. If he was having liver or kidney trouble, the drug could have accumulated in the boy's system. In that event, an immediate blood transfusion would be necessary to dilute the Dilantin.

Lab Technician Tony Ferinacci got a preliminary reading at 9:34 P.M. Joshua's Dilantin level was off the scale. A normal therapeutic range is 10 to 20 micrograms of Dilantin per milliliter of blood; Ferinacci's test could measure only up to 55 mg/ml. He recalibrated the machine to measure a greater quantity, then carefully ran a second test. Nine minutes later he pinpointed the level at 59.6 mg/ml, the highest he had ever seen. He immediately phoned the PICU.

The Unit's secretary remembers that Genene was standing at the desk when Ferinacci called. "I told the technician that we probably wouldn't be needing the results, and at that point, Genene, who was very angry, grabbed the phone, told him 'He's already dead!' and slammed the phone back down."

Before Ferinacci had even begun his tests, Joshua had suffered a second, fatal heart attack. The little boy was gone.

The Sawyers were told that Joshua had suffered a kidney failure that had allowed a toxic buildup of medication in his system. They left the hospital believing that the fire in their home had killed their son.

Pat Alberti was badly shaken by Joshua's death, but didn't know what to do about it. Suzanna Maldonado had already complained to the Unit's head nurse about Genene, and to the Unit's Director. Gossip had it that, as a result, Dr. Robotham was checking into the deaths in the Unit. The administration had been notified and was taking action. Alberti decided to keep her mouth shut and see what happened.

On Tuesday, December 15, at the beginning of each shift, every PICU nurse read and initialed a new directive in the nurses' log. Henceforth, all deaths and arrests in the Unit would be reported to both the PICU Director, Dr. Robotham, and Pediatrics specialist, Dr. German. Just four days later, Nurse Pam Sturm sent the first report. At 9:25 in the morning, on December 19, a four-month-old baby girl died after a difficult fight against hepatitis. Robotham scrutinized Sturm's account but found nothing unusual.

The next day—the eve of winter—a report of a second death landed on the Director's desk.

Four-month-old Carlos Olivarez had been in the PICU for several days. His family doctor had sent him in for a routine operation to correct a congenital defect in his intestines. In preparation for his surgery, the Unit's doctors had dedicated several days to reducing the inflammation and distension of his belly. On December 20, Carlos finally seemed healthy enough for the procedure, so he was sent up to the operating theater. Surgery began at 11:00 A.M.

As he worked, Surgeon Thomas Chapman explained the

simple procedure to the young doctors who observed or
assisted him. He removed the faulty section of the boy's
small intestine, patched together the cut ends, then stitched
the incision closed. Afterward, he sought out the boy's
parents to inform them that the operation had gone well
and that their son should have no more problems. When
the wound healed, Carlos would be better than new. Only
a mysterious scar would remain, with which someday he
could impress his friends. By mid-afternoon, Carlos had
been returned to the PICU.

Because Carlos seemed quite stable, Nurse Belko assigned Sally Benkert* to care for him on the Evening
Shift. Sally was still fairly new to the Unit and a little
unsure of the ICU protocols. She would probably still have
been out on the Pedi-General Ward if her friend, Genene,
hadn't persuaded her that the PICU was much more exciting and fulfilling work. Since Sally had transferred into the
Unit, Genene had done everything possible to teach her
the skills one needs in intensive care, but even though
Sally did her best to emulate Genene in all ways, she
would never be as adept a nurse. Belko compensated by
assigning Sally the easier patients.

Carlos turned out to be less stable than Belko had anticipated. Within a half-hour of shift-change, Carlos's
heart monitor went flat. The Code Team was unable to
revive him. He was pronounced dead at 3:58 P.M. His
parents refused an autopsy. Their baby had been through
enough.

Two hours later, Genene signed out and went home
with Charge Nurse Anderson's approval. No patient had
been assigned to Genene's care that day, and now the Unit
had one patient fewer. Anderson saw no point in having
Genene sit by with idle hands.

The next day, winter arrived in earnest. A cold rain
washed San Antonio, slowing traffic and dyeing everything grey. The downpour did not, however, prevent the
daily visit of Marilyn Zuniga's parents to the PICU.

Marilyn had been in the Unit struggling with a serious infection for six days—almost one-quarter of her lifetime. On December 21 at 4:25 P.M., shortly after the Zunigas left, Genene called a Code Blue for the little girl. Twenty minutes later, at 4:45, the Code crew gave up on Marilyn and went back to other duties. Genene unhooked the body from the monitors and pulled the IV lines. She then wrapped the baby in a blanket, called Security for an escort, and carried the body down to the hospital's basement morgue—the Cold Room.

Marilyn's parents wanted to know why their daughter had died, so they requested an autopsy. The medical examiner's radio-immune assay on the child's brain tissue revealed the presence of digoxin, a heart stimulant which, in large quantities, can cause heart failure. The drug's presence was minute—1.95–3.9 nanograms per milligram of tissue—but there was no notation in the child's charts indicating digoxin had been prescribed. It was possible, the examiner surmised, that the stimulant had been administered but not recorded during the frenzy of the little girl's final Code. In any event, because the amount was so small, mere billionths of a gram, the examiner decided the drug's unexplained presence was insignificant. He noted the cause of death as: "Cardiopulmonary arrest secondary to presumed sepsis [the uncontrollable spread of poisons from a localized infection]."

The day following Marilyn's death, Genene chose to look after a little girl named Dora Rios, whom Genene had cared for once before. Dora had been in and out of the hospital many times during her two years of life—many of the nurses had treated her at one time or another. Born with severe problems in her gastrointestinal tract, she had been subjected to multiple surgical procedures to correct the irregularities.

On December 21, Dora had returned to the Unit, suffering from diarrhea, dehydration, and possible peritonitis—a serious abdominal infection. She was placed in the bed in which Sally Benkert's patient, four-month-old Carlos Olivarez, had died the day before. The admitting physician prescribed IV fluids and an intense course of antibiotics.

On her second day in the PICU, under Genene's care, Dora was seized by an unexpected cardiorespiratory failure. She died at 8:12 in the evening. Genene remained with the deceased child, as always, preparing the body for the trip to the Cold Room. Before calling Security, she lifted Dora from her bed, cradled her in her arms, and for almost an hour, sat rocking the lifeless baby, crooning a wordless melody.

When Pat Alberti came on at 11:00 P.M. and found Dora's bed empty, she tracked down the child's charts. The final entry, in Genene's dark handwriting, read:

> A LEGEND IN HER OWN TIME. MERRY X-
> MAS DORA. I LOVE YOU.
>
>   JONES LVN.

"I showed that note to Suzanna. She didn't know what to do about it any more than I did. I couldn't figure it out. Why wasn't someone doing something about Genene? Three children had died in as many days; Genene was writing this weird stuff in the medical charts; she had started singing to the dead kids. I didn't know what to think.

"I figured I had to tell someone else—someone outside the Unit. Since I had been talking with one of the hospital's doctors—a psychiatrist—about some problems I was having coping with my teenager, I decided to tell him about Genene on my next visit. I thought that, as a doctor, he would be powerful enough to get something done. I also figured that he'd have to keep my name out of it because of doctor-patient confidentiality. I didn't want to be thought of as the one who's always blabbing, you know?"

On Christmas Eve, just two days after Dora's death, another of Genene's seriously ill patients died. Nine-month-old Paul Flores had been admitted with meningitis. At about 8:00 in the evening he began to bleed profusely. His blood pressure dropped, then his heart stopped. He was pronounced dead a little after 8:30 P.M.

In the span of fourteen days, the Unit had experienced seven deaths. What would later become known as the PICU's "Epidemic Period" was in full swing.

The Investigator

Why, when nothing was done, didn't anyone go outside the hospital and talk to the police?

All I know is that no one did.

I was talking to Murray Pollack about it once. He works in Washington, D.C., and he said, "You've got to understand the mentality of a large, bureaucratic institution. The cardinal rule is: 'Thou shalt not go outside administrative channels.'" He said everyone learns the lesson early that if you have a problem or complaint, you fill out the right forms and send them to the proper higher-ups. Then you let them handle it.

Some of the nurses told us that on different occasions, they did talk to some of the doctors, but those doctors for the most part just attributed it to personality conflicts among the nurses. According to Belko, the Unit's head nurse, it was all: "They're just jealous of Genene."

You have to bear in mind the residents' relationship

with that Unit is limited. They're there on a month's rotation and then they're gone. During that time they may see one or two kids die, but that's nothing out of the ordinary in and of itself. No resident was there constantly for six months or even three months. They weren't around long enough to pick up on the chain of events.

The attendings are available in case of emergency but otherwise they only come through on rounds—you know, when you go from patient to patient to patient with your handful of students. Robotham complained for some time that a good number of the pediatric attendings were more inclined towards research and/or their own writings than they were towards direct patient care. The most many of them did was fulfill a requirement that they had to review a patient's medical charts after a discharge or an expiration. How well they did that is a matter of debate. Look at the Sawyer case. That kid had an obviously toxic level of Dilantin present in his system when he died.

Didn't they explain the Dilantin concentration? They said it was due to kidney and liver failure.

Over a year later I asked Pollack—who was a devastating witness in the Santos trial—to take a look at that boy's charts. Murray didn't even have a question. He told me, "This kid was poisoned. Someone gave him a massive injection of Dilantin between 7:00 and 8:00 P.M."

And nobody even looked into it?

No, they didn't. I don't think they ever had any idea how to deal with it. It's like they couldn't accept what they were seeing. But in my mind, they should have stopped it with Joshua Sawyer. None of those other kids should have died.

FIVE

*His cries rent my heart, providing some
kind of sensual pity which I craved.*

Maurice de Guerin, Nouvelle
Revue Française

THE HOSPITALS IN SAN ANTONIO PROVIDE
medical care for a lot of Texas. For thousands of square
miles, San Antonio is the only community big enough to
support large, state-of-the-art medical facilities. Austin,
the state capital, is San Antonio's nearest neighbor, 80
miles to the north. Houston sits 200 miles to the east; Cor-
pus Christi, 150 miles to the southeast on the Gulf; and
Laredo, 150 miles to the southwest on the Rio Grande at
the Mexican border.

Fifty-five miles south of San Antonio, on the road to
Laredo, a sign designates a small cluster of homes as the
town of Pearsall, population 7,400. In the winter of
1981, thirteen of Pearsall's residents lived in the Santos
household: Esubio, Jesusa, and their eleven children.
Esubio was a farm laborer. Jesusa sold her own homemade dolls.

Late Christmas night after all the confusion of the holiday festivities, Jesusa finally found a chance to sit quietly
with her newest son, three-week-old Rolando. She saw
immediately that his slight cold had grown worse and so

decided to take him the next day to the clinica in nearby
Dilley.

The morning of December 26, Jesusa called her niece,
who had a pickup truck, to ask for a ride. Together, they
took Rolando to the tiny clinic that afternoon. The harried
medic told Jesusa not to worry, the baby had a cold. He
gave her a prescription and suggested that she wait a few
days, then bring Rolando back if he got worse instead of
better.

In a matter of hours Rolando was noticeably weaker, his
lungs more congested. Concerned by her son's continuing
decline and dissatisfied with the treatment he had received
in Dilley, Jesusa persuaded her husband that Rolando
needed to visit a doctor in the city. The next morning,
Esubio helped his wife and youngest son into the niece's
truck for the hour's drive north.

The doctor who examined Rolando at the Brady/Green
Walk-In Clinic that afternoon diagnosed possible pneumonia. He immediately started two IVs pumping the
antibiotics ampicillin and Gentamycin into Rolando's
bloodstream. The doctor then advised Jesusa and Esubio
to check their son into the county's hospital. With their
consent, he arranged for an ambulance to carry Rolando
the seven miles from downtown San Antonio to Medical
Center in the northwest outskirts of town. Rolando
was admitted to the PICU at 4:30 A.M., Sunday, December 27.

Dr. Dolores Majors, the admitting resident, followed
standard procedure for a probable pneumonia patient: she
attached Rolando to a ventilator that assisted his breathing,
adjusted his antibiotics, and then took blood and cultures
so the morning's attending physician could confirm the diagnosis. Dr. Majors assured Jesusa and Esubio Santos that
although Rolando was very sick, the treatment for pneumonia was virtually foolproof. If that was what Rolando
had—and she thought it was—then he ought to be fine
within the week.

Jesusa and Esubio spent the predawn hours of Rolando's

first night in the Unit dozing on the green plastic couches down the hall from the PICU. At about 7:30 A.M., December 28, Dr. Lorraine Barnes met with the Santoses to report that their son did indeed have pneumonia—specifically, trilobar pneumonia, meaning infection was present in three of his lung's five lobes. Dr. Barnes reassured the Santoses by repeating Dr. Majors's assessment: though their child's illness was very serious, it was also quite treatable. The doctor asked to keep the boy in the PICU until the course of antibiotics took hold. Satisfied that Rolando was now being well cared for, Jesusa and Esubio headed home.

Rolando remained behind, attached to a respirator, a naso-gastric tube, an arterial line to measure blood pressure, and three IVs. An apnea monitor kept track of his respirations, and a cardiac monitor recorded his heartbeat. He was semiconscious, his color was good, his vital signs stable, and his skin warm and dry. RN Carla Tieman, the first nurse assigned to Rolando's care, remembers thinking that this child was one patient who was sure to be just fine.

Since Jesusa and Esubio could not afford to make the trip into San Antonio each day to be with their baby, Jesusa made arrangements to keep in touch with the Unit by telephone. Because the Santoses had no phone of their own, they gave the Unit secretary their neighbor's number and promised to check in each day.

On the morning of December 29, when Jesusa made her first call to the PICU, the nurse relayed reassuring news: everything seemed to be progressing well. Six hours later, Genene took over Rolando's care.

At 8:16 P.M., Genene noted in Rolando's chart: "Questionable seizure activity with tonic [indicating stiffness or rigidity] movements of arms, and nystagmus [jerky, twitching movement of the eyes], followed by a flaccid appearance." Two hours after that, Rolando had a heart attack.

The Unit secretary, Mrs. Baxter*, contacted the Santoses who, in turn, called their niece to borrow the truck. By the time they reached Medical Center, Rolando's emergency was over. A medical resident explained that, following the injection of various powerful medications and a jolt of electricity, Rolando's heart had started up again. Since then, he had been stable.

The resident frankly informed Jesusa and Esubio that the doctors were baffled by the boy's setbacks. The results of a lumbar puncture failed to explain either his seizure or his lethargy, and a toxicological screen had not identified any trace of harmful drugs in his urine. In an effort to account for Rolando's strange symptoms, the resident suggested to the Santoses that their son might have an enlarged heart, or perhaps a hole that interfered with blood flow. Deeply worried, Jesusa and Esubio returned home.

On Wednesday, December 30, and Thursday, December 31, Jesusa's calls to the Unit elicited encouraging news: though Rolando had at times been quite upset and had a strange problem with irregular and heavy urination, he appeared to be improving. The nurse told Jesusa that her son would be going home in just a few more days.

Then, on Thursday's Evening Shift, after an uneventful day, Rolando again began to urinate excessively. Unlike his earlier bouts of diuresis, which seemed to taper off, this time the problem continued and grew worse. He became dehydrated. His blood pressure plummeted. His breathing grew labored and shallow. He slipped into a coma. The resident on call ordered Rolando's assigned nurse, LVN Jones, to resume mechanical ventilation and up the oxygen concentration. He added yet another IV drip to help maintain the boy's blood pressure.

At 11:15 P.M., Genene Jones went home and RN Margie Peace took over Rolando's care. She remembers: "He looked sick. The more tubes and wires, the sicker they are, and he had a lot. Overall, Rolando had been getting better, but when I got him, he wasn't doing very well at all."

As the New Year grew several hours old, Nurse Peace watched Rolando grow stronger. At 4:30 A.M. she noted in his chart: "Patient now very alert and awake. Appears to be in no distress."

Despite the holiday, Dr. Robotham was at his desk on January 1 shortly after sunrise, contemplating the problems left over from 1981. He realized he was losing the battle in the PICU. The gossip and feuding was completely out of hand. In the past few months, the Unit had lost some of its best nurses. The residents and med students seemed uncomfortable with their tours through Pediatrics and certainly less than enthusiastic. Robotham was also getting less support and cooperation from doctors in other departments. The teamwork and professionalism he had tried for so long to encourage had simply evaporated. Now it looked as if he might lose his position as well.

As of the first of the year, the Unit officially had a new Co-Director, Dr. Victor German. A short, eccentric man, full of humor, German was a popular member of the Pediatric faculty. Robotham liked and respected Victor German, but he was not looking forward to sharing his title as Director of the PICU with him. For two years Robotham had been begging for help with the Unit. Now it seemed he finally had some, but not the kind he'd had in mind.

On January 1, the day Dr. German began his duties as PICU Co-Director, he also started a one-month rotation in the Pediatrics Ward as one of the two attending physicians. The second pediatric attending was Dr. Ken Copeland. Since 1979, Copeland had been Medical Center's first assistant professor of pediatrics under Dr. Robotham. He had been the administration's first choice for Co-Director of the Unit but he had rejected the appointment for two reasons. First, he felt Dr. Robotham was doing a terrific job and, second, he was already too busy. Tall, angular, and distinguished, Copeland added a flamboyant presence to the ward.

During the last six days of December, Dr. Robotham had debated with himself whether or not he should tell the two new attendings of his growing uneasiness concerning certain nurses and the deaths in the PICU. He did not want to prejudice the doctors, to cause them to look for problems where none existed. Yet, uninformed, they might not spot unusual incidents. The fatality total for the last month of 1981 ended the debate.

Before German and Copeland's first shift, Robotham spoke with the two doctors in general terms about the kinds of problems the Unit had been experiencing. He suggested that they keep an eye out for any patient who suddenly took a turn for the worse or who suffered from seizures or bleed-outs that could not be easily explained. Neither Copeland nor German were surprised by Robotham's concerns. By that time, nearly every doctor in the hospital had heard rumors of the PICU's recent problems.

Kathleen Holland was one of the few who had not. She had not set foot in Medical Center for months. In November she had worked at Santa Rosa, in December at the Brady/Green. Now she was starting the year with a six-week rotation back at Santa Rosa. "I didn't hear about what happened to Rolando Santos," she says, "until the middle of 1983, when I read about it in the newspaper, like everybody else."

At 7:00 A.M. on January 1, Dr. Copeland took over attending's responsibility for Rolando Santos.

"As I recall, Rolando had been making steady improvement and continued doing well through the first half of the day. That afternoon, he was breathing so well I decided to remove his endotracheal tube and make him more comfortable. He was given a dose of Decadron, an anti-inflammatory agent, and he immediately began having a rather massive episode of diuresis—his urine output increased dramatically. He became paler and his heart rate slowed. His condition subsequently worsened into a hypotensive episode, that is to say, his blood pressure dropped to dangerously low levels. Eventually he stopped breathing and became unresponsive to stimuli—he went into a coma.

"Over the next few hours we stabilized the boy's blood pressure and circulation by keeping him perfused with fresh blood and volume expanders, but we were puzzled. We couldn't really understand why he'd had this rather massive urine output in the first place. Up till then, he had been doing very well. The following day we discussed it and thought that maybe the Decadron had been responsible—a possibility if Rolando's system was, for some reason, severely deficient in adrenaline. So, to check this theory, we gave him another small dose of Decadron. Nothing happened."

Something was wrong, very wrong. The child had been admitted six days before with pneumonia, and yet, in the last three days, he had suffered two cardiac arrests, two seizures, and at least two severe bout of diuresis. "It was a strange feeling," Copeland remembers. "I felt, momentarily, unsure of precisely what I should do."

Copeland resolved to keep a closer watch on the child and decided to make sure the whole Unit knew about it. The Unit secretary was told to inform everyone involved in Rolando's treatment that henceforth, Dr. Copeland was to have a daily report on the boy's progress.

For three days, Rolando grew stronger.

At 3:00 P.M. on January 4, Genene Jones again took charge of Rolando. The nursing notes Genene placed in the boy's chart indicate that, in the early evening, the infant became cyanotic—his nail beds and mucus membranes showed a bluish discoloration. She also recorded the results of an arterial blood–gas test which showed extreme metabolic acidosis (an accumulation of acid in the blood due to decreased oxygen metabolism in the child's tissues). To counter this acidosis, she raised the ventilator's oxygen concentration. Her notes record that his color improved.

Shortly thereafter, Genene noted in the charts that Rolando began to bleed sluggishly from various injection sites. After an hour his bleeding evidently slowed, then finally stopped.

For the next twenty-four hours Rolando had no problems, but Genene's notes for January 5 document another surprising setback at 6:00 P.M. His urine output again soared, his heartbeat accelerated, his blood pressure dropped, and his eyes twitched spasmodically. Fortunately, by shift's end, he was again stable. The nurses who watched over Rolando during the next two shifts experienced no problems. The last note, left by Susan McKinney, Rolando's nurse on the 7–3 shift on January 6, was positive: "2:30 P.M.—Color remains pink."

Less than four hours later, just after 6:00 in the evening, Rolando again began to have problems. Genene noted that he was oozing blood from his ankle—at the arterial line's insertion point—and from some of his other not-yet-healed wounds. By 7:00 P.M., he was bleeding freely from all his puncture sites. Genene summoned Dr. Richard Freese, the resident on call for the evening.

When Dr. Freese arrived, Genene directed his attention to the odd symptoms she had noted in Rolando's charts the previous evening. She then took the liberty of suggesting a possible diagnosis that accounted for the earlier symptoms as well as the child's present profuse bleeding.

"She told me she thought it was DIC—Disseminated Intravascular Coagulopathy," Dr. Freese later informed investigators. "I remember thinking, 'I suppose it's possible. I've never heard of DIC in a patient recovering from pneumonia, but nobody really knows that much about DIC.'"

Freese quickly reviewed what he had learned about the mysterious syndrome. A patient suffering from DIC bleeds, sometimes copiously—as a hemophiliac might. In the body's capillaries, the patient's blood cells randomly begin to clot. Circulation slows, the blood thins, and the finite number of available clotting factors decreases. The body's ability to dam its wounds diminishes. Blood oozes from unhealed injuries or, in more severe cases, from the body's fine mucus membranes. Usually, a bleeding episode follows some inciting event or overwhelming infection. Occasionally, it is associated with brain injury, and now and then it occurs in obstetrics. As far as Dr. Freese knew, Rolando did not fit into any of those categories. Still, the child was bleeding. Whatever the cause, it was imperative to replenish the circulatory system's clotting factors with an infusion of fresh-frozen plasma as soon as possible.

In Rolando's case, the infusion of plasma had no effect. He continued to bleed freely. At 7:16 P.M., Rolando's heart ceased to function. A nurse called the Santoses and informed them that their baby had, regrettably, passed away. Esubio made arrangements to drive north one last time.

At 7:59 P.M., after three full rounds of cardiotonic drugs and forty-five minutes of vigorous CPR, Rolando's heart at last resumed its work. After another twenty minutes his bleeding lessened and he stabilized. Stunned, the Unit secretary called the Santoses' number again, but the child's parents were already on their way.

The next day, Dr. Copeland received word from the lab confirming what he had suspected and feared: a great deal of heparin, a powerful, commonly used anticoagulant, had been in the boy's system, although the exact amount was not known. "I was aware," the doctor remembers, "that the boy had an A-line that was routinely flushed with heparin to keep it clear, but low-dose washes could not explain the kind of massive bleeding this boy had struggled through." Quietly, Dr. Copeland circulated through the Unit, asking several nurses how such a medication error might possibly occur. No one had any idea.

"I became convinced that Rolando had received more

than just a small, accidental overdose of heparin,'' said Copeland. ''It was at this point I began asking myself what I would do if it happened again. I decided to remove his A-line—thus eliminating any reason whatsoever for heparin to be used on the boy, and vowed that if he should start to bleed again, I'd give him protamine, heparin's specific antagonist.''

That afternoon, Pat Belko posted a notice instructing the Unit's personnel to ''Keep all bottles of heparin in the Medication Area, not at the patient's bedside.'' Mrs. Baxter recalls hearing Nurse Jones disparage the notice: ''Don't they think we know what we're doing?''

After Rolando's near-fatal emergency, Day Shift's Nurse McKinney took special pains to document the improvements she noticed in his condition. Her notes for Saturday, January 9, report that his skin was pink, his eyes equal and reactive, his fever down, and his A-line sutures dry. The congestion in his lungs was finally clearing. He was awake and alert much of the morning. He was, for the first time, hungry. ''I was happy for him,'' she said later. ''He was clearly through the worst of it.''

Around 3:00 P.M., as McKinney gave Rolando a sponge bath, she checked him carefully from head to toe. She found that when she squeezed his heel, it oozed slightly from the many punctures. She recorded the oozing in the chart, notified Dr. Copeland, took a sample from the area, and sent it off to the lab. On the way downstairs, the sample of blood clotted, eliminating the possibility of DIC. McKinney left at 3:30 P.M., confident Rolando was on his way to recovery.

At 4:00 P.M., Jones's nursing notes state that Rolando remained as McKinney had left him—stable and doing well. Just twenty minutes later, however, the boy was bleeding freely from all puncture sites. The first resident to arrive, Dr. Morena* incised an artery near Rolando's right elbow to obtain fresh blood for an accurate clotting study. Dr. Freese personally carried this sample of blood to the lab and placed it in the refrigerator, requesting the test be run as quickly as possible.

By 5:00 P.M., Rolando was in serious trouble. One shocked intern who witnessed the event reported: "Everywhere he had ever been scratched with a needle was just, well, bleeding, like a fresh, deep wound; blood was just coming out, trickling out from everywhere." Rolando was bleeding from his eyes, ears, nose, mouth, fingernail beds, rectum, penis, and from around his endotracheal tube; undoubtedly he was bleeding internally as well.

By 6:00 P.M., the results were still not back from the lab. Rolando's blood pressure was as low as the nurses had ever seen in a patient who was still alive. Plasma, packed fresh blood cells, and other volume expanders had not affected the boy's continuing loss of blood. According to Genene's notes, Rolando also exhibited subtle seizure activity, including lip smacking, rapid twitching of the eyes, muscle tension, and spasmodic convulsions.

The Unit's secretary located Dr. Copeland at home and apprised him of the situation. He excused himself from dinner and raced to the hospital. Esubio and Jesusa were also notified by the secretary and once again rushed north.

Just before 7:00 P.M., Dr. Copeland arrived at the hospital to join the residents in what appeared to be a death watch. Rolando lay limp, the ventilator pushing his bluish chest up and down.

"I found the boy to be hypotensive [his blood pressure was very low], and he was rapidly becoming hypovolemic [losing more blood than could be replaced]—his vital organs weren't receiving the necessary volume to remain perfused and functioning. He was grey, he was ashen, and despite applied pressure to numerous sites on his body, he continued bleeding freely. I was sure he would, very shortly, have a cardiac arrest and die.

"At that point," Dr. Copeland later reported, "I did two things. First, since we had been having some difficulty obtaining enough blood for laboratory studies, I performed a femoral artery puncture. I stuck a long needle into the large artery in the boy's leg and sucked out 10 or 12 cc's—a significant amount—specifically for lab studies. I then inserted a very small, tiny-gauge needle into a scalp vein.''

Standing over the child, Dr. Copeland paused momentarily. He strongly suspected Rolando had somehow been overdosed with heparin, but he couldn't be sure. If the boy's bleeding *wasn't* due to a heparin overdose, injecting protamine would be worse than useless. If Copeland's suspicions were incorrect, an overdose of protamine sulfate would kill the child.

''In my mind,'' Copeland explained, ''I had no choice.''

The endocrinologist drew up a vial of protamine and slowly eased 100 milligrams into the punctured scalp vein. He took several minutes to empty the syringe, infusing the child's system with enough protamine to counteract a massive amount of heparin. Nothing happened. Rolando's bleeding continued unabated.

Copeland drew up a second 100 milligrams. He pushed the potential poison a drop at a time until he had again emptied the syringe. Once more, there was no change. Whispers passed through the gathering audience.

''I was scared to death,'' Copeland recalled, ''but I was convinced that this was right, so I persisted.'' He drew up a third syringe.

Genene left the room. At the nurses' desk, Mrs. Baxter, the secretary, overheard her complaining about the doctor's tactics. ''She appeared to be very anxious and sort of, well, sort of disappointed by what was going on.''

The crowd at the cubicle's windows collectively held its breath. Slowly, Copeland began to inject the fresh syringe into Rolando. A third of its contents disappeared, then Copeland stepped back. A murmur washed through the audience. Rolando had stopped bleeding.

The amount of protamine needed to end Rolando's bleeding episode—230 milligrams—would later prove the child had been given an enormous overdose of heparin. A safe dosage for a child his age and size is about 125 units; Rolando had received at least 15,800 units, over *127 times* the safe amount.

Before returning home to his interrupted dinner, Copeland ordered Rolando removed to Pediatric's General Ward down the hall.

Shortly before 9:00 P.M., Jesusa and Esubio were allowed into the cubicle. Jesusa remembers that Rolando seemed terribly frail, nothing like the baby she had nursed before Christmas. "His skin was blue and hung loose on his bones. I thought he was going to die."

At the 11:00 P.M. shift-change, Jones briefed Alberti, informing her that Rolando had been bleeding, his blood pressure had bottomed out, he'd had to be reintubated, and he had, for a time, appeared lethargic. As she was leaving, Genene also mentioned that the administration of protamine had corrected the child's bleeding problem. "If he has any further oozing," she suggested, "you might want to try a little more."

That night, Dr. Copeland tried to think of some rational, medically understandable explanation for Rolando's episode. "It was annoying somehow; I was confused. I couldn't believe this was really going on. I called a pediatric hematologist, Dr. Paul Zelzer, in the middle of the night, and I said, 'Paul, tell me, please tell me, is there any possible explanation for this other than heparin administration? Could protamine correct DIC? Could it possibly correct some undiagnosed congenital hematological clotting abnormality?' He said no."

The next morning, when Nurse McKinney arrived for the 7–3 shift, she found Rolando awake, alert, and looking around. McKinney was still taking care of Rolando when Dr. Copeland returned that afternoon. Discovering that his earlier order had not been carried out, that Rolando was still in bed 553, Copeland turned to address the entire Unit: "I said I want this baby out of here, and I want him out *now*!"

Within minutes Rolando was rolled out of the PICU and admitted to the ward for less critically ill children.

By that evening, Rolando was breathing well enough that he was taken off the ventilator for the first time since his admission. Four days later, on January 14, after receiving care from nurses personally selected by Dr. Copeland, Rolando was pronounced recovered and sent home.

No one from the hospital ever mentioned to the Santoses that their son had been overdosed with heparin, probably on several occasions. For months, Esubio and Jesusa would worry about their baby's condition, convinced that he was suffering from some physical defect. Finally, in August 1983, they scraped together enough money to take Rolando to a heart specialist. The doctor assured them that there was nothing wrong with the boy's heart, nor was there any evidence to suggest his heart had ever had a hole or any other structural defect. He was a fine, healthy youngster.

That left only one thing from Rolando's stay at Medical Center Hospital for Jesusa and Esubio to worry about: the bill for $18,931.72.

Two days after Rolando's last crisis, Dr. Copeland confronted Dr. Franks and demanded something be done about the PICU's many problems. The acting chairman of the Pediatrics Department promised Copeland that he would get someone to look into it.

Franks called in Virginia Mousseau, the Health Science Center's director of nursing. A twenty-four-year veteran, Mousseau was tough and pragmatic; Franks knew she would be sensitive to the administrative issues involved. The chairman asked Mousseau to find out what she could from her nurses, to talk with Belko again and with the charge nurses. While she attended to that task, Franks intended to look over a few medical charts to see if anything caught his eye.

Franks also visited the hospital's executive director, B. H. Corum, to report on the situation. The Director asked Dr. Franks what he planned to do about Copeland's complaint and seemed satisfied when Franks outlined the plan of action he had arrived at with Mousseau.

Coincidentally, when Franks left the hospital that evening, he bumped into Marvin Dunn, dean of the university's medical school, on his way out to his car. Franks took the opportunity to tell Dunn, also, of the PICU's problems. Dunn did not seem unduly concerned. Like Corum, Dunn asked Franks to keep him informed.

The Investigator

He turned five this year. I call up now and then, see how he's doing. Favored red cowboy boots last time I saw him. Nothing wrong with him. No side effects at all. A miracle.

Have you ever thought about why a person would do such a thing?

Sure, I've thought about it. I'd guess everybody's thought about it.

I'm convinced that Genene had the desire to create a situation in which she became the heroine, and she knew enough about medicine to be able to do it. She'd take a look at the new admissions to find a kid with potential problems. Then, over the next few days, she'd write down some bogus symptoms. When an emergency occurred, no one was surprised. She *created* the situations.

I don't think it was her intent to zap a kid permanently, but to get him to a point where there was a crisis. She had a pretty good idea what effects the drugs she used would cause, so she knew exactly what measures to take and how to bring that kid out of it. She hit 'em with the CPR and hit 'em with the ambu-bag and, you know, got the right drugs in there, and brought the kid around. Then: "World, here I am, I've done it again."

She wouldn't say that, but she desperately wanted to hear others say it. And others did say it. Carla Tieman said it continuously, even after the first conviction. She said it right up, well, almost right up until she went into court to testify during the second trial.

She told you how good she thought Jones was?

Oh yeah, how miraculous she was, how great she was, how aggressive a nurse she was, how she really did know much more about treating a dying, almost-but-not-quite-yet-dead infant than the doctors did. A lot of those who'd seen Genene in action there in the PICU "saving kids" told me later she was one of the best crisis-nurses they'd ever seen. She really knew her stuff.

Sally Benkert was another that said this about her, although Benkert can in no way be compared with Nurse Tieman. Tieman was almost your perfect nurse—if you're dying, this is the lady you want doing her damnedest to save you. She'd know all the proper dosages to administer in just the right combinations to treat the infection or the seizure or the weakness or the system failure or whatever your problem was.

Pam Sturm was also very supportive of Genene. She was close to Genene. We had expected to have some trouble obtaining her knowledge of Genene Jones and the events in the PICU, and that proved to be the case. Pamela was a *great* nurse. I mean, she *knew* kids. She wouldn't condone anyone harming a kid, I'm convinced of it, but she also just couldn't believe that her friend, Genene Jones, would ever intentionally harm anyone, most certainly not a little, helpless child. She couldn't believe it. In her world, she and Genene saved lives.

Another part of it, I'm sure, was the fact that as long as Pamela was the floor supervisor, that is, working right there on any given shift with Genene Jones, there were no problems. In the summer of '81, Sturm transferred off the Evening Shift to the 7–3 Day Shift. When Belko transferred her over, that left—on the 3–11 shift—any number of inexperienced graduate nurses without a charge nurse. This facilitated, intentionally or not, a virtual takeover by Genene Jones on the 3–11.

Notwithstanding the fact that Genene was an LVN (and not credentialed to be in a supervisory position), she was the aggressive one, she was the experienced one, so she ran the 3–11. Every nurse up there told us that. There were nurses up there who quit, directly because of Genene Jones.

Was it clear from your investigation that no one else participated in creating the emergencies, that no one else shared in Genene's aberration?

Yes, it was absolutely clear. Absolutely. If aberration is the right word, I've never seen it in any person in my life to the extent that I've seen it in Genene Jones.

SIX

Did you expect a corporation to have a conscience, when it has no soul to be damned and no body to be kicked?

Edward Thurlow

TWO DAYS AFTER ROLANDO'S DISCHARGE, ON January 16, four-month-old Patrick Zavala underwent open-heart surgery. Patrick had a small hole in the wall between the right and left ventricles of his heart. With each cardiac contraction, blood that should have been pushed from the right ventricle into the lungs passed uncleansed directly into the left ventricle and into the stream of outgoing blood. Since birth, Patrick had been suffering from a lack of energy and periods of hyperventilation coupled with minor respiratory arrests.

The corrective surgery was relatively simple, but to perform it, the surgeon needed to stop the patient's heart, then restart it with a jolt of electricity once the muscle had been sewn together. Patrick's parents and pediatrician had been reluctant to subject him to this trauma, so they had waited to see if the hole would close on its own.

As the months passed, however, and Patrick's problems continued, the pediatrician decided it was time to intervene surgically. He advised Patrick's parents to take him to the experts at Medical Center Hospital. At 8:15, the morning of January 16, two young surgeons—Drs. Kitten and Bennet—opened Patrick up and sutured the hole in his heart. The Cardiothoracic Surgery Division Chief, Dr. Kent Trinkle, remembers observing the operation. He thought it uneventful, smooth—"first class." He was confident the boy would recover completely.

Late in the day, Surgery released Patrick to the care of Pediatrics, and he was assigned to the PICU's bed 551. To ease the stress on his irritated respiratory system, he was intubated and attached to a ventilator. IVs fed him antibiotics and anesthesias.

During Patrick's first full shift in the Unit, the 11–7 Night Shift ending on Sunday, January 17, LVN Eva Diaz kept close watch on him. Because of a recent personal loss, Eva had a special fondness for the tiny male babies in her care. Highly competent, hardworking, and easy to get along with, Eva was a popular member of the Unit's nursing staff. She had been with the Unit almost since its inception and brought a wealth of experience to her care of Patrick.

At the beginning of her shift, Eva undertook the slow, uncertain task of adjusting the ventilator's oxygen level and rate of respiration to obtain a perfect match with the child's own natural rhythms. By mid-shift, she had worked out the adjustment: the little boy seemed to be doing fine. At shift-change his vital signs remained strong. Eva labeled him "stable" and went home confident she had seen Patrick through the worst.

During the day, Patrick remained stable as the doctors and nurses gradually eased back the respirator's Breaths Per Minute (BPMs), letting the boy's diaphragm take on more and more responsibility. He appeared to be healing nicely. That night, Dr. Ng, the physician assigned to care for Patrick during his stay in the Unit, received a call from Nurse Jones.

"She told me that shortly after they had taken Patrick off the respirator, at about 6:00 P.M., he had developed some difficulty breathing. Evidently Dr. Morena, the resident on duty, had ordered Patrick reintubated and put back on a ventilator. Genene said that when the tube was replaced, she'd noticed that Patrick was not responding to the pain of intubation—he hadn't gagged reflexively, which is the normal response. She said she thought the lack of response indicated the possibility of neurological damage. So I told her to increase both the oxygen concentration and the BPMs and said I would be right in.''

Jones followed Dr. Ng's instructions, and Patrick improved. Jones, however, then sought out Dr. Morena and insisted he send the child to Neurology for a CAT scan.

"I told her," Dr. Morena recalls, "I didn't see any reason to take a patient who was recovering from surgery and cart him down to a different floor of the hospital for a neurological test that didn't have anything to do with his diagnosed medical condition."

The child stayed.

A short time later, on the other side of the PICU, Jorge Montoya called a Code Blue. His assigned patient, Raymond Gonzalez, a child very sick with meningitis, had gone into cardiac arrest.

For the first time anyone can remember, Jones did not jump in to help.

When Morena went to assist with the Code, Jones approached a doctor from Neurology who was at the nurses' desk, completing notes on another of the Unit's patients. Jones outlined to the physician Patrick's earlier lack of gag response and suggested a CAT scan. The neurologist knew that Morena was tied up in a Code, so he decided to handle the matter himself.

He asked Jones if the patient was stable enough for the trip to the CAT scan room. "She said, 'Hell yes, he's stable; I wouldn't suggest it if he weren't stable.' So I called Nuclear Medicine and arranged to have the boy seen immediately." Jones loaded Patrick on a gurney and whisked him out of the Unit.

While waiting for the CAT scan to warm up, Patrick's heart started beating rapidly, then irregularly. He began to wail at the top of his lungs. His body jerked about frantically. Then his heart stopped.

Jones called a Code Blue and began CPR, ordering drugs from the startled technicians.

"We told her we didn't keep those kinds of drugs in Nuclear Medicine, and she started swearing. She was massaging the kid's chest and screaming at us to get her to the elevator when the others arrived."

In response to Jones's Code, Nurse Anderson and Drs. Kitten, Parks, and Ng rushed in from different parts of the hospital. The doctors took over, injecting the cardiac stimulants they had snatched up on the way. The group moved into the elevator, heading for the PICU and its emergency equipment.

"Genene was crying," Anderson remembers, "then she picked up this syringe filled with saline—salt water—and emptied it over the boy in the sign of the cross, like she was baptizing him. I had never seen anything so . . . bizarre."

The medics managed to get Patrick back to the PICU, but the baby's stitched-together heart never resumed its work. He was pronounced dead at 9:50 P.M. Still crying, Jones carried the child's body around the Unit for a quarter of an hour, then moved into the break room to cry alone.

At 10:50 P.M., Eva Diaz arrived for work and was puzzled by the empty bed in 551. She walked to the break room, where a number of nurses were chatting while they waited for the shift-change briefing to begin. She asked what had happened to her patient. When she learned Patrick had died, she shook her head in disbelief. Behind her, Jones squeezed into the crowded break room just in time to overhear Eva blurt out her grief and frustration: "What did Genene do to him?" Eva, realizing what she had just said, quietly mumbled an apology to no one in particular and slipped out of the room.

Like Eva, Pat Alberti also wondered what had happened to the Zavala boy. She went searching for Dr. Morena, who was preparing to head home. "Morena looked real angry—his eyes narrowed up. But the only thing he said to me was that he'd be real interested in seeing the results of the toxicology screen. 'The last time I saw him,' he said, 'before she snuck him out of here, the kid looked strange, like he was drugged.'"

Early the next morning, a group of curious nurses and doctors attended the Zavala autopsy, including Nurses McKinney, Mendez, and Alberti and all three doctors who were present for his death—Drs. Kitten, Parks, and Ng. The pathologist was surprised by the unusual audience for her work and wondered what she would discover during her examination. The autopsy turned up only one minor irregularity, however; there seemed to be some blood between the brain and the skull. The heart was in good condition, healing well, the spinal fluid clear. In the end, the pathologist could not pinpoint the cause of death, so without directing blame at the surgeons, attributed it to surgical complications.

During the course of the autopsy, Dr. Kitten overheard Dr. Parks mumble something to Dr. Ng about the need for a toxicology screen on Patrick. The remark struck Kitten as odd, and he later asked Parks why the doctors would be interested in screening a surgery patient for poisons.

In cautious undertones, Parks explained to a stunned Kitten—who evidently hadn't yet heard—that there had been some problems in the PICU recently, including over-heparinization. The Pedi-doctors now followed an unwritten policy of checking into all questionable deaths.

When Dr. Trinkle received the inconclusive postmortem, he began to get angry. Just a week earlier, another of his surgery patients recuperating in the PICU had arrested and died for no perceivable reason. The surgeon wanted to know why these two patients went bad. He began walking the halls asking questions.

"In a matter of hours, I had picked up a great deal of information about nursing staff problems in the PICU, and a failure by some of the doctors to respond adequately to those problems. So, I went to Pediatrics' acting chair, Dr. Franks, and I asked him what the hell was going on with the PICU. He told me it was being taken care of.

"I didn't think that was a good enough answer, so I told him I had three surgery patients in the PICU and I'd yank them all out of there and send them to Neonatal if he couldn't give me a better explanation."

Trinkle's threat was a potent one. If the chief of Cardiothoracic Surgery pulled his three patients out of the Unit at once, the news would be all over the hospital in hours. Franks worked out an agreement with Trinkle: the difficulties experienced in the Unit would be brought to the attention of higher authority, and action would be taken.

When the surgeon left, Franks sat down and drafted a memo to Marvin Dunn, summarizing the escalating situation. He reported that Robotham's chart review, begun in early November, had failed to substantiate the rumors of "purposeful nursing misadventure." However, on "January 9, 1982," the memo continued, "we were able to document that a child in the Unit began to bleed as a result of heparin overdosage." He advised Dunn that, because of this incident, he "had returned to a position of not knowing whether there is a problem" in the PICU. Franks concluded by informing the dean that he was initiating a review of the PICU's morbidity-mortality rate.

That evening, when Nurse Diaz arrived for work, she was told that she would no longer be working in the PICU; Eva was to be transferred to another Unit. Nurse Jones had lodged a complaint that Diaz had actually accused her of being responsible for the Zavala child's death. Nurses Benkert and Peace had supported Jones's allegation.

Diaz was given the opportunity to read the three written complaints. The first, in Genene's dark handwriting, stated:

ON 1-17-82, EVA DIAZ WAS
WORKING THE 11–7 SHIFT IN THE
PICU. THE PT. SHE HAD TAKEN

CARE OF ON 1-16-82, HAD EXPIRED
ON 1-17-82.

SHE WAS HEARD BY MYSELF TO
QUESTION TWO OTHER NURSES
ABOUT THE DEATH. AFTER SHE
WAS TOLD THE BABY HAD
EXPIRED SHE MADE THE
FOLLOWING COMMENT. 'WHAT IN
THE HELL DID SHE DO TO HIM'
REFERRING TO THE NURSE WHO
HAD TAKEN CARE OF THE INFANT.
/S/JONES

The other two statements corroborated Jones's account.

Eva Diaz's sudden removal from the PICU shocked her co-workers and heightened the feelings of tension and distrust. Many of them considered her one of the best nurses in the Unit. If it could happen to Eva, they told each other, it could happen to anyone.

The next day, on January 20, Trinkle paid an early morning visit to Dr. Howard Radwin, president of the hospital's Medical-Dental staff. The surgeon repeated to Radwin what he had learned recently about the PICU's problems. He persuaded Radwin that the problems in the Unit were threatening patient care and required immediate attention.

Radwin dictated a memo dated January 21, 1982, addressed to both Dr. Robotham and Judy Harris, the director of Nursing for Maternal Child Health Care (Belko's immediate supervisor). Radwin instructed the two administrators to "investigate the nature of Trinkle's concerns" over the quality of care in the PICU. In eleven days, on Monday, February 1, at 10:30 A.M., the pair was to report their findings to a committee that Radwin would assemble. President Radwin forwarded copies of this memo to senior administrator B. H. Corum and his assistant, Associate Director John Guest. Radwin wanted to speak personally with the medical school's dean, Marvin Dunn, however, so informed him over the phone of the 10:30 A.M. meeting on February 1.

Radwin's plans, coupled with Franks's memo, snared Dunn's attention. He called Franks and Corum, and together they decided they should act immediately, before Radwin's investigative committee convened. They agreed to an emergency meeting of key administrators the following Monday morning, January 25, 1982.

Three days before the administrator's scheduled meeting, on Friday, January 22, a five-month-old boy under Jones's care began to show symptoms of DIC. Within a half-hour he was bleeding freely, and the blood loss was beginning to weaken him. His blood pressure dropped and he lost consciousness. Unfortunately, Dr. Copeland was not on hand to diagnose the child's problem. In another hour, the baby was pronounced dead of a cardiac arrest.

A medical student assigned to the PICU that night drew a blood sample from the dead child for a toxicology screen. He later told investigators that a heavyset nurse with light brown hair volunteered to run the sample to the lab while he went to dinner. The two vials were never logged in.

The next evening, another baby assigned to Jones suffered a heart attack. This time the Code Team was able to pull the boy through. Two days later, he was sent home. He was safe.

The Investigator

So, after the Santos incident, which was a documented case of heparin overdosage, Dr. Dunn called a meeting and a number of administrators discussed what was to be done. During that meeting—

Can I short-stop you there and put that all into a more comfortable perspective? As a result of the Santos events, internal inquiries were conducted by the doctors—the Medical Center and the UT Health Science Center being synonymous in this respect. The hospital and the top-level administrators made some inquiries into what had happened, that's true. They established lab values—they had the hematology reports. They knew beyond a shadow of a doubt that the kid had been overheparinized on two occasions. I'm sure it happened on three occasions, but the proper tests were performed on two occasions: the 6th and the 9th of January, 1982.

They chose to remain somewhat aloof. They didn't pin Genene Jones down, although the concern was ob-

vious. Their inquiries faltered. No decisive action was
taken at the time. And this is why I stopped you. In my
opinion, the meeting you mentioned was not a result of
Rolando Santos. The kid recovered, he was released
and that, essentially, was it. It wasn't until the subsequent death—under very mysterious circumstances—
of Patrick Zavala on January the 17th, 1982, that these
people finally took some action.

Trinkle *insisted* on knowing what was going on. Trinkle is a hard-nosed, aggressive doctor who won't put
up with any bullshit. He was very adamant about getting to the core of the matter: why did Zavala die? And
that's what prompted the series of meetings that com-
menced on January 25th, 1982.

SEVEN

An official man is always an official man, and he has a wild belief in the value of reports.

Sir Arthur Helps, Conversation
in a Railway Carriage

NOBODY WILL EVER KNOW FOR SURE EX-
actly what was said at the January 25 meeting except the
participants, though public statements, memoranda, grand-
jury testimony, and investigative interviews provide an
outline of its substance. The administrative heads of the
hospital and the medical school—B. H. Corum and Marvin Dunn respectively—both attended. So did Virginia
Mousseau, the administrative head of Nursing, Bob
Franks, head of Pediatrics, and John Guest, the hospital's
associate director and assistant to Corum. The administrators also asked Dr. James Robotham to attend to supply them with the details of the recent events in the Unit.
The administrators probably also expected him to account
for these events in some way, to defend himself against
the implication of incompetence.

The PICU Director covered several key points. He
started by explaining that PICU personnel first noticed an
increase in the incidence of ventricular arrhythmias, flaccidity, and bleeding episodes some five months earlier.
Two nurses had brought the increase to his attention in

October, but he had heard the same observation made independently by residents, attending physicians, and other nurses. Some had also expressed concern that many patients seemed to experience these medical emergencies in twenty-four-hour cycles. A child might have a cardiac arrest one evening and then not have any real problem until the following evening when he or she would have a second or third arrest. Robotham also discussed the decline in the Unit's morale and the problems this had created: gossip; accusations of negligence; residents refusing to work with certain nurses. Cooperation between the PICU and other departments had virtually disappeared.

Robotham stated that he dealt with what he identified as the cause of these problems by introducing numerous safeguards designed to reduce the possibility of accident. All medications had been removed from the patients' rooms. New procedures required nurses to report all deaths to both him and Dr. German. Since December, he had instituted a policy mandating a toxicology screen for any patient who suffered an odd or unexpected medical emergency. Within the past mouth, the nurses had been instructed not to inject any medications without a second nurse present. In addition, Robotham had done the chart review, which the assembled group had already seen. The Director then summarized the Santos case, explaining that the child had experienced a severe bleeding episode due to heparinization. He also told the assembled administrators about Surgery's concerns regarding the Zavala case.

Finally, Robotham related his attempts to remove from the Unit the nurse he felt was the source of many of the problems. He mentioned a "personal history of emotional instability and burnout," "inappropriate emotional investment" in work and patients, "mothering dead children," plus a record of psychosomatic illness and family problems. Nevertheless, he concluded, his requests to transfer this nurse from the Unit had been refused by Nursing.

Bob Franks reportedly contributed at this point, describing his meetings with Ken Copeland regarding the Santos

boy, and just a few days later, with Kent Trinkle regarding
Patrick Zavala. Franks, or perhaps the nursing administrator, also told the group that Pat Alberti had spread
rumors of the problems outside the Unit to one of the Center's psychiatrists, who had evidently seen fit to forward
the information and identify Alberti as the source.

Informal notes from the meeting showed that, after
some discussion, the group came to the conclusion that the
"unexplainable events" in the Unit were due to one or
more of just three possibilities. First, the PICU could be
experiencing a run of bad luck—a statistical bunching of
emergencies and deaths. A second possibility was that the
Unit as a whole simply was not working properly. Maybe
staff members were not as well trained as they should be;
maybe they were careless, even negligent. The third possibility considered: Somebody might be killing babies.

The meeting broke for lunch and reconvened later that
afternoon with the hospital's malpractice attorney, Paul
Green, joining the group.

It was reported that the morning's discussion was repeated in its entirety during the second session, including
the information about Santos and Zavala. The solution the
participants arrived at, with the help of the attorney, was
to conduct another internal investigation. Robotham mentioned that a former teacher of his, Dr. Alan Conn, from
Toronto's Children's Hospital, was in town on a sabbatical. Conn seemed like the perfect choice to head the
investigation they contemplated because Children's Hospital had just been embroiled in the investigation and prosecution of one of its nurses accused of injecting children
with drugs. The administrators told Robotham to give
Conn a call.

All of the participants at the January 25 meeting knew
or should have known that under Texas law, "any person
having cause" to believe that child abuse had occurred is
required to report it to law enforcement authorities. A year
later, attorney Paul Green explained in a statement to the
press that he had advised those attending the meeting that

there was insufficient evidence to warrant such a report. Evidently, all present at the meeting felt that this advice was sufficient to relieve them of their individual responsibility. Not one of them ever took the information to any law enforcement agency. Not then, and not at any time since.

The following day, Corum briefed Dr. William Thornton, chairman of the board of the Medical Center Hospital, plus a number of other board members, on the results of the previous day's meeting. The board assented to the proposed plan to bring in Dr. Conn.

On Wednesday, January 27, Dean Dunn met with Dr. Robotham and Dr. Conn to explain the hospital's circumstances. Conn agreed to assist and the next day met with Dunn and Corum to outline the study.

Conn wanted to line up a team of specialists: three doctors and three nurses. He felt strongly that nurses would be better at evaluating the nursing disharmony in the Unit than any doctor. Corum, however, balked at the cost of bringing six experts to San Antonio from all over the country. Having just been involved in budget meetings, he knew he didn't have the money—he'd have to lift it from some other section in his budget, and the prospect didn't make him happy. Dr. Dunn evidently persuaded him by promising to take a look at the medical school's budget to see if it could spare a few dollars to help out.

Dr. Conn began calling his colleagues immediately, convincing them to fly down for a few days of review and investigation. Within hours, he assembled a panel of six. Official letters of invitation went out on Friday, January 29.

Three days later, on Monday, February 1, the committee meeting that Radwin had scheduled two weeks earlier at Trinkle's request finally convened. By this time, however, the plans put into action by Dunn and Corum had left the committee with little to do.

Dr. Robotham informed them on behalf of the administration that Dr. Conn had been invited to the hospital to review the PICU. After a brief discussion, the group reached an agreement that there was "no threatening situation in the Pediatric Intensive Care Unit which would require immediate intervention" and that Conn's "review of policies and procedures would suffice at this time."

The next day, in a press release issued by Community Relations Officer Jeff Duffield, the hospital officially announced that "in February . . . an evaluation will be conducted of services in the Pediatric Intensive Care Unit by Dr. Alan Conn, a visiting professor at the University of Texas Health Science Center at San Antonio." The release went on to quote Dr. Corum's comments on Conn's visit: "This is part of the on-going review of patient care programs that will help assure us and the community that we are delivering the highest quality of patient care. Dr. Conn will head a group that will thoroughly review the Pediatric Intensive Care Unit and make recommendations that will be key for future planning."

Once the Conn committee was announced, tension in the Unit increased noticeably. The nurses were now reluctant to prepare or administer *any* treatment without a witness. Everything was double and triple-checked, first by a second nurse, then by a doctor. Tempers flared. Morale struck bottom.

Everybody seemed to know that Genene was the object of suspicion. "They're out to hang me," Genene told her friend Jorgé Montoya one day. "They might as well let me go."

RN Chris Cuellar remembers Genene as "tired. Weary. Despite the fact she had recently had a one-month leave, I thought she needed a break in her routine, needed to take it easier." Chris asked Genene why she continued taking the sickest patients.

"Belko and I talked about it," Genene told her friend, "and we decided that if I stopped taking the sickest kids now, it would look like I was admitting guilt."

About this time, Genene worked up the nerve to confront Dr. Robotham, her former mentor, and requested to speak with him privately. She had noticed he had become extremely cool toward her, and, despite repeated requests, had failed to write her a letter of recommendation. In Belko's office, alone, Genene asked him if he thought she was doing something to the Unit's patients.

Robotham answered her. "Yes, I do."

"Why?" she asked. "Why would I do something like that?"

"I don't know."

Late Sunday afternoon, Valentine's Day, 1982, Dr. Conn's review team arrived. Dr. Robert K. Chrone, director of the Multidisciplinary ICU at Children's Hospital Medical Center of Boston, brought his unit's head nurse, Joanne Geake. Dr. G. A. Baker, PICU director for the Hospital for Sick Children in Toronto, brought Marion Stevens, the hospital's ICU coordinator. Dr. Russell Raphaelly, the medical director of the PICU for the Children's Hospital of Philadelphia, brought Sheri Whaples, head nurse of their PICU complex's Acute Unit.

On Monday, February 15, thirty-five days after Rolando left the PICU and close to a month after Patrick's death, what would become known as the "Conn On-Site Review" began.

Early Monday morning, at the start of the inquiry, Corum, Robotham, and Dunn briefed the review team on both the hospital and the university's concerns. They asked the reviewers to do their best to sort out what was happening in the PICU. What they needed, they explained, were some solid recommendations for improvement.

Dr. Robotham appears to have provided considerable input to Dr. Conn and, possibly, to the rest of the team as well. Several of Robotham's handwritten memoranda outline the information that he supplied the team. His composite list touched on every problem afflicting the PICU, but for Robotham, the "bottom line issue centered around one nurse," and presumably he made that point clear to the reviewers.

For three days, the team toured the PICU, as well as other units in the hospital. They met with representative PICU nurses, residents, house staff, and physicians. They also reviewed some medical charts. Each night, the reviewers met back at their hotel, the upscale Granada Royale Hometel on Briaridge, to discuss the conclusions reached that day. The following morning, their notes were typed up by Dr. Corum's secretary and eventually assembled into an official report.

During the course of the review, Pat Belko phoned Dr. Holland and told her that, for the most part, people unfriendly toward Jones were being scheduled for interviews by Conn's committee. She asked if Kathleen would go in as a friendly witness. Kathleen, who had been away from the Unit for three months and knew very little about the intervening events, was happy to provide positive information regarding her experiences with Genene. She let the team know that she was available to be interviewed.

On February 17, she answered questions for half an hour but was never able to deliver the testimonial she had mentally prepared. To Kathleen, it seemed that the team was more concerned with Robotham's skills as the Unit's leader than any other issue.

From the beginning, Dr. Dunn had been explicit in his request that before Conn's team of experts left, they give him some hard, solid recommendations that he could implement immediately. Accordingly, late in the afternoon on February 17, Dr. Dunn held a "debriefing session" for the review team in his office. There, after their two and one-half days of listening to hearsay testimonials, the seven-person jury did their best to distill an acceptable, coherent, pragmatic solution to the problems besetting the center's PICU.

The team could not be sure which of the three possibilities—statistical bunching, less than optimum efficiency, or deliberate wrongdoing (or any combination thereof)—accounted for the PICU's difficulties. They did conclude, however, that the level of organization, the level of competence, and the level of supervision in the Unit was inadequate across the board.

They also felt that the majority of events could very possibly be attributable to medical or nursing inadequacies, but not all. In at least one instance, the nursing personnel harbored either malignant intent or were grossly negligent. The team offered the opinion that the hospital should presume that the PICU's problems could be caused by any of the three possibilities and proceed accordingly.

The team suggested some specific, immediate action that would collectively address all of the possibilities. Because so many problems and rumors seemed to center on Genene Jones, they recommended the hospital get rid of her, as well as a second nurse they termed "disruptive"— LVN Patricia Alberti. Apparently, the Conn team viewed Pat's determination to call attention to the PICU's problems—even if that meant going outside standard administrative channels—as conduct not appreciated in a loyal employee. It was pointed out that the hospital could avoid any legal problems for unjust termination by simply "upgrading the Unit," instead of firing Jones and Alberti. Changing the staffing prerequisites to RN level would eliminate the two problem LVNs with no hint of discrimination or arbitrary action.

The team further advised that the administration appoint a new head nurse, a full-time physician-director, and, at the same time, place the PICU under the overall directorship of an interdepartmental committee. They explained that this form of supervision was common practice in many pediatric centers. Because a large proportion of a PICU's patients are admitted after an operation, three departments—Surgery, Anesthesia, and Pediatrics—are routinely involved with these patients' welfare. The team therefore recommended that the interdepartmental committee be composed of representatives from these three departments.

Another recommendation was to conduct a second, broader chart review. They suggested that a team of three respected individuals—two outsiders and one insider—hold additional interviews and review every PICU patient's chart going back a full year. Unlike Dr. Robotham's chart review (which had gone back just six months and focused only on deaths), the additional review should be directed at questionable incidents as well as deaths. The team felt that if someone was engaged in nursing misadventure, he or she might not necessarily be trying to kill a child but might only be trying to create a crisis. If the reviewers started from this premise, a pattern might appear that would not necessarily show up by looking solely at patient deaths. The team also expressed their doubts that anything would turn up; they respected and supported Robotham's clinical competence. Since he had concluded that nothing could be found, then there was probably nothing to find.

On a more fundamental level, the team questioned whether the hospital even had a need for a PICU when it functioned at such a low census. The team's members all shared the opinion that, to justify the financial and physical support a PICU required, it should consist of at least ten to twelve beds filled 60 percent of the time. Medical Center's PICU was operating with a much lower patient occupancy rate. The team suggested the Unit's patients be relocated to the Neonatal and Surgical ICUs, so the Unit could be closed down for a short period to allow physical as well as administrative restructuring. "If you restructure the Unit so it's an effective, top-flight Unit," the team's report suggested, "then you'll get the heart cases and the transplant cases, and the Unit will quickly become cost effective." A shutdown would permit a smoother transfer of power and change of personnel, and it would create a sharp break between the old and the new PICU, putting to rest some of the uneasiness doctors felt about the facility.

Before the debriefing session broke up and the team returned to their respective responsibilities, they concluded with some specific suggestions and comments: "At the very least, a senior physician (not an intern) should be assigned to the Unit twenty-four hours a day; full support should be given by nurses and house staff; and nurses should be rotated onto the Day Shift from time to time, in order to give them the benefit of day rounds with the physicians. Management seminars and assertiveness trainings should be made available. Structured meetings should be initiated where doctors and nurses can get together and communicate in a stress-free atmosphere about the good things as well as the bad. This will help alleviate the strong adversarial relationship that presently exists between staff nurses and both Pediatric and Surgical house-staff members. The importance of role models and strong, effective leadership is also drastically needed."

Dr. Conn's preliminary report included a recommendation that LVNs Jones and Alberti, specifically, be terminated from employment at the hospital. The document furnishes no reasons for recommending their removal, although Dr. Dunn's notes from the exit interview on February 17 reflect that the team felt Jones was "the center of the storm." Again, Alberti's recommended termination appears to have been motivated primarily by a bureaucratic dislike of "Whistle blowers." Curiously, when the final report was prepared, the pointed recommendation regarding Jones and Alberti had been transformed into the less actionable suggestion that the Unit be upgraded to an all RN-staff.

The Conn committee disbanded early Wednesday evening, February 17, and for the next few days, the Medical Center experienced a period of great unrest. Dr. Franks, hearing that the well-liked Dr. Robotham was to be removed from his hard-earned directorship of the PICU, tendered his resignation. The Surgery and Anesthesia department heads balked when they heard about the interdepartmental plans for the PICU—they didn't want to become embroiled in what they viewed as strictly a

Pediatrics problem. Dr. Dunn took it upon himself to smooth out these difficulties.

On Monday, February 22, five days after the completion of the on-site team's review, hospital administrators met to consider the team's analysis and recommendations. This ad-hoc ICU committee was chaired by Dr. Arthur McFee, a pleasant, popular doctor from the Surgical Department who was the director of the hospital's efficient Surgical ICU.

The first meeting accomplished little. Dr. McFee, experiencing a hint of the frustration and impotence that had plagued Jim Robotham for years, scheduled a second meeting for the following day.

The participants at this second meeting felt obliged to reject the Conn team's suggestion that the PICU be closed. "The closure of the Unit, without provisions of some other alternative, has been ruled out by the hospital as politically, morally, medically and financially unfeasible." Since the Conn team had provided detailed recommendations about temporary alternative sources of care for the PICU's patients, the political infeasibility of such a move was the most persuasive factor.

The Unit would remain open, but most of the team's other recommendations were put into effect. All committee members were also in agreement that since the hospital's long-range intention was to establish a twelve-to-fifteen-bed Unit that would serve as a Pediatric Referral Intensive Care Unit for all of southern Texas, total reorganization was needed, from physician coverage to nursing management, from policies and procedures to physical reconstruction.

By the end of the day, the committee had worked out the Unit's administrative reorganization. Corum and Dunn were to oversee the ongoing Pediatric ICU committee. Dr. Jan Puckett, an anesthesiologist with a special interest in young children's respiratory problems, was designated the new PICU Medical Director, in effect replacing the far more experienced and credentialed Dr. Robotham.

Robotham retained the title of Pedi-ICU Co-Director. The position was subordinate to Dr. Puckett, a young woman who was considerably Robotham's junior in experience and credentials.

In the PICU, the nurses were still waiting for the other shoe to drop. The Conn committee had come and gone, some changes had been instigated, but they still didn't know what, if anything, would happen to them.

On the morning of February 24, one-month-old Fernando Jimenez was admitted to the PICU suffering from a systemic bacterial infection. The baby was grievously ill, yet his doctors were optimistic. They gave his frightened parents—a young couple, just past being children themselves—reason to hope for their only child.

That evening, under the care of Jones, Fernando suffered a cardiac arrest at 10:10 P.M. The Code Team managed to revive him.

The next day, on February 25, again under the care of Jones, Fernando went down for the second time, arresting at 8:20 in the evening. Again he pulled through. At 11:00 P.M. that same evening, at shift-change, Fernando arrested once more. Miraculously, the severely weakened child hung on. During the next two shifts, he began to build up some strength, although the tremendous pain and physical shock of three cardiac arrests in little more than twenty-four hours had left him pale, limp, and tired.

On Friday, February 26, reassigned once more to Genene's care, Fernando suffered a fourth arrest, at 5:15 that evening. He was pronounced dead at 5:37 P.M.

Three days later, on Monday, March 1, 1982, the PICU's interdepartmental committee met for the first time. For the most part, the committee's members were the same as those in the ad-hoc committee. Dr. Arthur McFee was again installed as chairman. At the first meeting, it was agreed that as of March 10, and for an indeterminate time, the number of beds in the Unit would formally drop to four. After much discussion, and despite obvious reluctance, the committee consented to Virginia Mousseau's proposal that Nurse Belko be retained as the manager of the PICU.

Dr. Robotham was conspicuously absent from this initial meeting. Over the preceding two weeks, he had found himself less and less a part of the decision-making process concerning his Unit. In a six-page letter drafted the following day, March 2, and addressed to Dr. Dunn, he put his frustrations into writing.

For the record, Robotham detailed the many ways the university and hospital had failed to fulfill their promise to provide him with full support in his attempt to create a functional multidisciplinary PICU. Of the Pediatric faculty, he charged, only 50 percent made sufficient efforts to assist him, and of those only two or three worked consistently to improve care and develop a "minimally adequate care and teaching system" for the Unit. The Surgery staff seemed less than cooperative, with Neurosurgery ranking at the bottom of the list.

Characterizing ancillary care and support in the Unit as ranging from adequate to abominable, Robotham advised, "The hospital requires top to bottom changes in personnel and attitude, which is now hopefully in progress." He went on to outline his efforts to provide teaching for the PICU nurses and mentioned his repeated requests to Nursing that they deal with Genene's apparent burnout. He also informed Dunn of his unsolicited reactions—some favorable, some unfavorable—to the Conn commission's findings and recommendations.

The last two pages of Robotham's letter responded to the unfounded gossip and rumors then circulating around the hospital that he had been preoccupied with his own research, neglecting the PICU and attempting to cover up the question of foul play in the Unit.

"From the time the first suspicions were raised," he asserted, "I was bringing this information to Dr. Franks." It was Franks, Robotham charged, who had ruled the problem a nursing administrative matter that could result in a libel suit if the hospital made unfounded accusations or insinuations. Robotham had done what he could in the Unit itself, instituting policies of "vigorously investigating" every death or unexpected emergency, discussing all problems on rounds in front of House Officers, students and nurses. "Trying to ignore a potential problem," he protested, "should be the last thing I could be accused of."

Robotham ended his letter with the charge that the hospital's sudden flurry of activity in response to the Conn team's findings and subsequent lack of action, except to relieve the Director from his position, had unfairly damaged his reputation both locally and nationally. "Few other faculty members," he concluded accurately, "have worked as hard to better the school and the hospital."

For years Robotham had lobbied in vain to muster both departmental and financial support, to no avail. Now his replacement, Dr. Puckett, was receiving complete support. In one of the new PICU interdepartmental committee's early meetings, the following points became policy: (1) The Director controls all admissions and discharges; (2) the Director may consult with any specialist in the hospital regarding any patient in the Unit; (3) Pediatric and Surgical faculty will make rounds at least once daily to check their individual patients, accompanied by the Director or senior resident in the Unit; (4) resident PICU coverage will never be less than second-year level; (5) faculty call schedules in Pediatrics, Surgery, and Anesthesiology will be available to the PICU Director; (6) four additional, full-time faculty members will be recruited, as well as two PICU and two SICU fellows; (7) additional salaries at $20.00 an hour will be made available for senior residents to cover the PICU and SICU until regular full-time resident coverage becomes available; (8) an office is to be constructed within the Unit for both Dr. Puckett and a senior resident; (9) the PICU's equipment will be updated.

Suddenly, everything was possible.

At about noon on Tuesday, March 2, Nurse Belko passed the word that the hospital's top nursing administrator wanted to talk to the PICU nurses at the 3:00 P.M. shift-change—something that had never happened before. Nurses from other wards were brought in to keep an eye on the Unit's patients while nurses from the two shifts listened to their boss.

Virginia Mousseau began by introducing herself and telling them how proud the hospital was of the work they had all been doing. They had helped make the Unit one of the city's finest ICUs—but the administration wanted to make it better still. The hospital had decided to implement the Conn team's many recommendations, so, before the end of the month, the Unit would be upgraded to an all-RN staff.

A murmured gasp passed through the small audience—more than half of those present were LVNs, not RNs. What would happen to them?

"If you want a scapegoat," Genene spoke out, rising to her feet, "take me. We all know you just want to get rid of me. Let me go and let the rest stay."

Mousseau assured the group that the upgrade was not meant to be directed at any one person. Based on the review team's findings, all the hospital's Units would soon be strictly RN staffed; the Pedi-ICU was simply the first to change over. She explained that each LVN would be given the opportunity to transfer to some other position within the hospital.

Nursing administrators began to meet with the Unit's LVNs immediately, discussing with each nurse his or her individual situation. When Genene's turn came, she was told that there were no pediatric positions available at the hospital and asked if she would like to work in some other position.

"No, I would not," she said, accepting the alternative: Voluntary Termination, Eligible for Rehire.

On Wednesday, March 10, a standard letter of recommendation was prepared for Jones, which Belko signed.

By Friday, the PICU's committee received Mousseau's report that "both LVNs regarded as most sensitive in the functioning of the PICU either have, or will soon, depart the Unit and hospital." Presumably the LVNs referred to are Jones and Alberti (rather than be reassigned, Pat Alberti had also chosen to terminate voluntarily.) The PICU committee's writings did not discuss the reasons these two nurses were considered the "most sensitive" nurses in the PICU, and there has never been any indication that Alberti was anything less than a very capable and dedicated nurse.

By March 13, Genene Jones had only three more shifts to work in the PICU. That Saturday, Dora Noyola, a pretty, four-month-old baby was placed in Sally Benkert's care on the 3–11. Just before 6:00 P.M., Dora arrested. Nurse Jones was the first to rush into her cubicle to begin CPR.

Three hours after Dora was carried to the Cold Room, Genene's own patient, a fair-haired, ten-month-old girl, also suffered an arrest. At 9:40 P.M., CPR was discontinued, and Crystal Baker joined Dora Noyola below.

Two days later, on March 15, 1982, Suzanna Maldonado arrived for her 11–7 shift and found a notation in the PICU log directing her to check her mailbox. There, she found a rectangular note on which someone had printed:

YOUR DEAD

Suzanna showed the note to Pat Belko. The head nurse took a pen, obliterated the message, and told Suzanna not to worry about it.

The next day, however, another note appeared in Suzanna's mailbox. On a different kind of paper, someone had printed, in squared-off, block letters, a single word:

SOON

Frightened now, Suzanna turned the note over to the hospital's Security Department. They were intrigued by the note and Maldonado's description of the previous message, but not alarmed. Maldonado was told that, for as long as she liked, they would be happy to escort her from the building to her car. Other than that, however, there wasn't much they could do.

The threat notes were quickly common knowledge in the Unit. Belko and Anderson both asked Jones directly if she had been involved. She said she knew no more about it than anyone else.

On Thursday, March 17, Genene Jones made her last appearance in the Unit, stopping by to pick up her paycheck and to say good-bye.

After Dora Noyola and Crystal Baker, no other PICU patients died in March. In April, the Unit suffered only one death; in May, none. It seemed that Medical Center had solved the PICU's problem. The epidemic of death had ended. The administrators congratulated themselves, and the hospital's Publicity Department spread the word about Medical Center's newly reorganized facility for critically ill children.

One doctor remained unconvinced that the situation in the PICU had been adequately addressed. In mid-April, Ken Copeland informed Dean Dunn that he was prepared to resign if the administration did not inform law enforcement authorities about the Santos overdose. Dunn hastened to assure Copeland that, according to Dunn's best information, the hospital's attorney, Paul Green, had already taken the matter to the district attorney. Copeland accepted Dunn's assurance.

Jim Robotham also was troubled by the way the hospital had handled the Jones affair. In late April, before he returned to Maryland with his family, he sent a letter to Virginia Mousseau, asking her to review and reevaluate Genene's long history of problems. ''Although I have no official administrative responsibility for Ms. Jones,'' he wrote, ''I do feel that there should be adequate documentation in her records of the stresses she experienced so that she will be properly protected and judiciously supervised at any future place of employment.'' The nursing administrator evidently did not agree with Robotham; no additional comments were placed in Jones's file.

A year later, when San Antonio's medical examiner, Dr. Vincent DiMaio, was told that 122 patients had died in Medical Center's PICU between 1979 and 1982, he called a press conference. He announced that despite explicit laws demanding that any suspicious death be reported to his office, Medical Center had not reported a single PICU death since DiMaio took office over two years before. The county coroner had never been officially notified of the unusual deaths of Jimmy Sawyer, Dora Rios, Carlos Olivarez, Patrick Zavala, or any of the others.

''One almost feels,'' DiMaio said, ''that they considered themselves above the law.''

The Investigator

The fact of the matter is that *to this day*, we, the DA's office, have not yet received *any* reports from the Medical Center Hospital, the UT Health Science Center, or any other medical authority that anything—including their behavior—was even questionable in regards to the Pedi-ICU.

Were there any other children, besides Rolando Santos and Joshua Sawyer, where you had documentation of misadventure from lab tests showing overdoses where there had been normal doses before?

Yes. A kid who didn't die was a child everybody referred to as "the little Down's syndrome baby," Albert Garza. This was in October of '81. He was the epitome of the bleed-out events, at least those preceding Rolando Santos in January of '82, three months later.

Albert Garza just bled-out like a stuck pig—day in and day out—under the care of Genene Jones, and they had her nailed. They had the syringe. Dr. Larry

Houghuis pinned her down. Jones and Houghuis were at loggerheads throughout. Houghuis was a super-confident, super-bright, astute young resident. Jones hated his guts and he didn't think too much of her. But he was aware enough of the scene to back off of any real confrontation. Until this incident.

Dr. Houghuis told me, "It was at that point I knew she was doing something wrong, I just didn't know how she was doing it. No one had caught her doing it, but she had to be infusing this kid with heparin. *Why*, I had no idea."

This kid was bleeding through the eye sockets, the ears, the rectal opening, and everything else, you know? Just *bleeding*. No clinical reason. Same thing that took place with Santos later on.

There are other cases of bleedings—not quite that severe, but cases of inexplicable bleeding—none of them clinically diagnosable, or explainable. Now, there are events that take place during the course of a patient's stay that are not clinically explainable, but a reasonable explanation for them is usually definable. With Jones's patients, however, there were many cases in which no clinical explanation could be found. Too many. And they weren't all bleedings. There were arrhythmias and so-called "seizures"—you know, there are seizures and then there are seizures. Natural seizures in kids are difficult to evaluate. You know how kids are, they kind of look a little spastic anyhow at three months old when they're crying or when they get agitated or excited. Jones would scream "seizure!"

You see, Jones had inexperienced nurses, graduate-level nurses, working with her on the Unit. For them, if Genene said it was a seizure, then it was a seizure. This set the groundwork for her to go ahead with her "treatment" of that kid.

Theoretically, the doctors have to order the meds, but she would *insist* that the docs push *her* meds. If the doc said: "Well, wait a minute, I want to run some tests, I want to be sure. I just don't want to be pushing meds indiscriminately. Seizure or no seizure, he's going to make it." Genene would just let loose: "God-damned stupid-ass doctors," and other stuff like that, right to the guy's eyeballs. She really developed a very real, tangible hatred towards select doctors and, in numerous cases, really put the bad mouth on them to the other nurses.

That kicks back into the earlier thing we talked about: motivation. I believe it was multifaceted. There was no one particular motive to this whole case; it was a combination of things. One of the aspects was her hatred towards certain people, and she could develop an *intense* hatred—frightening. Keep in mind, I caught it third-hand, and even so, I could feel the heat of that hatred as it was described to me by different people, including people who were close to her and who were willing to answer our questions, based on their observations and perceptions of her over the months and years they worked together.

Houghuis she hated with a passion. Another young doctor, one of the few who came to us voluntarily, uh, I can't think of her name right now; I remember her because she was very pretty. Genene just hated her. I mean, with a more intense hatred than imaginable. And once Genene tried to set her up. It's crystal clear that she tried to set her up by encouraging her to push a drug that was called for, but not in the quantity that Genene drew into the syringe. The doctor, in the face of Genene's overpowering urgings more than anything else—she was just a PI-1, a first-year resident—pushed it and, of course, she was in the presence of other doctors, it was a Code situation, and Genene instantly berated her for pushing too much.

The woman—oh, I remember now, her name was Dr. Richards—she stopped, and everybody looked at her and said, you know, "*What* are you *doing*." She was the "fall girl," okay? She never forgot that. That was one of the reasons she came forward, because she was concerned—not really for what Genene had tried to do to her, but, after things really started opening up and she realized that Genene was involved in so many of these unexplained, untoward events—she was concerned that Genene might indeed be a wacko.

So you think that Genene was using some of these incidents as a way of "getting at" the doctors she hated, that that was part of her motivation for torturing these kids?

What you're getting at is best illustrated, I think, by Dr. Larry Houghuis. In very clear, unadulterated terms—and I'll try to paraphrase it as closely as possible because it made sense after, and during the course of, the investigation (we had others allude to this same thing)—he said something to the effect that he began to suspect in about October of 1981, that if you were in good graces with Genene Jones and you got along with her, your kids were going to be all right, but if you didn't, the kid stood a good chance of dying. He put that in about as clear and simple and precise terms as anyone I've ever spoken with.

Genene was particularly angry at Houghuis because Houghuis didn't kowtow to her, he didn't yield to her. He said, "Hey, I'm the doc." He didn't have to say it, 'cause, see, Houghuis has the type personality where it comes across very clear without him opening his mouth: He's the doc. He's not pompous or anything, he's just, you know, when he walks in the room, you know the doc's here. And this was when he was a resident, okay. He'll probably be one of the top-notch medicos in the field, I'm convinced of that, because he's got that kind of solid determination to be good at what he does, plus he's very bright.

What was the attitude or the general impression you

got in interviewing these people who worked in the PICU with Genene? Were they scared by what was going on—the probing, the fact that there was an official investigation? Did they seem at all angry or suspicious?

Yeah, they did. First of all, the tendency most folks have towards law-enforcement personnel, I can deal with that, I can get through that, you know. It's usually very easy to establish rapport with most folks. Most people are susceptible to the stroke; most people are basically honest. People are dishonest when they have something to hide, or when their defensive mechanisms are needed, or at least perceived as being needed. When they pop out, the person is revealed to be sensitive to that area of questioning. It's involuntary; it's a reaction the body has. So, by asking questions and getting reactions, you create a complete picture—an overall understanding of the subject of your investigation. That's basically what we do.

And most of these people really weren't in that category, okay? Openness and frankness created a favorable response in most all these people. These are ordinary folks. They're working folks. They work hard and believe in what they're doing—and they're not very well paid for the work they do in that rat race they have to go through at that hospital in Pediatrics. They have a tremendous amount of pressure on them just by virtue of the fact that they've got *little kids* that they're trying to keep alive. And these are *sick* kids. A Pediatric Intensive Care Unit is just exactly what it sounds like. It is *intensive* care. Around-the-clock medications, monitoring, and treatment.

Once we reached these people, by sufficiently explaining to them the seriousness of finding out the truth of what went on, they agreed to lay it on the line. They realized that their information was going to be documented, and that it was absolutely necessary. They gave us forthright information. We told them, "Never mind that you can't give us the actual dates and names and whatnot, tell us what you remember." We got honest testimony, and we got the circumstances down.

Did everyone at the hospital cooperate with you?

No. Overall, with exceptions, the further down the hierarchical structure we got, the more cooperation we received, and the more obvious the acknowledgment for the need for patient care. Most of the nurses we spoke to and a good number of the resident personnel were very helpful. Once we got up to the professorial level, the need to protect the bureaucracy often became more of a hindrance to us. And it became obvious that the hospital's lawyers had spooked a number of doctors. I think they were very subtly encouraged not to volunteer too much information through some casual comment to the effect that, "be careful what you say, there may be malpractice implications in it for you, too."

Let me point out a prime example of how this happened. Early in the investigation I got together with one of the doctors out there and asked him to describe what really goes on in there—the scenario. I called him, "When can you be free for a couple of hours?"

He said, "I'm never free."

"OK, how about Sunday?"

He said okay and devoted Sunday afternoon to me. He even came downtown. He wouldn't talk into a tape but I just wanted background, so that was okay. I said, "Give me an education," and he opened up.

After just a few minutes, I was thinking, "My God," you know? I just started jotting down the terms I didn't know and the key medical phrases I thought I was going to be interested in. He mentions heparin, and I think: "What the hell is heparin? What's it from? What's it used for normally?" I remember he mentioned digoxin, and digoxin to me sounded like a candy bar. So, we're going through all this stuff and I'm trying to get a little background, and he ends up giving me about a five- or six-hour dissertation.

We established a good enough rapport that he says, "All right, I'm going to help you in any way possible."

I said: "We're going to have to talk on tape. We're going to have to get down and dirty. Are you willing to do that?"

He says, "Yeah."

"You're gonna have to give me the whole background again, put it on tape, and then we'll get onto some precise things from there."

He says, "Great."

We shook hands, and I was as confident as I've ever been that I've got a shortcut to learning a new routine. These are professionals, and I had no idea what an ICU was all about. What's the medical field all about? What about the docs, how do they work, how do they think? What are these meds all about? How does that place function? He was going to give me everything he could about all this.

It wasn't too long after that—a week, maybe two—I contacted him, and the wall was up. He refused to furnish the interview. The doctors who refused to cooperate with us, I felt, were just pawns in the hands of other individuals who were making long-term decisions about what was best for the community. If they don't like what I'm saying, to hell with them.

Nobody seemed to care about those little kids out there. You know, they're not even capable of complaining beyond a cry or a yelp. Some of 'em were probably too sick to do even that—couldn't even articulate a complaint. At least an adult can say, "Hey, that nurse came over here and stuck something in my arm and it made me woozy," or, "it made me bleed. What was that?" You don't have that with little kids. These kids are from a few weeks, well, some of them were just a few days old, but mostly they were from a few weeks to a year or two years old. Joshua Sawyer was one year old.

Where was the concern for the patients—those tiny, helpless kids in the PICU—when these events were going on? Where was the concern for the kids on January 25th when they acquiesced to some stupid-ass decision by an attorney to *not* report these highly suspicious events to law enforcement?

They could have so easily lifted the burden off their shoulders at that point. From a moralistic standpoint, they *should* have done that, yet they didn't. They sat on it. Morals and morality aside, the *intelligent* thing would have been to report it and then they could have said, you know, "If the DA doesn't go with it, we nevertheless reported it."

That's what makes me bitter, because—what do they call it? their doctors' oath?

The Hippocratic Oath?

Yeah. I think they bastardized it to: "The Hippo-critical Oath."

PART 2

The Discovery

Kathleen's Kerrville Clinic

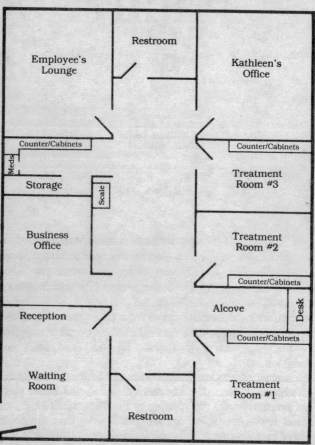

EIGHT

Things are always at their best in their beginning.

Pascal, Lettres
Provinciales, *No. 2*

AUGUST IN TEXAS BRINGS A KIND OF MADNESS to the air that most locals don't seem even to notice. With the dawn, city and country come alive with the Texas summer's music—the constant shuddering and throbbing of awakening locusts. Each day thousands of the large, green, iridescent insects crawl from their cocoons to shake their soft wings dry. Within hours they spread themselves to the wind, their wings flashing blue and gold, black and crimson.

August of 1982 was filled with that kind of madness for Kathleen Holland. Despite more than two-and-a-half years of preparation for the opening of her Pediatrics Clinic, the final few weeks found her working harder than she could have ever imagined. All the pieces she had labored to pull together were finally falling into place—all at once. Day after day, Kathleen signed for a torrent of deliveries: equipment, furniture, medications, office supplies, construction materials. The carpenters banged away, filling her rooms with counters and cabinets. Paint spread across the walls, carpet appeared underfoot. Kathleen's naked, leased space bloomed into a doctor's office.

In her rare quiet moments, Kathleen wondered how she had ever found her way to the life she was now beginning. It hardly seemed possible that she was the same person who, so long ago, started down the road to this place and time. The child she had been seemed a stranger, as if her past belonged to someone else. That girl back in Albany, New York, that other Kathleen, had been predestined for some different life. At sixteen, Kathleen had dropped out of school, grieving over her father's sudden death. Stubbornness alone drove her to return and finish her senior year. Then, for twenty months she filled her time working as a clerk-typist. When she had returned to school—remedial courses at the community college—it had been, at least in the beginning, more to please the man she loved than to fulfill any ambition of her own.

Now, thirteen years later, Kathleen's slow-born dream of opening her own pediatrics clinic was just days from becoming a reality. Her staff—an experienced pediatrics nurse from San Antonio and a receptionist/office manager with a delightful cockney accent—were already on the payroll, working hard to help Kathleen with the final preparations. Although carpenters still labored over the built-ins for the two examining rooms, by the second week of August 1982, the Clinic was almost complete. The refrigerator and cabinets were filled with all the paraphernalia a doctor's office required: tongue depressors and cotton swabs, plastic gloves and paper gowns, syringes, prescription pads, bandages, medicines, batteries, thermometers—Kathleen was confident nothing had been forgotten. Pristine *Highlights* magazines lay on the waiting room's pint-sized picnic table. Sleeping babies nestled against Madonnas in the framed prints hanging over the Naugahyde couches. On the mural in the children's corner, a road twisted through a dark forest, past knights and dragons, princesses and thieves, leading at last to a distant castle in the sky.

Kathleen's Clinic lacked only patients.

"The day the Clinic opened," Kathleen recalled later, "Monday, August 23, I had only one patient. On Tuesday, I had my second, that was Chelsea McClellan. Chelsea's mother, Petti, had called in the late morning to ask for an appointment and the receptionist, Judith Johnston,* told her to come right in." The Clinic's staff was still waiting for the McClellans an hour later. Kathleen asked Judith to call again. Judith reported back to the doctor that Petti had been waiting till after the lunch hour because she thought they would be out. "I told her, mum," said Judith, "that we don't go to lunch until the babies are all taken care of." Kathleen thanked her receptionist for saying just the right thing.

"Mrs. McClellan and her daughter arrived at about 1:00 in the afternoon," recalls Kathleen. "I took them back to my office so we could sit down and get to know each other."

The mildly worried mother across the desk from Kathleen was a soft-spoken, open-faced brunette with full lips that turned up in an easy smile. Petti was a little younger than Kathleen but no longer a girl; she spoke simply, with the easy drawl of the Houston suburbs. The little girl in Petti's arms was a charmer—blond curls, blue eyes, and the chubby pink body of a healthy fourteen-month-old. The child looked all around and seemed to want to touch everything within reach. She was a little fussy, but when her gaze first connected with Kathleen's, she broke into a brazen smile.

Petti seemed almost embarrassed as she explained her problem to the new doctor, "It isn't anything, really. Chelsea has a little bit of a cold is all. You know, a sniffle. But, if you could give her something that would help . . ."

"I noticed a hint of uneasiness in her voice," Kathleen later testified, "so I asked her if there was some special reason she was concerned about the cold.

"She told me that she was sure everything was fine, but

that about six months earlier, Chelsea had had a cold that turned into pneumonia, so she wanted to be careful. From there, we went into Chelsea's history.''

In June 1981, two months short of a full nine-month term, Petti had begun to bleed. Reid, her husband of one year, had rushed her to Kerville's Sid Peterson Hospital for an emergency caesarean section. ''I was afraid I was going to die,'' remembers Petti. ''I was so weak. As soon as Chelsea was born, the doctor sent me off in an ambulance to a bigger hospital in Fredricksburg.''

Chelsea Ann, the McClellans' premature daughter, was also in trouble. She weighed just two pounds, four ounces, and her lungs were badly underdeveloped. She was having difficulty breathing. The medics placed her on a respirator and she improved, but when the respirator was disconnected, she turned blue. The doctor diagnosed hyaline membrane disease, a form of acute respiratory distress common in premature infants. Chelsea was transferred immediately, via helicopter ambulance, to San Antonio's Santa Rosa Medical Center, where more sophisticated care could be administered. In the Neonatal Intensive Care Unit, she was placed in a crib and attached to IVs and a respirator.

Daily, Reid had traveled the long miles between the hospitals in San Antonio and Fredricksburg, questioning the doctors, offering the two women in his life whatever comfort his presence might provide. After just a few days, Petti recovered much of her strength. Their daughter's progress was slower, but by the third week of her life, Chelsea was eating well and breathing on her own. Although still underweight at four pounds, six ounces, she seemed to be thriving, so the doctors discharged her to her parents' care.

Petti and Reid were overjoyed. Though each already had a son, both had dreamed of a little girl to complete their family. In a few months, when they were sure Chelsea was fully recovered and safe, Petti went to her gynecologist to have herself sterilized by tubal ligation. There would be no more children.

At eight months, Chelsea came down with a cold she couldn't shake. The doctor in Kerrville diagnosed pneumonia. He advised Petti to take Chelsea to a San Antonio hospital. Petti's good friend, DeAnna Armour, volunteered to chauffeur mother and daughter to the city. DeAnna remembers that a terrible electric storm raged during the long drive south. The road was treacherous, washed with the downpour. Both women were anxious, tense, but Chelsea didn't seem to care in the slightest. Sick as she was, DeAnna recalls, "she laughed and played the whole way, grabbing for the steering wheel." The doctors at Santa Rosa kept Chelsea in their care for ten days, until they were sure the ampicillin had wiped the infection from her lungs.

"We'd been talking a long time," Kathleen recalls, "and Chelsea was beginning to get impatient. Petti was having a hard time holding her still."

Chelsea's struggles to escape the confines of her mother's arms were interrupted when a smiling woman poked her head in through the open door. "Mrs. McClellan, would you like me to take Chelsea while you and Dr. Holland finish talking?"

"It was the office nurse," Petti remembers. "I'd never met her before that, but I figured it would be okay to let her take Chelsea for a few minutes."

Genene Jones whisked Chelsea off Petti's lap. "Come on you," she said, lifting the laughing child high into the air, "let's go play."

Later, Kathleen looked back on that afternoon and identified the moment things began to go wrong. As she continued to talk with Petti, Kathleen faintly heard her nurse, down the hall near the front of the Clinic, say something rather odd: "Don't go to sleep, baby. Wake up. Wake up, Chelsea. Don't go to sleep."

"I lost track of what Petti was saying," Kathleen recalls. "I was asking her to repeat herself, when I heard Genene say: 'Dr. Holland, would you come out here now, please.' I knew there was some kind of problem because I recognized a sense of urgency in her words."

When Kathleen entered the treatment room she saw Chelsea, who had been bouncing with energy less than five minutes before, draped across the examining table, dusky and not breathing. Genene, proving herself to be as efficient in an emergency as Kathleen remembered, was already holding an oxygen mask to the child's face. "She had a seizure," the nurse reported. "She stopped breathing."

Kathleen slapped her stethoscope to the child's chest. The heartbeats were strong and regular, although beginning to slow; the muffled rush of functioning lungs, however, was entirely absent.

"Bag her." Kathleen almost barked the two words instructing Genene to continue using the ambu-bag to force air into Chelsea's lungs, then she rushed out to summon help.

Her receptionist was still out to lunch, so Kathleen commandeered the aid of the carpenters at work in the second and third examining rooms. "Get help *now*. I have an emergency." Without waiting for a response, Kathleen dashed back to the treatment room. The doctor took over the ambu-bag but realized immediately that the child was not receiving adequate ventilation. Chelsea appeared quite mottled and was still not breathing on her own.

"All right, let's intubate," she said.

"Okay," said Genene after the slightest of hesitations. "The tubes are down there."

Kathleen pulled open one of the table's lower drawers, grabbed the appropriate-sized sterile tube, ripped open the package, and moved toward Chelsea's head.

"What are you going to intubate with?" Genene asked. "The laryngoscope still hasn't arrived."

Without the laryngoscope—a device that allows one to see inside the throat to safely wedge the curved metal tube tightly into place—there was a real danger of tearing Chelsea's vocal cords or perforating her esophagus. Kathleen, instead, chose to insert an oral airway—a plastic contraption that would at least keep Chelsea's tongue from falling back and blocking her throat.

As they worked, Genene briefed the doctor. "We were playing on the floor in the reception room—rolling a tennis ball back and forth—when she suddenly slumped over. I thought she'd just gotten tired, so I picked her up. In my arms, she laid close, snuggling up and loving me. But after a moment or two, I sensed there wasn't any movement, so I leaned her forward. At that point I realized she wasn't breathing—she was cyanotic. I started mouth-to-mouth resuscitation, called for you, and brought her in here."

With the airway in place, Genene was now able to use the ambu-bag to respirate Chelsea effectively. Her color began to return. Kathleen slipped down the hall to talk to the child's mother.

"A seizure?" Petti repeated. "What do you mean, 'she's having a seizure'?"

"Don't worry, everything's under control." Kathleen hurried back to the front of the Clinic.

"I wondered what in God's name was going on," Petti recalls. In a fog of panic, she moved out into the hall in time to see Dr. Holland disappear into the front examining room.

At 1:22 P.M., in response to the carpenter's plea, a nurse from the neighboring office arrived. She slipped into the room past Petti, who was crying silently in the doorway watching. "I'm Terry* from Dr. Webb's office next door," she advised them. "The paramedics are on their way."

Terry took over bagging, freeing Genene to start an IV. Kathleen requested 2.5 milliequivalents of bicarbonate to help counteract the acidity building up in the child's sluggish circulatory system.

"At this point," recalls Kathleen, "Chelsea began to seize—have some jerky movements in her arms and legs. Then she became tonic—straightened out and exhibited quite a bit of tone—quite a bit of stiffness. She was no longer completely limp as she had been just a few minutes before. As the paramedics arrived, I was giving a dose of Dilantin—an anticonvulsant given for seizures—because my impression was that Chelsea was having a seizure that was compromising the return of normal respirations. I felt that if the Dilantin stopped the seizure activity—as it should have—her breathing would return more quickly and bagging would be easier in the interim."

Kathleen watched expectantly, but despite the Dilantin, Chelsea did not resume spontaneous respirations.

The paramedics arrived at the Clinic just three minutes after the 1:22 P.M. call. Their trip to Sid Peterson Hospital's Emergency Room was equally swift. Petti sat in front with the driver while Genene and Dr. Holland rode in back with their patient. The paramedic in the rear hooked up a cardiac monitor and attached a bottle of D5W to the IV line Genene had already started. Twisted around in her seat, watching every action, Petti prayed.

By the time Chelsea was admitted to the Emergency Room, at 1:35 P.M., she already seemed to be doing much better. Evidently the Dilantin had calmed the seizure after all. Chelsea now had strong spontaneous respirations and a good, pink color. Bagging was discontinued and a simple oxygen mask was placed over her face.

In the lobby, Petti called her husband. Reid McClellan dropped everything and sped to Kerrville. As Petti left the phone booth, a nurse approached. "If you want to, you can go into the ER. To be nearby."

Petti stopped just inside the doorway. Tears welled up, blurring the sight before her.

"Chelsea was laying there on the stretcher, trying to get the mask off her face. But her little arms, they were just sort of flopping around—she didn't have any coordination. It was so strange. She would reach up for that mask but her arm would go either to the side of her face or fall halfway down. It was terrifying. She just . . . there was no coordination. She didn't have any. Her arms. They were just flopping around."

Once the child's vitals stabilized, Kathleen left her to the care of the ER personnel, then led Petti back out into the lobby. The doctor needed more information. Kathleen strongly suspected that Chelsea was suffering from some seizure-related illness, perhaps metabolic, but needed further corroborative evidence before deciding on treatment. She asked Petti for anything in her daughter's past behavior that was even the slightest bit out of the ordinary.

Petti closed her eyes, forced her thoughts away from the present emergency, and searched her memory. She found nothing.

"Please," Kathleen persisted, "however insignificant."

Petti offered what seemed like trivialities. Chelsea had, on occasion, held her breath when she was angry. Once, Chelsea's brother, Cameron, had run into her, knocking the breath out of her, but she started breathing again when the babysitter blew into her face. There had also been one or two occasions when Petti had had a little trouble rousing her daughter from sleep, but that was all she could think of, except that sometimes Chelsea would sit in her crib and "just sort of stare off into space."

"Thank you, Mrs. McClellan. When your husband gets here, I'd like to talk with him, as well."

Kathleen knew that the types of behavior Petti had described were all considered potential evidence of seizures, which are often very subtle in children. Coupled with Genene's clinical description of the emergency's onset, the doctor felt confident that Chelsea was indeed suffering from some kind of seizure disorder.

About forty-five minutes after entering the hospital, Chelsea was transferred from the Emergency Room to the Intensive Care Unit. There Kathleen gave the little girl a thorough physical. Although a bit cranky, Chelsea seemed fine. Kathleen ordered an array of additional tests.

It was nearly 2:30 before Reid and Petti were finally permitted to visit their daughter. Reid entered the ICU fully expecting to see his baby lying limp in bed, near death. Instead, Chelsea greeted them both with a bright smile.

"Even though she had IVs in her foot and head, and a couple of those heart monitor things stuck to her, she was standing up in the crib, holding on to the railing, and rocking back and forth," Reid remembers. "When she saw us, she smiled and crinkled her nose—she always did that when she got excited—then she raised her arms and said, 'Mama' and 'Daddy.' God, she was such a happy little kid."

Shortly after 3:00 P.M., when the sixth floor's charge nurse, RN Martha Carlson, arrived for her Evening Shift, as always, she quickly scanned the beds. Martha remembers Chelsea catching her eye and smiling.

"I was quite surprised because I'd never seen a child in the ICU standing up in bed smiling at strangers thirty minutes after being admitted. It was unusual to say the least. In my eyes, Chelsea simply did not appear to be a sick child." Over the next few days, Martha's impression was reinforced. "If you came into the room and held out your arms to her, Chelsea would hold out her arms in return and move toward you. She was constantly standing up and walking around the crib, and she was always playing some kind of game. She was one of the friendliest, most outgoing, smartest babies I've ever seen.

"I found all this rather odd, but I didn't want to cause any trouble. When Dr. Holland first came to town, we were all pretty impressed and excited, and sort of bent over backward trying to make her feel welcome. If she thought this child needed special care—and from what we'd heard had happened in the doctor's Clinic, it sounded like the child *did* need special care—we wanted to make sure she got it. And she did get it; she just didn't appear to need it."

For ten days, from August 24 to September 2, Chelsea

was poked, prodded, X-rayed, and scanned. To rule out the possibility that the seizure had been the result of some infection, Dr. Holland ordered a painful spinal tap, a urinary bladder tap, and a full series of blood tests. The hospital's small lab ran blood cultures to screen for bacteria, serum amino acids, and urine amino acids. They also ran a ferric chloride test used to identify possible metabolic disorders. Every test Kathleen ordered came back negative; nothing abnormal could be found.

During this time, Chelsea was rarely if ever without someone by her bedside. For the first couple of days, Petti took time off from work and stayed there herself around the clock. When Chelsea's elderly babysitter, Bardetta Kreiwitz, came to visit, she noted Petti's fatigue and sent her home, insisting on taking her place.

"She needed to rest," recalled Bardetta. "I didn't mind. Chelsea was, well, she was a special child, a true little angel. I remember she had this habit of, well, if you were busy doing something, she'd sit and watch you, and when you looked up—catching her watching you—she'd burst out laughing. She liked little games like that."

Petti's friend, DeAnna, also took turns watching Chelsea. "Dr. Holland had left orders that anybody— Petti, me, a nurse, whoever was in there—observe Chelsea closely. There was a sheet of paper taped to the wall next to Chelsea's crib, and if she did anything unusual—even if she was asleep—Dr. Holland wanted it written down: what happened, how long it lasted, and all like that. But I never did write anything down because I didn't notice her doing anything unusual. As far as I saw, there was nothing to write down." Despite the IVs attached to the little girl's head, DeAnna reported, "If she wasn't sleeping, she was just happy and playing and laughing all the time."

Kathleen was perplexed. Her fourteen-month-old patient had a history that included pneumonia, at least one reported breath-holding spell, and various other possible subtle seizure signs; the little girl had almost died right in her office. Yet now, nothing seemed to be wrong with her.

"In my mind, that left only the possibility that Chelsea had some kind of neurological problem that just hadn't been picked up yet. I wanted more sophisticated tests run." Kathleen sent Chelsea home on oral Dilantin—to prevent any future seizures—and arranged for Petti to have Dr. Mackey, a neurologist Kathleen knew in San Antonio, give Chelsea a complete neurological workup. It was scheduled for Monday, September 20.

Petti felt so grateful to Kathleen and Genene for having saved her little girl's life, she didn't know how to express it. She went around spreading the word among all her friends, to anybody who would listen, really. "Take your kids to Dr. Holland," she said. "She's the best thing since canned beer."

The Investigator

Did you have an opportunity to work with Dr. Holland? We met with her recently, but she seemed, still, very hesitant to talk openly.

Yeah, well, I guess she's had enough of it. Interesting woman. This whole deal cost her her career. I mean, it's an uphill battle now. There's nothing like getting your socks knocked off about two weeks into being a doctor. Right on through the Georgetown trial, she was scared to death; very tight, very structured, particular and precise in her answers. Very quiet. She had a heavy, heavy wall around her. She didn't really know what was going down and was, in fact, very close to being indicted. I had the impression that the grand jury up there blamed her for what happened as much as they blamed Genene Jones. They couldn't accept the likelihood that she didn't know what was going on, that she wasn't part and parcel to it. But, as best as can be evaluated in a criminal matter, I just can't conceive of Holland being the one that pushed those needles. That's just not the way it developed. Not at all. Kathleen was always one step away.

NINE

Something wicked this way comes.

Shakespeare, Macbeth, IV.i.

DURING ALL THE YEARS OF KATHLEEN'S MEDI-
cal training, no one had ever told her what to expect from
a small-town pediatrics practice, nor had she ever thought
to ask. When she opened the door of her Clinic, she didn't
know how many patients to expect, or how long it might
take to build up a client base. She didn't know whether the
parents that she met would like her well enough to return.
She didn't know how difficult it would be to manage a
business and practice medicine at the same time. Most important, after years of coping with San Antonio's sickest
children, Kathleen didn't know that Kerrville's oldest doctor had never, in more than forty years, had a single pediatrics patient who had suffered a respiratory arrest in his
office.

Kathleen was just trying her best to handle each new
problem as it occurred, and by Friday of the first week,
she was ready for the reprieve of the weekend.

For three or four months, if things went as Kathleen
anticipated, weekends would be the only time she would
have a chance to be with Charleigh, her new husband. The

house they were building together just outside Center Point, fourteen miles to the south of Kerrville, was not much beyond the cement foundation. Though Charleigh stayed there "for security reasons" seven days a week, sleeping in a tent, conditions were still too primitive for Kathleen to join him every night. Without a bed and a shower, she could not be presentable for work each day.

Bill Schick, Kathleen's business manager, had offered a practical solution, both for Kathleen's housing problem and for her nurse's. Genene had had difficulty finding a rental in Kerrville that would accept both children and pets. Schick proposed that Kathleen buy a house in town that she could lease to Genene for the amount of the monthly mortgage payment, on the condition that a bedroom be reserved for Kathleen's use five or six nights a week. As a consequence, Kathleen not only saw Genene all day long at work, she became a kind of fifth member of Genene's household at night.

The other four people living in the Nixon Lane house constituted an eclectic group. There was Genene, of course, and her two children, nine-year-old David and five-year-old Amanda.* To take care of the children while she was at work, Genene had invited Bonnie Gunderson,* a troubled, pregnant woman of eighteen, to move in. On occasion, Sally Benkert—Genene's friend from San Antonio—also stayed at the house. Sally had moved up to Kerrville several months before to take a job at the local hospital and to be near Genene. She apparently was having trouble inducing the local power company to hook up to her small mobile home, so Genene suggested Sally feel free to stay with them until the connection was made.

Though it was an added stress to be surrounded constantly by virtual strangers, Kathleen did what she could to make the best of, even enjoy, her circumstances. "I appreciated the efforts Genene made to create a homey, Christian atmosphere. We said grace before meals; everyone had chores; we played games together in the evenings."

Perhaps because of their long, forced companionship,

the two women quickly became better friends than they otherwise would have. In some ways, they had much in common: a blue-collar upbringing, the death of a cherished father at a young age, a passion for medicine. Kathleen learned over time to laugh at Genene's earthy humor and to accept, even appreciate, her aggressive approach to life. Genene, for her part, had a protective, loyal admiration of Kathleen, as if Kathleen was everything Genene wished she had become.

Still, by the end of that first week, Kathleen was longing for the upcoming workday to be over so she could escape—away from the Clinic, away from her prepackaged family, away from the demands on her time and attention, and back to the comfort of Charleigh and the countryside. It would be a long day.

Early on Friday morning, August 27, eighteen-year-old Nelda Benites became alarmed over the worsened condition of her one-month-old daughter, Brandy, who had been sick for about a week with dark diarrhea. "She hadn't been eating well," Nelda remembers, "and she had been crying a lot—too much." Nelda and her husband, Gabriel, decided to take Brandy to Sid Peterson's Emergency Room, where they were referred to Kathleen Holland's Clinic. Kathleen had made her policy clear to the local medical community: she would not turn away any patients based on a lack of insurance or an inability to pay.

Kathleen and her nurse received the family in the waiting room shortly after 11:00 A.M. Genene took the child from Nelda's arms and carried her into the front treatment room. Kathleen noted that the little girl seemed ashen, suggesting acidosis, and was very lethargic. "Although she was awake, she didn't appear to be very alert, and because Nelda was very upset, I was concerned. I got a real quick history, had Judith, my receptionist, take care of the necessary forms, and went right on in to check her over."

Kathleen placed the O_2 mask near the infant's face, then

conducted a complete physical, looking for anything out of the ordinary. She noted that Brandy did not fuss as much as a child her age normally did while being examined. When Kathleen started gently probing the baby's abdomen, Brandy began to whimper. Kathleen went on alert. "I thought: Here's a three-month-old baby born two months premature. She has a three-day history of bloody diarrhea, is now acidotic and has a tender, distended belly. All of this suggested a serious condition, such as volvulus (which is a twisted intestine) or N.E.C.—necrotizing enterocolitis (an infection of the bowel wall, sometimes seen in preemies, that compromises blood flow)."

Standing in the doorway separating the waiting room and the central corridor, Kathleen explained the situation to Nelda and Gabriel. "It could be a simple viral infection, but it could also be serious. I'd like your permission to admit her to the hospital for more tests."

As Kathleen talked with Brandy's parents, Genene prepared the baby for the transfer to Sid Peterson Hospital by starting an IV. From the first day, Kathleen had set the policy that any child transferred to Sid Peterson from her Clinic would arrive IV'd, intubated if necessary, and accompanied by two or three vials of blood already drawn for immediate analysis. Not only did she want to ensure a safe delivery, she wanted to make sure that there would be no delays in treatment once the child reached Sid Peterson. The hospital staff had always been very candid about being far more accustomed to dealing with adults and senior citizens than with children. Kathleen saw no sense in leaving these often delicate procedures to medics unfamiliar and uneasy with pediatric medicine.

When Kathleen returned to the examining room—two to five minutes later—she noted that an IV had been started and Genene was drawing the second vial of blood. She also noticed, however, that Brandy was now worse off than she had been minutes before—her color was more ashen; her fingers and toes were a deeper purple-blue. Kathleen twisted the valve of the green oxygen tank to increase the O_2 flow, placed the ambu-bag's mask firmly over the child's face, and pumped a few times. Brandy's color improved somewhat, but when Kathleen stopped bagging, the child immediately lost ground. "With each breath, she breathed more and more shallowly. I remember thinking of the phrase that we had used in training to describe the progression to apnea in an acidotic infant— 'pooping out.' She just looked pooped—like she was really tiring out. Then, all of a sudden, she stopped breathing altogether, and went limp."

Genene rushed to the phone. Instead of the slow, comfortable trip to the hospital as they had originally planned, Brandy now required an emergency transfer.

In the few minutes it took to reach Sid Peterson's ER, Brandy resumed breathing on her own and became more alert. The X rays Kathleen ordered revealed an area of intestine that appeared suspicious, but established nothing conclusive. The doctor did the best she could with the few facts she had obtained, settling on a working diagnosis of N.E.C.: "That explained most of her problems."

After talking with Nelda and Gabriel again, Kathleen arranged for a transfer to San Antonio, where a more thorough evaluation could be made by Santa Rosa's Dr. Ratner, a pediatric surgeon Kathleen respected. "If this was in fact N.E.C., a specialized surgical intervention might be necessary at short notice."

Still breathing on her own, Brandy—now intubated, IV'd, and attached to a cardiac monitor—was reloaded aboard the ambulance. Because of her susceptibility to motion sickness, Kathleen followed in her own car while Genene Jones, EMT Phillip Kneese, and RN Sarah Mauldin (the assistant director of Sid Peterson's Respiratory Department), accompanied Brandy in the ambulance's cabin.

As they left the hospital's parking lot, Sarah specifically recalls Brandy was breathing "okay." Just a few miles down the road, however, the nurse noticed that the infant's ribcage did not appear to be moving up and down. She put her hand on Brandy's chest. She felt no movement, but the bumpy road made it difficult to be sure. "I asked Genene to take a look."

Jones examined the child for a few moments, then told Sarah she thought Brandy was breathing fine. Sarah relaxed.

"Look," said EMT Kneese, pointing to the cardiac monitor.

The ambulance pulled to the side of Interstate 10 about halfway between Kerrville and Comfort—the next small township to the south—and stopped.

Kathleen pulled up directly behind, leapt from her car, and opened the ambulance's rear door to discover Genene leaning over the stretcher doing compressions. Brandy was in full arrest.

"Stop CPR," she ordered as she climbed inside and put her stethoscope to the child's chest. "I heard a sluggish beating, as though the heart had just started coming back, or had been back for just a short while."

"Medications, Doctor?" asked Genene, her hands already into the doctor's black bag.

"No, I don't think so," replied Kathleen, for the quickening heart also sounded strong. "How long to San Antonio?"

"About forty-five minutes," offered the driver.

Kathleen turned to Genene, "Let's just go with a dose of bicarbonate. Bag her now and then just to help her out." She turned to the driver: "The most important thing is to get her to the hospital as quickly as possible."

Kathleen returned to her car and the caravan continued south. Inside the ambulance, the driver radioed his dispatcher, requesting that Santa Rosa be advised via telephone of their problems—the ambulance was still too far out for direct radio contact. Sarah took the first shift pumping on the ambu-bag, breathing for Brandy. Phillip kept an eye on the cardiac monitor. Almost absently, Genene asked: "Are there any clean syringes on board?"

Sarah later recalled thinking: "A syringe? What for?"

Phillip, familiar with the contents of the ambulance, quickly double-checked a few of the smaller compartments. "Sorry, no syringes."

Genene nodded. Very purposefully then, she inserted a second IV in the child's foot—even though the IV in Brandy's arm was flowing smoothly. Neither Sarah nor Phillip questioned her. "Since the ambulance didn't carry any IV sets, she had to have brought it with her," Phillip later clarified. "And, so . . . since she, well . . . it's hard to explain, but she was aggressive in the sense that at all times, she gave the impression that she knew exactly what she was doing. I just figured the kid needed it for some reason which I wasn't aware of."

Shortly after this second IV began to flow, Genene picked up Brandy's leg and let it fall back to the stretcher. "It dropped like a lead weight, completely limp," Phillip remembers.

Genene then turned to Sarah, looked her in the eyes, and, as Sarah recalls, "with a kind of breathy excitement, said: 'The kid's gone bad. Bag like crazy.' And I did."

After twenty minutes, Sarah relinquished the ambu-bag to Phillip, who breathed for the pale but stable child until he, in turn, relinquished responsibility to a Santa Rosa nurse, thirty minutes later.

It was left to Genene to tell her boss the details of the second crisis. Kathleen did not hear the whole story of what occurred in the ambulance until nearly a year after the event.

The Clinic had had its second cardiopulmonary arrest, but Kathleen did not connect the two events. In her mind, the children presented entirely separate medical problems, both with distinct histories of potentially serious symptoms. "Brandy I'm not sure about. Even now," Kathleen says. "In my mind, she is the most, uh, nonsurprising. She was a two-month-old preemie—one month out of the womb—with a three-day history of diarrhea, blood in the stools, and was ashen in the waiting room. I wasn't the least bit surprised when she arrested. I was disappointed, certainly. I mean, don't get me wrong, I was not *undismayed* over the episode, I wasn't *unconcerned* by it, but neither was I surprised medically. Whether or not Genene had anything to do with Brandy's arrest, I don't know. I guess I'll never know."

A Parent

It's not that we think Holland ever did anything deliberate to the kids. We just think she should have seen something. She should have suspected something was up. I mean, she must have heard some of the gossip down in San Antonio. And when these crises started, you'd think she would have put two and two together, you know?

So, you blame her for what happened to your child.

I don't *blame* her, exactly, I just think she should have seen it. Why did she give that woman so much authority? Why didn't she pay more attention when Jones was sticking all those kids with needles? Why did she let Genene go in the ambulance instead of going herself? I don't know. All I know is I take my baby in to see a doctor and I expect that doctor to be able to take care of everything, to protect her.

These other doctors in town say she ought to have noticed it. They say the town hasn't had a single respiratory arrest before. Dr. Holland should have known, should have suspected. She should have supervised that woman more closely. Why didn't she know enough to see that all these emergencies were too much of a coincidence? I realize she was just a new doctor, but I trusted her. I put my baby in her hands, and all this stuff happens—God only knows if it'll have some lasting effect, my child being so hurt, confused, and afraid. Someone has to be responsible for that. It was Dr. Holland's office; she should have been supervising everything.

So that's why we're suing. Someone has to be responsible.

TEN

*There are temptations that require all of
one's strength to yield to.*

Elbert Hubbard
The Philestine, XX. 86

JAMES AUGUST PEARSON WAS A SPECIAL
child. Strangers saw only his problems, which were many
and grave. He was cruelly deformed, his skeleton crumpled
into harsh angles. He was tiny, weighing just twenty-two
pounds at seven years of age. He was severely retarded,
unable even to speak. And he was chronically ill with a
potentially fatal heart defect, constant respiratory problems,
and occasional seizures. His doctors had been predicting his
imminent death since the day of his birth.

Jimmy's family knew the child behind the many problems. They remember a sweet and gentle soul who had
endured long years of pain and isolation. Though his hand-
icaps limited his ability to communicate, he was loved
and, they felt, he loved in return.

On the morning of August 30, 1982, Jimmy suddenly
started to seize uncontrollably and continuously despite his
antiseizure medication. His mother, Mary Ellen, rushed
Jimmy to Sid Peterson Hospital where the ER nurses asked
Dr. Holland—who had arrived at the hospital not long before—to take a look at the youngster. "At the time,"

Kathleen recalls, "I was tending another patient, six-month-old Christopher Parker." Mrs. Parker had brought Chris to the Clinic that morning, concerned by his raspy breathing. Kathleen's quick examination of the boy's constricted air passages persuaded her that he should be checked into the hospital for twenty-four-hour observation. She obtained Mrs. Parker's consent and arranged for an ambulance transfer. It was just after Chris—stabilized and calm—was carried up to the Pediatrics Ward that Mary Ellen pulled up outside the ER doors.

"Oddly enough," Kathleen recalls, "I'd treated Jimmy years before, during my residency." Already familiar with the little boy's problems, she quickly stabilized Jimmy with an injection of 1 milligram Valium and 0.1 milligram phenylephrine via his IV, and attached a nasal cannula which blew a steady stream of oxygen into Jimmy's lungs. After a phone consultation with the two San Antonio physicians overseeing Jimmy's case, Kathleen told Mrs. Pearson they all felt it would be best to transfer Jimmy south to Santa Rosa Hospital. Kathleen then called Fort Sam Houston in San Antonio to arrange for a transport via an army helicopter ambulance.

Throughout the United States, the army's MAST units (Military Assistance to Safety and Traffic) supply medical-evacuation services to both military personnel and the civilian communities surrounding their bases. MAST personnel, all highly trained emergency medics and pilots flying VH1 Hotel Medivac Hueys (sophisticated helicopters designed and built by Bell Industries specifically for the military), respond to all kinds of requests for emergency airlift services, including ambulance transfer from remote townships to large city facilities.

On Tuesday, August 30, 1982, Sergeant First Class David Maywhort had first refusal on all distress calls directed to Fort Sam Houston. Sergeant Maywhort, the MAST platoon leader of the 507th Medical Company stationed at the fort, was both supervisor and instructor for the medics in his unit. Despite the fact that his duties had been demanding more and more of his time in recent years, he took pride in the fact that he always managed to log enough missions to meet the monthly quota of hours required to maintain status as a flight-ready specialist in emergency medical evacuation. At that time, in 1982, probably fewer than twenty-five people in the world were as capable as Sergeant Maywhort of stabilizing a Coding patient and keeping him or her alive long enough to get to a hospital.

The fort's logs reveal that at 12:32 P.M. that day, the MAST unit received a call from a Kerrville pediatrician named Holland, requesting transportation to San Antonio for a seven-year-old male suffering from a sudden onset of uncontrollable seizure activity. The transport sounded challenging and the day was perfect for flying: "Clear blue and 22." Maywhort snatched up the mission for himself.

"We lifted off immediately and touched down at the VA Hospital's helipad in Kerrville," Maywhort later testified. "That's about a mile and a half, maybe two miles from Sid Peterson. When our ambulance arrived at the hospital, we were greeted by a nurse and Dr. Holland. The doctor informed Sergeant Garcia—the crew chief—that there was an additional patient, Christopher Parker, who also needed transport and asked if that would be possible."

Since placing her call to Fort Sam Houston, Kathleen had decided that Christopher, still suffering from respiratory problems that had been alleviated but not corrected by the administration of vaporized epinephrine, would be better off under observation in a San Antonio hospital. Concerned that Christopher might experience an episode of respiratory distress during the hour-long drive to San Antonio by ambulance, she opted to send him along with Jimmy via helicopter.

"Garcia told the doctor that we'd have to check the boy out," Maywhort continued. "At this point, I followed the nurse upstairs to look over Christopher while Sergeant

Garcia went with the doctor to check on our scheduled pickup.''

The army's policy governing the MAST transport program leaves flight command decisions in the hands of the flight medics. They alone determine whether or not a transport will take place. ''The flight medic philosophy,'' Maywhort explained, ''is to transport a patient if it will do some good. Our goal is to provide a stable transportation from point A to point B, so we're reluctant to transport a very unstable patient or a patient whose life is going to be endangered by the flight, especially if he could be maintained in a fairly stable condition at his present location. The only time we really alter that thinking is when we know, or are reasonably certain, the patient is going to suffer greater injury or death if we *don't* transport him.

''An additional concern on these civilian missions is the overall circumstances. Unfortunately, when we're called in to a small community (and this happens a lot, in my opinion), the facility may be trying to unload a terminal patient—they'd rather he died somewhere else. So, in each case, it's our responsibility to ascertain whether the flight is warranted. The army doesn't want to be in the position of continually delivering corpses.''

Although Sergeant Maywhort was the senior medical officer on board the flight, Sgt. Gabriel Garcia, as the crew chief originally assigned to the flight, was officially in charge of the mission. What he said was law (unless something went wrong with the craft itself, in which case the pilot, David Butler, became the commander). Like Maywhort, Sergeant Garcia was an advanced medical specialist with over three-years experience in the field. He and Maywhort had flown together on many previous missions; they respected each other as individuals and medical professionals.

''After Dr. Holland explained the situation and Maywhort went upstairs,'' Garcia recalled, ''I entered the ER to inspect the Pearson boy—a poorly developed seven-year-old child with obvious multiple orthopedic deformities. He was only about a yard long and weighed about twenty pounds. As I recall, Jimmy's overall consciousness level was at best semiconscious—he was more or less in a postictal state [a drowsy postseizure condition] the entire time. I talked with Dr. Holland and the boy's mother about what type of treatment he'd been given, what medications he'd been on, how much O_2 he needed, how his behavior today differed from his past norm—generally, how stable he was physiologically. All things considered, he seemed to be in pretty good shape, though he did appear to be having some sort of respiratory distress—he had a lot of fluid in his bronchials and his breathing was labored. You couldn't help but see the strain of his accessory muscles trying to draw the oxygen in. Unquestionably, he was a sick child, but his mother said these symptoms were fairly normal for him. So, looking at the flight time from Kerrville to San Antonio, I felt comfortable that we could, in fact, deliver the boy to San Antonio in as good a condition as he was when we started. I told the doctor we'd take him.''

In the Pediatric Ward, Sergeant Maywhort found Christopher and checked the baby's vitals. "The nurse informed me that he was a four-month-old child who had just suffered an episode of respiratory distress, but when I saw him he was having no trouble breathing at all. He seemed very healthy. I'm still not really sure why they wanted him transported, but as it seemed fairly obvious that we weren't going to have any problems with him, I didn't see any harm in it.''

Maywhort tucked Chris into an incubator and carried him downstairs, where he recommended to Garcia they go ahead and transport both boys at once. Sergeant Garcia turned to Kathleen and questioned her regarding the worst possible scenario: If both patients developed problems at the same time, what were the priorities? "Dr. Holland told us to treat Christopher Parker first.''

Kathleen introduced the sergeants to Genene and informed them she would be accompanying the two patients south. "After a bit more discussion," Garcia remembered, "the doctor was called away and I found myself alone with the nurse. As I recall, she smiled rather gravely and said, "I think we may have some trouble with the Pearson boy. I think he may go sour."

Two ambulances were used to transport everyone to the helipad. Sergeant Maywhort accompanied the Parker boy in one while Garcia rode in the second with Jimmy Pearson and Genene. During the short ride, Garcia reminded Genene—the newest member of the flight's medical team—about some of the things one must keep in mind regarding patient care in a helicopter. "I didn't go into a lot of detail, because my impression was that she was an experienced nurse—in every way she presented herself as a highly competent, flight-practiced RN. But I do recall reminding her about the impossibility of oscillating in flight—listening to the lungs or heartbeat with a stethoscope. It can't be done. Not only is it awfully loud in that cabin (there isn't a whole lot of soundproofing in a military vehicle) but the stretchers the patients lie on are directly connected to the aircraft's frame, and the engine's vibrations transfer right through the litter into the patient's body, up the stethoscope, and into your ear. You can't hear a thing.

"I also told her exactly what we'd expect from her if there was some kind of emergency, be it aircraft failure or medical problems. I reminded her about how the headset worked once connected, and about how she shouldn't interrupt the pilots unless absolutely necessary. It was just a quick briefing. She gave me the impression that she knew about it all already.

"Sometime in there, I noticed she had brought a paper bag along and I said, 'Do you have everything?'

"She said, 'Yes.'

"I said, 'What do you have?'

"She said, 'Well, I have these things,' and held up the bag.

"I said, 'Do you mind if I look?' I wanted to make sure

I knew about everything that would be available in case there was some kind of emergency, and I was curious as to what she thought she might need. I reached in and in addition to a laryngoscope, some tubes, and a bagging mask, I found a preloaded 3-cc syringe, which she indicated was filled with Neo-Synephrine, and a bolus of lidocaine [a local anesthetic also known as an effective antiarrhythmic].''

"Secure in the rear?"
"Secure."
"Lift-off."
The passengers filled the Huey's small cabin. Christopher, snug in his incubator, was strapped directly to the cabin's rear wall while Jimmy was secured in the litter immediately above, both lying perpendicular to the direction of travel. Sergeant Garcia and Genene sat facing the stern, with about six inches between their knees and the two patients. Sergeant Maywhort and Sgt. Ken Torrongeau sat behind the rear wall in the Huey's two gunports, their eyes scanning the skies for other air traffic.

The mission's pilot, David Butler, banked around smoothly until they were headed southwest, roughly parallel to and slightly to the west of Interstate 10. As the helicopter rose to four thousand feet, Maywhort, peeking into the cabin from the starboard gun-port, watched the patients closely for any adverse reaction to the change in air pressure or the motion and noise of the aircraft. Neither seemed affected.

About this time, Maywhort waved for Garcia's attention, indicating to the crew chief that he should turn on his mike. Because Maywhort was patched into the ship's intercom system by way of a Y-connector, he could not speak through his headset unless Garcia first activated his microphone.

"What's up?" Garcia asked.
"How about moving the Life-Pack to the upper berth? The Parker kid doesn't seem to need it. He's asleep."

"Roger."

The Life-Pack 5 is a small, eight-pound, portable heart monitor, specifically designed for use in a helicopter. Its filters and insulation enable the pack's scope to render an accurate reading of the heart's electrical activity despite constant interference from radio waves, the engine's explosions, and the rotor's vibrations shuddering through the craft.

In minutes Garcia attached the three color-coded, foam-cushioned adhesive pads to the appropriate locations on Jimmy's tiny chest and turned the monitor on. As always, there was some distortion present, but Garcia knew how to read past the deviant lines and noted a normal rhythm of seventy to eighty beats per minute.

About five minutes later, roughly halfway to San Antonio, Sergeant Maywhort again turned from scanning the sky to find Genene hunched over the patient in the upper berth, her stethoscope pressed to the boy's chest. She seemed anxious. "I waved to Sergeant Garcia again, got his attention, and indicated in sign language that he should see what the nurse was doing. He said he'd find out."

Again Sergeant Garcia unstrapped himself, stood up, and moved to the patients. The crew could hear pieces of what was being said, but only through the microphone in Garcia's headset; Genene's mike was never activated.

"What are you doing?" Garcia asked.

Genene answered him with a look suggesting contemptuous exasperation.

"I was sort of stunned, really," recalls Garcia. "I looked at her trying to use her stethoscope on this poor kid, and it was just absurd. I said, 'You can't do that.'"

"Of course I can," Genene yelled, returning her attention to her patient.

"But, you can't hear anything through that."

"I can hear fine," she shot back, pulling her stethoscope from her ears. She began to gesture frantically. "He's going bad," she shouted, as Garcia did his best to match fragments of words with the movement of her lips. "He's in trouble. He's having another seizure. Look at him, he's turning black. He's going to arrest, just like I said he would."

Maywhort recalls that Jones "seemed somewhat agitated . . . not upset or anything, just agitated. Kind of excited, like something important or, well, *exciting* was going on."

Genene grabbed her paper bag and returned to her seat.

"Garcia, what the hell is she saying?" asked Maywhort.

"I'm not real sure. Something about the kid going bad—seizing—but he looks all right to me. How about you?"

Maywhort acknowledged that Jimmy seemed fine.

Garcia checked the Life-Pack's oscilloscope. Despite the interference skewing the tracing, he could see that the boy's regular pattern was unchanged. He reached down and turned the scope toward Maywhort, who also found the waves reflecting a normal sinus rhythm.

Genene was again at the litter listening intently with her stethoscope as Garcia tried to explain that whatever she thought she was hearing, it wasn't anything to be concerned about because the boy was doing just fine. Genene shrugged him off.

At this point, Garcia and Maywhort engaged in a non-verbal discussion about how they were going to handle the situation. Clearly they were dealing with an undertrained, perhaps incompetent civilian. Contrary to all evidence that told them the boy was as stable as when they had left, she was insisting that her patient was having serious problems. "It's not easy for us, as flight medics, to just interfere with a medical person who has been assigned to fly in our aircraft with his or her patient," Sergeant Garcia explained. "It invariably causes a lot of political problems with different hospitals and doctors. So, once we do it, once we begin to insinuate ourselves, to interfere with the course of treatment, the patient is, from that moment on, solely *our* responsibility. We have to follow it all the way through to the end, and we have to be right. It's sort of like a mutiny.''

As Garcia again turned to check the monitor, Maywhort and Torrongeau saw the nurse pull out a syringe and, holding it up, empty it of air.

"Stop her!" they yelled from the gun-ports as Genene quickly injected its contents into the boy's IV port.

Garcia, standing directly behind Genene, but unable to see just what she was doing, could not bring himself to intervene. "It isn't our practice," Maywhort later clarified, "to slap people around in the aircraft, to prevent them from doing what they were sent along to do. It takes an extreme deviance from accepted procedure for us to step in and overrule a medically trained passenger. On a basic level, they're the ones who are in charge of their patients. However, technically, since it's a military aircraft, we're ultimately responsible. While I could see what she was doing, I couldn't reach her; I was in the gun-port. While Garcia was close enough to have stopped her, he couldn't see what she was up to.''

Maywhort bellowed, "Mark time," to alert the pilots that something significant was going on in the cabin, that there wasn't time to talk about it, that it was serious, and that they should note the time. Genene pulled the empty syringe from the IV and tossed it into her paper bag.

Turning, and gesturing expansively with her hands, suggesting "no big deal," she yelled at Maywhort: "It's Neo-Synephrine. To dry the mucus. Help him breathe easier." She returned to her seat.

Maywhort and Garcia shared their shock through their eyes. They felt certain that the child needed no additional medication and Neo-Synephrine certainly did not have much to do with the seizure Genene had just been screaming about. Further, they had every reason to believe that the nurse had, for some unknown reason, tried to deceive them—they both knew she had not heard anything through her stethoscope. Greatly concerned, they hovered over the child.

Minutes ticked by; the child seemed unaffected. Then Garcia noticed a change. Jimmy's chest retractions began to get deeper, and his skin began to mottle and turn blue. Garcia looked at Maywhort, who indicated he also saw the change. Then Jimmy's respirations grew shallower and increased in pace.

Genene popped up from her seat, her face glistening with sweat: "He's having a seizure!"

"He's having a heart attack," Garcia countered, noticing the monitor—the BPMs were increasing, scattering, diffusing. "Mayday. Mayday," Garcia intoned as he pushed the black button on the Life-Pack's face, activating a printout of the scope's readings. "Mayday. Find me some room, Butler. I've got an arrest back here." It was not wise to work on the boy in the cramped quarters of the cabin—they needed to land and open the bay doors.

Butler scanned the terrain below while activating his radio transmitter. "San Antonio Tower, this is Medevac two-four, approximately four-zero miles northwest of your station. We are making an emergency landing—patient medical emergency on board. Repeat: patient medical emergency on board. Notify Kerrville Veterans Administration, Sid Peterson Hospital, and Santa Rosa Medical Center. Will recontact when airborne. Over."

"Medevac-two-four, this is San Antonio Tower. Roger. Good luck. Over."

In the chopper's crowded, swaying cabin, Garcia looked the boy over closely. Jimmy had stopped breathing, and the scope was now reflecting ventricular fibrillation. The boy was in grave danger.

Genene pushed Garcia aside and placed the mask of her ambu-bag over Jimmy's face. His deformities, however, prevented a tight seal. Maywhort, standing on his seat, motioned her aside and, leaning into the cabin over the top of the litter from his gunner's port, his back pressed up against the cabin's roof, he initiated mouth-to-mouth resuscitation. As the chopper dropped from the sky, Genene sank into her seat.

Butler spotted a small, nearly-level pasture between two hills and in seconds set the craft down between the scrub oaks. "The field appeared to be cultivated and had a slight downgrade. I remember some high-tension wires that I had to navigate around. I also recall spotting a couple of men on horseback watching us from a nearby hillock."

Garcia flung the left door wide and Sergeant Torrongeau jumped from the gunner's well to pull open the door on the right. Moments after touchdown, Jimmy, despite the numerous wires and tubes connected to the various parts of his body, lay on the floor of the cabin. Maywhort crouched over the boy while Genene and Garcia, both standing on the aircraft's skids, leaned in through the doorway. Genene pulled the endotracheal tube from her paper bag and tried to intubate Jimmy, but she could not get a tight fit. Garcia took the tube from Genene's hand and deftly inserted it around the warped tissues. Instantly, Maywhort attached the ambu-bag and started to pump.

"Prepare for lift-off," bellowed Garcia.

As everyone piled back inside, the endotracheal tube worked itself loose. Garcia considered replacing the tube but decided they had been on the ground long enough. He told Maywhort to handle ABCs—airway, breathing, and circulation—and ordered an immediate lift-off.

The doors slammed shut. The engines whined. "Secure in the rear?"

"Secure."

"Lift-off."

As they climbed, Garcia ordered Butler to reroute to Methodist Hospital in northwest San Antonio. It was the closest.

Crouching near the forward cargo compartment, Maywhort held Jimmy in his lap and continued respirating the child while Garcia began cardiac compressions. "We paused intermittently to check for return of pulse," Garcia recalled, "but basically, we just kept up the ABCs until we delivered Jimmy to the ER at Methodist Hospital about twenty minutes later."

Between compressions Garcia recalls noting Genene white-knuckling the left-hand crew-member's seat. "She seemed a little pale and appeared to be going through some kind of hyperventilation syndrome. It looked like she was, well, it's hard to describe. Sure, it was a frightening experience, and anybody might pant, but she looked more, well, you know, *excited*. I asked her if she was all right, and she replied that she felt a little airsick."

Sergeant Garcia would later testify that upon landing atop Methodist Hospital, he vaguely recalls seeing someone consolidating the Life-Pack's printout and the empty syringe into Genene's brown paper bag—but he cannot recall who this was. Neither the bag nor its contents were ever seen again.

Jimmy's mother, Mary Ellen Pearson, who had driven down from Kerrville, beat the helicopter to Santa Rosa Hospital by more than an hour. It was late in the afternoon before she finally saw her son rushed off the helipad by the army medics. Genene spotted her and walked with her down to the ER.

"What I remember most vividly is her appearance," Mary Ellen would later report. "She was trembling. She was pale. She had an unusual—I can't explain the look she had in her eyes. It was something I've never seen before. She was 'up.'

"The first thing she told me was that Jimmy was fine, then she went into the flight. She said that shortly after take-off it'd become necessary for her to give Jimmy some Valium for his seizures. Then, about halfway through the flight he'd stopped breathing, and they'd had to make an emergency landing in a cow pasture to save him.

"Then, I remember, she made a sort of joke about the cows not producing milk for the next twenty years because of Jimmy and the helicopter. And then—I'll never forget—she looked at me and said: 'It was one of the most exciting afternoons of my life.'"

Since Kathleen was not Jimmy's regular doctor, none of the medics aboard the helicopter or in San Antonio thought to provide her with a followup report. Again Kathleen heard the story of the crisis-in-transit from her nurse. And no one else. "It sounded exciting. When I heard how Genene had literally saved that kid's life, I remember thinking again about how much my motion sickness affects my life. I wished I could have gone along to take care of my own patients."

Jimmy, Mary Ellen Pearson's son—a boy born with five major structural defects and a genetic orthopedic problem that limited his bone growth, a boy whose every joint was stiff, who probably could not hear, and who saw no better than a normal child sees under water—spent the remainder of his days in hospitals. Seven-and-a-half weeks after his one and only helicopter ride, Jimmy, not quite eight, finally succumbed to complications stemming from his defects and an overwhelming infection. During his short, troubled lifetime, the only respiratory or cardiac arrest he ever suffered was on August 30, 1982.

Nick Rothe

How was it that you got involved in this case?

There's a writer by the name of Jones who wrote *From Here to Eternity* and some other things; in particular, he wrote something about airplane pilots that I've always admired called *Fate Is the Hunter.* I believe fate is going to get you when it's your time for something, and I got hunted down. "It was fate" explains how I ended up working with Ronnie Sutton as co-prosecuting counsel for the Genene Jones murder trial.

I don't think I've ever heard of it happening before—not in Texas anyway—where two DAs from neighboring counties work together on *any* thing. It can get complicated. But it worked great for us. We developed what we referred to as a mutual-assistance pact and essentially ran a joint investigation. Shared everything. I think the San Antonio investigators handled almost all the interviews, for both counties—and there were hundreds of people to talk to. We also had our end to develop, the Pearson case for example. We developed that down here in San Antonio. Completely.

But that happened up in Kerrville?

The incident started there, yeah, but it ended down here. They landed here. All those people who we needed to call in to testify before a grand jury lived here in San Antonio. The hospitals are here and the MAST guys are all over here at Fort Sam. So I went ahead and worked that part of the case up from scratch.

And that's why you questioned those men during Chelsea's trial?

Right. See, I was the one who'd talked to them; they told *me* what happened, not Ronnie. Plus, I had a personal interest in that one. Jimmy was a real special kid. His parents gave me a little framed picture. I keep it in my office.

What you've got to understand about this whole thing is that . . . is that Genene is . . . you need to . . . Okay, sure, I don't know her very well because, as a prosecutor, you don't normally talk to the defendants much. But I think probably the best idea you can get of her is to compare what she says happened up in that helicopter and what the MAST medics say happened.

See, these army medics, they're the top of the line. I mean, I've had *doctors* tell me, "Hey, if I get hurt, I hope they send the goddamned medics from MAST before they get any *doctors*, cause those guys'll keep me alive." They're just dynamite. One of 'em was a Vietnam medic, I think, and the other one was . . . Well, as a matter of fact, Maywhort is an instructor now at one of the universities where he teaches traumatic nursing and such. He's also a professor in the military school for training medics in air-evac. I mean, these guys are awesome individuals. They are totally under control. They live by the numbers.

When I hear that Genene said, "They let the kid turn

black and then when I tried to get them to do something, they said, 'Ah, let him die. He ain't gonna make it anyway,'" well—

[THE SPEAKER SHRUGGED]

You know who was sittin' there suckin' on that kid's mouth—spittin' out all that junk? Those two army guys—while she was sittin' over in the corner, wipin' her face, trying to keep from throwing up. Either she was airsick or she was . . . something. But the things she said they said . . . I mean, those guys are professional lifesavers—they don't let anybody die if they can help it. Somebody dies with them, it's not because they didn't try *everything* that could be done. Especially a baby. Hell, until I told 'em, they thought she was a registered nurse, with air-evac training. That's the way she presented herself to them.

I asked them, "Did you know she was an LVN?"

They went: ". . . Oh my God."

It's part of a picture she paints: Genene's version of reality. She's been quoted as saying that she feels sorry for me and Ron. She claimed Sutton was obsessed with putting her away, that he *had* to get her feather in his cap. She says I was forced to put her away by Millsap. It was my assignment. Millsap presumably wanted a big win to make a name for himself, get reelected, maybe run for president.

She makes it all up and when people don't buy it, she can't believe it. She's bananas, totally bananas. Got to be.

ELEVEN

*It is too late to be on our guard when we
are in the midst of evils.*

Seneca

ON FRIDAY, SEPTEMBER 3, THE EARACHE
twenty-one-month-old Misty Reichenau had had for four
days was better, but her mouth sores were worse. When
Misty would not stop crying, not even to eat, her nineteen-
year-old mother, Kay, decided her daughter had more than
a cold. A little after 10:00 in the morning, Larry
Reichenau called their family doctor, Dr. Duan Packard,
whom Misty had seen only days before. Dr. Packard's office informed Larry that the doctor was out of town and
referred them to the town's new pediatrician, Dr. Holland.
Kay called the Clinic and spoke with Judith. They set an
appointment for 2:00 P.M.

Shortly after 1:00 that afternoon Sally Benkert brought
by a home-cooked lunch for the Clinic's staff, to celebrate
the end of the second week of business. The women were
in the rear staff room polishing off the remains of the picnic when the front door's bell chimed. Judith went forward, returning promptly to inform Kathleen that their
2:00 appointment had arrived.

Kathleen went out to the waiting room to meet Misty,

Kay, and Kay's mother, Karla Jenson. As Kathleen looked over the sick child, Kay informed the doctor and nurse that Misty—wailing a constant high-pitched cry—had been running a fever of 102 to 103 degrees for four days. Kay explained that Dr. Packard, a few days before, had prescribed some antibiotics to help Misty fight her ear infection, yet the little girl's mouth sores had gotten progressively worse in the last day or two.

"She must be real sick," Kay told the doctor, "because she's stopped eating, and Misty has always been a real good eater."

Kathleen offered to take a closer look and ushered them into the front treatment room—the other two still weren't completed. Kathleen quickly inspected the child's eyes, ears, nose, and throat. "I also listened to both lungs, her heart, her abdomen, and checked her basic, overall neurological status in terms of motion."

As the doctor palpated the child, Genene pointed out that Misty seemed to be holding her neck rather stiffly.

Often when children get upset or anxious, they will resist flexion of the neck, especially when a stranger tries it, so Kathleen asked Kay Reichenau to rock her daughter in her arms for a few moments to calm the baby. When Misty was relatively quiet and secure, Kathleen tried to gently roll the infant's head forward. Misty resisted and wailed still louder. "Even after she had been in her mom's lap for quite a while," Kathleen later recalled, "she still held her head way back most of the time. She didn't want to let it fall down forward."

Kathleen leaned against the exam table and carefully explained to Kay that, due to Misty's continuing fever (in spite of the antibiotic treatment she had been receiving) and taking into account her stiff neck, one of the things they had to consider was the possibility of meningitis—an infection that develops between the two membranes that cover the brain. Kathleen thought Misty exhibited classic symptoms: a history of persistent fever, ulcers in the mouth, irritability, a high-pitched cry, and a stiff neck.

The antibiotics that had been prescribed for Misty's ear infection may have temporarily weakened the meningitis bacteria without being strong enough to eliminate it.

"Of course," Kathleen said, "it's possible it *isn't* there. This might all prove completely inconsequential or just co-incidence, but we need to be sure that we eliminate that possible diagnosis, because a meningitis that has only been partially treated is a very serious matter." She explained that if the prescribed antibiotics do not completely destroy the meningitis bacteria, the infection can very easily re-bound. In such instances, the afflicted children usually suf-fer serious neurological problems. Kathleen recommended that Kay send her daughter to the hospital for further tests.

"But I think we've caught it in time," Genene volun-teered. "It's not too advanced, not too serious."

Kay was unsure, nervous. "She's not going to die, is she?"

"No," Kathleen assured her, then told Genene to pre-pare Misty for the trip to Sid Peterson, reminding her to draw up some blood for the hospital. They would want to begin the cultures immediately, to see just what infection Misty was fighting. Kathleen then stepped out into the hallway and moved toward the Clinic's office to handle the necessary paperwork and to ask Judith to call an am-bulance. As she mentioned the word "ambulance," Kath-leen could see out of the corner of her eye that Kay became upset, so she added: "Make it clear that this is a nonemergent-basis request." The doctor picked up a pad and began jotting down a few notes.

Kay moved out into the waiting room and spoke with her mother for a few moments. Reassured that everything would be all right, Kay returned to the treatment room. As she entered, Genene turned abruptly.

"Please step out of the room, Mrs. Reichenau," Jones said, moving away from the table and her patient. "It's hard on a mother to watch their child get an IV inserted," she told Kay. "I know, I've got two of my own. Why don't you wait out in the reception area. Misty's going to be all right.''

Kay elected to stay with Misty. "She was scared," Kay remembers. "I mean, she was sick and it's only natural. I thought I might be able to calm her somehow just by being there. So, I went ahead and helped hold her still. Dr. Holland came back in about then. I was leaning over Misty—she was lying on the table—and I was holding onto her left arm while the nurse put the IV in her other arm, and I was just sort of leaning over her head, talking to her—more or less just trying to keep her from seeing what was going on and to calm her down.''

"When I returned to the examining room," Kathleen later testified, "Genene was placing the IV in the baby's scalp. I assisted Mrs. Reichenau in holding the child still. Shortly after the IV was started, Misty—who had been screaming throughout the procedure (which all children will do)—suddenly stopped screaming and, for a short period of time, went limp.''

Kay would later recall vividly what happened after Genene put the IV in her daughter's arm. "Misty was looking at me—her eyes were open and she was looking right straight at me—and there was a terrible look in them, like she was scared real bad. It happened just twenty, thirty seconds after the IV started flowing, something that short. It wasn't a long time, but it was long enough that I knew. Misty had been crying and screaming, and then she just quit everything. She was just lying there like in midair. I hollered. I said, 'There is something wrong here. Misty is not breathing.'

"Genene made some comment about how, yes, Misty was mad, but she was more likely just holding her breath, kind of having a temper tantrum. But I was holding her arm and I knew she was just limp, just totally out of it. She was still, uh, 'looking' at me, but there was no movement whatsoever. Anywhere.''

Kathleen recalls that "shortly after the IV was inserted,

Misty was crying and then just suddenly took a deep sob, stopped crying, and stopped breathing. I was holding her arm, trying to keep her still, and could feel her slowly go limp and then—I think it was then—I noticed that her spontaneous respirations had ceased. At the time, this appeared to be a typical breath-holding spell.

"Now, when I say 'limp,' I am looking back in retrospect. At the time, I was not analyzing this as an episode of limpness. I was trying to use that bit of information to help me analyze, characterize, and identify the problem Misty was having. Some children, when they get agitated, will start crying and then either voluntarily or involuntarily—we really don't know which—take a deep breath and hold it, actually stop breathing for a moment. Usually, the child will, after a period of time, lose consciousness. He then goes limp and, after a short period of time, starts breathing again. I knew that I had felt the child sort of slowly go limp, yet she had some tone in her muscles, so I thought that Misty was probably having a seizure, but I also remember thinking, 'it might just be a breath-holding spell.'"

"When the doctor said Misty might have just been holding her breath and then passed out," recalled Kay, "I told her, 'No. Misty is not breathing. There is something *wrong*.' That's when they asked me to leave the room."

Sally Benkert then stuck her head in the door to see if she could be of some help. Sally would later testify that when she entered the room "the child was slightly cyanotic in the face. Her teeth were clenched, her eyes were rolling back up in her head, and she looked very stiff; her hands were clenched, turned in toward the body, and her extremities were trembling. She was shaking all over." Sally also recalls that, at this point, Dr. Holland was trying to hold down the child and maintain an airway while Genene tried to get an IV started. Kathleen, on the other hand, insists that it was she who started the IV.

Kathleen yelled out the door for Judith to change the ambulance call from a nonemergent one to an emergent one and asked Sally to assist with the oxygen mask. The IV in place, Kathleen tried and failed to intubate the child: "Her teeth were clenched," Kathleen remembers, "and she kept biting down on the laryngoscope blade."

To help facilitate the intubation, Genene suggested Kathleen use succinylcholine. Kathleen later recalled that "in the midst of all the immediate attention I was giving the procedure, I said something to the effect: 'No, no, I don't know the dose off the top of my head. I want to do this without it.'"

At the first mention of the need for the drug, however, before Kathleen thought to stop her, Sally asked Genene where the drug was kept and rushed off to fetch it from the clinic's refrigerator.

"When I returned, just a few moments later," Sally testified, "Genene was pushing what appeared to be Dilantin—I noticed an open syringe of Dilantin laying on the table, partly used. I stopped at the counter, picked up an empty syringe and asked Dr. Holland how much she wanted of the succinylcholine." Sally further testified (although Kathleen denies) that Dr. Holland shot back a request for 2.5 cc's. "I raised the vial," Sally continued, "and aimed the syringe when Genene said: 'No, wait. You really mean *1*.5.' And they argued for a bit. Genene felt 2.5 cc's was a little too much to give Misty because she was only two years of age and looked to be approximately twenty or twenty-five pounds. The proper dosage is three milligrams per kilo, so, in Misty's case, the more correct dosage would in fact have been closer to 1.5 cc's."

Kathleen asserts that she simply told Sally that she would intubate without succinylcholine, and then did so. Since the succinylcholine was no longer needed, Sally deposited the syringe on the counter near the sink and tucked the vial behind the cottonball dispenser, out of the way.

"It's hard for me to recall specifically" says Kathleen, "—I find that I tend to get Rolinda and Misty and Chelsea confused at times in my mind—but, I believe the EMTs arrived while Misty was still moving around quite a bit, displaying quite a bit of tone. I recall that her movements at the time were consistent with the term tonic-clonic— jerking about mixed with periods of increased tone or rigidity. She was salivating profusely, so much that I was afraid the tape securing her endotracheal tube would become too wet to hold the tube in place. We used the EMT's portable suctioning device to clear her mouth, but the tube slipped out anyway. I was going to leave it out, but she was breathing shallowly, so I re-intubated for transport.''

Kay Reichenau was told that her daughter had suffered both a respiratory arrest and a seizure. The EMTs explained to the frightened mother that she would not be allowed to ride along in the ambulance. They advised her to make arrangements to meet them at Sid Peterson's ICU.

When Kay next saw her daughter, about two hours later in Sid Peterson's Emergency Room, Misty was alert and fighting the tube in her throat. ''She was overbreathing through it,'' Kay remembers. ''Her eyes were wide. She was scared.''

Kathleen calmly explained to Kay that she would wait to perform the lumbar puncture test for meningitis because of Misty's earlier seizure, and because Misty's anterior fontanelle (the soft spot in the front of a baby's head) was completely calcified and closed. This was not unusual for a baby Misty's age, but was an indication that Kathleen should proceed with caution.

Kay then learned that Dr. Holland had arranged for a MAST unit to fly Misty down to one of the big hospitals in San Antonio. ''I wanted to go along,'' Kay said later, ''but she told me that I couldn't, that Genene would be the only one allowed in the helicopter with Misty.'' Only medical personnel are allowed in the helicopter with the patients under MAST policy.

When the medevac arrived in San Antonio that afternoon, Misty's admitting physician found her ''agitated, breathing on her own, and struggling against the breathing tube,'' which he promptly removed.

Over the next five days, Misty's doctors performed an expansive assortment of tests, almost all of which proved negative. An equivocal spinal tap led the physician in charge, Dr. Mackey—a specialist in diseases relating to the central nervous system—to concur with Holland's diagnosis of a possible early meningitis. Neither Dr. Mackey nor Kathleen could explain, however, why Misty had, on the afternoon of September 3, suffered a respiratory arrest.

Mary Morris

You met Genene in LVN school, isn't that right? You two were in the same class, from June of '76 to June of '77?

That's right.

After you two graduated, when did you next see her?

Well, I saw her at the nursing test, but then I didn't see her again until Saturday, September 11, 1982, at Sid Peterson Hospital. It was something like a little after two o'clock in the morning—I was in charge of the sixth floor that night—I got a call that we were getting a patient by the name of Genene Jones.

I told a couple of the aides, "I used to go to school with a girl by that name. I wonder if it's the same person." Since it wasn't too busy (and it's one of my responsibilities anyway) I went into her room to help admit her and get her settled in. And as I walked through the doorway she said, "Well, Mary Morris."

I smiled back and said, "Well, Genene Jones." So

we knew each other immediately. She was evidently having trouble with an ulcer. Very painful. And because ulcers can be very serious, she was encouraged to stay in bed for at least a week. My understanding is that she did not.

What did you two talk about?

I asked her what she was up to. She said she was in town working for a pediatrician, a Dr. Holland, helping her open a clinic. And I thought that was interesting. Then she mentioned that she was also up there to help start, then take charge of, a Pediatric Intensive Care Unit there at Sid Peterson.

I couldn't understand that. I said, "Well don't get your hopes up too high. First of all, I don't know if either the state or the staff at the hospital will let you do that. I'm not sure of the laws, but I know the hospital has an *RN* in charge of our one ICU, not an LVN."

She then said, rather adamantly, "Well, that's what we're going to do. And we're going to staff it with all LVNs."

I said, "Well, the other thing is, Genene, sure, we have sick children, but I don't know if there are *enough* sick children here in the area to constitute a need for a Pediatric ICU." By that time I'd been working the sixth floor for a couple of years (that's where most of the children went, the sixth floor) and I just couldn't imagine this working out.

That's when she said: "Oh, they're out there. All you have to do is go out and find them."

TWELVE

If there were nothing else to trouble us,
the fate of the flowers would make us sad.

> John Lancaster Spaulding,
> Aphorisms and Reflections

"AS A RULE, PETTI WOULD DROP OFF HER TWO youngest, Cameron and Chelsea, at my house on her way in to work," recalls Bardetta Kreiwitz, the McClellans' grandmotherly day-sitter. "She usually got there between 7:00 and 7:30 in the morning and we'd have coffee. She'd pick them up, oh, anytime between 5:00 and 6:00, depending if Petti had to stop at the market or something; she always did that first.

"On Friday, September 17, Chelsea was first through the door. She marched right into the kitchen, sat down on my lap, and started drinking from my cup of coffee. She had on a red and white gingham dress with lace on it, and a matching bonnet. She had been out of the hospital a little over a week. She still had a little head cold but seemed to be in much better spirits. Chelsea always liked for me to fix her breakfast, so I fixed a bowl of cereal. Petti put Cameron to bed—he had the flu—then we sat down and talked awhile."

After Petti left, Bardetta stroked Cameron's head and chatted with him for a bit, until he started feeling sleepy.

She slipped out then and got down on the floor with Chelsea, to play. "She used to love to play little games with her looks—sort of like tag, but with her eyes, like peek-a-boo. She couldn't talk yet, but she was thinking all right.

"And oh, she had a temper. She could stomp her foot harder than I could if she got mad. Her face would flush and she'd sort of cry, well, more like yell really—there weren't any tears in her eyes. But I would never let her get away with that, and she knew that. All I had to do was point my finger at her and say, 'Don't start it, Chelsea. Don't start,' and she would blow it right off. She was such a special child."

After some play, Chelsea looked a little drowsy, so Bardetta fixed her a glass of Tang and put her to bed. She went right to sleep.

Chelsea was still asleep when Petti returned at about 9:30 A.M. to pick the two kids up for their 10:00 appointment with Dr. Holland. Petti had been worried about Cameron; "the flu knocked all his strength right out of him."

"Come on, honey," said Petti, lifting Chelsea from the bed. "Time to go."

Bardetta remembers: "Petti was leading Cameron by the hand and carrying Chelsea against her chest, her arm under her rump—you know what I mean; Chelsea was looking back over her mother's shoulder. As they went out the front door, Chelsea was laughing and waving and telling me 'bye and everything. Maybe she was a little sleepy still, but she was fine."

The McClellans arrived for their second visit to Kathleen's Clinic a few minutes late, so Petti was relieved to find that the doctor was also behind schedule. "She's been held up at the hospital, but she ought to be here directly."

Judith, noticing Petti pull out a pack of Virginia Slims, said, "You can go on into the back room, if you'd like, Mrs. McClellan. Otherwise, you'll have to go outside; there's no smoking in the waiting room."

"Oh, fine. Come on kids, let's move into the other room." They joined Genene in the staff lounge. The nurse greeted them warmly and, after a quick chat with Petti, volunteered to take the children's vitals while they waited for the doctor to arrive. Height, weight, and temperatures took about ten minutes. Chelsea weighed eighteen pounds, twelve ounces.

Sometime after 11:00 A.M., Dr. Holland arrived and found the McClellan trio in the rear lounge chatting with Genene and Judith. "When I walked in," she recalls, "Chelsea was investigating the carpet."

"Good morning," said Kathleen. "I'm sorry I'm late. I hope you haven't been waiting long."

"Not at all," Petti assured her.

Kathleen recalls that "even though the appointment was for Cameron, I was still looking for something that might help explain Chelsea's seizure." She gave Chelsea a quick examination, but found nothing out of the ordinary. Even the little girl's sinuses were within normal limits, though she did have a slightly runny nose. "What's the baby's temp?"

"She's afebrile," replied Genene. "It was only a hundred."

Chelsea was fine.

"I discussed the childrens' vaccination needs with the mom briefly," Kathleen recalls, "then left the staff room and went across to my office in order to record the information I had just obtained. Before entering the office, I turned and told Genene to go ahead and give Chelsea two routine infant immunizations: a diphtheria/tetanus and an MMR."

"She was sulking," Petti recalls of her daughter. "Her eyes were wide. When Genene reached out for her, she started to whimper.

"Genene said, 'Why don't you wait outside Mrs. McClellan. I know most mothers don't like to see their babies get shots.'

"I told her that I would be going on in with Chelsea, to

be with her while she got her shots. I said, 'It doesn't bother me to watch my kids get shots.'"

Petti remembers that Genene did not seem at all pleased and turned about sharply. "She got sort of huffy."

Together, mother and daughter followed Genene into the foremost treatment room where two syringes awaited them, already prepared. Genene raised the syringe to check the amount of fluid one last time, informing Petti that the first shot would protect her daughter against tetanus and diphtheria, while the second was an inoculation against measles, mumps, and rubella.

Genene dabbed Chelsea's thigh with an alcohol swab. "Okay, hold her hands."

Petti did so, cradling Chelsea in her lap, speaking softly in loving, reassuring tones as the nurse pushed the first needle into the child's upper left thigh, emptying its contents. Chelsea wailed.

Within seconds, Petti noticed that Chelsea was acting strangely. "'My God,' I thought, 'what's happening?' It seemed she wasn't breathing right, and her eyes were looking at me funny. She was sort of whimpering—it was as if she was trying to say 'Help me,' but couldn't."

Petti stammered to the nurse, "Something's wrong. Do something."

"She's just mad about having to get the shots," Genene replied, as she prepared the second syringe. "It's nothing. She's reacting to the pain."

"No, stop. She's not acting right. She's having another seizure!"

Genene, intent upon administering the second injection, ignored Petti's outburst. Instead, she quickly dabbed the child's other thigh and imbedded the second needle while softly mumbling, "I have to give her this other shot."

As the empty syringe left Chelsea's leg, the child was no longer breathing. Her pink cheeks were beginning to blue.

"I looked at her," recalls Petti, "and I could see she

was trying to say 'Mama.' I thought, 'Oh God, she wants to say 'Mama.'

"Chelsea then went limp; just like a rag doll, just like Raggedy Ann—that's exactly what she looked like, just limp. She was still looking at me, but it didn't look like she could see me. Her eyes were all strange looking and they weren't like they were supposed to be. They weren't like they were supposed to be."

"This can't be happening," Petti insisted to the nurse. "She's not sick. *Cameron's* sick. *She's not sick!*"

"Just as I was signing my name to Chelsea's chart," recalls Kathleen, "Genene filled the doorway. She was wide-eyed and asked me if I would please come look at Chelsea. I didn't know what to think. She kind of hustled me along and told me quickly that Chelsea had gotten upset with the shots, had gotten mad, and was breathing shallowly. She said: 'I gave her a little bit of O_2 by mask and she seemed to pink up and do better, but now she's breathing shallowly again.'

"As I entered the examining room, I saw Mrs. McClellan standing at the end of the table near the oxygen tank, rocking Chelsea in her arms, almost bouncing her, while holding the oxygen mask to the child's face. At first I just observed for a moment and generally took a look at the child's color—which was good at that point—but her respirations were shallow. She was not completely limp; she was moving her arms some.

"I suggested to Petti that we put Chelsea down on the table, so we could administer the oxygen more accurately and efficiently. We began bagging in the hope that she would respond and pick up the respirations herself. At this point Chelsea went momentarily limp—just for a short while—and then had what appeared to be a seizure, a contraction of her arms."

"Genene," said Kathleen, "80 milligrams Dilantin."

"80 milligrams Dilantin."

Petti stood watching as an IV was inserted into her

daughter's scalp, then Kathleen instructed her to tell Judith to call both an ambulance and Sid Peterson—they would be taking Chelsea to the ER again.

Emergency Medical Technician Tommy James, a veteran paramedic, and his partner, Steven Brown, received Judith's call at 10:55 A.M. The ambulance arrived at the Fine Medical Building at 10:58 A.M. "When Steven and I walked into the examining room," recalls Tommy, "I noticed an infant on the treatment table being ventilated—a nurse was assisting her breathing with a mask and bag. The nurse told us that the child had suffered seizures, was in respiratory distress, and that we needed to transport her to the Emergency Room of Sid Peterson.

"We had brought in a stretcher, a heart kit, and an O_2 bottle. We connected the airway to our bottle, while the nurse placed the child on the stretcher. We then proceeded to the vehicle, ventilating her on the way."

The ambulance sped off seconds later. Petti again rode in front with the driver. In the rear, Tommy James manned the ambu-bag while Genene Jones monitored Chelsea's vital signs. Dr. Holland tailed the ambulance in her private car. As they exited the parking lot, Tommy slid back the glass partition separating the rear cabin from the driver's compartment: "Lights and siren."

At the hospital, Genene carried Chelsea inside. It was 11:07 A.M.

Within twenty-five minutes of the injections Genene gave Chelsea at the Clinic, an angry little girl was once again in the hands of the experts of Sid Peterson's Emergency Room. Kathleen recalls that by this time Chelsea was "moving quite a bit, moving her extremities quite a bit, in fact, was beginning to fight the presence of the endotracheal tube. I ordered 0.8 cc's Valium, IV, and she calmed down. We then changed the endotracheal tube to one size larger for a more appropriate fit." Through it all, because the child still seemed to be breathing shallowly at best, Tommy continued assisting her with gentle compressions on the bag linked to the oxygen tank.

Kathleen's notes mention some slight twitching in Chelsea's eyes, but the child's color, heart rate, lungs, and reflexes all seemed to be normal. Kathleen was now convinced that Chelsea had some sort of neurological problem and advised Petti to check Chelsea into a San Antonio hospital immediately, rather than wait until the following week for the tests that had already been scheduled.

Because both Petti's car and her son Cameron were still at the Clinic, RN Cleo Meadows, assistant director and nursing supervisor for the 7–3 shift, asked Mrs. Northington* of the Social Department to drive Petti back over. As they were leaving, Genene said she would hitch a ride with them since she wanted to pick up both Dr. Holland's purse and her own.

"We were at the Clinic just a few minutes," Petti testified. "While I called Reid, my mother, and Mrs. Kreiwitz, Genene raced from room to room, collecting different things for her black bag. I told Cameron somebody would be by to pick him up in just a few minutes, and we left."

In response to Petti's calls, Reid and Petti's mother sped to the hospital. As before, by the time they arrived, Chelsea's emergency appeared to be over. "I told Reid they'd pretty much handled it the same as last time," Petti remembers. "I also told him about Chelsea's eyes and her strange movements. I had been worried, but, as she seemed to be coming around, we relaxed."

Kathleen called San Antonio and arranged for a bed, then called Fort Sam Houston, but the MASTs were delayed on another call. "It would have been more than a two-hour wait, or something like that, before they would even be able to head in our direction." So Kathleen spoke with the EMTs, and an intercounty ambulance transport was arranged.

Thirty to thirty-five minutes after they first arrived at the Emergency Room, Genene and Tommy wheeled Chelsea's gurney back out of the ER to the rear of the ambulance. Genene pushed; Tommy pumped the ambu-bag. Kathleen recalls that as Chelsea left the ER, "she looked quite stable, very pink, and, I felt, fairly comfortable. I had considered extubating her, but decided it was better to have a good airway in place for the ride, since her seizures had previously given us so little warning."

Two hours after the McClellan trio had walked into Dr. Holland's Clinic for Cameron's flu appointment, Chelsea began her second ambulance ride of the day. "We drove out north on Sidney Baker toward the interstate," recalls the driver, Steven Brown. "Then we turned southeast on I-10 toward San Antonio."

Heading down the highway at Code Two—lights but no siren—the same crew escorted Chelsea as had that morning. Also as before, Dr. Holland followed closely behind. Reid and Petti brought up the rear of the speeding caravan, passing the miles in silence.

In the back of the ambulance, Tommy James kept a constant eye on Chelsea's heart monitor. To ease the child's still shallow breathing, he pumped the respiratory bag. Genene monitored the child's blood pressure and pulse. Once, when they hit a bump, Genene cautioned Tommy: "Be careful we don't lose that tube. If we lose it, we'll never get it back."

Less than ten minutes after departure, just eight miles down Highway I-10, at mile post 517, Chelsea's heart monitor stopped its steady electronic beeping and started a piercing drone. Chelsea, not yet two, was having a heart attack.

Steven recalls, "I was driving along and everything seemed to be real good when I noticed a lot of movement going on in back. There was a lot of—well, you know, I heard things being pushed, like boxes or something. In the rearview mirror, I got eye contact with Genene Jones."

"Pull this son of a bitch over!" she shouted.

The caravan halted.

Steven jumped out, ran to the rear, motioned for Dr. Holland, and opened the door. "As I recall," Kathleen later said, "I saw the EMT bagging Chelsea, and Genene doing external cardiac compressions."

"She's straight-lined!" Jones snapped.

After imploring his wife to stay in the car, Reid, too, ran to the flashing vehicle in time to hear the nurse's pronouncement. Turning, he saw his wife moving toward the ambulance. He intercepted her and walked her back to their car.

Inside the ambulance, Kathleen Holland placed her stethoscope to Chelsea's chest. "I ordered them to stop CPR for a moment so I could listen for a heartbeat. There was none. I palpated to see if I could feel a heartbeat, but I could feel none. I then jumped on the stretcher and began doing compressions myself."

Tommy continued pumping, breathing for the unresponsive child; Kathleen ordered the standard emergency drugs. Genene reached into her black bag, gathered a number of syringes together, then injected Chelsea with epinephrine, calcium chloride, and sodium bicarbonate. There was no response.

"Get me to a hospital, quick," Kathleen said as a second round of stimulants was administered.

"Which one?" asked Steven, adding the sirens to the lights and pulling back onto the highway.

"The nearest."

Steven radioed his office who, in turn, telephoned Comfort Community Hospital to advise them that an ambulance would be arriving momentarily with a Code Blue emergency.

At 1:05 P.M., less than ten minutes after Chelsea's arrest, they all skidded to a halt in front of the small, one-story hospital.

The staff ushered the group through the first door on the left into the tiny Emergency Room. Dr. Holland, Genene, and Steven Brown took turns pressing on Chelsea's chest while Tommy James remained at his post, pumping the air-bag.

Kathleen conferred with the doctor present, Dr.

Shepleigh, on the available medications, and together they calculated the differences between the adult solutions the hospital had available and the dosages suitable for Chelsea's needs. "I gave the child two rounds of 5 milli-equivalents bicarb, .8 cc's epinephrine, and 2.5 cc's calcium chloride, all through her IV," Kathleen says. "I hoped these stimulants would jolt the child's system into activity, but there was no response."

In the Comfort ER, after six rounds of the cardiotonic meds, Kathleen racked her brain for anything she might be missing. "We thought about using shock, but the size of the paddles they had there were too large to use on a patient Chelsea's size."

Kathleen tried a dose of lidocaine, and it was effective. Chelsea's heart started up, but only briefly; a few moments later, it sputtered still for the last time.

Reid and Petti waited in a room across the hall. "We were in there awhile," Petti remembers, "I don't know how long. At one point Reid went out and talked to the driver. I guess Steven must have told him something because when he came back in, he kept saying that I had to get, you know, prepared, 'just in case.' I didn't know what was happening. I got real mad at him. I was so mad at him. I told him not to talk like that, that there was *no* way Chelsea could die. There was *no* way. She wasn't sick."

Those attempting Chelsea's resurrection in Comfort kept up their efforts for a total of thirty-five minutes. At that point, explained Kathleen, "Chelsea's pupillary response began to get, what we call, 'sluggish.' It was slow. And when that begins to happen, when the pupils are not responding to light, then significant brain damage, as a result of the prolonged lack of oxygen, becomes a high probability. I pronounced Chelsea dead at 1:20 P.M.

"It's a doctor's responsibility at times like that to stay strong for the family. I went out to talk to them then, to tell them we'd done all we could."

In shock, Petti would later not remember much of these

events. Tommy recalls however, that Petti was crying. "Nurse Jones brought the baby out, wrapped in a blanket, and gave it to the mother. She was in a rocking chair, and began rocking the baby, whispering, 'No, no, no. She'll wake up in a minute. She's done this before. Wake up, Chelsea. Wake up.'"

Shortly thereafter, Genene, cradling the dead child to her breast the entire way, returned to Sid Peterson in the ambulance with Steven and Tommy. When they arrived at the hospital, the nurse in charge of the Emergency Room escorted the EMTs, and a sobbing Genene, downstairs. The body was logged into the morgue, then the ambulance returned Genene to the Clinic.

Kathleen stayed on in Comfort, attending to the necessary forms and details. When she signed the death certificate, she identified the cause of death as "Cardiopulmonary arrest, due to seizures of undetermined origin."

Back at the Clinic, in the office's log, Genene summarized the event:

> . . . CPR DISCONTINUED. PARENTS
> INFORMED OF DEATH BY DR. HOLLAND.
> BABY TRANSPORTED FROM COMFORT
> TO SID PETERSON HOSPITAL BY EMS
> AND MYSELF, AND TAKEN TO MORGUE.
> I WOULD HAVE GIVEN MY LIFE FOR HER.
>   GOOD BY CHELSEA.

Petti and Reid McClellan

(PETTI) One thing I learned from this was just how much I read in newspaper articles is completely false. It was a real eye-opener. Most of those reporters simply *make it up.* I sometimes wondered why they asked us questions at all, because if we didn't answer them, they just wrote what they wanted to put in there anyway.

(REID) And they twist your words real bad. I feel very uncomfortable sittin' here and talkin' seriously with you, unless I somehow know that the *truth* is going to be told. What actually happened. The thing is, I'm gun shy. I've had my words twisted, and now I'm sittin' here talking to you, and I really couldn't care less what you think about the way I look, the way I am, because it's really not going to make any difference. It's not going to make me a better person. It's not going to bring Chelsea back.

She was the most beautiful baby you've ever seen. You can turn and look behind you at the collage on the wall there. Cameron made that.

Do you view the world any differently now?

(PETTI) I do, a lot. The things that I never thought about, or that I always took for granted, I don't anymore. Little things, you know, that you encounter every day but just never pay attention to. For instance, you never think about something really bad happening to somebody you love. Oh, maybe your grandparents, you know, but not those making up the younger part of your family. You never think of anything really bad happening. Especially me.

I mean, my daddy died, but I was just, what? four or maybe five. Nothing really bad has ever happened to me. It hasn't. It really hasn't. Up until Chelsea.

I mean—I grew up just like any typical American from a middle-class family, you know? I was a cheerleader in high school, and just very ordinary, very Texan. Nothing very dramatic or tragic ever happened to me. And death—I never thought about death one way or another. I wasn't afraid of it, but I never thought about it either. Especially where it concerned my kids. You know, it never—even when Chelsea was born, and I was so sick. I had lost so much blood and I was just so weak. Even then, I never did think about anything happening to Chelsea, you know? I never thought about anything ever happening to Chelsea.

Even that day in Comfort, Reid was trying to tell me, you know, "You've got to be ready for this." And I just got *furious* with him, really furious. Because it just—it just did not—it never entered my mind, not even fleetingly, that anything really bad could happen. Sick is one thing, but *bad?* No. No, it never entered my mind. So, like I said, I look at life a lot differently now.

I get up in the morning differently now. My motto is: "Take one day at a time, do everything you can, and be as happy as you can. Live from one day to the next."

(REID) Myself, I've finished all the complaining that I'm going to do. 'Cause it makes no difference. I aim to take care of what I've got left.

I'm very thankful for all this. I've got her, and my two boys. I think that's more important than anything I could tell you about the past. It won't change anything and they're more important. That's the way I feel about it. We've got to live on here. I've talked to some people, you know, that seem to be more intelligent than me, but they all tell me pretty much the same thing: you've got to make your own decisions. Nobody can tell you nothin'. They can't tell you anything.

It's kind of a hard thing to sit back and listen to you wanting to do a book. I'm sitting here realizing, "They ain't gonna let it die. They just want to keep on pushin' it." You know?

We understand, and that was our major reason for hesitation in coming here tonight, or in contacting you at all.

(PETTI) It seems like it would be sort of hard to write the book and *not* talk to us. It seems like Chelsea would turn out to be more like an object than a real person who was a member of a family.

(REID) And there were things that—you wouldn't believe what this child did. She was so . . . with it. She was better, I mean, she was ahead of her class. She was number one sitting in her seat in front of the teacher, you know? And at fifteen months, that ain't bad. She was a fine baby. A *fine* baby. I'd like you to read something that my father wrote. It's fantastic.

Before my father got into politics, he was a minister. And he did something here that really came from the heart. I want you to read that. It's the eulogy he gave at Chelsea's funeral. Since you're writing a book, you ought to stick that in.

(PETTI) Another friend gave me a poem. It was just beautiful. I've still got that too, and Scott Monroe's note. He's Ron's assistant. He wrote us a poem during the final arguments. I don't know how he did it, I mean he was sitting there right in the middle of it, and he wrote this beautiful little eloquent note.

(REID) In the middle of the final arguments. Fantastic man.

I wasn't a witness, but they wouldn't let me in that courtroom for the trial anyway. They said I'm hostile, I'm crazy, I'm a nut. But I can't see a father in the world acting differently.

I was there for the final arguments though, and, oh man, those lawyers, they just rip your heart out. I'll tell you, they convinced me. See, I was raised, and have always lived the opposite way: an eye for an eye, and a tooth for a tooth. I can't, I *can't* just *forgive* something like this! But, they showed me. They showed me. Justice *does* work.

THIRTEEN

I am overcome of evil.

Euripides, Medea, 1.1077

NINETEEN-YEAR-OLD LYDIA EVANS KNEW nothing of the McClellans' tragedy that Thursday. Like most of the rest of the world, she would not hear the details for many months. All she knew was what Dr. Holland's receptionist told her over the phone.

"Hello, Mrs. Evans?"

"Yes."

"Ah, good, Judith Johnston here," she said in her lilting accent. "We've just received word that Dr. Holland won't be going into San Antonio after all; the ambulance is turning around. So, if I may, I'd like to 'un-cancel' Jacob's appointment. That is to say, if you'd still like to bring Jacob in a bit later, that looks to be quite possible."

Lydia said that would be fine. Her son, Jacob, five months old, had been irritable and cranky for over a week, and Lydia was at her wits' end. "I felt like there must be *something* I should be doing for him, but I didn't know what. See, he was teething, and nothing seemed to please

him—he just cried and hollered constantly. The day before, September 16, I'd called to see if I could get him in
to see his normal pediatrician in Fredricksburg, but he was
out of town and would be for another week. I then called
the doctor who'd delivered him, and after he'd asked me
several questions, he told me that he frankly couldn't
imagine that anything could be really wrong with him.
Jacob had been such a healthy baby, right from birth, the
doctor felt sure it was just the teething. That made me feel
better and I stopped worrying about it.

"A little later, my sister Elizabeth called. I think I was
doing the ironing, and during the course of the conversation, I happened to mention how irritable Jacob was. She
suggested I bring him in to the terrific new pediatrician
there in Kerrville—Dr. Holland. Well, I was busy and I
. . . well, I said something like 'Yeah, that might not be a
bad idea,' but Jacob had more or less settled down just
about then, so it was really just one of those polite dis-
missals, you know? I wasn't as worried about him as I had
been earlier.

"We hung up after a bit, and I put Jacob in his crib for
a nap. It must have been about a half-hour later, I got a
call from Dr. Holland's office. Ms. Johnston said that
Elizabeth had called them and let them know that I would
probably be calling about Jacob, and was there anything
they could do? Well, I was a little impressed—such concern, such consideration. I set up an appointment for the
following morning."

Lydia's sister, Elizabeth, picked Jacob and his mother
up early that Thursday morning, September 17, chauf-
feuring them into her Kerrville home for a visit before the
appointment. A little while later, Jacob's grandparents—
Donald and Loretta Lardie—arrived. They had earlier
promised to give mother and son a ride to the doctor's,
then home. Upon arrival, however, Mrs. Lardie told
Lydia that the doctor's office had reached her just as they
were leaving the house: Jacob's appointment had been

canceled. There had been some kind of medical emergency. Doctor Holland would be out of the office for the rest of the day.

"We stayed there for a while, at my sister's house," recalled Lydia, "just visiting, and it wasn't too much longer—I hesitate to try and guess at the time that elapsed, but it wasn't too much longer—the Clinic called us back (my mother had given them my sister's number). The receptionist informed me that the ambulance was returning and offered to reinstate Jacob's appointment. I said, 'Fine,' and my mother and father drove us in as we'd planned. We got there sometime between 3:15 and 3:30."

Judith greeted Jacob's family and told them that Dr. Holland was still at the hospital "making some arrangements," but the nurse would see them.

"Ms. Jones came out from the back of the office then," Lydia recalls, "introduced herself, and said that we could go ahead and do the preliminary work on Jacob. Dr. Holland was due back any moment.

"We stepped into a hallway where we went through the normal procedure of weighing and measuring and taking Jacob's temperature. I told the nurse the whole story, of how Jacob had been very irritable and that at times he would just scream, and how my doctor was out of town and the other doctor—the doctor who'd delivered him—didn't feel there was anything wrong. While I talked, my mother helped the nurse hold Jacob on the scale. It was all pretty normal. She kept asking questions about his history—how he had been when he was born and all that I could remember about what'd been going on with him since he'd been irritable. I remember that she kept coming back to his eyes—looking into his eyes—and feeling his head, she did that a lot. She seemed concerned and mentioned something about his left eye not responding to light properly, that the pupil was sluggish, or something like that, though the right eye, she said, seemed to be all right.

I'd never noticed any problems with Jacob's eyes, and I really didn't see any problem then either—but I wasn't really 'double-checking' her.

"Several times she repeated, 'Don't have nystagmus, Jacob, that is not any fun.' After the second or third time she said that, I asked her what she meant. She said nystagmus was a side-to-side movement of the eyes that indicated seizurelike activity."

At this point Genene told the mother and grandmother that she felt it would be prudent to run some tests. Although she certainly didn't want to alarm anyone, where children were concerned, she said, it was always wise to be conservative. Then she turned and left the room.

"I assumed it was to call the hospital and get in touch with Dr. Holland," Lydia says. "She came back three or four minutes later and told us that Dr. Holland had authorized her to go ahead and take some blood samples for tests and to put in an IV needle. They wanted to transfer Jacob to Sid Peterson. The tests sounded like a good idea, but the IV worried me. I thought maybe she wasn't telling me everything, that something was really wrong with Jacob, so I asked her why she had to put in an IV needle."

"In case he goes into a seizure," replied Genene, "while they're running the tests on him."

"I was stunned," Lydia recalls, "and for a moment didn't know what to say. 'He's never had any problems like that,' I finally said. 'Jacob's never had a seizure before.'"

Genene said, "With the kinds of tests they'll be running, you can't always be sure how a baby'll react."

"Well," said Lydia, slowly, "I don't know if I want them to go into any kind of tests like that."

Genene reached out and put a reassuring hand on Lydia's forearm. "I know how you feel, but don't worry. He'll be fine." She then urged both women toward the treatment room's doorway. "Now ladies, I need to get him ready for the hospital. I'm a mother too, and I know how it is to watch your child when he's unhappy. I think it'd be better if you waited out in the lobby. He'll probably cry out when I take his blood.''

Mrs. Lardie spoke up, ''Lydia can leave if she wants to, but I'll be glad to stay and help.''

''No, I'm sorry,'' insisted Genene, ''it's against our policy to have a relative in the room when we're performing any delicate procedure.''

In the waiting room, the two women were telling Jacob's grandfather what had happened, when Jacob began to scream. ''It was not the normal crying of a baby,'' his grandmother recalls. ''It was a scream. It was a terrified cry. He screamed several times, and then, in mid-scream—as though it were just cut off—there was nothing, just dead silence.

''My husband was seated, and I noticed the pained expression on his face—he had heard the screams too—so I went over to him and touched him, and he looked at me and said, 'Honey, Jacob is gone.' I looked at Lydia then, and I didn't think—I still don't—that she was, at that moment, quite aware of what had happened. She had to have heard, but she looked kind of blank, like she hadn't let what'd happened fully register. I walked over to her and said, 'Honey, something is wrong with Jacob.'''

Lydia raised her head slowly. ''What? What's wrong?''

''Jacob's stopped crying.''

They heard a sudden flurry of activity in the back of the Clinic, then Judith called the hospital and asked for Dr. Holland.

Mrs. Lardie pushed into the central hall demanding to know what was going on. ''The door to the examining room was open, and I saw Jacob lying on the table totally still, not moving at all, limp. I thought he was dead. Genene was apparently administering mouth-to-mouth re-

suscitation. At that point the receptionist told me to go
back to the lobby and not get in the way.''

Judith closed the door to the waiting room behind Mrs.
Lardie, then moved back into the reception area and made
another phone call. Moments later, a nurse from the office
immediately next door rushed through the waiting room,
quickly followed by two EMTs.

Dr. Phillip Webb, the newly established family practi-
tioner who was in charge of the neighboring office, arrived
shortly thereafter. ''I observed a five-month-old baby lying
on an examining table flaccid, limp, cyanotic,'' he recalls.
''There were two paramedics in the room, Nurse Jones
was in the room, and my nurse was in the room. The child
was not breathing at all. As I came through the doorway, I
heard Nurse Jones inform the EMTs that she had tried to
intubate the baby but had been unsuccessful. She saw me
then and asked if I would. I did so immediately. I then
listened for a heartbeat; it was slow but present. We then
picked the child up and moved quickly toward the ambulance.''

After completing the paperwork at Comfort, Kathleen
had driven to Sid Peterson to attend to the forms that had
to be filed in connection with Chelsea's death. She also
checked in with Judith and was informed that the Evans
family had been contacted and would be keeping their appointment after all. Drained from the events of the day,
Kathleen asked the receptionist to send the Evanses to Sid
Peterson as soon as they arrived at the Clinic. The message was given to Genene.

''While I was at Sid Peterson arranging Chelsea's autopsy,'' Kathleen recalls, ''I kept waiting to hear from the
ER about Jacob's arrival. I had just finished up and was
heading out the door, when one of the hospital's operators
stopped me and said there was a message that there was
some emergency at my office, and I was needed, STAT—
shortest turn-around time.

"I ran out to my car, jumped in, and drove very quickly back to the office. The first thing I noticed turning off Water Street was the ambulance in the parking lot.

"I parked, jumped out of my car, and headed toward the building, but before I got there, the ambulance honked its horn and the back door opened. The physician who had the office next to mine hopped out, pointing back into the cabin: 'I had to intubate him.'"

Dr. Holland climbed in and asked Genene: "What the hell happened?"

"He came in with bulging fontanelle and had a seizure," she replied, pumping the ambu-bag. "I had to call the doctor and nurse from next door. He ordered 180 milligrams of Dilantin." She coughed slightly and rolled her eyes. "I knew that was too much, so I only gave him 80."

Lydia Evans and her parents drove to the hospital ahead of the ambulance and waited for it outside the hospital's emergency entrance. When the ambulance arrived, the driver got out, ran around to the rear, and opened the door. The second EMT jumped out then, turned, and offered an assist to Genene, who ignored him and simply leaped down. It was at this point that Lydia, in a mild state of shock, saw her son for the first time since Genene had asked her to leave the Clinic's examining room. He was hanging utterly limp in Genene's arms.

While Kathleen Holland and the ER team began work on their new patient, Genene pulled Lydia Evans aside. "She said she needed to tell me what'd happened back at the Clinic," recalls Lydia. "We sat down and she said that she had not started taking blood—hadn't even inserted the IV needle yet—when Jacob, lying on the examining table, simply started to scream. She said he arched his back and turned blue. His breathing stopped, then his heart stopped."

Later in the ICU, after Jacob had been stabilized, Kathleen double-checked Genene's initial recorded observations of the child. The front of Jacob's head was rather large for his age, and there was a slight separation between the fontanelle bones, as Genene had said. It could be a normal variation, but in a child who has had a seizure, it becomes a more notable idiosyncrasy. Based upon the symptoms Lydia had supplied Judith with when she called for the appointment, Kathleen initially had suspected the screaming episodes were nothing more than tantrums about which the first-time mother was overly alarmed. In light of the seizure in the office, however, coupled with the enlarged fontanelle, and the rapid eye movements Genene had reported, Kathleen was now concerned about the possibility of a slowly developing hydrocephalus—fluid accumulating within the skull—or possibly meningitis. Kathleen asked Mrs. Evans to leave her son in the hospital for observation and tests.

In the six days Jacob stayed at Sid Peterson, the doctors turned up nothing that could explain his respiratory arrest. Dr. Holland referred Jacob to Dr. Mackey, the neurologist in San Antonio. Dr. Mackey failed to find any cause for the episode or any evidence that Jacob had a seizure disorder.

Kathleen had had four cardiac or respiratory arrests in her Clinic in the space of four weeks but, she maintains, "I still didn't suspect anything because I didn't connect the incidents in my mind. That wasn't the way I'd been trained to think. To me, each patient was completely distinct, with separate symptoms, different histories. I never thought, 'My God, I've had four emergencies in X number of days, or two respiratory arrests, or two *anything*.' I had no yardstick. I know that's hard for people to understand, looking back on it, but in my experience, children with the symptomology these kids had *often* went on to develop serious problems."

As the months and then years slid by with no recurrence of the strange problems Jacob suffered in Kathleen's Clinic, his parents allowed themselves to accept the certainty that his emergency was artificially induced. They finally stopped worrying. No passage of time, however, could ever erase Lydia Evans's memory of her son's screams as he felt his ability to move, even to breathe, slip away.

A Mourner

They held the service at the funeral parlor. I think there was about thirty people there. Reid was trying to take care of Petti. She seemed really lost; my heart just broke for her. At some point, I saw that nurse go up and give her a shot of something. I guess it was something to calm her down. It seemed to help.

It's frightening to think of, isn't it. We all thought it very decent of the doctor and her people to attend, you know, to take the time to show they cared. Reid and Petti even took out a newspaper ad, to thank them publicly for all they had done for Chelsea. It was hard for them to believe Jones was responsible, hard for all of us to believe.

It was a beautiful service. Chelsea's grandfather—and I believe that was Reid's daddy—gave the eulogy. I don't think I ever heard a more moving tribute. Someone told me he used to be a minister, which I don't doubt. He was such a beautiful speaker—just reached out and touched your heart.

Do you remember what Chelsea's grandfather said?

Not very well— Just a little, you know. He said— He was talking about how we all have a purpose in this life, something to accomplish. Then he talked about how much Chelsea had accomplished in her short life, how much joy and love she brought to the family. He said that all of us had been touched in some way by her life; and that's really true, don't you think?

Yes, we do.

He read this little poem about how God had only loaned Chelsea to Reid and Petti for a little while, to help their hearts grow bigger. And now God had taken her back. He said something like— How Chelsea had joined her great grandfather in heaven and how he probably was already teaching her how to play poker. I remember that, because people kind of smiled, you know?

I'm butchering what he said pretty badly. I wish I could remember it better. It was just very moving, very loving. I know I had tears on my face and a lot of the other ladies did too. It was very beautiful.

It was a fine thing for Chelsea's granddaddy to have done.

FOURTEEN

No one is made guilty by fate.

Seneca, Oedipus, *1.1019*

THE MONDAY FOLLOWING JACOB'S ARREST and Chelsea's death, the Clinic was closed. Everyone attended the funeral. The heat and humidity of mid-September pressed down upon the mourners like a second gravity. Chelsea was buried among the wild oaks in Kerrville's Garden of Memories cemetery.

On Tuesday, September 21, the Clinic reopened. Two days later, September 23, yet another ambulance was dispatched to Kathleen's Clinic. The patient was a five-month-old baby girl, Rolinda Ruff, who had been suffering from diarrhea and was dehydrated and listless. While Kathleen was starting an IV to replenish the fluids Rolinda had lost, the baby appeared to have a breath-holding spell: she sobbed deeply, then she stopped breathing entirely.

When Rolinda arrived at Sid Peterson, several physicians made a point to be on hand. During the week since Chelsea's death and Jacob Evans's emergency, the doctors at Sid Peterson had begun to share their misgivings about the events in Kathleen Holland's Clinic. Dr. Duan Packard, Sid Peterson's chief of staff and the dean of the Kerrville medical community, awaited the young doctor and her patient in the ER, along with Drs. Earl Merrit and Larry Adams. Dr. Frank Bradley, the hospital's anesthesiologist, was just finishing in surgery when the ER Code Blue was called. "I went to see if there was anything I could do to help out. I was standing at the bottom of the stairs when three or four medics came bursting through the Emergency Room doors in a hurry, carrying a child. They went down the hall and placed the child on a gurney. I could see that the child was having what we call diaphragmatic respirations— jerky respirations.

"Dr. Holland announced that because of the trouble she had had with the child, she was going to intubate— place a tube into the windpipe. Dr. Merrit was standing next to me at the time, and I heard him comment, 'Looks like the child is beginning to breathe all right now.' Dr. Holland started into the child's mouth with a laryngoscope blade, which is a flat blade with a light on the end so we can see the larynx. As she did this, the child started making gross motor movements, which were purposeful but not totally controlled. She had shoulder motion and elbow motion, but I noticed no fine motion, no fine control such as wrist or finger motion at all. I watched the child start jerking her shoulder, acting like she was trying to cough, then she flipped her arm up and finally got it to her mouth.

"It struck me, as I stood there watching the child, that she was exhibiting that same type of behavior that I see all the time in the operating room when an intubated patient, coming out from under the paralytic effects of suc- cinylcholine, ineffectually reaches up for the tube—be- cause the tube hurts and it gags you. While these movements are clearly purposeful, the patient is unable to accomplish his or her purpose because, though he has regained *proximal* muscle control, he hasn't yet metabolized the drug enough to have *distal* control.

"To me, it appeared as if the child was coming out from under the effects of succinylcholine and I mentioned this to Dr. Mason, the Emergency Medicine specialist there at Sid Peterson. He urged me to talk to Dr. Packard."

Bradley found a willing listener in Packard, whose attention had been drawn to Dr. Holland's Clinic for sometime, since the incident involving his own patient, Misty Reichenau. After listening to Bradley and reflecting on what he himself had just witnessed, he called Dr. Joe Vinas (who, like Dr. Holland, had graduated from the University of Texas medical school in San Antonio and had trained at Medical Center Hospital). Packard asked Vinas to investigate Holland's professional history.

That evening, shortly after 6:00 P.M., Vinas called an associate, Dr. Terry Ryan,* a member of the Thoracic and Cardiovascular Surgery Department at MCH. As a professional courtesy, Ryan agreed to tell Dr. Vinas what he knew. He remembered Dr. Kathleen Holland as a competent and interested doctor, if perhaps somewhat overzealous.

Vinas mentioned generally some of the problems they were having, then told Ryan of the rumors that one of the nurses at Sid Peterson had passed along to him that afternoon: Genene Jones had been employed at Medical Center during a time of heparin overdoses and other apparent problems in the PICU. Could Ryan possibly find out anything more about this?

"He called me back a short time later," Dr. Vinas later recalled, "and told me: 'Looks like you've got a baby killer on your hands.'"

"He explained that there had evidently been an inordinate number of deaths and arrests in their PICU the year before which in some way seemed to revolve around LVN Genene Jones. He then indicated that he would prefer to not personally forward me to anyone directly involved in that investigation. He thought that might prove somewhat embarrassing for him; but he felt certain I would know who to contact. I indicated that I did, and that it was no problem, and thanked him for his help. I then phoned Dr. Arthur McFee.

"Dr. McFee was very kind. After I explained the situation briefly, he indicated he would be more than happy to help and began sharing with me some of the details of their investigations. He indicated that the findings were disturbing. Genene Jones was the common denominator in the questionable occurrences at Medical Center, some of which had culminated in the rather inappropriate deaths of certain infants. There was, however, no *criminal evidence*—at least, not enough to substantiate criminal charges. He said that they had decided to remedy the dilemma by releasing all the LVNs and retaining only registered nurses in the PICU.

"I immediately relayed this information to Dr. Packard who called an emergency meeting of the executive committee at Sid Peterson."

"There was just too much smoke," Dr. Packard said later. "I've been in practice here for over forty-three years, and I've never had a respiratory arrest. To the best of my knowledge, up till this time, there'd never been one in Kerrville at all. Something had to be very wrong."

Those attending the emergency meetings on Thursday, September 23, agreed things would have to change. The hospital's administrator, Tony Hall, called Dr. Holland and told her the committee expected her the following day, Friday, at 1:00 P.M. "Be prepared to talk about your Clinic and the patients you have treated at the hospital."

The next day, Tony Hall joined the executive committee (including Drs. Packard, Vinas, and Bradley) as they waited for the new pediatrician to arrive.

Kathleen stepped in. The room was quiet. Eleven men faced her, seated around an oblong table. Kathleen took the one empty seat at the near end.

Dr. Packard began. "A good number of children seem to be getting sick in your Clinic. Could you tell us why you think that might be happening?"

Kathleen, tense but focused, pulled out a neat stack of three-by-five cards on which she had listed each child's history, symptoms, and treatments. After briefing the panel on her emergency patients, she told them that she appreciated their concern and would welcome any advice; however, as far as she knew, nothing out of the ordinary had happened.

"Then they asked me about my frequent use of an antibiotic that only I seemed to know had come back into favor for use on pediatric patients. They asked me about the use of succinylcholine in the Clinic; I told them I'd never used it. Never. They suggested I might be over-utilizing their PICU, which struck me as odd. They passed along several complaints they had received regarding both Sally Benkert's and Genene's aggressive attitudes. I apologized for both nurses and promised to speak to them about it. They asked me about the competence of my office personnel—whether I trusted them. I answered yes."

Kathleen's beeper went off, and she left the room to find a phone. She returned a few moments later to inform them that Jimmy Pearson, now back in the hospital's ICU, was suffering a respiratory arrest. She apologized, excused herself, and at the door asked: "Would anyone care to assist me?"

No one volunteered.

Before the meeting broke up, the remaining doctors agreed that their suspicions outweighed Dr. Holland's explanations. As Packard and Hall left the meeting together, the two further agreed that it was time to bring others into the matter. Hall called the Board of Vocational Nurse Examiners (responsible for licensing vocational nurses) and spoke with the nursing board's investigator, Ferris Aldridge. The investigator told Hall that he did not feel this was a matter for board investigation but would locate the proper authority for him. Aldridge began to make the phone calls that would eventually put him in touch with Texas Ranger Joe Davis.

When Kathleen returned to the Clinic, Genene asked her about the meeting. "I told her that they'd asked about my approach to pediatrics, about my intubation criteria and techniques, and about my understanding of seizures. I mentioned that they asked about succinylcholine—did I keep it in the office, had I ever used it. I also told her that they had expressed some concern about her aggressiveness and asked whether I trusted my office personnel.

"At that point, she became upset," Kathleen recalls. "She said, 'Somebody's starting rumors,' or something to that effect."

On Saturday and Sunday, September 25 and 26, Kathleen stayed at the house site in Center Point with Charleigh. She returned to the Nixon Lane house early Sunday evening, shortly after dinner. During the course of idle conversation before retiring, Genene told Kathleen, "Oh, by the way, I found that missing vial of succs."

"What missing succs?"

"Remember, the vial of succs that was missing."

"Genene then proceeded," recalls Kathleen, "to recall to me a day when she had reported this vial missing, and how I ordered her to have it replaced. My recollection of that day's conversation was somewhat different in that I did not remember it being one about any potentially dangerous drug. I clearly recalled a sense of the benign nature of the drug I heard her report as missing. Succinylcholine would never fit that characterization.''

The doctor, vaguely disturbed, asked, ''So, where was it?''

''In the lower drawer of the crash room's table, under the paper lining.''

''How did it get there?''

''I don't know.''

''Well, okay, good. At least it's found.''

''At this point,'' Kathleen remembers, ''I was definitely uneasy. All of a sudden the Clinic's missing medication turned out to be the same medication mentioned by the Sid Peterson committee. It was about then that Genene started to volunteer all kinds of information. I didn't know what to ask next, so I just sat silently. Genene just kept on talking.''

''There's only one problem,'' Genene was saying, ''the cap has been popped.''

''How did that happen?''

''I don't know.''

''Well, was it in the drawer? Maybe it came off when it was dropped in the drawer.''

''No.''

''Well then . . . where is the cap? How did it get popped?''

''I don't know. You know we've had a lot of people in and out of that office lately.''

Kathleen's uneasiness increased. '''Suspicious' isn't really the right word, but I was beginning to wonder. Something wasn't right. I remember just staring at her, listening, occasionally nodding. She was looking down at the table mostly. She'd look up at me for just a moment, then look back down again quickly.''

''But anyway,'' Genene said, smiling, ''it's okay, I checked it against the replacement vial and all 10 cc's are there. If somebody wants to draw it up, they can draw it up. It's all there.''

"She sort of stopped for a moment with that statement," says Kathleen, "and I kept sitting there. A long time ago, someone said, you know, when people start offering you a lot of unsolicited information, it usually signifies something. I just didn't know what. The last thing I remember hearing her say was: 'Oh yeah, I checked, and there are no holes in the stopper.'"

Kathleen was unnerved. "That night I thought back over the kids, and I kept coming back to one thing in my mind. All the children I had seen personally had one common denominator: they had all been limp—some only for a short time, but they had all experienced a period of flaccidity."

The next morning, Monday, September 27, with no appointments scheduled till after noon, Kathleen followed her regular procedure, stopping off at Sid Peterson to check on patients before heading for the Clinic. Genene was just leaving for lunch with Sally when Kathleen arrived at 11:30 A.M.

Kathleen dropped her purse and coat off in her office, then went to the refrigerator. She opened the door and pulled out the two vials of succinylcholine. "They looked fine. I held them up to the light and saw that there was a very, very slight difference in the meniscus—the dip in the fluid—but that could have easily been due to the internal shape of the bottle. I was about to put the two vials back when I tipped them toward me and glanced at their tops. One was completely sealed by the plastic cap. The other, the vial in my right hand, had a popped top with two distinct puncture holes in the center of the vial's red rubber stopper.

"I didn't know what to do. I freaked out. I recall walking around the office, more or less just pacing back and forth, wondering what exactly I should do, who I should call—and what I would say."

Sometime after 1:30 P.M., Genene returned from lunch.

She seemed in good spirits. She had a ribbon in her hands which she'd tied into a bow. She told Kathleen that she had been to visit Chelsea McClellan. (Petti, who also happened to be at the cemetery that day during lunch, saw Genene kneeling at her daughter's gravesite. "She was rockin' back and forth, sobbin', and callin' out Chelsea's name over and over.")

Kathleen asked Genene to accompany her back to the refrigerator. "Genene, would you please take out the two vials of succs."

"Okay."

"Now look at them."

"Yeah."

"All right, now look at the tops."

"Yeah."

"What about the tops?"

"So?"

"There are holes there. Where did those holes come from?"

"I don't know."

"Genene, you told me last night there were no holes, how did—"

"There were a lot of people in that room that day."

"In what room? What day?"

"The day Misty Reichenau seized."

"Genene, I didn't use succs on Misty."

"I know, I know, but don't you remember, I asked you if you wanted to use it because you were having trouble intubating."

Kathleen stopped for a moment, searching her memory. "All right, I remember you asking me if I wanted to use it, but I also remember saying no, I couldn't remember the dose off the top of my head and I wanted to try intubating without it. And I did finally get her intubated without it."

"Yes, I know, but I had Sally go get it out of the refrigerator in case you changed your mind."

Dr. Holland telephoned Sally and asked her to come down to the Clinic immediately. Kathleen met Sally in the reception area and together they walked back toward the refrigerator. "All right now, Sally, Genene tells me the day Misty seized, you came back here to the refrigerator and grabbed a vial of succinylcholine. Is that right?"

"Yes."

"All right. Tell me what you did with it. In fact," Kathleen handed Sally a capped vial of saline, "*show* me what you did with it."

They walked to the front examining room. "I popped it on the way," said Sally, reenacting her movements, "then got ready to draw, but you guys wouldn't give me a dose. You were arguing over the dose."

"Okay, so you didn't draw any out. What did you do with it then?"

"I put it back here, behind the cottonball dispenser," said Sally placing the vial out of the way, behind the jar, itself already close to the wall.

"My last question," Kathleen later said, "with both Sally and Genene present was: 'Well, then, how did the holes get in the stopper?'

"They both replied: 'I don't know.'"

Kathleen thanked Sally for coming down, then left the room. After she replaced the vials in the refrigerator, she turned and almost bumped into Genene standing in the alcove's archway. "How am I going to explain those holes, Genene?"

With what Kathleen later described as a coolly defensive demeanor, Genene said, "I don't think you should explain them at all. I think you should just throw it out. Tell them we lost it. We won't be lying if we say we lost it. We *did* lose it. I know we found it again, but they don't have to know we found it. Just throw it away."

"Genene," Kathleen said, as calmly as she could,

"medically and legally, I can't do that. For my own peace of mind, I can't do that."

At this point, Judith announced the arrival of the afternoon's appointment. Kathleen left abruptly to lead the mother and child into the front examining room, shutting the door behind her.

After Kathleen ushered her patient out the door, at about 3:00 or 3:30 that afternoon, Genene walked up to her and said, "I did a stupid thing at lunch."

"Oh?"

"I took a bunch of doxepin."

Kathleen looked Genene squarely in the face (something she had not done for more than an hour) and saw that Genene's eyes were glazed and the lids drooping. "How many did you take, Genene? How many?"

"I don't know. Not many."

"How many, Genene?" Kathleen's voice began to rise.

"A couple. I don't know. A few."

"Where is the bottle?"

"At home."

Kathleen called Nixon Lane, but the bottle of antianxiety pills could not be located. Kathleen forced herself to look through her nurse's purse, and the bottle she found there—labeled as originally holding thirty pills—was empty.

"How many did you take? Did you take them all, Genene?"

Jones was blinking slowly. "No, I only took a few. I threw the rest away. I'm just feeling a little down."

"Genene, you have to go to the hospital. I'm calling an ambulance."

"No, don't do that," she said, stretching out on the couch in the central hallway. "I just need to lie down for a while."

"I'm sorry, Genene," replied Kathleen, her voice tight and shrill, "you are going to the hospital." While Judith called Sid Peterson, Kathleen rushed next door to Dr. Webb's office. "My nurse has just told me that she has taken an overdose of doxepin," she announced, in mild hysterics, but with great finality. "Number one, I am not an adult doctor, and number two, I wash my hands of this woman."

The EMTs arrived at Dr. Holland's Clinic for the last time shortly before 5:00 P.M. Kathleen watched as her nurse was carried out. The woman she saw was a stranger, someone of frightening, unknown possibilities.

The doctor returned to the refrigerator, opened the door, and stared at the vials without touching them. She thought about Chelsea. She wondered what would happen now. She sensed that those two vials represented a future that held more trouble than she could imagine. She shut the refrigerator door, walked to her office, and called Drs. Joe Vinas and Frank Bradley. "I need to talk to you," she heard herself say. "Please come to my office, now. It's urgent."

"I arrived about 5:15 P.M.," Dr. Vinas remembers, "and Dr. Holland invited me right in. She appeared to be very upset. She told me she felt as if she were being questioned by Sid Peterson, not only as a doctor, but also legally, and as a person, regarding her involvement in the numerous arrests at her Clinic. She informed me that she had just fired Genene Jones because Jones had attempted suicide that afternoon and, more importantly, because Dr. Holland had, just that morning, found a vial of succinylcholine which had obviously been opened and which had obvious needle marks in its top. She then produced the vial and while there were certainly two separate puncture sites, it appeared to me as though a needle had been pushed through the membrane a number of times—entering by way of the same two holes. The vial, however, was full.

Dr. Holland told me she had no knowledge of this vial

being opened and she specifically denied the use of succinylcholine during the Misty Reichenau arrest when the
drug had been fetched by an acquaintance of Genene's
who just happened to be in the Clinic at the time.

"She was in a defensive posture during the entire interview. One of the things she wanted to make sure I understood was that she had given Genene the opportunity to
work with her only because Medical Center Hospital had
recommended her favorably. Dr. Holland said that she was
told: 'It would do Genene some good to get up there in a
different environment.'

"Dr. Bradley arrived about then and the three of us discussed the situation concerning the succinylcholine. We
went through Dr. Holland's requisitions and found that she
had ordered and received three vials of the drug from Pampell's Pharmacy. One of the vials was missing.

"Dr. Holland indicated some surprise over the number
of vials and felt that she had not really intended to order
that many. Though Dr. Holland's name appeared on each
of the slips for billing purposes, two of the three had been
signed for by Genene Jones.

"At that point, we called the hospital administrator,
Tony Hall. He came down and took charge of the two
vials, along with about five other opened (some punctured)
vials of saline solution. He turned them over to the Department of Public Safety the following day.

"As we were all leaving the Clinic, Dr. Holland noticed
three boxes in a corner of the office, stuffed with baby
clothes and toys. They had evidently been dropped off by
Mrs. McClellan a few days before. Dr. Holland began to
cry then. 'My God,' she said, 'if Genene killed that baby,
I'll never forgive myself.'"

Late that evening, Tony Hall contacted Texas Ranger
Joe Davis, who had been asked by Investigator Aldridge
of the Board of Nurse Examiners in Austin to look into Sid
Peterson's complaints against Dr. Holland's Clinic. Hall
informed Davis that Holland's nurse was in the hospital as

a result of a suicide attempt. "I thought these things might be preying on her mind," Davis recalled, "and that she might be ready to talk about it all, so I went on over there about ten o'clock. We chatted a bit, and she denied having done anything wrong, explaining that the seizures in the Clinic were only normal incidents—that they quite often occur with children. She told me, 'The Sid Peterson staff just doesn't know about kids—they're upset because they don't know anything about pediatric care.' As for the succinylcholine in the office, she denied ever having injected the drug into any patient.

"Just before I left, I asked her if she would be willing to take a polygraph test, to which she responded, 'I will, if Dr. Holland will.'"

The following morning, Tuesday September 28, at 10:00, Genene arrived at the Clinic in her uniform.

"What are you doing here?" asked Kathleen.

"I work here, remember?"

Kathleen was speechless. "I was all alone with her, and it was frightening. She frightened me. I didn't know what she was capable of, you know? I thought: 'How can I say this gently and still make sure she'll go away?'"

"Genene, I think that with all that's happened, it would be better for both you and for me if you didn't work here any more."

Genene became abusive. Angry. Threatening. She challenged Holland to take a polygraph test. Before storming out of the Clinic, she looked Kathleen in the eye and said in a low voice, "There's only one thing I'm sorry for: somebody convinced you that I'm guilty."

A short time later, Ranger Davis called from Tony Hall's office to warn Kathleen that Jones had been released from the hospital.

"No kidding," Kathleen commented, and told the Ranger about her confrontation with Genene. When she returned the receiver to the cradle, Judith appeared in the door, "Genene is on the other line and wants to talk to you." Holland refused. A few minutes later, Judith returned to hand Kathleen a note that Genene said she had left for her in a drawer in the office. Thinking that Joe Davis might still be in Tony Hall's office, Kathleen immediately called the administrator's.

"Davis just left," Hall told her.

"My former nurse left a letter, and I want him to come take it."

"What's it say?" Hall asked.

Kathleen tore the envelope open and began to read aloud:

> THERE ISN'T ANYWAY TO EXPLAIN TO
> YOU WHY THINGS ARE GOING TO
> CHANGE. SOMETIMES, AS WRONG AS IT
> MAY SEEM, YOU HAVE TO EXCEPT
> WHAT LIFE DISHES OUT.

"WHEN YOUR OLDER," the note went on to promise, "YOU WILL BE ABLE TO UNDERSTAND WHY."

Confused now whether this part of the note was even intended for her, Kathleen read on, unthinking. Genene confided her plan to "GO AWAY," but explained that this didn't mean "I DON'T LOVE YOU." Kathleen continued in halting tones: "MY LOVE, IS SO DEEP, AND STRONG, IT WILL LAST FOR ALL ETERNITY." At this point, shocked and uncertain, afraid even to consider what Tony Hall must be thinking of Genene's ramblings, Kathleen stopped reading. "What is she *saying?*" she protested. "I don't know what this is, but I can't . . . Look, if Davis wants this letter he can come and get it. I don't even want to *touch* it."

The letter that Kathleen refused to finish for Mr. Hall went on for several disjointed paragraphs that became increasingly infantile in tone. Genene asked Kathleen to explain to her children how much she loved them. "IT'S

SUCH A STRONG LOVE, I CAN'T PUT IT ON PA-
PER.'' She also asked Kathleen to ensure that her two
children were placed with good people with lots of love.
"I'M NOT GUILTY OF MURDER," she avowed, but
said that "DADDY'S WAY IS RIGHT"—it would, she
felt, somehow take "ALL THE PRESSURE OFF YOU
AND THE SEVEN PEOPLE, WHOSE LIFE I HAVE
ALTERED."

Dissolving into delusion, she claimed "NO ONE CAN
HURT ME WITH MY DADDY." Her deceased father
would, she wrote, straighten everything out, "AND THEN
WE'LL GO HOME." There would be no more problems for
Kathleen and "NO MORE NIGHTMARES FOR ME."

"I'M GOING WITH DADDY BECAUSE I MISS HIM
AND WANT TO BE WITH HIM," she closed. "HE'LL
TAKE CARE OF BOTH OF US." The note was signed:
"I LOVE YOU, GENENE."

Late that afternoon, Ranger Davis returned to Kathleen's Clinic to pick up the curious letter. He and Tony
Hall then met Genene at the Nixon Lane house. The
Ranger and Administrator escorted Jones to Austin for her
polygraph test. After a short series of questions, the examiner evaluated Jones's exam. He concluded that for several
pertinent questions, Jones had given responses that indicated deception.

Before the close of business on Tuesday, Kathleen was
notified that pending the outcome of an investigation, she
should consider herself removed from Sid Peterson's medical staff and barred from the hospital itself.

On Wednesday, at 11:00 A.M., Texas Rangers arrived at
Kathleen's Clinic to escort the doctor to the Department of
Public Safety's headquarters in Austin. Her interview with
DPS investigators began at 1:00 in the afternoon, and for
the next five hours, Kathleen detailed everything she knew
about the seven emergencies in her Clinic and about the

few rumors she had heard concerning Jones's activities in Medical Center's PICU.

Shortly after 6:00 P.M., one of the investigators asked if she would agree to a short lie-detector test, to which Kathleen responded, "Sure." Rangers strapped her into the same chair Genene had occupied the day before, then the investigator stepped forward, and to Kathleen's surprise, read her her rights. The familiar words, which Kathleen had heard so many times delivered by TV cops to TV criminals, shocked her to the realization that she, too, was considered a suspect in Chelsea's murder.

As calmly as she could, Kathleen answered the examiner's two-dozen questions, then, at his request, answered them a second time. While the examiner evaluated the responses, the rangers disconnected Kathleen from the machine.

"Well," the examiner bluntly informed Kathleen a few minutes later, "looks like we've got a liars' contest here."

Like Genene before her, Kathleen had not passed the test.

The drive back from Austin was long and quiet. As they neared Kerrville, Kathleen asked Ranger Davis to stop off at the Clinic so that she could pick up the few things she had asked Bonnie Gunderson to gather for her from the Nixon Lane house. For the next few nights at least, Kathleen intended to stay in a Kerrville hotel.

"I felt this crazy compulsion to check and see if Bonnie had remembered my toothbrush," Kathleen recalls. "I don't know why, but it was all I could think about—as if it mattered somehow."

Kathleen unzipped an overnight bag, and saw immediately on top two medicine vials and a note.

"I remember I jumped back from the bag as if I'd been burned," says Kathleen, "and really just lost it. I was really freaked. I was kind of yelling at the two rangers: 'That lady's trying to frame me,' I said.

'You picked me up, these bags weren't here then. I know nothing about them. I just now opened this bag. Test it for fingerprints. I've never seen this stuff before in my life!'"

The vials proved to be saline. The note was from Genene, written shortly before Kathleen left for Austin. In the note, Genene admitted that she had given medicine once without a doctor's orders and had, on occasion, changed the potency of medications, making them slightly weaker or stronger, as she saw fit. Genene also informed Kathleen that she had failed her polygraph and fully expected Kathleen to fail hers as well. "I may go down for this," she wrote, "but I won't go down alone."

PART
3

The Excavation

FIFTEEN

*"Ah, the Americans are sly and clever,"
said Tan, whereupon the Americans present broke out into uncontrollable laughter.
The interpreter explained to Tan that the
Americans themselves never thought of
themselves as either sly or clever.*

> Bernard B. Fall, Last
> Reflections on a War

LIKE AN ACTOR, THE CRIMINAL INVESTIGATOR
constructs the thoughts and motivations of his subject out
of pieces of himself. He must be able, empathetically, to
recreate the truth of a crime before he can uncover it. The
investigator therefore enters into an uneasy communion
with the criminal born of the intimacy of understanding.

A detective and a district attorney are both criminal
investigators, but different kinds. The detective has a more
connubial relationship with the events as they really happened. His goal is to *find* the truth; therefore, all facts are
of equal merit to him, each one a part of the whole story.
The lawyer's task, however, is to *expose* the truth—to
persuade a jury—so the lawyer judges the facts with a
more cynical eye. What will be useful, what will help obtain a conviction—that is how the lawyer assesses the
fruits of his investigation.

In 1982, Ron Sutton was district attorney for Kerr
County, including the principal township of Kerrville. Affable but guarded, with a Texas drawl and a rural lexicon
of words and phrases, Sutton is a sophisticated cousin of

that good ol' country boy who you would not want sitting across from you at a bargaining table: Before you know it, he has your wallet, watch, shirt, and shoes, and you are smiling, thinking you got the best of the deal.

At six feet and some 240 pounds, Sutton looks like the former football player he is. Ruddy-faced, thick-necked, with a shock of thinning, blondish-grey hair, the uncomplicated personality he projects is contradicted by a pair of shrewd eyes beneath a heavy brow. "I learned how to think in law school," he says. "How to think logically, reasonably, in straight lines, about the subject of my own choosing. I enjoy it, the law; it's both my vocation and my avocation."

Thirty-eight years old in 1982, Sutton had spent the previous sixteen years learning the art of lawyering. In 1977, Sutton took on the job of district attorney for the five counties north of San Antonio, more than 800 square miles of thinly populated Texas Hill Country. He's held the position ever since.

"Of course, it's a lot of work," Sutton says. "I spend a lot of time runnin' down the road. But, I like the casualness. You'll notice that when I'm just doing work here around the office, I don't put on a coat and tie. I detest ties. They choke me."

Like most of the attorneys in this part of Texas, Ron is a native, grew up around Junction, and was graduated from Baylor University, then Saint Mary's Law School in San Antonio. "After graduation I did some research for a retired chief justice, then started doing criminal defense work. Didn't like that much. Then I became a county attorney, which was more interesting, but I got dissatisfied with it. There wasn't enough action. I like to to keep busy. I ran for judge along in there and got beat—and that was probably the greatest thing that ever happened to me. Because then I was ready, when, in September of '77, the governor appointed me district attorney. I'm still not sure quite how that happened. I was lucky, I guess. Anyway, even though I wasn't too inclined toward the idea at first, I

said, 'Well, okay, I'll try that.' And to my surprise, I got
to enjoying it.

"Of course, there's a lot more money out on the other
side, but hell, there's a challenge to it that I love. You
know, putting together a case like the Jones case, it's, uh,
well, I don't quite know how to describe it. I love it. To
build a case from scratch—finding out what happened,
then figuring out how you can present it all to a jury and
have it make sense—that's the most challenging thing in
the world. To get in a courtroom and really go to *work* on
something is, for me, a tremendous challenge and very
exciting. You're under enormous pressure; especially
something this big where it takes so long to present it all.
You get tired as hell, but I don't know, it just seems like
you're doin' the right thing, especially when you're putting a murderer away. It just *feels good*, you know, even
though it's so hard. You don't get a whole lot of thanks
for it, but, you do get some personal satisfaction."

"In regards Chelsea's case," Sutton says, "I was concerned at first that these people—the hospital, the nursing
board—might be alarmists, you know? I mean, I didn't
know, maybe this type of thing *does* happen. Maybe this
child died naturally, and they're just alarmists. So, I tip-
toed in.

"The case shook loose in late September, '82. On the
24*th*, the hospital guys started making inquiries. On the
27*th*, Kathy Holland turned over the vials. That same
week, she and Jones took their lie detector tests. Then the
DPS—Department of Public Safety (our police force)—
sent over its test results on the vials. The next Tuesday,
October the 5*th*, Ranger Joe Davis tracked down Genene
specifically to discuss the succinylcholine. He read her her
rights, then took a written statement from her.

My name is Genene Jones and I was employed by Dr.
Kathleen Holland, as an office nurse. My employment
started on 8/15/82 and ended on 9/28/82.
Office medication were ordered by me, as ordered by

Dr. Holland, on 8/18/82 from Pampell's, which included one (1) 10cc bottle of succinylcholine.

This vial of succinylcholine was subsequently lost or misplaced on 9/3/82, after the incident in the office with Misty Reichenau. This medication was not used on this child, but was discussed by Sally Benkert (nurse employed by Sid Peterson Hospital—ICU).

A few days later, I asked Dr. Holland if she wished to order a second bottle of succinylcholine. She stated, "yes," so second bottle was ordered by myself from Sid Peterson Hospital pharmacy. The bottle was not picked up by me. It is unknown to me who picked up this order.

Sometime during the week of the 19th of September, the original vial of succinylcholine was found by me and returned to the ice box. It was found in the bottom side drawer of exam table in [the front treatment room], along with two tubes of blood. Dr. Holland was notified the day I found it. A day or two later, Dr. Holland asked me to look at the original bottle. The bottle had two puncture marks in the rubber entry point, which was not noticed by me when I found the bottle.

Dr. Holland then asked me, how the puncture marks got there. I stated I don't know. I then asked her the same question. She stated she did not know.

Dr. Holland at this time called Ms. Benkert and requested that she come to the Clinic, which she did. Dr. Holland then questioned Ms. Benkert.

At the time I left, there were two bottles of succinylcholine in the office. The original and the second one, which was ordered when the original was lost or misplaced.

I have no knowledge of any further orders of succinylcholine. The original was delivered, and I don't know who picked up the second bottle.

"The lab report that the DPS sent me on the two vials of succs," Sutton recalls, "showed the punctured vial had been diluted with sodium chloride—saline solution; its concentration approximately one-sixth that of the other bottle. That same day, I learned that the hospital people had discovered that Holland's office had in fact placed three orders—not two, but three orders—for succs.

"At this point, I realized that something had gone wrong there at that Clinic. We had the missing succs, and there were different stories as to what had happened to it. A vial of the stuff had been tampered with and I knew the results of the polygraphs. I had two good suspects; I just didn't know which one or the other (or maybe both) was involved."

On October 7, the battle of Ron Sutton's life began when he advised Ranger Davis that he was going to start a grand-jury investigation into the McClellan matter. "I told him it was to meet on Tuesday, October the 12*th* in Kerrville and that I wanted Dr. Holland, Tony Hall, Dr. Packard, and Petti McClellan served with subpoenas."

The use of the grand jury offered Sutton several advantages. Since no one was allowed into the grand jury's chambers except witnesses and officers of the Court, he could begin his investigation in relative privacy, and there maintain some degree of control. The testimony was under oath and subject to perjury penalties, yet the witnesses would be without the benefit of legal counsel, and therefore somewhat at his mercy. All testimony elicited would be rendered indelibly into written transcripts, so witnesses could be held to their stories. In addition, all witnesses were forbidden to reveal what transpired in those secret chambers, affording the district attorney some protection against the contamination of shared stories.

Sutton had already determined that there were a good half-dozen incidents targeted as "questionable" by the hospital's administrators, so he stipulated in Dr. Holland's subpoena that she produce those children's medical records before the jury. This subpoena served to instigate hostilities and distrust between the district attorney and Dr. Holland that persisted for many months, to the detriment of both sides.

While Sutton slowly began to get his teeth into this strange case, Kathleen was struggling simply to keep on functioning. A numbing unreality seemed to have settled over her life. Ordinary tasks had taken on an absurd aspect; she staggered under a crushing sense of futility and impending failure.

She had understood from the first that, rightly or wrongly, the blame for these events would be laid at her door. She had forced herself to call her malpractice insurance carrier, but was unsure even of what to say to the pleasant-voiced woman who asked her to describe her problem. "How do you tell someone you think your nurse killed one of your patients?"

The insurance carrier referred Kathleen to one of their medical malpractice attorneys, William Dickson Wiles. Wiles, a kind-hearted middle-aged man who had been doing malpractice defense work half his life, remembers his initial conversation with Dr. Holland as "one of the most bizarre stories I had ever been told."

At the end of nearly two hours of conversation, which was mostly listening on the attorney's part, Wiles suggested Kathleen retain a criminal attorney.

"Criminal attorney?" Kathleen protested, "I haven't done anything wrong."

Wiles did his best to reassure his new client. "You don't have to be a criminal to need a criminal law specialist." Wiles knew that Kathleen faced a long series of grand-jury appearances, interrogations by law enforcement, possible suspicion regarding her knowledge or complicity, and potentially, even indictment. She would need an expert guide through this mine field. Wiles put Kathleen in touch with Jack Leon, one of the criminal defense attorneys in San Antonio.

Leon gave his new client the advice all criminal attorneys give all their clients, hoping the warning is not already too late and praying the client is neither too arrogant nor too pigheaded to heed it: "Don't tell them *anything*.

They may try to hang you up on this. Don't volunteer any information. Don't provide them with any records—legally they're privileged documents, anyway. I'd also like to remind you, Doctor, that you are facing potentially millions of dollars in civil lawsuits here. Keep your mouth shut and you won't have to worry about making any mistakes."

Kathleen was unhappy with the advice. "But I haven't done anything wrong," she argued, "I haven't got anything to hide."

Leon remained adamant. "It doesn't matter whether you have or haven't. A grand jury can indict you using *only a piece* of what you've said, *taken out of context*. Get yourself indicted and then you've really got problems, problems that will cost you a lot of money to resolve. Do yourself a favor: Don't say anything."

Mr. Leon didn't anticipate he would be able to prevent Kathleen's testimony forever, only long enough to negotiate with Sutton. He wanted immunity from prosecution in exchange for complete cooperation. Sutton said no. "If she hasn't done anything, she's got nothing to worry about from me. But I'm not giving anybody immunity."

On October 4, therefore, when Joe Davis stopped by the Clinic with the grand-jury subpoena, Kathleen told him she would make no further statement and, upon advice of counsel, would not provide the requested medical records, because they were privileged documents.

Sutton wasn't willing to accept Kathleen's refusal. He drafted a medical records release form and sent Joe Davis out with a dozen copies of it—Sutton intended to get a written release for those records from the parents of every child who had experienced a crisis at Kathleen's Clinic, thereby eliminating her claim of privilege. On October 11, Joe Davis returned to Dr. Holland's office with a new subpoena and the signed releases in hand. Kathleen turned over her complete file for every patient specified: Chelsea, Misty, Jimmy, Brandy, Jacob, and Rolinda.

The next day, the nervous doctor made her first appearance before Kerr County's grand jury. Attorney Sam Bayless, Jack Leon's associate, had given her explicit instructions: After each question she was to request an opportunity to consult with her attorney who would be waiting just outside the grand-jury chambers; she was to repeat the question to Sam as close to verbatim as possible; she was to invoke the Fifth Amendment in response to any question her lawyer designated.

Sutton asked Kathleen to identify herself and she complied. He showed her the records she had given Joe Davis the day before: "Are these your office records?"

"Yes."

"Are these records full and complete, without any additions, changes, or modifications?"

Again, Kathleen answered affirmatively.

On the next question, however, she dutifully requested to consult with her attorney. Sutton, evidencing great frustration, let her go. Kathleen stepped outside and repeated the innocuous question to Bayless, who wrote it down in his notebook. "Take the Fifth," he instructed.

"Sam, let me answer the question."

"Take the Fifth," he repeated. "If you answer some of the questions, you may lose the privilege. We've got to establish a pattern."

When Kathleen returned, Sutton repeated the question. Kathleen pulled out a small, folded-up piece of paper from which she read: "I respectfully decline to answer on the grounds that the information may tend to incriminate or degrade me."

The district attorney burst out: "Incriminate or degrade you! Are you afraid your answer will tell us something you don't want us to know?"

Kathleen again read from her paper.

Sutton did what he could to shake Kathleen from her stubborn assertion of the Fifth, asking her harmless questions, berating her when she continued to read her prepared statement: "Do you really think telling us when you graduated from medical school is going to incriminate or degrade you?''

Kathleen never rose to the bait: ''I respectfully decline to answer . . .'' She sat stoically as the district attorney snapped that he had half a mind to cite her for contempt, and in response to his next question she again read from her slip of paper.

Angry, Sutton sent the witness home, then began the process of persuading the grand jury to charge the doctor with contempt. Her invocation of the Fifth was the cause, but not the basis for the citation; Kathleen was entitled to claim the privilege. Sutton found another hook on which to hang his charge of contempt.

The next morning, Kathleen, along with the rest of the Hill Country, learned from the newspaper that Kerrville's new pediatrician had been charged with contempt for her failure to cooperate with the grand jury's investigation into Chelsea McClellan's death. Specifically, the grand jury charged Kathleen with failure to comply with the subpoena's notice to produce the medical records of certain patients.

Kathleen was understandably confused by the contempt charge; she had turned over every document requested in the subpoena. Jack Leon quickly found out that the charge was based on a technicality: One of the questions Kathleen had declined to answer before the grand jury was whether she had made any alterations to the medical records she had turned over to Joe Davis. The grand jury, Sutton argued, therefore had no way of knowing whether Kathleen had fully complied with the subpoena or had instead deleted or altered the records. Three weeks later, on November 5, the contempt charge was finally heard before the Honorable Murray Jordan. Kathleen's attorney pointed out to the judge that Kathleen had, at the beginning of her testimony before the grand jury, sworn that the records were ''full and complete, without any additions, changes, or modifications.'' Therefore, the question that was the basis for the contempt charge was duplicative, already asked and answered. The contempt charge, Leon argued, was unfounded.

Judge Jordan concurred with Leon's position and dismissed the case. Unfortunately, the local Kerrville paper did not carry the story of Kathleen's exoneration on its front page, as it had the original story of the contempt charge.

Kathleen's business, already noticeably shrinking, began to fall off heavily after the press coverage of her alleged failure to cooperate with the grand jury. For the first time, she felt the weight of community suspicion. She forced herself to institute the practice of starting every patient consultation with a speech that began: "I don't know whether you've heard about the investigation regarding the children who got sick in my office, but I think you should be informed before we go any further." Most parents stayed; some did not.

Genene Jones had already left Kerrville behind. She and Sally had vacated the Nixon Lane house within a week of Genene's dismissal. They took the kids, Bonnie Gunderson, and all Genene's worldly goods, shoe-horned them into Sally's trailer, and headed north 100 miles to San Angelo. There, she and Sally set up in a trailer park and hunted down new jobs.

On October 18, Sutton butted up against his first brick wall. He and Joe Davis dropped by Sid Peterson Hospital to interview and take statements from all the people who had been present in the ER at the time of Chelsea's second attack. One of those interviewed was Dr. Frank Bradley, the doctor who had recognized the possibility that Rolinda Ruff had been fighting off the effects of succinylcholine rather than recovering from a seizure. Bradley was the first to explain to the lawmen just what kind of drug they were dealing with.

"At that time," Sutton recalled, "Bradley advised me that if it *was* succinylcholine, we were in trouble, because succs *rapidly* disappears in the body. He told us: 'It's untraceable. If that's what happened, if succinylcholine killed this child, you'll never prove it. It cannot be found.'"

Remembering the moment later, Sutton sat back and took off his glasses. "You know, this case hit the front pages in Paris, Hawaii, all the Scandinavian countries, Japan, Canada, seems like everywhere. And it wasn't, I don't think, simply because what happened was so bizarre, but because it was bizarre *and at the same time* involved this strange drug: succinylcholine—synthetic curare. Y'see, with this drug, you remain conscious. It doesn't 'knock you out,' it just paralyzes you. You can't move in the slightest, no matter how much you want to. If no one treats you, you die of suffocation—utterly immobilized, and *completely conscious*. That's part of the nightmare of this. Especially for the mothers.

"I had succinylcholine once, when I had my tonsils out, back before I graduated from college. What surgeons are supposed to do is give you the anesthetic so that you're 'out,' unconscious, before the succinylcholine takes effect, so you never experience it; but if they don't time the shots just right, the succinylcholine'll take effect first—before the anesthetic kicks in—and that's what happened to me. I'll never forget lyin' there on the table and the doctor telling me to count back from five to one. I started, then all of a sudden, I couldn't breathe! I was lyin' there, lookin' at him, and I was tryin' to tell him, you know, 'Hey, I can't breathe, there's somethin' wrong! I'm dyin'!' But I couldn't, I was just . . . helpless. Then the anesthetic took effect, thank God, and I went under. It only lasted a few seconds, but I remember. Scared the hell out of me."

Ron Sutton took a long look at the significance of Frank Bradley's information. He realized he now faced two challenges. If he couldn't provide the jury with a murder weapon, he was going to have to rely on a case built entirely on indirect, circumstantial evidence. The prospect was daunting; it was always easier to obtain a conviction when the jury had some concrete and direct evidence of the crime. Sutton knew, therefore, he was going to have to work like hell to prove Dr. Bradley wrong; somewhere there had to be someone who could trace this untraceable drug. He put the word out, through the rangers and through discreet associates, that his office wanted any and all information about succinylcholine.

At the end of October, Kathleen's husband, Charleigh, broached the subject of divorce—only, he explained, to protect his separate property from becoming embroiled in the lawsuits they both knew were coming. Kathleen tried to see the wisdom in the request but couldn't help feeling betrayed. She tried to refuse, but Charleigh was firm. "I wanted to make sure," he later explained, "that even if Kathy lost everything else, she would still have a home to come to."

Hating to do it, feeling inexplicably dirty, Kathleen found the cheapest available attorney to file for a simple, sixty-day, no-fault divorce. Her marriage to Charleigh Appling was legally terminated before the end of the year. They had been married just six months.

Sutton, meanwhile, ground on with his investigation, constantly scheduling time to call witnesses before the grand jury to build up a legal record of the events while they were still fresh in everyone's minds. At night, he labored over medical texts and pedantic articles in medical journals, gathering the necessary knowledge to deal with the subtleties of the case. Dr. Bradley helped with this, as well as Dr. Vinas, but they were not the doctors who had witnessed all the events firsthand. Sutton remained frustrated that Kathleen refused to cooperate, but continued to decline to grant her immunity. "It's just not something I do."

In the middle of December 1982, Sutton finally found time to drive into San Antonio to interview Dr. Kathleen Kagan-Hallet, the pathologist who had performed a detailed examination of Chelsea's brain as part of the autopsy. Dr. Kagan-Hallet informed Sutton that she had not been aware of his investigation. It was her opinion, she explained, that the child's death was due to atypical Sudden Infant Death Syndrome.

"I then asked her," Sutton recalls, "if she felt, based on her evaluation of the baby's tissues, that *if* a shot had been given which contained succinylcholine, could that have possibly caused or contributed to the child's death? She seemed a bit taken aback, but advised us yes, if such a shot had been given, it could probably be linked very directly with the death."

Sutton asked the pathologist to review her findings in light of such a possibility and to inform him of any change in her verdict.

A few days before the Christmas holidays, while attending a pathologists conference at Medical Center Hospital, Dr. Kagan-Hallet mentioned her odd conversation with Sutton to one of her fellow pathologists, Dr. Corrie May. May, a former employee of Medical Center, made the connection between the names of Jones and Holland and the previous year's problems in the Center's PICU. Disturbed, she brought the Kerrville investigation to the attention of her current boss, San Antonio's medical examiner, Dr. Vincent DiMaio.

Alarmed by the implications, DiMaio relayed the information to a newly appointed assistant district attorney, Nick Rothe, who in turn carried it straight to San Antonio's newly elected DA, Sam Millsap, who had been in office less than two weeks—since 12:01 A.M., the first of the new year. Millsap immediately opened an investigation into the strange report.

In the last week of January, 1983, San Antonio's grand jury began to hear testimony regarding the events that the press would eventually christen, "The Baby Deaths Case."

Sam Millsap

I took office January 1st, 1983. As I recall, it was sometime before the end of the month that I was approached by the medical examiner here in San Antonio. His basic message to me was: "I'm glad you're here, strange things have happened at the Medical Center Hospital. I don't know exactly what's going on, but what I do know are two things. Number one, they're not complying with the law which requires that a medical examiner perform an autopsy when death occurs under certain circumstances (which are specifically enumerated in the medical examiner's statute). And number two, there's scuttlebutt in the medical community that babies are dying out there at that hospital. I've looked over the files, and there are cases I should have been doing autopsies on, but officially I've never heard anything about them. The autopsies are either being performed privately or not at all."

So, just two or three weeks in office, I had to make the decision that we would go ahead and take this thing on. As we got deeper into it, it became clear that the conflict was not just between my office or the legal system and Genene Jones, but also to some extent between the prosecutors and two of the most powerful institutions in this community: the Bexar County Hospital District and the University of Texas.

In the state of Texas, there is no organization that is more powerful than the University of Texas. None. It's like this great hulking presence that's just always there, and it's everywhere, and its power is just enormous. So, initially, my role was to make the decision: "OK, we're going to get into this thing, and if we have to, we'll take on these institutions 'heads up.'"

I made that decision, I think, naively.

Firstly, going into this case, I didn't have any earthly idea whether we would, ultimately, discover something prosecutable, so there was a certain amount of risk there. And secondly, I had no idea that I would end up being pitted—in a personal way—against these institutions. The UT system is kind of like the Chinese government: they just assume that they're going on forever. It doesn't make any difference what kind of little blips they have on their personal Richter scale along the way, I mean, it's: "We're always going to be here. DAs come and go, and he's a problem right now, but we'll be here when he's gone." So they just play like nothing's really happened.

My continuing role, all the way through the process, was to set policy and make decisions as to how the case would be staffed. With whom and to what extent it would be staffed. One of the best decisions I made in that regard was assigning [the Investigator] to this case. He is a great investigator. A wonderful investigator. He would be horrified if he knew that I was telling you this right now, but let me say that in many, many ways, he is really the star of this whole thing. I mean, you've got to have guys like Ron Sutton and Nick Rothe who walk into the courtroom and say what needs to be said. You've got to have that. I mean, there will never again be a closing argument like the closing argument Nick Rothe made in Georgetown. I mean, it was just . . . I sat there and cried, literally cried, in the courtroom when Nick was making his closing argument because it was like, uh, you know, well . . . it was really orgasmic in a lot of ways. That's a strange way to describe it, I know, but I mean it really was. It was *moving*. And both Ron and Nick did fantastic jobs, but they wouldn't have had anything to say if not for [the Investigator]. And see, that's the bottom line. You can have the greatest lawyers in the world, but if you don't have the kind of resourcefulness and relentless pursuit of truth by somebody like [the Investigator], then the lawyers don't have anything to say.

In addition to staffing decisions, I had the role of getting funding from my commissioner's court for this specific case. This was a difficult proposition, because the Medical Center Hospital is an arm of county government. So, in effect, what I was saying to the county commissioners when I went down there and told them I've got to have X number of dollars to conduct this investigation—what I was saying to them was: "I need this money to investigate *you*."

How much did it end up costing?

Oh, God. I don't have any idea. I would be afraid to even—I mean, it was just incredible how much it cost. See, most people in this city are a lot more concerned with robberies and muggings and assaults. Those are crimes that affect them directly, and they expect the person administrating this office to coordinate efforts such that those problems are somehow lessened or, when they do occur, dealt with. Cases like the Jones case cost a lot of money; they're not always too popular with businessmen.

What did you think when DiMaio came to your office

with this story? What was your reaction; how did you feel about it?

Well, I had lots of reactions—well, I shouldn't say 'lots of reactions.' I had reactions at different levels. The dominant reaction that we all had, I think, in the early, like first ten days of this thing, was: "It's impossible, it cannot be true. There's got to be some rational explanation for this rumor. Who would—or could—kill babies in a PICU?" And even after we got the various reports and saw in black and white that there was substance to the rumor, still, there's a normal human tendency to grope in a situation like this for a rational explanation. Because to do otherwise is to admit the existence of an absolutely monstrous and very threatening situation.

People are at their most vulnerable when they're in a hospital situation, and the reason you go to a hospital is to be cared for, not to risk being murdered. To the extent that one accepts the possibility that these things can happen, you really place yourself at risk from an emotional standpoint. And just the incomprehensibility of someone with snakes in her head going around killing babies is so bizarre and unreal, it's hard to deal with. You reject it. "My God," you say to yourself, "it just *can't* be true. There's *got* to be some other reason why these things are happening. There *has* to be some rational explanation." So that's one reaction I remember.

Another reaction I recall very clearly was, "My God, why me?" I kept asking myself, of all the places in the Western world where something like this could happen, (a) why does it happen in San Antonio, and (b) why in the world does it confront me when I'm less than thirty days into this office?

I'm really not sure if Vincent DiMaio were to walk into my office today and say, "We're back on the track, we got the same kind of thing going on," I tell you the truth, I'm not sure I'd have the courage to do all the things that I did before. Because you get to a point where you know, well let me put it this way: if what you want is to be the champion, you've got to want it more than anything else. More than *everything* else. And if you want it that much, you might be able to fight over and over again and never lose, but when it's all over, you might find that the price you've paid is a little steep. Like a boxer who's taken too many blows to the head—he may be the champ, but he's also punchy; he's got a few screws loose. I think that can happen to a DA, and I was taking those punches all the way through this case.

Why did you take it on?

My personal test for any decision is this: If my nine-year-old son knew as much about this situation as I know about it, would he be proud of the decision his daddy made or would he be ashamed? That's my test.

We understand that the only action your office ultimately pursued was to prosecute Jones for overdosing Rolando Santos. Why is that?

Look, the argument can be made that from a moral standpoint, a human standpoint, anybody who knew what Jones was doing and participated in the decision to send her down the road, putting her in a position where she could harm additional babies, is guilty of murder—specifically, the murder of Chelsea McClellan. But legally, from a *causation* standpoint, that doesn't hold. Even if all of these people had said, "Genene, you're a dirty rotten bitch, we're going to the district attorney and we're not ever going to give you a letter of recommendation," it's possible that she still might have killed Chelsea McClellan anyway.

Think about B. H. Corum, Marvin Dunn, Virginia Mousseau, Pat Belko, Judy Harris—these are all people who I consider basically honorable people. These are not burglars, rapists, robbers, murderers, embezzlers. These are good people who got caught up in a situation that they didn't know how to deal with and didn't have the moral fiber to deal with it in the way it should have been dealt with.

On the part of many people at the hospital you have at all points in this process an overbearing concern with two things: (1) the image of the hospital and the medical school, you know, the medical community and the effect that the revelation of all of this stuff would have on that image, and therefore on themselves as an involved part of the whole, and (2) the great concern about the biggest of all bugaboos for doctors: malpractice.

I like to believe that every human being has a point beyond which he will not be pushed, beyond which he will not compromise. I hope that everyone has a point where he draws the line and says: "OK, now we play hardball. I don't know what the consequences are going to be, but I cannot continue to exist without saying: This is what I believe." The sad thing is that nobody understood, except just a handful of people, that all it took was for one person to say, you know, "I am not going to let this go on. You solve this problem— first of all you deal with the problem, admit that it exists, and deal with it, because if you don't, I'm going to blow the lid off this place." But nobody did that. No one.

SIXTEEN

I am not a crook.

Richard Nixon, 1973

"I WASN'T ON BOARD AT THE TIME THE GRAND jury first began questioning witnesses," the Investigator recalls, "so, later I went back and read the transcripts from those early testimonies. One that has always stuck in my mind was Dr. Dunn's. And not just because he was later held in contempt of the grand jury.

"I've heard lots of people testify in my life, both informally, while taking statements and just talking with people, and formally, under oath. Most people are a little nervous. Tense. Even if they have nothing to hide, their defenses are up when they're talking with an official. Dunn, on the other hand, was, well, a rather remarkable witness. Very few times does he lose composure. He's gracious. He appears calm, even comfortable. Rarely does he answer a question with one sentence, and often speaks for long periods of time without prompting. Overall, what impressed me the most, I guess, was how much it appeared that he knew just what he wanted to say that morning, said it, and left. Granted, the lawyers didn't really know what they were looking for then (this was right at the beginning), but Dunn was in control of the situation. And that's not necessarily where you want a witness to be in a murder investigation.''

"Good morning," began the young assistant district attorney drafted to warm up the witness and get the examination started. "My name is Luis Vallejo, and as I told you earlier, I work for the district attorney's office." Two other, senior assistant DAs—Nick Rothe and Terry MacDonald—sat behind Vallejo, listening and making notes. "You do understand that this is an official meeting of the grand jury of Bexar County, Texas?"

"Yes, sir," replied the slight, bespectacled, bearded gentleman. It was 9:46 A.M., February 3, 1983.

"I will get straight to the point, Doctor," continued Vallejo, '' so we don't waste your time and we can expedite the matter. We are interested in specific information that we have received concerning a possible investigation by a team of doctors—either from out of state or out of the country—into an unusually large number—or an inordinate amount—of deaths in your Pediatric ICU. We understand that there was an investigation, and a report made. Are you familiar with this report?"

"Yes."

"Could you please tell us what prompted the investigation?"

"I will be glad to. [But first,] let me explain to the members of the grand jury, if I may, who I am and why I was involved with that. If that is all right.''

"Doctor, that is an excellent idea. I should have asked you myself. Could you please state your name?''

"Yes. I am Dr. Marvin Dunn, and I am the dean of the University of Texas Medical School here in San Antonio. The medical school uses several hospitals for teaching purposes, which include such hospitals as Santa Rosa and the V.A. Hospital, but our primary teaching hospital is Medical Center Hospital. That hospital is owned and operated by the hospital district for the county. We have an affilia-

tion agreement with the hospital such that the medical
school provides the professional staff—the doctors, in
other words. This includes both the faculty (who are fully
trained physicians) and also the resident staff (who are
known as 'house staff'—doctors who have graduated from
medical school but who are in the process of completing
anywhere from three to five years of training in their various specialties). Then, additionally, we have medical students there. Have you talked about what a Pediatric ICU
is?''

''No, sir,'' replied Vallejo.

''Then I had better explain that, also, because I think it
will be helpful to you. We have learned through the years
that some patients are just extremely sick and really require (or may require) heroic means to pull them through,
and you can't do that by just putting them in a bed and
having a nurse come by and check every three or four
hours. So, we have established—and some of you may be
familiar with this, so indulge me if you are—what are
known as Intensive Care Units, and I will refer to those as
'ICUs.'

''An Intensive Care Unit usually only has a few beds.
Ours happens to have about four beds at the present time
in Pediatrics, and they are monitored by nurses all the
time, and usually a physician is either there or nearby.
These babies and children are very sick, and they usually
have specialized procedures going on to keep them alive.

I am sorry that you were not able to tell me the subject
to be discussed beforehand, because I could have brought
information about dates and whatnot. So, though I have
sworn to tell truthful answers, don't hold me to precise
dates, because I will just try to recollect those, and if you
need precise dates, I will be glad to get those for you.

''I became dean there, and this is a precise date, November 17, 1980. At that time, Dr. Phillip Brunell was the
chairman of the Department of Pediatrics in the medical
school. Dr. Brunell resigned as the chair in July of 1981,

and we recruited his replacement, Dr. John Mangos . . . in the summer of 1982.

"From July of 1981 until Dr. Mangos came here permanently, Dr. Robert Franks was the acting chair for the Department of Pediatrics.

"Dr. Franks came to see me the first time, about—it was early January of 1982. As I recall, we were both going out to the parking lot together, late in the afternoon. And he said, 'I simply want to alert you that something is going on in the Pediatric ICU. I don't know what it is, but we have got to look into it, and I am looking into it. As soon as I find out [anything], I will let you know.' I said, 'Good.'

"It was about the following week, I believe, that he came back to see me and told me what he had been finding out, and I asked him to put it in writing, which he did. This would bring us to about the second or third week in January. Okay. Now, what had been going on?

"First of all, we had only had the Pediatric ICU open for about a year. In the course of the year, we had more and more patients admitted there, for a variety of reasons. First, was simply because we had not had one before and the doctors were [just beginning to recognize] its value and were using it more. Secondly, there had been an epidemic during the winter, as I recall, flu or something like that— but some disease in which we had an unusual number of admissions—and there had been several deaths. More than had occurred a year before, and that concerned some people.

"Looking into that, and what I suspect that you are interested in, I don't think the number of deaths really was an issue. It was something that simply came to people's attention. The reason for that is that if you look at the number of patients admitted and the severity of their illnesses, the actual number of deaths that occurred is not out of the ordinary. It was just that we didn't have such sick children the year before and the number admitted had not been so high.

"I would like to ask you to focus with me, not on the deaths, but on the incidents that were occurring. They had a, well, I am going to call it a number of incidents—and it probably is not that great a number, it is just that you don't expect these, so when you have even several, it is out of the ordinary. Incidents had been occurring that couldn't be explained or at least couldn't be explained to our satisfaction. Now what am I talking about?

"Well, [suppose] you have a child who has a heart condition and is in the Intensive Care Unit because of the heart condition, and then develops heart failure and the heart stops. Well, you expect that sort of thing to happen. But, if you have a child in there who does not have a heart condition, but has some other condition, and it has an irregularity of heartbeat and the heart stops, that's unusual, okay. The second [kind of incident], and the kind of thing that I believe had occurred more—" Dr. Dunn stopped a moment, then started again.

"Most of these children who are in there are extremely sick, as I have said. For example, they may have had their heart operated on, and during the course of the heart operation, they hook the child up to a pump so that the pump circulates the blood through the body while the surgeons work on the heart (because the heart can't pump the blood while they have it opened and are working on it). Now, when you do this, you have to put something into the blood to keep the blood from clotting; otherwise, it will clot and plug up the pump. The common drug used is called heparin. So, they put heparin in the blood, and it keeps the blood from clotting while they are working, but then, when they get through, you want to get rid of the heparin, because, after all, it is important that the blood clots. . . . If the blood won't clot, strangely enough, it will begin to ooze through into the intestine and it may ooze through the vessels in the brain, so you don't want anyone to go around with blood that won't clot. You have just made someone a hemophiliac. So, what do they do? Well, there is another drug that will neutralize heparin, so they [administer that to the patient]. But you have to be very careful you don't put too much in, because if you do, all the blood will clot."

"What is the name of that drug, sir?"

"Protamine sulfate is the common one that is used. So, you neutralize a lot of the heparin, but not all of it, and then, you let the body metabolize the rest of it. That is the safe way to do it, and we know about how long it takes for the rest of the heparin to be detoxified by the liver. But, during that interval, a patient may have bleeding problems; so you watch for that.

"So, let's say that you expect [these bleeding problems] to go on a little in any patient who has had heart surgery for, say, twenty-four hours. But if that patient starts to bleed two days later, or three days later, then how do you explain that? Well, maybe they have a liver problem, and the liver didn't metabolize [the drug]. There are ways to explain it, but at the same time, that bothers you when that sort of thing happens.

"Now, to complicate matters, in the cases that we were concerned with—these very sick infants and children—in almost every case, are not able to eat. So, they have to have intravenous feedings and fluids and sometimes special drugs (if they have a serious infection—serious enough to be in [an ICU]—we may be giving them an antibiotic so potent that it has to be given intravenously). These kiddos don't have so many veins that you can just go in and stick a needle in every time you need to give them an IV. So, you do what is known as a 'cut-down': you surgically cut through the skin, locate a vein, and put a plastic catheter—a polyethylene [tube]—into the vein and put a stitch around it, and that is the lifeline to the baby. . . . Whenever you need to give fluids, then, you give them through that catheter and you don't have to worry about getting a vein if you need it in a hurry.

"Well, you have to keep that catheter, that polyethylene

tube, open when you are not giving fluids. When you give fluids, it stays open. When you stop giving fluids, the blood that will come right up to the tip of that catheter will clot, and then your tube is plugged. The way you get around that is that you inject just enough heparin solution into that tube—the theory is, you go right to the end, and then one drop beyond, okay. So, that tube now has a heparin solution [in it,] and the blood comes up to it and it won't clot. [After any] medication is given or fluids are given, the nurses take a small amount of heparin solution and just rinse [the port, the catheter, and the] vein out. Not enough so the child [begins to] bleed, but enough to keep the tube open.

"Well, some of the children that developed bleeding episodes had those tubes in there. So, one possibility was that in rinsing out the tubes, too much heparin had been used. Or, for a little tiny infant, you use a very weak solution of heparin, but in a three-year-old child that might be in the next bed, you might use a more concentrated solution. The question was, well, maybe somebody picked up the wrong bottle and used the concentrated solution.

"Now, I can't recall all the several instances that occurred, but these will suffice to give you some examples of the kinds of things that we were dealing with, all of which could be explained somewhat—like the liver didn't detoxify the heparin as soon as it should, or somebody may have picked up the wrong bottle, or too much was used. But at the same time, when you have several of these occurring, you are really obligated to wonder about what is going on.

"What had brought this to Dr. Franks's attention, and in turn to me, was a case [in which,] as I recall, three different things happened that couldn't be explained in any way like this. For example, the child had a bleeding episode, as I remember, and didn't even have a tube in. He did not have a known heart problem, and yet [manifested] some heart irregularity. And, I think the third instance was that for reasons that none of us could figure out, the child became paralyzed and couldn't breathe. In each case, what happened was recognized very quickly in the ICU and heroic means were taken to deal with it, and the child lived, and the child, as far as I know, is still alive today. But the physician who was responsible for that child was extremely upset over these things happening, and he had no explanation for it. He moved the child out of the Intensive Care Unit, and the child did very well after that.''

"Was it the same doctor in all three instances?"

Dr. Dunn was not quite sure what was meant, nevertheless, he attempted to clarify. "As I recall, it was Dr. Copeland."

"On all three?" Vallejo evidently believed that Dr. Dunn was referring to three different patients instead of just one—presumably Rolando Santos.

"Well, it was his patient and therefore— And I don't believe he was there at the time the three happened, okay. But he was the senior physician responsible for the patient. And so, then, he moved the patient out.

"He [then] went to Dr. Franks and said, 'Look, a lot of things that have happened, you know, can [be explained] one way or another, whether [those explanations are] the reason or not. But in the case of my patient, [those explanations] cannot explain any of [his problems]. You have got to look into this.' And that is when Dr. Franks came to me and wrote a memo and said very briefly what I have taken a lot of time to tell you. This, as I say, was about the third week of January, of 1982.

"Well, I'm not a pediatrician, so I would not hold my competence out to be the one to investigate these matters, but I certainly understand the problems very well. And I called a meeting for the following Monday.

"As I recall, Dr. Franks's memo came to me about Wednesday of one week, and I called a meeting for Monday morning of the following week to get the principles [together]. And these included Dr. Corum, who is the executive director of the hospital (in fact, of the hospital district), Dr. Franks, Dr. Robotham, who was the senior pediatrician at the time in charge of the Intensive Care Unit, Virginia Mousseau who is the senior nurse for the hospital and in charge of all nurses. I believe that John Quest was also at that meeting, but I am not sure, Mr. Vallejo.''

"What was his last name?"

"Quest," repeated Dr. Dunn, incorrectly identifying John Guest. "He is the senior associate director of the hospital district."

"Quest, as in Q-u-e-s-t?"

"Yes, sir. He is Dr. Corum's associate. I believe he was there. The others for sure were there. And in one way or another, by that time, we were all aware of what the general problem was, and we tried to sort through what information we had—what we knew for certain, what we didn't know, and how we were going to approach this problem.

"It seemed to us, at that time, that there were three possibilities. One was, that statistically we had had some unusual bad luck. That may seem cavalier to you, but let me explain what I mean. There are certain surgical procedures [for which] one expects a mortality of say five out of every thousand. Appendectomies, for example: a common procedure, and very few people die [from them], but in the course of a long period of time, some people do, and believe me, we really can't explain it. And just take that figure of five in a thousand, and you can go to Boston or Cleveland or Los Angeles and you will find that every time you get one thousand appendectomies, five people have died, plus or minus whatever. Now in your own hospital, you may do two hundred appendectomies a year and you would say, 'Okay, we would expect one a year might die.' If you have one death a year, you don't worry that something strange is going on. And, of course, in five years, if you do one thousand cases, you expect five. What happens if in one year you have three? Is it going to be that in the next two years you have none and then in five years, you still only have five and just statistically three came at once?

"[This] was a possibility. That everything that had happened (with the exception of that one case that I have mentioned—which was not a death but even so, we couldn't explain it) with that exception—all of these things could be things that might have happened anyway, and just by chance, [or by means] we didn't understand, they all came at once. That was one possibility.

"The second possibility was that we simply were not running a very good Intensive Care Unit. We thought we were, but maybe we weren't. Maybe our personnel were not as well trained as we thought they were. Maybe they weren't being as conscientious and maybe they weren't watching these children. [Maybe] the child that could have been watched and cared for a little bit more here, was not being watched and then got into big trouble down the line. So, maybe we weren't having the quality control that we needed.

"The third possibility was that somebody was doing something deliberately that they shouldn't be doing. And, except for that one case, we didn't have any reason to think that somebody was doing something deliberately. But that was still a possibility and we really didn't know which one it was."

At this point, Assistant District Attorney Nick Rothe stood and addressed the administrator. He too (like Vallejo earlier) was confused about just how many patients Dr. Dunn had been referring to. "Excuse me. Which case are we talking about? The sudden paralysis?"

"Yes," answered Dunn. "The one that developed paralysis and then had a heart problem. Don't hold me to the medical specifics, but there were about three [separate problems] in that one case, and I think those were the three. And fortunately, the child did not die. At the same time, if the child had died, we might have had an autopsy and have been able to explain why all three happened.

"Well, we could not let this go, you know, just overlook it and just say that time will tell. We decided at that meeting that we would invite a team of experts to come down and [take] a very critical look at our Intensive Care Unit, our personnel, and our procedures in these cases that we couldn't explain. [Maybe] we were too close to the situation to really make those judgments because Dr. Franks—when this had begun to come up (with matters being brought to his attention back in the fall)—had had people in the department look at individual cases. And he tells me that they would come back and say, 'Well, you know, I can't explain it for sure, but it could be this or it could be that.' Okay.

"We were fortunate at that time to have a visiting professor from Toronto, Dr. Cown, and—"

"How do you spell that?"

"C-o-w-n," said Dr. Dunn, incorrectly identifying Dr. Conn. "And I believe his first name is Alan, and he goes by A.W. Cown."

"And do you have any recollection of what institution he is with?"

"Oh, yes."

"Where is that?"

"He is with the Toronto Children's Hospital. Easy to remember because that is probably the most prestigious children's hospital in the world. A fabulous institution. He had been the director. He was taking a sabbatical leave—which institutions give, as you know, to senior professors to go to another institution to do study and research—and he had been interested in coming to ours. So, we were really quite honored to have him, and it was fortunate that he was here. So, we asked him, since he was an expert in this area, if he would head up an investigatory team for us, and he was willing to do it. Partly because he is a very good person at heart, and secondly, they had had a similar circumstance up in Toronto and he was very sensitive to the fact that you can get blind-sided by these things."

"Doctor," broke in Terry MacDonald, suddenly interested, "let me stop you. Are you familiar with the details of the 'similar circumstances'?"

"Not in great detail."

"Could you explain to the grand jury what details you are familiar with?"

"Well, I don't know what the final outcome of it was, but there was—I'll put it in a sense (and I think this is the way it was, at that time anyway)—[it was] alleged that a nurse was giving infants some drugs (and I don't remember the drug, it might have been digitalis) which created a heart problem, and I don't know if she engaged in heroic means to revive the children or whether some of the children died or not, but that had occurred, and he was very much aware of the problems. Not simply that that had occurred (or was alleged to have occurred), but he was aware of [the difficulties they'd had pinpointing the cause:] is this a medical problem that we have missed, have we not managed the patient well, or is somebody doing something?"

MacDonald asked, "He was familiar with the situation where they were investigating an intentional act?"

"Yes."

"So, he would have expertise into the third possibility that you have related to the grand jury?"

"Oh, absolutely. Absolutely. And that is probably the reason he was willing to take his precious time from a sabbatical to head up a team and do this.

"The second thing that he did for us, and I think it was due to his sensitivity about this, was that he was able to obtain for us—on very short notice—three of the top people in the country in this field, and he simply—I'll tell you who they are, if I can remember for sure."

"If not, I assume you have records pertaining to this investigation at your office."

"Yes, sir."

"And at a later date, would you be able to provide us with copies of those records?"

"When we get through, why don't you tell me what you

need and we can work out how to go about getting it to you]." The dean continued his briefing, naming and identifying the members of Conn's committee. "I think you could ask any pediatrician and he will tell you that [these people are] the top in the country. And so, Dr. Cown and these six individuals came, I believe it was February the 15*th*. Right in the middle of February."

"Of '81 or '82?" asked MacDonald.

"'82. So, Dr. Franks brought this to my attention sometime in the early part of January. I got his memo in about the third week of January and that is when we had our meeting: on that Monday, which would have probably been the last Monday in January. And then we got the team down here within three weeks after that. They spent three days. They went through the Intensive Care Unit, I'd say, very meticulously. They watched the procedures being performed, looking at the skills of the individuals. They met with all of the staff: nurses, RNs, licensed vocational nurses (LVNs), the residents, house staff, and the physicians. They reviewed the key cases that we had been troubled by, and they made a report. I guess that is where we started, when you asked me about the report."

MacDonald, who had picked up another tantalizing phrase in the dean's testimony, asked, "Doctor, do you recall you said, 'key cases.' How many cases were you concerned about?"

"I don't recall how many they reviewed, but I know they reviewed in great detail the one that I just told you about—Dr. Copeland's case."

"That was the one with—"

"Three incidents that couldn't be explained by anybody, and I will come back to that because that was part of their investigation."

"Doctor," asked Nick Rothe, confused and somewhat incredulous, "are you telling the grand jury that we are primarily talking about only three instances and one death?"

"No. No."

"There were more?"

"First of all, we don't know how many cases we are talking about because things happen all the time to patients and you think you understand the reason for it and you go on. But maybe you don't understand the reason for it. Now, the three instances [I've been talking about] occurred in the same patient."

"Oh, in *one* patient." Rothe finally understood.

"Yes. One patient."

"Well, how many—you don't know how many other individual patients there were that were suspect—that you couldn't explain?"

"Well, it becomes a spectrum."

"Well," Rothe confronted Dunn squarely: "I understand it could have been anywhere from seven, eight, ten, or twenty instances."

"Don't hold me to this," Dunn responded, "but let's say—within the course of the whole time—a dozen."

"Twelve?"

"Yeah. Because [in] looking back, [you start to find other possibilities.] You say, 'Well, golly, if this has happened [here], I had a case back in July and there was something there."

"Doctor," Vallejo asked, "was there a written report at the conclusion of this investigation?"

"Yes, sir. There was."

"Is that something that you would still have in your possession?"

"Yes, I do."

"So, we can get that report—"

"Let me ask you a question—which I think I know the answer to, but— I don't know that the university's lawyers would have any reason for not releasing it, but if the university's general counsel has a problem, I assume that you could subpoena it."

"As a matter of fact," said Rothe, "I spoke to the university's attorney on the phone yesterday, and at the conclusion of our investigation today, I intend to call him again. He expressed his complete interest in cooperating with us fully. I am sure that will not be a problem.''

"I personally have no problem at all for you having it and if they have no problem with it, that's fine.''

"That report,'' Vallejo persevered, "would it contain the number of cases they looked into?''

"I'm not sure it says how many they looked into. Let me address that in a different way, which may help you. Let me just tell you what they said in their report, and since you will have the report, you can read it for yourself. I will just paraphrase it in general, because we also had quite a lengthy discussion with them in addition to the written report.

"In essence, they said they didn't know which of the three possibilities [the PICU was experiencing] either, but because they couldn't tell which of the three it was, they thought we needed to take some deliberate action. And one of the recommendations that they made was that we staff the Pediatric ICU strictly with registered nurses. Why?

"Licensed vocational nurses, known as LVNs . . . have had less training than RNs, but in many cases they have had extensive experience. So, there is nothing wrong with having LVNs working in an Intensive Care Unit, especially if they have had experience, and the ones we had did have significant experience.

"[In any event,] there had been comments made about one or two of the LVNs as being individuals who might have done something wrong. We couldn't get any hard evidence that anyone could really point their finger at.''

MacDonald interrupted the doctor. "Could you elaborate on that, sir? There might have been instances?''

"Yes. We heard from one nurse that one of the LVNs was killing babies, okay?''

"Who did you hear that from?'' asked Rothe.

"That came thirdhand from a nurse to a doctor, and then, to our [January 25] meeting that I mentioned.''

"Who was the doctor that information came from?" Rothe asked.

"I don't remember. I just remember that at that meeting it was said that there was a nurse who'd said that 'one of the LVNs was killing babies.' Quote, unquote."

"Is there any way," Rothe asked, "of going back into your records, or do you know of anyone that was at the meeting that might recall the *name* of the doctor or the—"

"I could probably reconstruct that, but let me finish up the conversation at that point about that issue."

"Please do." The lawyer sat down again, scribbling a note on the yellow pad in front of him.

Dunn picked up where he'd left off. "[Upon] looking into [this accusation]—and I can't recall who related this at that meeting—[it was discovered] that the nurses had a very major personality conflict with each other and there was a lot of jealousy and a lot of backbiting. And, apparently, this was true. There was a lot of interpersonal conflict, and critical things quite apart from this issue had been said about one another. And this [accusation] had been attributed to the fact that there had been untoward instances [of medical emergencies] and this had been the comment: 'She is doing something that she shouldn't be doing to those babies.'

"Nevertheless, one cannot dismiss those things. The team, when they were here (and we had done this also, but they verified it), tried to look for patterns. That is, [for example], did all of the unexplained instances occur during the 3–11 shift, or the 11–7 shift? And there was not a clear-cut pattern so that one could say, 'Yes, everything that goes wrong, goes wrong on the 3–11 shift,' and therefore, we could look for somebody there that is doing something irregularly.

"Nevertheless, it doesn't rule out [the possibility] that somebody on a given shift [was] doing something, because they can always give a drug that doesn't take effect until later. So, we didn't want to rule out that possibility.

"Nevertheless, because of a comment like I just mentioned, the fact that some of the [incidents] had occurred on a given shift, [the fact that] one of the LVNs had been involved in resuscitations on at least several instances—"

"Let me interrupt you for just a moment," Rothe broke in. "The name of the nurse in question?"

"I am not absolutely certain, but I think it is Genene Jones. Can I check that and confirm that?"

"Sure," Vallejo reassured him. "That's one of the things we can put on a list when we conclude our interview."

"May I borrow your pad here?"

"Sure. We will ask you to please confirm a lot of the things we are discussing today, and we will get back with you later today or tomorrow."

"May I ask you," said the jury's foreman, "how did you remember that name?"

"Because it came up in our discussions several times," said Dunn.

"This week, or several years ago?" continued the foreman.

"No. It was one year ago. One year ago. And then, the other [consideration] was whether or not there was enough that this person should be discharged. Well, the nurses work for the hospital district [not the medical school], so that was not an action that I could take, but I could at least have some influence on it.

"The team felt," Dunn continued, "that we should remove the LVNs from the ICU. There was not enough evidence, from what they could see, to say that somebody had done something wrong, but one could not take a chance."

"Just a minute doctor," said Rothe. "Let me interrupt you again. You said that the team suggested that all of the LVNs should be removed, yet you specifically recall Genene Jones. Was she dismissed from the ICU?"

"All of the LVNs were."

"All of them?"

"Yes, sir."

"So, Genene Jones just went out with the flow when they all went. But Genene Jones was the subject of the remark about an LVN killing babies, I would assume?"

"I think so. I think so. Let me confirm that. One of them was, and I believe it was her."

"Okay, but you independently recall her name in particular?"

"Yes."

"I assume you probably don't recall any of the other names of the LVNs?"

"As a matter of fact, I remember none of them."

"But you remember that one?"

"Yes."

The attorney asked the dean to return to his previous train of thought.

"I think I was giving you a kind of summary of what the team recommended and, as I say, we had a lengthy discussion with them after they finished their visit, and so part of what I am telling you may be verbal and part may be written in the report, so I may give you more than you actually read in that report.

"They recommended that we put a new director, physician-director, in the ICU, and they recommended that we put the ICU under the directorship of an interdepartmental committee. . . . [They] recommended that we set up a committee with representatives [from] three departments: Surgery, Anesthesia, and Pediatrics, and that that committee oversee the [Pediatric] Intensive Care Unit. And we did that. And we also made Dr. Arthur McFee (M-c-F-e-e) the chairman of the committee. Why Dr. McFee? Dr. McFee is a professor of surgery and he is the director of the Intensive Care Unit for surgery; so, all surgical patients—with the exception of small children who may need to be in the Pediatric ICU—go to his Intensive Care Unit. The team, when they were here, looked at our Surgical Intensive Care Unit and talked to the staff and Dr. McFee, and said that it was a simply superb ICU, and it was well run, and Dr. McFee had extraordinary competence, and we would be well served to make him the chairman of the committee to oversee the Pediatric ICU. And we accepted their recommendation on that, and did that.

"So, we set up the committee and made Dr. McFee the chair, and that group, to this day, is still responsible for the Pediatric ICU. That has been about a year. We recruited, from within our own staff, Dr. Jan Puckett (which is P-u-c-k-e-t-t, I believe). She is an anesthesiologist but has a great interest and expertise in respiratory problems in infants and children and therefore was a very logical person to put in charge of the ICU, and we made her the physician-director of the ICU, and she still serves in that capacity.

"And then, we took (I have forgotten how many, but) at least two of the key nurse supervisors in the ICU and had them visit other Intensive Care Units in the United States—and I can't give you the details of how many, but one or two—so they could see how other Intensive Care Units were run, and what procedures they used and what controls and checks and balances they used."

"Doctor," said Rothe returning to his earlier subject, "after the LVNs were relieved, or dismissed, from the Unit, at that point, do you have any information as to the wake of incidents or unexplained problems subsequent to their replacement by registered nurses? Did the problems cease or did they continue?"

"To my knowledge, we have had no problems with unexplained and untoward events [since]."

"When we are talking about unexplained problems like blood clotting and respiratory seizures, to your knowledge, were there any deaths that occurred in the ICU?"

"During that previous period?"

"Yes, sir."

"I don't recall this with any certainty, but I think what could be said is, there were some deaths [for which] everything about the events leading up to the death of the child could not be fully explained."

"Were these deaths similar in nature, or were these different types of situations?"

"I don't recall the details. I have not gone through all of the cases. Now, let me jump ahead and see if I can answer your question by giving you a rough answer. (You can tell I am a university professor, because I give rough answers rather than answering questions.) Another recommendation of the team [concerned the fact] that we had focused our attention on cases within the past six months. The team said that there was not enough evidence that they could see, in the cases that they reviewed, to come to any definitive conclusion. However, [they suggested] maybe we had been shortsighted in only reviewing all of those cases for six months, and we should go back for a full year, and if we went back for a full year, we might find some instances—either untoward instances or deaths—[about which it might be said,] 'you know, at the time that bothered me, but I didn't think anything about it, but putting it all together now, so and so.' Okay. That's the first point.

"The second point [the team made was,] (and your question now triggers that in my memory), they said, 'you have been focusing on deaths. Maybe it is not the deaths that are important. Maybe it is the untoward instances. Maybe you really haven't had any deaths (or a significant number of those beyond what you would expect), but maybe you have had a lot of instances that you have overlooked. So,' they said, 'go back and look at all the cases.'

"Well, Dr. Franks had looked at probably all of the cases. He was the acting chair. Dr. Robotham had looked at them, and other members of the faculty who had been disturbed by all of this had looked at them, and they said: 'We are too close to it. We can go over and over those cases and still may not find anything new. Let's get some fresh insight into this.'

"And so, when Dr. Mangos came on as the new chair for the department, not having had anything at all to do with this, and knowing none of the individuals or doctors (except just in meeting them as he was being recruited in coming here), we asked him once he got here, [along with] one of the senior nurses in the hospital (and I do not recall her name at this minute, but who was not involved with any of this), and John Quest, who is the associate executive director of the hospital district [to look at charts]. We got an administrator, a senior, world-renowned pediatrician, and a nurse who was not involved, to independently go through all of the PICU's cases for the past year, and see if they could come up with any sort of pattern beyond what had already [been found].

"And they have been doing that for some time and, quite frankly, I do not know if they have reached a final conclusion on that, but the last time I checked with them, they had not found anything beyond what had already been turned up. But, that was the effort, to go back and try to see if there had been a pattern there."

"Doctor," said Nick Rothe, "let me ask you a couple of questions. You have indicated that your analysis of the situation was that there were three possible explanations. One was bad luck. What was the second?"

"Second is that our training and control and performance was not up to standard."

"All right," Rothe continued. "And the third was that someone could possibly be doing something?"

"Was deliberately doing something."

"I believe you told the grand jury that the net result of the report by an eminent physician from Toronto was that you could not determine a pattern and you could not specifically find that the cause of this problem was any one of those three things. Is that correct?"

"That is, with any certainty."

"Therefore, it would follow then—would it not—that there existed then, and there exists now, the possibility that it was any one of those three things."

"Or a combination."

"Or a combination of them, yes, but *including* an intentional act by someone, in effect, someone engaging in criminal activity of some sort. That is still possible today, is it not, sir?''

"That's right."

"All right," Rothe continued. "To your knowledge, did anyone in the hospital district connected with this investigation ever report any of this to anyone outside the hospital—"

"Well—"

"—such as the San Antonio police department, the Bexar County district attorney's office, or any criminal investigative agency, with a view toward the possibility of number three?''

"Yeah. The day that we had the meeting (that Monday that I told you about) that I had called, in Dr. Corum's office, and we set up the strategy for how to approach this—"

"About when?'' interrupted the foreman. "Monday, about when?''

"It would be the Monday of the last week of January.''

"Of 1981?''

"Yes. No, of '82. One year ago.''

"All right.''

"I raised this question,'' continued Dr. Dunn, "because none of us were sufficiently knowledgeable about the law to know at what point one should or should not—or must or must not—report such a thing. And, so, we asked the hospital attorney to meet with us, and I believe it was that same afternoon. And Dr. Corum was there and I was there and I don't recall if anyone else was there.''

"Who was the hospital attorney at that time?'' asked Rothe.

"I think it was Paul Green that came, but I will have to check that.''

"All right.''

"And we laid out to him everything that we knew at that time—what we had discussed that morning—and raised this question and left it with him. We would keep him informed of what we found (if anything) different, and that he should deal with the district attorney's office in terms of providing information that was appropriate to be provided.

"Now, I believe at a subsequent meeting—and I cannot tell you when this was but—I believe that [Green] told Dr. Corum that he had talked to someone in the district attorney's office, and whether he had given them the entire story or asked a hypothetical question or what, I don't know, but he was satisfied that the information we had would not yet be sufficient and that it wasn't appropriate to report. That's the extent."

"Yes, sir." Rothe scribbled a note, then looked up at the dean. "In all of the instances that we are talking about, sir, these unexplained, untoward problems, assuming—and I think we have to—that there were some deaths involved, what, if you know, was listed as the cause of death in those instances?"

"I don't know. I don't have that information."

Rothe pressed forward. "Would it be the practice of the medical school and the hospital—Medical Center Hospital—where you have an unexplained death (that is, one you can't put any kind of tag on), is that not, sir, a case for the Bexar County medical examiner?"

"Yes, sir."

"To your knowledge, were any of these untoward instances and deaths ever reported to the Bexar County medical examiner?"

"I don't know."

"Could you determine that, sir? Or would you have to ask someone else?"

"It would not have—"

"Or would it not have been your responsibility to do so?"

The implicit accusation hung in the room. The dean addressed it firmly.

"No, sir, it would not. I would be glad to pursue that for you, but I am kind of the second person removed from that. I can tell you that the faculty are all quite aware of the requirement to report [such] cases to the medical examiner, and in the majority of instances, they are very faithful about doing that, [although] there have been instances, quite frankly, in which they have failed to do that. I think it is no malfeasance on the part of the faculty or the house staff that [such a failure] occurs."

"Is it possible," Rothe continued, "that in these untoward instances that we are talking about—without regard to any malfeasance—is it possible that they were not reported to the medical examiner?"

"Yes. And it is also possible that at the time of death, the physician thought he knew [the cause]. For example, I don't know if there were any deaths following cardiac surgery, but I think there probably was one during that time, because the cardiac surgeon was one who had come to Dr. Franks and said that he was troubled about the care in the Pediatric ICU. Let's assume that there was a death following cardiac surgery. Well, open-heart surgery on these small babies—there is a high mortality anyway."

Rothe clarified his inquiry, "I am directing my question to untoward, unexplained deaths, and not that type of thing."

"But all I am saying," Dr. Dunn responded, "is that in retrospect, one might say that that death wasn't fully explained, whereas at the time, they said, 'Well, we think we can explain it,' and not report it."

"Have there been any of these untoward events subsequent to January of 1982?" Rothe asked.

"None that I am aware of."

"They've stopped?"

"Well, let's say subsequent to February, because February was when we had the team in and took our action."

"And, also," the district attorney pointed out, "those things stopped subsequent to your removing the LVNs from the ICU?"

"Yes," Dunn confirmed.

"And that included Genene Jones?"

"See, a lot of things happened at the same time," the dean explained. "That happened—we removed the LVNs, which included that person, whether that is the correct name or not. We put a new director in. We sent our nurses to get additional training, if you will. We put [the Unit] under the scrutiny of a group of experts. And that epidemic of respiratory infection we had in the winter didn't come back. So, a lot of things happened at once. Therefore, we couldn't come to a conclusion then about, well, 'We took this action and it stopped, therefore, there was a relationship.'"

"So, again, as you have pointed out," Rothe summarized, "there were three possible things that could have happened—including criminal activity—that could explain these things, and there were three or four things done to alleviate the situation, so any one of those remedial measures may have resulted in the sudden stop in these untoward incidents?"

"That's right."

"The only common string that you saw in these, well—" Rothe shook his head and abandoned his question. "Your specialty is what, Doctor?"

"Pathology is my specialty."

Rothe thanked the dean, and Luis Vallejo resumed the questioning. "Doctor, have you ever come into contact with, or heard of in any way, the name of Dr. Kathleen Holland?"

"Yes. I'm not sure that it is [the same] Kathleen Holland that I have heard about, but you can tell me if it is the correct one. I believe Kathleen Holland took her pediatric training here at Medical Center Hospital in the medical school. Is that correct? Is that the one?"

"Yes, sir."

"And I have been told recently that Dr. Holland is in practice in Kerrville, and that she hired Genene Jones to work for her and that there were some untoward incidents there and that there was a grand jury in Kerrville looking into it."

"Did her name surface at all during the investigation headed by the doctor from Toronto?" This was an important question for the investigators; Vallejo found himself repeating it. "Did her name surface at all during this investigation?"

"To my knowledge, no. It never came to my attention."

"Have you any information or knowledge of whether or not Dr. Holland was assigned to the Pediatric's ICU or just in the Pediatrics Ward during the time of these unexplained instances?"

"I have no knowledge that she was."

"Do you have any knowledge or reason to believe that she and Genene Jones in any way were connected?"

"None at all," Dunn assured him. "The only connection that I am aware of is what I have heard, and that is strictly hearsay—that she had hired Genene Jones to work for her."

"Doctor, would it be a fair statement, or an unfair statement (or, should I say, an accurate or inaccurate statement), to say that these unexplained deaths— Let me rephrase that." Vallejo went on more carefully, "Would it be accurate to say that the deaths in the ICU had, in fact, quadrupled during a certain period of time in the last two to three years?"

"I don't know if 'quadrupled' is the correct number; it had increased. However, as I recall, when one looks at the number of cases admitted for the two periods of time, and the degree and severity of the problems of the children, it was not considered to be out of bounds."

"Then," Rothe broke in again, "let me ask you this, Doctor: If that was the case, why did the hospital feel constrained to utilize a Toronto expert, two people from Boston's Children's Hospital, et cetera, to investigate a situation in which, if you put the stats together, was not out of the ordinary?"

"Well, for two reasons. One is, like I was saying about operative deaths, that [when] you expect [a certain number] over a five-year period, and you get three in one year, you are bound to say, 'Wait a minute, let's take a second look at that.' So, that's one point, because just because you think you can explain something medically, doesn't mean you are always right.

"The second part—and this was what [lay at the heart of the matter]: that one case that did not die but had three unexplained events; *that* you could not explain away. We could not find a medical explanation for those three events."

At the time, the significance of this last admission slipped by Rothe and the other attorneys. The prosecutor was concerned with clarifying another point.

"But would the hospital go to the expense and effort to bring people from Boston's Children's Hospital, and so on, to investigate one unexplained death in the Unit? This was not, sir, the result of one incident was it? It was much more than that."

"Well, of course, it wasn't the result of one incident. It is [just] that there is one incident that is clear-cut that we couldn't explain."

Again the admission went unexamined. The attorneys were more interested in uncovering a flood of unexplained deaths than focusing on one unexplained illness that had not been fatal.

"But that is not what precipitated the investigation, is it?" Rothe prodded.

"Well, actually, it was. You see, up until that point, you could always find some explanation that could explain what had happened in each of those [questionable instances]—even though it might not be a highly probable one, or one that you are willing to accept quickly. But, if you asked the question, 'Is there any explanation for that?'—'Well, yes, there is.'"

"My point is this, though," Rothe seemed slightly frustrated, "that one particular case, granted, had three problems with it that nobody could explain, but all of this reporting and all of the conversation we have had thus far was not with the view toward explaining that case, was it? But rather with the view toward explaining the overall increase in these untoward problems on the Pediatrics Ward, right?"

"Sure."

"So, it was not any *one* thing, it was a multitude of things, is that correct? And the increased numbers brought your attention to it—can we put it that way?"

"That's right."

"For whatever the explanation may have been, criminal activity or otherwise?"

"Right," the dean concurred.

"Let me ask you another question," continued Rothe. "Do you know, or are you aware of any autopsies performed on any of the infants who may have died during this period of the investigation?"

"Uh-huh."

"And if so, by whom were those done?"

"I don't know the answer to that."

"Do you know how many of those were done?"

"No, sir, I don't. I don't have that information."

"One other question. Regarding these unexplained incidents, deaths, or whatever they may be," asked Rothe, "what is it going to take for us to get the medical records of those particular cases that were the subject of the initial investigation?"

"Let me be sure I understand your question, because it may have two parts to it. Are you asking about how you can identify the specific cases, or are you asking about how you can obtain the physical records?"

"Both. Can you identify them, and would you be able to provide for this grand jury medical records dealing with those untoward and unexplained incidents?"

"Okay, as an individual, I cannot. As a grand jury, you can do it. I do not have the names of the cases. . . . You may have to get several people to put all of these together for you. Dr. Robert Franks, who was the acting chair of the department, while he probably does not have a comprehensive list of the names, and he probably does not, he can put that together. And the physical records are the property of the hospital district, so you have to get those through Dr. Corum, the medical records. And, at the moment, I don't know how many of those records are in the physical custody of Dr. Mangos, John Quest, and the nurse.''

''But they are in a file, are they not?''

''Yes.''

''By that, I mean,'' Rothe clarified, ''we can—there is a source of information for the names of the individuals who were the subject of this investigation by which we can then go to the medical records or technicians or whoever they are and get those records?''

''Yes. Understand that you start out with one case that is the peak of the iceberg (and that is the one that I keep telling you about), and then you get into a group of cases in which there are instances that are difficult to explain but can be explained. And then, you go on down to the rest and you will have to ask the question, 'Were there things that occurred there that we thought we understood and explained but we really shouldn't have accepted that?' So, you have got this kind of an iceberg. They can cut off the top for you in terms of the ones that were the object of major concern.''

Rothe asked Dunn briefly about Sudden Infant Death Syndrome, whether it is common in a child Chelsea Mc-Clellan's age. Then Vallejo went over the list of documentation the district attorney's office would like the dean to supply.

The dean expressed some concern about obtaining the documents from other people—wouldn't that constitute a violation of his oath not to reveal what was discussed before the grand jury? Terry MacDonald assured the dean that he was free to ask any questions about information he had been instructed to gather, and, if he felt the need, to discuss the entire substance of his testimony with an attorney.

Vallejo requested three things: a copy of the Conn report, a list of the doctors and nurses who made up the Conn review team, and the name of the doctor who told the administrators of the nurse who had come to him with reports of a death nurse in the PICU.

Rothe stood when Vallejo finished. He still had one question to ask the dean. He later recalled, "It was central to the prosecution. I'd been thinking about it all morning: when I would ask it, how I would slip it in—and here was the spot. I had to ask it now . . . and my mind went blank. But I was already talking."

"Now, Doctor," Rothe said, "this is a question, this is not a request: how would we go about. . . ." His question trailed off. He started again: "For example, Genene Jones's name has come up . . ." and pacing, he paused again.

Dunn encouraged him to go on, "Yes?"

"How would we go about . . ." Nick stopped a third time, tapping his forehead with a pencil.

"Then I turned on him," Nick said later, "and asked him straight: 'Is it possible to compare her name to the cases in question? Is there any way to determine whether or not she was on duty, and whether or not she had any contact with these patients?'"

"Yeah," replied the dean.

"How could we do that?" asked Rothe, resuming his seat, ready to write.

"Let's see what the simplest way would be. In the early investigation that we did, and this . . ." Dunn now paused for a moment. "I am talking about when Dr. Franks had heard about this (even before he came to me and had some of the people in the department look at the cases), they were looking for patterns like that, and I suspect they may have that as a specific answer for you."

"Let's ask Dr. Franks about that," Rothe said to his colleagues.

"If they fail in doing that," continued Dunn, "you can get from the hospital, the duty roster, number one. Secondly, if you have the medical records in your possession . . . see, the nurses, in charting [their patients,] have to sign their name for any incident that occurred, and certainly in some of these cases, there is no question that she was the nurse that had been involved.''

"But there would be nothing to keep her from handling a patient without putting her name on the record would there?" Rothe asked. "It could have been another nurse's charge, but she could come in and handle the patient."

"Well, yeah. Except, if the records are kept properly. . . . Let's make an assumption that something happened to a child, and she is not the nurse in charge of the child but she finds the child and engages in heroic acts. The nurse who does do the charting should note: 'Mrs. Jones found the child and did so-and-so.' So, that should be in the records."

"I assume the record would also contain a notation regarding any doctor or nurse who used any heroic action to resuscitate the child. If, for example, a doctor were called in, or if a nurse came in and assisted?"

"Yeah. That should be in the notes."

MacDonald, realizing the lunch hour was overdue and that the attorneys had pretty well covered every question they knew to ask, spoke up: "Does any member of the grand jury have any questions that they would like to ask?"

"Yes," a woman juror responded. "Who puts the information on the charts for each patient?"

"There are actually two sets of notes, so if you look at any of these medical charts—I am glad that you asked the question—there are nurses' notes and there are doctors' notes, and they are kept in separate areas. The nurses keep a running log when they come on duty and make rounds and see the patient, and they make a little note about the condition of the patient at the time they came on duty, and what medications they give, and anything special that happens, and that sort of thing. And then, there is a separate section for doctors' notes, where physicians will write about the condition of the patient, further treatment that is to be given, usually a note about what they expect to happen, and then, there is a third section of the chart which is called 'the orders,' and if a treatment or a drug is to be given to a patient, the doctor writes [in the orders], 'Give this patient this drug, this amount, this frequency,' and then, when the nurse picks up that order and acknowledges it, she initials it. And then when she gives the medication or the treatment, she should write in their notes that she has given the drug."

The same juror then asked, "Would there be any chance that the nurse or the LVN could tamper with the chart?"

"What do you mean by 'tamper with'?" asked the dean.

The juror hesitated, unsure of exactly what she did mean. "I mean, I guess, why would they necessarily have to write down what was actually done?"

"Well, now, there are two issues here. One is that, you know, they can write anything that they want to, but I think most of us are aware that charts become legal documents really, because of malpractice suits and whatnot."

"But LVNs can write the information," the juror persisted.

"Yes," Dunn confirmed. "Whoever is the responsible person. Most nurses and doctors know that they should never, ever, go back and change an entry in a chart. If they have written something incorrectly, they should not go back and scratch it out, they should make a note that that entry was incorrectly entered and whatnot. So, to answer your question, yes, a lot of people can tamper with charts, but they sure should not, and I think most of them don't."

"And the charts could be made available, if necessary?" concluded the juror.

"You are the grand jury, and I guess you can subpoena anything you need."

Rothe took over the questioning once more. "Doctor, in the case where Genene Jones . . ." He paused and scratched his forehead. "You said there was a connection and—I think it was the particular case that you were talking about, where there were three incidents. Was she involved in that one?"

"I'm not sure that she was in all three," said Dunn.

"But she was involved, or was at least in attendance on a number of those?"

"Well," said Dunn, "let me go back to your original premise [of] a minute ago, about the fact that there are unexplained incidents along the way and she had been involved in some of those, but not all—in some of them."

"So, if she had been involved," Rothe continued, "we would expect to find a notation by Genene Jones about the incident or whatever it happened to be, right?"

"Or, if she was not the nurse responsible, the other nurse would write that [Jones] had found the child."

"All right. Thank you, Doctor." And Rothe sat down. He had heard enough. He needed those charts.

The foreman then asked, "How many nurses would there be, approximately, 'per shift,' I guess is the way you would phrase it."

"I think that at the time there were . . . we had eight beds—I think—at the time, and there were generally two nurses on duty on an average, and there may have been three."

"Would those have been RNs or LVNs?" asked the first juror.

"It varied. It varied from time to time as to how they rotated the people. As I recall, when all of this started and I began to ask the people in the nursing service about Genene Jones, their comment to me was that 'She is an LVN, but she has had a lot of experience and she is probably more capable than many RNs,' and then [there would be] a pause and they would say, 'But that is one of the problems that we have, because there is a lot of jealousy between her and RNs, because she feels that she knows more, and, in some cases, she does.' So, she may have been the senior nurse on some of the shifts that she was on. I just don't know about that."

"Doctor, do you know how long she has been a nurse or what her background is, or anything?"

"No. I don't know anything about where she went to school, or her training, or her experience, other than what I have told you."

"Dr. Dunn was later held in contempt by the grand jury," the Investigator told us. "Not for his testimony on February 3, but because of his failure to turn over some documents. After the grand jury talked with Dr. Mangos and Dr. Franks and some of the other doctors at Medical Center, they issued some broadly worded subpoenas, in an attempt to pull in whatever documentary evidence they could.

"Some eight or nine months later, we began hearing rumors of a 'Conn I report,' a 'preliminary report,' in other words, an earlier version of the document Dunn had given us back in February—Conn's final report. This preliminary report, Conn I, contained some statements which showed that Medical Center had a specific interest in Genene Jones's activities back in February of 1982.

"We ran a bluff on the hospital administration. I was sent in to see B.H. Corum, and I told him: "We know that there was a Conn I report and we want it. Where is it?" Corum said he had heard of its existence but did not have it. A couple of days later, Dunn appeared before the grand jury to answer some additional questions and produce some other unrelated records. 'Coincidentally,' he also brought in the missing Conn report along with some detailed notes about his exit interview with Conn's team. You know, it was, 'Oh, by the way, I found these too. They were misfiled.'

"This was in *November*. We'd been sweating blood for months trying to put the story together and these documents contained some crucial pieces of information.

"Well, the grand jury wasn't too happy with the fact that the hospital had withheld this evidence, so they held Dunn in contempt. Slapped him with a fine, which was no big deal. I'm sure the loss of face hurt worse. In a way, Dunn was sort of a fall guy—obviously, he wasn't the only one who knew of the existence of these documents."

The Investigator

How was it that you came to be involved with this case?

I came in, I guess, probably three weeks after the information was finally reported. Late Friday afternoon, the third week of February, 1983, I was notified that we had a 5:00 meeting in Sam Millsap's office with some of the chief attorneys. And that caught my attention: "Five o'clock on a Friday? Who the hell meets then?" You know, "What's up?" See, the whole thing started . . . see, Sam Millsap . . . let me give you some background on this. Sam Millsap was sworn in as district attorney of Bexar County, January 1, 1983. I was sworn in that same night, as were all the other new people who came on board with Sam.

Sam Millsap hired you?

No, not him personally, the persons on his staff who hire investigators. I think I probably brought the most experience to the team. I had been in both military intelligence and army criminal investigations for years. I ran felonies, and I'd guess I probably worked more murders while I was in the army than most any ten military investigators. It was sophisticated, and we were dedicated. We were pros. This investigation, for instance, was at once both difficult and rather simple. From the standpoint of running it to its logical conclusion, that *would have been* rather simple; I just don't believe we ever really did that. From the standpoint of going out there and getting your hands on the information, that was difficult because of all the politics interwoven throughout virtually all the activities.

And obviously, this is *not* the way to run an investigation. You don't start, day one, with the grand jury. You go out there and you ask questions, you beat the bushes, and you set your mind to learn a new system—the medical profession. You find out just who you're going to talk to first. Even if somebody doesn't want to talk to you, you can find out what the extent of their knowledge in certain areas will be, either by virtue of their position, their tenure, et cetera. You can kind of break it down and find the logical structure in which the issue under investigation took place.

But the lawyers *started* by calling in the powers that be at both the hospital and the UT Health Science Center. With hindsight, one can easily see that it was all meaningless testimony. Nobody knew anything. "Of course," they said, "we had these deaths, but nothing inordinate went on. Of course there's nothing 'untoward' occurring in the Pedi-ICU." The general tone of the earliest testimony was that they were almost indignant about being asked the questions.

Anyway, I first heard about the case at that Friday evening meeting. Once I was briefed, I immediately knew that this was going to be a real giant undertaking, because then Kerrville came into perspective. What little I had heard about Kerrville, I then connected to this. I said, "Gentlemen, this is going to take some time."

"About a month?"

"Month, my ass. Closer to a year."

Well, it ended up there was about sixteen, seventeen months of pure investigation. It wasn't easy, but it was the right thing to do.

SEVENTEEN

My dear fellow, life is infinitely stranger than anything which the mind of man can invent.

Sir Arthur Conan Doyle; Sherlock
Holmes addresses Dr. Watson

THE MAN SAM MILLSAP CHOSE AS THE KEY DE-tective on the Jones case—the Investigator—has, in the thirty years of his career, mastered the guise of a harmless, good-natured, hard-working but unexceptional law enforcement officer. He favors polyester and looks at all times slightly rumpled. He speaks with a Midwestern accent in roundabout fashion, reaching his points as if by accident. His face is bland, with all evidence of aggressive inclinations carefully wiped from it. He seems, in a word, unimpressive, but is in fact an unflinching and uncanny judge of the human soul. His only marked characteristic is his steadfast integrity. One gets the sense that after years of witnessing the cost of others' compromises with the devil, the Investigator has learned the value of a black-and-white morality.

"For the first three months of the investigation, we were really just getting our feet wet. The first step, always—and the most important—is getting out there and meeting the people. While every person's got his own idio-syncrasies, deviation from the norm gets to be pretty easy to spot. The idea is to constantly push for more information, more contact. Make people uncomfortable, see how they react. You watch for alarm, defensive reactions, tension, nervousness, sensitive areas. You observe, and you get to understand their motivations. Gradually, a mosaic of what must have happened gets formed. Hopefully, by the time the case is closed, the mosaic is clear enough so that the resulting report will be solid enough to put an end to a bad situation.

"In every case, the question we're ultimately trying to answer is: 'What happened?'"

Sam Millsap called the first meeting of the Jones task force on Friday, February 18, 1983. The dawn of Saturday the nineteenth found the Investigator still reviewing the documents he had been handed the night before. He knew from the beginning that one of the major problems this case would present was how to cope with the masses of information the investigators were going to have to pull together.

"I'd started an alphabetical listing of names immediately, and it was already lengthy. On the way home I'd stopped at the five-and-dime and bought a red leatherette 1983 journal. I keep a personal log when I get involved in an interesting case, and I knew this was going to be interesting from the word go. I think of it as a perpetual memo and make an entry every night.

"When I'd finally finished digesting the initial papers, it must have been 6:00 A.M. My wife was up. We had coffee together. Then I made the first entry. It was long as I recall. The first usually is."

INVESTIGATOR'S LOG: 1st DAY, FRIDAY, 2-18-83.

At 5:05 P.M., was reminded of oaths to office, then informed would be looking into a case involving questionable deaths of several infants and young children at the Medical Center Hospital—part of the University of Texas's Health Science Center, here in San Antonio. Instructions dealt with confidentiality of information and

Kathleen Holland on the steps of the Georgetown courthouse. (*Photo by* Austin American-Statesman)

Genene Jones leaving the courthouse after the guilty verdict. (*Photo by* Austin American-Statesman)

Genene Jones during an interview after her trial. (*Photo by Jay Godwin of* Austin American-Statesman)

Ron Sutton talking with the press while waiting for the verdict. (*Photo by Larry Kolvoord of* Austin American-Statesman)

Jim Brookshire talking with the press after the verdict. (*Photo by* Williamson County Sun)

The Honorable John Carter outside the Williamson County Courthouse. (*Photo by Jay Godwin of* Austin American-Statesman)

Bo Holmstedt after testifying about his testing procedures. (*Photo by* Williamson County Sun)

Unidentified servant of the court and Sergeants Maywhort, Garcia, and Torrongeau on their way to the courthouse. (*Photo by* Williamson County Sun)

Sam Millsap speaking to the press during the San Antonio trial. (*Photo by* San Antonio Express-News)

Nick Rothe speaking to the press during the San Antonio trial. (*Photo by* San Antonio Light)

The Medical Center Hospital complex in northwest San Antonio. (*Photo by author*)

The Williamson County courthouse, Georgetown, Texas. (*Photo by author*)

The razor-wire capped fences around the Mountain View Unit of Huntsville's Prison for Women. (*Photo by author*)

"Dr. Kathy's" pediatrics office in the little yellow house in Kerrville, Texas. (*Photo by author*)

severity of implications involved. Copies furnished of all
relevant documents obtained or generated to date.

Documents tell of a Dr. Kathleen Holland and of a
Nurse Genene Jones, who—while officed in Kerrville—
are suspected of having caused or induced respiratory
seizures in eight infant patients in their clinic. The
paralytic succinylcholine a possible cause; drug apparently
untraceable during autopsy. Both Dr. Holland and Nurse
Jones deny having used the drug in their treatment of these
children. Department of Public Safety polygraph exams
indicate deception from both Holland and Jones on
relevant questions.

PICU REPORT, 2ND DRAFT, DATED 1/83:

So-called Mangos Report explains the findings of a
survey by medical staff personnel of ninety-four records
for patients cared for in the PICU during a lengthy
"questionable period," approx. '81–'82. Thirty-one kids
expired before leaving the PICU. Thirteen records of key
interest. Stats reflect eleven of fifteen infant deaths
occurred during the 3–11 Evening Shift. Jones usually
worked this shift. On the basis of this report, writer
concurs with notion that Jones's presence on duty in the
PICU during infant deaths could be attributed to: (a)
coincidence; (b) Jones volunteering to care for the very
sickest infants; or (c) negligence or wrongdoing on the part
of Jones.

The Mangos Report the Investigator referred to in the
first entry of his log was the same one Marvin Dunn had
spoken of before the grand jury. The still-not-completed
report had been assembled and turned over to the district
attorney. The document would become the skeleton
around which the investigators would build their case.

The brief report contained the results of an ostensibly extensive review of patient medical records conducted by the new
Pediatrics Department chairman, Dr. John Mangos, with the
assistance of Medical Center's assistant director, John Guest,
and RN Jean Foster. These three individuals had divided
among themselves medical histories of ninety-four children,
purportedly every child who had died unexpectedly or suffered

some questionable incident in the PICU during a period roughly corresponding to the year 1981. Each team member independently reviewed his or her share of the charts, culling out the most puzzling cases. The team then together prepared one-paragraph histories of these children; the summaries eventually formed the core of their final report.

In all but these sixteen cases, the reviewers concluded the questioned death or Code had been reasonably consistent with the child's medical condition. Even in the selected cases, the medical crisis, as summarized, seemed less than alarming.

Joshua Sawyer, for instance, was one of the children whose PICU stay was noted in the report:

> THIS ONE-YEAR-OLD BOY WAS ADMITTED TO MCH ON 12/8/81 BECAUSE OF SEVERE SMOKE INHALATION DURING A FIRE IN HIS HOME. HE WAS IN A STATE OF RESPIRATORY FAILURE WHEN SEEN AT MCH AND WAS INTUBATED AND PLACED ON A VENTILATOR. HE WAS MONITORED FOR INCREASED INTRACRANIAL PRESSURE AND HAD MILD SEIZURES. HIS NEUROLOGICAL STATUS REMAINED POOR DURING THE COURSE OF HIS HOSPITALIZATION, AND HE DEVELOPED CARDIAC ARREST ON THE EVENING OF 12/12/81. HE WAS RESUSCITATED FROM THE FIRST ARREST BUT SUCCUMBED TO THE SECOND ONE AND WAS PRONOUNCED DEAD AT 9:22 P.M. NURSE G. JONES WAS IN ATTENDANCE WITH THE PATIENT DURING THE FINAL EVENTS.

Oddly, no mention was made in this summary of the extremely high level of Dilantin lab technician Tony Ferinacci found in Joshua's blood, or of the "kidney failure" theory advanced to account for it.

Rolando Santos also merited a one-paragraph summary in the report:

> THIS FOUR-WEEK-OLD BOY WAS ADMITTED TO MCH ON 12/27/81 FOR THE TREATMENT OF "TRILOBAR" PNEUMONIA AND RESPIRATORY FAILURE. WAS PLACED ON

RESPIRATOR IN THE PICU. ON THE FOURTH DAY OF
HOSPITALIZATION HE HAD SUDDEN SEIZURES. CAT SCAN
WAS NORMAL. THE SEIZURES WERE FOLLOWED BY CARDIAC
ARREST. EPISODE OF HYPOTENSION ON SIXTH HOSPITAL
DAY. BLEEDING FROM PUNCTURE SITES AND PROLONGED PT
TIME WAS DETECTED. ON 1/6/82 HE HAD ONE MORE SUCH
BLEEDING EPISODE (ASSAY FOR HEPARIN WAS POSITIVE). ON
A THIRD EPISODE, PROTAMINE CORRECTED THE PROBLEM.
WAS TRANSFERRED TO THE FLOOR ON 1/12/82 WITH
CLEARING OF ALL PROBLEMS AND ON 1/16/82 WAS
DISCHARGED HOME.

To anyone familiar with the course of Rolando's stay in
the PICU, the summary seems almost cavalier in its casual
assessment of his problems and its virtual disregard for the
incontestably massive amount of heparin proven to have
been in the boy's system at the time of his last emergency.

At the conclusion of this case-by-case analysis of the
sixteen questionable incidents (which did not include Patrick Zavala or any infant who died after him), the Mangos
team noted that "Nurse G. Jones was present during the
final events occurring during the P.M. (3–11) shift of nursing in all these cases." The report also pointed out that of
the fifteen other deaths that occurred in the PICU during
1981, eleven occurred during the 3–11 shift.

The team acknowledged that Jones's frequent association
with the Unit's crises certainly was troubling, but reiterated
Pat Belko's observation that Jones habitually cared for the
Unit's sickest patients. They went on to comment that they
were impressed by the fact that "G. Jones had written some
of the most legible, detailed, and informative nursing notes,
always documenting medications, procedures, and the presence of physicians. In only one case (#8, Dora Rios)," the
report continued, "Nurse Jones went beyond the professional standards and wrote a rather emotional note at the end
of her nursing comments about the death of the child."

The Mangos report concluded that Jones's connection to
the deaths of their targeted patients "could be coinciden-

tal"; however, "negligence or wrongdoing cannot be excluded."

However superficial the Mangos report would prove to be, it was a way into the maze of San Antonio's Baby Deaths Case. The Investigator had 16 leads— 16 names, 16 medical charts to compile, 16 babies about whom to question doctors, nurses, and parents. It was a start.

Kathleen's life seemed to have bottomed out at the end of 1982. Her patient load dropped to four or five children a day. Her bills outpaced her income. Her creditors grew more insistent in their requests for payment of overdue accounts. Her divorce from Charleigh became finalized December 31.

The new year, however, brought an upswing. Business had started to pick up again. After three months of temporary agency nurses, Kathleen found a permanent nurse— an open-hearted, older woman who seemed almost instantly to have adopted Kathleen. In mid-February, when San Antonio's grand jury began its inquiry into the Jones case, Kathleen's lawyer was able to persuade them that his client had little of value to tell, especially in light of the Fifth Amendment privilege; Kathleen was excused from appearing. The insanity of the events in her Clinic was beginning to recede, if only slightly.

Then, on February 15, 1983, Kathleen had an unexpected visitor at her Clinic. His business card identified him as Ted Dracos, a reporter from a San Antonio TV station. He had come, he informed Kathleen, to ask her some questions about her former nurse, Genene Jones.

He seemed like a very pleasant young man," Kathleen recalls, "for about ten seconds."

"We've got this information," Dracos began in a friendly, half-apologetic way, "about some rather mysterious deaths in Medical Center Hospital's PICU—where you were working along with Genene Jones before you worked together here at your Clinic—and in light of the fact that you and Genene Jones are presently under suspicion of murder here in this county—''

Kathleen excused herself, then went back to her office to call Jack Leon. The attorney told her not to answer any questions. ''*Be nice*,'' he advised. ''For God's sake don't antagonize the press, but don't answer anything.''

Kathleen returned to face the reporter in her waiting room to explain in as diplomatic a fashion as possible that her lawyer would not allow her to speak with the press. Dracos became a little less affable. He told her he had obtained certain information, and he really thought it would be in Kathleen's best interest to review and comment upon it. With or without her input, however, he was going to broadcast the story. Kathleen politely declined. ''I really wish I could help you, Mr. Dracos, I really do, but I just can't. I've got to follow my attorney's instructions.''

The next evening, Wednesday, February 16, Ted Dracos, a newsman whose audience had come to respect his often shocking and confrontational exposés, broadcast the first installment of his exclusive report on mysterious deaths in Medical Center's PICU and their connection to the events in Dr. Holland's Kerrville Clinic. The following day, every news source in town was on the story. ''Tot Death Probe Shakes Hospital,'' screamed the headlines. For the first time, San Antonians learned that a baby killer might have been stalking the halls of their county hospital a year earlier.

Three days later, on Tuesday, February 22, Public Relations Officer Jeff Duffield issued a short statement to the press prepared by Dr. William E. Thornton, chairman of the board of managers for the Bexar County Hospital District.

MUCH HAS BEEN PRINTED AND SAID DURING THE PAST WEEK ABOUT ALLEGED OCCURRENCES IN MEDICAL CENTER HOSPITAL'S PEDIATRIC INTENSIVE CARE UNIT AND IN KERRVILLE DURING 1981 AND 1982. WHILE THE HOSPITAL DISTRICT IS PROUD OF ITS ACCOMPLISHMENTS IN THE PAST AND OF OUR PEDIATRIC INTENSIVE CARE UNIT, WE HAVE

WITHHELD OFFICIAL COMMENT. IT HAS BEEN REPORTED
THAT THERE ARE GRAND JURY INVESTIGATIONS IN PROCESS.
THE HOSPITAL DISTRICT HAS BEEN FULLY COOPERATING
AND WILL CONTINUE TO COOPERATE FULLY WITH SUCH
INVESTIGATIONS. WE WANT THE TRUTH TO BE FOUND AND
WILL ASSIST THE LEGAL AUTHORITIES TO OUR UTMOST IN
THAT EFFORT. BUT TO ASSIST IN THE SEARCH—TO FIND
THE TRUTH—WE MUST HONOR THE CONFIDENTIALITY AND
SECRECY OF A GRAND JURY INVESTIGATION. TO DO
OTHERWISE MAY DO AN INJUSTICE TO AN INVESTIGATION
AND TO THE SUBJECTS OF SUCH EFFORT.

WE HAVE NO EVIDENCE OF ANY INTENTIONAL
WRONGDOING, AND WE HAVE PROVIDED THE APPROPRIATE
AUTHORITIES WITH ALL THE INFORMATION WE HAVE
AVAILABLE.

Dr. Thornton also consented to be interviewed by the
broadcast media. On the 6:00, 10:00, and 11:00 news programs, he assured San Antonians that their "institution
was professional."

The county's medical examiner, Dr. Vincent DiMaio,
was not as charitable in his television appearance. He informed the television cameras that he had never been advised of any questionable infant deaths at Medical Center
Hospital and strongly implied that he should have been,
since failure to notify the medical examiner's office is a
violation of state law.

The Dracos story broke just before the Investigator's
initial witness interviews were scheduled to begin; the investigation team, therefore, had already lost the possibility
of conducting a low-key quiet inquiry. Now every witness
was acutely aware of the potential ramifications of each
question asked and each answer given.

Genene's sometime babysitter and housemate, Bonnie
Gunderson, was one of the first to be interviewed. She
proved to be a very talkative witness; however, the value
of her information was tempered by the Investigator's
sense that the young women had an active imagination that
was not always sharply differentiated from memory.

Suzanna Maldonado was quietly helpful, telling the Investigator of the information she and Pat Alberti had discovered in the Unit's Log Book. Another early subject, a nurse who had worked the 3–11 with Genene, showed open hostility when questioned. She complained that she felt she was being forced into a corner, that the Investigator was trying to pressure her into blaming Genene for the deaths in the PICU. She consistently refused to consider the possibility that anyone would, for any reason, intentionally injure a sick child.

Very quickly, the Investigator began to develop a picture of the issues he faced, of the medical knowledge he would have to acquire, and of the people from whom he was likely to encounter resistance.

On Thursday, February 24, San Antonio's grand jury heard from two witnesses from Kerrville: Genene Jones and Sally Benkert.

"She danced all over their heads," the Investigator would later say of Jones's San Antonio grand-jury appearance. "She was very confident, led them right to the topics she wanted to cover, then sang the same song she'd already been singing about Kathleen's Clinic for months: There were problems at Medical Center Hospital, all right, but they didn't have anything to do with her."

Genene complained about the graduate nurses who were not qualified for the positions they held in the PICU. She talked about the communication gaps between hospital departments and the feuding between Pediatrics and Surgery. She spoke of residents who, afraid they might lose face by admitting they didn't know what to do, instead instituted improper treatment. She even went so far as to bad-mouth specific doctors and nurses, insinuating they were responsible for certain dangerous incidents, which she recalled for the jury.

Afterward, William Chenault, the attorney who had helped Genene with her divorce four years earlier and who was now handling this "patently ridiculous case" as a favor, refused to discuss, or allow Genene to discuss, specific questions, "since grand-jury testimony is secret, by law."

"I have no comment, gentlemen," is all reporters heard from both Genene and her friend, Sally, before they quickly disappeared into a waiting car. Chenault, however, took the opportunity to criticize the press and to direct attention toward other issues, and away from his client.

"The media shouldn't start naming people when nothing has been done. There hasn't been any criminal action on the part of anybody, either in San Antonio or in Kerrville. And I don't think there was ever any negligence on the part of Genene. She is a fabulous nurse.

"As far as the Kerrville case goes, I don't think there is any relationship between the medical care received and the death of the child. In San Antonio, well, in the first place, the numbers floating around are totally wrong. The sources the press has are not correct. It increases every time I see it. I've seen five, I've seen twelve, I've seen thirty-two, I think I even saw forty-seven somewhere. Before you're through, you're going to have us connected with every kid who died at Medical Center Hospital during the past five years."

Referring to Dr. Conn's early 1982 investigation into the Unit, Chenault said, "They looked at all the records, at the autopsy reports on all the children, and they pointed the finger at nobody. Why my client is being singled out, I just don't know."

A frenzy of publicity followed Genene's grand-jury appearance and it caused Kathleen's practice to nose-dive. As February ended, she reached a new low of only two or three patients a day. Kathleen's nurse kindly suggested that the doctor take care of other more necessary bills before she pay the nurse's own salary. "I don't need it right now, Honey, and it looks like maybe you will."

Kathleen also started to get phone calls in which the caller was derogatory or vaguely threatening, or failed to say anything at all. For the first time, she felt frightened. The press seemed determined to sensationalize the case as much as possible. She began to wonder, "What if my side of the story never comes out?"

Support came from odd sources: a letter or postcard from a stranger, kind words from the parents of her remaining patients, the overwhelming generosity of her nurse. Kathleen surprised herself by finding solace in an unexpected source: a Bible a mother had given her when the troubles had first begun, five months earlier. She sat down one evening, opened to the first page—Genesis— and began reading. "I'd tried reading the Bible once before, when I was a kid, but I didn't have much use for it. I guess you have to be ready for it. It gave me a real sense of how God is always present in our lives."

At the beginning of March, 1983, Millsap announced his decision to place Assistant District Attorney Nick Rothe in charge of the Jones case in San Antonio. Rothe, a former criminal defense attorney, had been persuaded by Millsap to try the other side of a case for a change. Of average height, build, and looks, the most enduring impression Rothe leaves behind is one of intensity. That intensity, coupled with an aggressive, restless mind, made him an ideal choice to handle the difficult investigation ahead. In his first official act, he took firm control: Each day at 8:10 A.M., all attorneys and investigators involved were to congregate in his office for a strategy and debriefing session. For a year and a half, they would see each other more regularly than they saw their families.

By the second week of March, the media had fallen into an almost daily rhythm of updates on the Baby Deaths Case. Reporters hounded Jones relentlessly, but she seemed to thrive on the attention. Speaking from Sally's trailer home, Genene constantly reiterated her position: If there had been some outside cause behind the many deaths during her employment in the San Antonio PICU, it was nothing more than inexperienced doctors and nurses—it had nothing to do with her. "I *trained* most of the girls that came through that Unit.'' As for the emergencies in Kathleen's Clinic, that had been mere coincidence and not at all unusual. All the fuss was just ridiculous. She had not murdered anyone. ''I just can't believe people could think that about me. I am a mother and a nurse. I love babies.''

While Genene spoke long and vehemently of her innocence, calling her own press conferences and frequently generating headlines, Kathleen maintained an increasingly reluctant silence. Her attorneys, Jack Leon and Sam Bayless, continued to caution her against wading into the fray. They knew from experience how damaging an unfortunate phrase taken out of context could be.

In addition to constant harassment from reporters, she continued to receive calls from the lunatic fringe, promising reprisals Kathleen did not want to know about. Kathleen installed an unlisted private line at the Clinic and refused to take any calls except those regarding her patients.

In mid-March Kathleen received the summons on the first lawsuit filed in this matter. The McClellans were suing her—not Genene, not anyone else—for seven million dollars, alleging she was the cause of their daughter's death. Kathleen also received two weeks' notice from her landlord at 320 Water Street. He hadn't been paid in months and could no longer carry the loss. Charleigh urged her to call it quits. ''No one will rent you space. Cut your losses and get out. Start up somewhere else. You're just throwing good money after bad.''

Kathleen refused to give up. ''I've got to stay. Somehow. If I leave, it will look like I'm running away.''

She said much later, ''I guess you could say I chose to make a stand. I guess I figured it couldn't get any worse.''

During his third week of interviews, the Investigator spoke with Virginia Mousseau, the senior nursing administrator at Medical Center who had attended the January 25 meeting the previous year. She told him she first began hearing about problems in the PICU as early as September or October of 1981, from Pat Belko and Judy Harris. Then in

late October, Dr. Franks also mentioned to her the possibility
of questionable deaths and specifically raised Jones's name
in connection with them. Mousseau, however, felt the way in
which Jones had recently been singled out by the press was
unjust. She gave the Investigator nothing to support a suspicion that Jones had ever harmed any of the PICU's patients.

At the end of that week, the Baby Deaths investigation
changed quarters. In the face of the press's rabid interest in
the case, Rothe grew concerned about the safety of the
records generated by his investigators. The records included
reams of confidential and highly emotion-charged materials;
Rothe did not want the documents' integrity or confidentiality compromised. He obtained sole use of the Old
Jail, a building a few blocks from the courthouse long out of
use as a lockup. The investigative team would not be as
comfortable there, but their files would be considerably
safer.

As Millsap's subordinates began to dig into the case, the
district attorney realized how intimately his investigation
was connected with Ron Sutton's. Perhaps because of his
inexperience in the office, he conceived of a rather novel
proposal. Recognizing that Sutton did not have adequate
manpower or funding to develop the case with the dogged-
ness required, Millsap proposed a joint investigation conducted under the auspices of both the Kerr and Bexar County
DAs. Sutton readily agreed; he knew he could use the extra
help. Millsap was relieved. He wanted a conviction in this
case, and while he did not know yet how good a country
lawyer Ron Sutton was, he had faith in Nick Rothe.

As their first act under this "mutual assistance pact,"
which directly benefited Sutton, the Bexar County team
undertook the investigation of the Jimmy Pearson helicopter
incident. To begin, the Investigator called Fort Sam Houston
in an effort to set up interviews with the MAST crew but
experienced some difficulty cutting through military red
tape. *"Matter resolved through intervention of Mr. Rothe,"*
he wrote, *"still an active member of the United States Army
Reserves. Will make initial contact next week."*

Gradually, through interviews with doctors of all specialties, pathologists, lab technicians, nurses, secretaries, record keepers, and administrators, the San Antonio investigative team began to get a feeling for the issues and institution they were confronting. "The case," recalls the Investigator, "was brand new territory for most of us: emergency medicine; research and development futures; the personality and mentality of a doctor, a nurse, an administrator."

Daily, cartons of medical records were delivered to the Old Jail; all were read, sorted, collated, charted, and filed for accountability and easy access. Interviews continued, from informal discussions over coffee to sworn grand-jury testimony.

On March 11, 1983, RN Carla Tieman, a nurse who had been graduated from UTHSC's nursing school in 1980 and who had worked with Jones at Medical Center, called the DA's office and expressed a desire to appear before the San Antonio grand jury to "show the other side."

Throughout her testimony on March 16, Nurse Tieman expressed sentiments and rationale supportive of her friend, Genene. Tieman explained that she had, since Jones had moved north, "remained on very good terms with Genene, who I believe was, in the old days, the most experienced nurse on the 3–11." Tieman admitted that she began to note the escalating number of deaths in the Unit in the fall of '81 but dismissed rumors that Jones was to blame.

"By the winter of '81, the entire nursing staff picked up on the regularity of deaths and the fact that they occurred, for the most part, on the 3–11," Tieman told the grand jury. She felt, however, that the Evening Shift's problems could be attributed to some degree to inexperienced nurses. She also subscribed to the theory that kids are more likely to go bad during the late afternoon or early evening.

"It appeared to me," the Investigator later said, "that she was continually trying to convince herself on this last point, and we soon found out that an increased 3–11 mortality theory was a highly debatable rationale."

By the end of the first month of the San Antonio investigation, the team had reports or records of forty-three infant deaths in Medical Center's PICU between January 1, 1981, and March 13, 1982. A little more than 74 percent of these deaths had occurred during the 3–11 shift.

"Interesting information at the time," recalls the Investigator, "but before too many decisions could be made, we needed more data; we needed a broader base. Assignments were directed toward establishing: (a) names of nurses attending patients at time of expiration; (b) names of doctors attending patients at time of expiration; (c) initial diagnosis of patient at time of admission; and, of course, (d) any additional interesting variables."

On March 25, the Investigator finally spoke with head nurse Pat Belko. Like the others, Belko said she first began hearing rumors about infant deaths in the fall of 1981. The Investigator recalls that "she appeared very defensive of Jones and charged that we were not conducting any pro-Jones interviews." Initially Belko denied LVN Eva Diaz had been transferred from the PICU after a confrontation with Jones. Only later, after considerably more questioning, did she remember some vague details, but maintained that Diaz was not really terminated from PICU work per se; rather, she explained that "conditions and tensions in the Unit were best served by keeping Jones and Diaz apart."

On March 30, nineteen-year-old Bonnie Gunderson, who had shared the Nixon Lane house with Jones and Holland, appeared before Sutton, Rothe, and the Kerr County grand jury. The first hour of her testimony was largely innocuous, then she began to settle down and give the grand jury some provocative answers.

When Rothe suggested that it seemed "pretty weird" that so many seizures at the Clinic occurred while Jones was around, Gunderson agreed, frankly speculating that Genene may have been inducing emergency situations because "she wanted to be somebody." The procedures then took a bizarre twist when Bonnie turned the discussion to six seances that the Clinic's receptionist, Judith Johnston, allegedly conducted for Genene and her friends. "Two were with Tarot cards," she said, "and four with a Ouija board." Gunderson said she did not actually attend or participate in these sessions, preferring instead to accompany Jones's children to a neighbor's for T.V. and talk. Nevertheless, she felt able to describe these alleged sessions in detail, claiming that the lights were turned out, candles lit, and the participants sat in a circle, holding hands. The purpose of these sessions, Bonnie blithely asserted to a roomful of incredulous lawyers, detectives, and jurors, was to "contact spirits who then talked with the dead babies."

Evdently someone thought a story like that was too good to keep quiet. Within days, the newspapers flaunted teasing headlines that proclaimed: "Witchcraft Rumored," and "Witchcraft Denied in Tot Death."

The Investigator later asked Kathleen Holland about these alleged seances, and as expected, Kathleen firmly denied such things had ever happened. She conceded that Judith and Genene had, on a couple of occasions, played with a Ouija board as "a parlor game, an amusement." The rest of Bonnie's story, however, she characterized as "utter rot—a complete fabrication."

The Kerrville DA turned up a second intriguing development in the latter half of March. Through his contacts in the DPS, Sutton had tracked down a pathologist who had participated in the only other known murder trial involving succinylcholine: Dr. Fredric Reiders, of Philadelphia. Reiders had steered Sutton toward a second scientist, Dr. Bo Holmstedt, a Swede, who had helped develop succinylcholine three decades earlier and who had purportedly devised a way of tracing the supposedly untraceable drug.

Although Sutton was excited by the information, Reiders warned the DA that the possibility of definitively establishing the presence of the drug in Chelsea McClellan was tenuous at best. Reiders informed Sutton that most of the solutions used by pathologists to preserve tissue samples rendered Holmstedt's proposed test ineffective. Therefore, the preserved tissues from Chelsea might be untestable. If they were, then Sutton was probably out of luck. Chelsea had been buried six months earlier; Reiders had little expectation that new tissue samples could be obtained by exhumation. Sutton concentrated his hopes on the tissues taken and maintained by Severance & Associates, the pathology group that had performed Chelsea's autopsy.

The Investigator, meanwhile, did what he could to look into Bonnie Gunderson's sensational accounts of seances and witchcraft. Since he had been unable to track down Judith Johnston to confirm or deny Bonnie's report, he made an appointment to interview her ex-husband, who spoke of Judith with a fond tolerance. He revealed that Judith was originally from the Chicago area—"Her cockney accent is a complete phoney." He told the Investigator that one of the key reasons his marriage to Judith went sour after several months was her disagreement with him on moral issues. "Judith was into meditation," he reported, "and believed in the doctrine of the Eckankar group." He understood Eckankar to be a loose-knit philosophy that minimizes the importance of biblical teachings and espouses a kind of freedom from moral strictures.

With a dogged fixity of purpose, the Investigator sent to Austin for one of the many files maintained by the state on various small religious organizations or sects. The file he received described Eckankar, a society headquartered in Las Vegas, Nevada, as espousing a philosophy of total free spirit and a belief that evil does not exist. The Investigator referred to the telephone book for a local chapter, and on Tuesday, April 12, went so far as to attend an Eckankar recruitment meeting.

"Writer seemed to be the only newcomer," he noted with meticulous detail. "Four persons present, including head of local group, an elderly man of about seventy; intelligent, conversant, and well versed in the cosmic area.

Appeared to be comfortable in casual clothes, including
tennis shoes. The leader's forty-minute spiel about the
teachings of Eckankar—presented before and after an
introductory film which dealt mostly with the general
background of the man who evidently started the group on
a nationwide front—struck the Investigator as fluent and
cohesive. He noted that the Eckankar philosophy is that
the truth lies only within the individual, who finds it in
himself.

"No indication of mysterious or sinister goings-on," he
concluded. "No heavy sales pitch, and the emphasis
continued along the lines of individual truth must be found
within . . . present all-important. No price or cost factor
discussed."

The meeting appeared to have put an end to the Investigator's curiosity about the metaphysical tangents for
the duration of the investigation. "Starting with Bonnie
Gunderson's testimony, these events took on a rather oc-
cult flavor for a while," recalls the Investigator. "Seances, witchcraft, premonitions, ETs, telepathy. The press
made a big deal out of it. For me, it was just another angle
that had to be checked out. My conclusion," the Investigator finished with a crooked smile, "was that the
Eckankar angle was something less than significant."

By mid-April of 1983, San Antonio investigators had
thirty-five taped or written interviews (with forty-five more
scheduled), and the transcripts of twenty-five grand-jury
witnesses on file. Flowcharts were being prepared so that
relevant information could be easily assimilated by someone less familiar with the facts and personalities involved.

Numerous doctors and nurses had by this time described
Jones's behavior under various circumstances as bizarre,
hysterical, overly aggressive, belittling of select staff personnel, and deceitful. To the investigators, it appeared she
might be a thrill seeker and someone who wanted to be the
center of attention.

According to the Investigator, the DA's snowballing

files on the Baby Deaths matter also contained an abundance of information suggesting that the hospital administration had failed to respond in a timely manner to employee complaints about questionable deaths and treatment of PICU patients.

On April 19, Genene Jones married nineteen-year-old Garron Turk, a recent high-school graduate. They had met in March at the Park Plaza Nursing Home in West Texas City, outside San Angelo, where Genene was employed, training nurse's aides to change patients' clothes, make their beds, and give them baths. Garron had been one of her pupils. James Loudermilk, owner of the nursing home, said of Genene, "I thought she was real friendly and conscientious, concerned about the health of the patients. And I'd like to make it clear that she did not work in patient care. Not here."

The newlyweds' whirlwind courtship slipped by Garron's stepfather, Jay Chatham, of Odessa. "His mother and I did not attend the wedding," he said. "Didn't know about it." About Genene he remained silent. "I had occasion to lay my eyeballs on that woman only once, and for the sake of my stepson, I won't say anything."

On the last day of April, Kathleen, Charleigh, her office nurse—Kathy Marshall—and the friend who gave Kathleen the Bible, all congregated at the Clinic with a flat-bed truck, boxes, and masking tape. Kathleen and her crew attended to the dismantling of her Clinic, while her landlord hovered in the background. Mid-way through the day, a reporter stopped by to see if Dr. Holland would answer a few questions. Even though Kathleen declined the interview, he stayed on to lend a hand with the move. At the end of the day, Kathleen's pediatric Clinic was stripped, except for a single chair and a wall-paper mural of a castle in the sky.

"I went back in for the resting chair," Kathleen recalls,

"and— I looked around— All gone. I sat down in the chair and cried. I felt like I'd lost."

In the early part of May, Bonnie Gunderson—who had rejoined Genene's household with her new son, Travis— had a severe reaction to the dinner she was eating. She slumped over in a seizure; her hostess had to rush her to the same ER that, just weeks before, had treated young Travis, a victim of sudden respiratory arrest.

Sutton, meanwhile, received some welcome news from Dr. Reiders: Dr. Holmstedt, the Swedish scientist reported to be the only man in the world capable of locating trace quantities of succinylcholine in a corpse, had agreed to assist with Sutton's investigation. Sutton was delighted.

"He was expensive, but the way I look at it," Sutton explained, "if you want to discuss the New Testament with somebody and Christ is around, that's where you gotta go."

Reiders also had some bad news, however. The chemical solution used to preserve the tissue samples taken from Chelsea's body during the autopsy was not compatible with Holmstedt's procedures. If Sutton wanted the Swede to run his tests, they would need fresh samples.

"For me," Sutton recalled, "the hardest part of this whole thing was having to ask those poor people if I could dig up their daughter. I didn't like doing that. But it had to be done."

Reid and Petti gave their reluctant consent. At 8:30 A.M., on Saturday, May 7, the earth above Chelsea's grave was broken. Twenty minutes later, the casket was lifted from its bed. The exhumation was performed by Drs. Vincent DiMaio and Fredric Reiders, assisted by Dr. Theodore Boyce, Kerr County's health officer, and was completed by 9:45 A.M. The body was in an excellent state of preservation.

Reiders took the new tissue samples, packed in dry ice, back with him to Philadelphia. The following evening, he caught a flight for Europe.

When the news of their daughter's exhumation leaked

out, the McClellans were forced to cope with an ever increasing barrage of intrusive reporters, sensationalized press announcements, and sympathetic friends. One day in the late afternoon, Reid's boy, Shay, answered the telephone just ahead of his father at the other end of the house. Reid picked up the extension in time to overhear a reporter ask his seven-year-old how he felt about his sister's death.

"He had to leave home," says Reid. "We had to send him back to his momma. He couldn't handle the fact that someone *murdered* his little sister."

For seven days, Sutton waited restlessly for word from Sweden. "I believe it was May 14," he recalls. "It was about 6:30 or 7:00 A.M., when, uh, well, I happened to be in the bathtub that morning. Now, ever since Reiders took off, I'd been just like a kid waiting for Christmas. The phone rang and— I had the telephone in the bathroom with me, never went anywhere without it. I was laying there in the tub, the phone rang, and this foreign operator says, 'You have a call from Sweden,' and I splashed water all over the house."

Dr. Holmstedt had found succinylcholine.

In San Antonio, the grand jury continued its inquiry into the events at Medical Center Hospital. On May 19, Pat Belko was finally asked to testify. The Investigator recalls that "from the start she appeared sensitive to questions related to why it was that two working nurses in the Unit were the persons who initially and most diligently tried to determine what was causing the numerous deaths. After a scant thirty minutes, Belko requested legal counsel and the interview came to a halt."

That same week, Kathleen received a phone call from Jack Leon. The Kerrville grand jury was issuing another subpoena for Kathleen, compelling her to appear on May 25. Leon sketched out the game plan for his client. "We're going to handle this one just like we did the last one—you take the Fifth."

Kathleen balked. She knew her friends and neighbors in Kerrville would view her continued assertion of the privilege against self-incrimination as an admission that she had something to hide. "Jack, I can't. With all the publicity that there's been in San Antonio, if I don't tell my side now, this thing is going to destroy me."

Leon wouldn't budge. "You can't risk it. I won't permit it."

Kathleen agonized about the matter for several days, then called her malpractice attorney, Dick Wiles, by now a trusted friend and advisor. "Tell me if my thinking is wrong," she pleaded. "I need to have someone help me with this decision."

Wiles hesitated, then gave his honest opinion. "I'm talking to you as a friend now, not an attorney. I think you should risk it. If they indict you, they indict you, but you're killing yourself just sitting around and waiting to find out, and there is just as much possibility that you might clear yourself."

When Leon heard Kathleen had decided to talk, he told her he could not continue to represent her unless she signed a Release that stated she was testifying against his advice. Kathleen agreed to sign anything he asked; she was not changing her mind.

The night before her appearance, Charleigh tried to dissuade her from her decision to testify. "You're paying those damn lawyers a lot of money, you ought to follow their advice." Kathleen was firm. She spent a sleepless night, then met her attorneys early the next morning. Leon's associate, Bayless, had driven up from San Antonio with the Release from Liability, which Kathleen signed. Dick Wiles had also come to Kerrville to spend the day with Kathleen at the courthouse, hoping to provide her with some moral support.

They waited all morning for Kathleen's appearance, and then all afternoon. Kathleen was not called until 4:00 P.M.

"When I first started testifying," Kathleen remembers, "Ron Sutton was just firing the questions at me. He was very hostile. If I tried to provide some background information or give what I thought was a complete answer, he would get agitated. He'd tap his foot, he'd roll his eyes. He'd start to interrupt, then sigh and let me continue. He was obviously frustrated.

"At some point in the second hour, suddenly the hostility was no longer there. Ron started listening to the answers I was giving. I think that he could see that I was honestly trying to give him the information he needed. At 6:00 P.M., when I walked out of that room, I had the sense that I wouldn't be indicted—that I had made the right choice."

When Kathleen finally left the grand jury room, Sam Bayless and Dick Wiles each took one of her arms to shepherd her through the crowd of reporters surging up to get a photo or a quote. The three had no comment for anyone until a newsman shouted: "Is it true your client was given immunity?"

Bayless stopped short to find a microphone. "My client doesn't *need* immunity."

When Sutton left the courthouse that evening, his mind was on other matters. The previous day, a police informant had called Sutton to let him know that Genene, who had been missing for over a week, had turned up—at the home of a relative of her young husband. Sutton, afraid Genene was preparing to disappear, decided to bring his suspect in. He called Sgt. Bob Favor and Capt. Maurice Cook of the Texas Rangers in Midland late in the afternoon, just before Kathleen began her testimony. He advised Favor that Genene and her new husband "would most likely be found in a silver and blue 1983 Ford Ranger bearing 1983 Texas licence plates SV 6772."

Later that evening, Favor and Cook parked outside a modest home in Odessa, Texas, just twenty miles from the New Mexico border. As they approached the residence, they observed a silver and blue medium-sized pickup backed into the garage, its hood protruding from under the partially closed door. The truck appeared to be loaded down with a bed and numerous boxes of personal belongings.

The officers knocked at the front door, identified themselves, and asked if a Genene Ann Jones was present.

"Yes," answered a young woman, who opened the door wider. "Come in. There's more tension in this house than you can imagine."

"After the usual wailing and gnashing of teeth," Sergeant Favor recalled later, "we took her in."

During Genene's first night in custody, in the Ector County jail, she began to bleed. She announced to her jailers that the trauma of her false arrest had caused her to miscarry her husband's child.

The following morning, William Chenault, Genene's attorney, told the press: "They put her in a cell with a whole bunch of other women, and I guess five or six of them decided to beat up on her. It wasn't a very pleasant experience."

Capt. George Olesh of the Ector County jail countered both stories offered by Genene and her attorney. He explained that Jones had been in a cell by herself all night long. "When we have prisoners for another agency, we try to keep them separate. The bleeding was due to her menstrual period."

Later that day, Ranger Joe Davis drove north to Odessa to take charge of Jones and escort her back to Kerrville. Once they got underway and out onto the highway, Genene complained to Davis about her miscarriage. "It was all Sutton's fault," she said. "You can tell him: We're even now."

"That," says Sutton, "was the nearest thing to a confession we ever got from her."

Kathleen Holland

The emotional low point for me in all this was probably the night before appearing in front of the grand jury for the second time. I can't think of any single moment when I was closer to the bottom. But there were other lows when I had to wrench myself up by the shirt collar and tell myself: "You have got to just stand up to this. You've got no reason to run from anything.

Channel 12 did a "follow-up interview" one year later and they asked me: "Why did you stay? Why didn't you go somewhere else?"

And I told them the same thing: "Because this is my home, and I had nothing to run *from*."

I knew that I had done nothing wrong, and I felt that if I stuck it out long enough, the rest of the community would finally see that.

Do you feel that that has become clear?

[Long pause] Not at this point in time. Part of it is because Kerrville is still a small town. Kerrville people still read the Kerrville newspaper primarily, and that's the perspective they get. And while I can't prove this, it always seemed that there was not a single negative thing about me that did not make the front page of the Kerrville paper, and there was not a single *positive* thing about me that appeared anywhere else but the back page. So, does the community of Kerrville know? Perhaps more now than just after the trial, despite all the publicity surrounding the trial, because of word of mouth. My patients go out and stand up for me. There are mothers who bring their kids to me (some of whom have been coming to me since I first opened the Clinic), who have stood and literally fought for me. They've argued with people, gotten angry with people, and told them: "Don't say anything about her unless you've been to her and you know. If you've never gone to her, then just don't say anything."

What do your detractors say?

"You take your child to *who*? Don't you *know* that she's the *one*?"

But because of what I did with my patients from the time the investigation started, I've never had anyone who answered with anything else but: "I know. She told me all about it." See, they weren't finding out something new. They could say, "Yeah, I knew all about it; she told me. And my kids sure like her."

What have you learned?

That I am stronger than I thought I was. And I think a lot of that I learned after I got some confidence from rediscovering my faith in God. I really think that helped me to keep up the courage. There were a lot of pressures around me to just get out. I was not fighting only the people around me who thought I was guilty, but also people who were close to me who were advising me to run. I felt stronger in my decision to stay after I started reading the Bible.

I guess I also learned about reading between the lines a little more. The biggest mistake I made—many times I guess—was my not reading between the lines. And I'm referring primarily to the institution's response. I didn't read between the lines when they asked all LVNs to leave because they were upgrading the Unit.

As a result, in my own life, I now try very hard to say what I mean, and not leave things unsaid, between the lines, for people to have to ferret out.

Do you trust people less?

[Long pause] Perhaps not less, but not as soon. I don't think it would be fair to trust less, and I wouldn't be comfortable with that. It's a question of where that trust is placed, and when. But it's either there or it's not. Maybe now I just have to have more evidence before I say "okay."

Do you think of yourself as more cynical?

Yes and no. I think . . . I don't know, that's hard to answer. I guess I'm more cynical in some respects, but I think I've taken my cynicism and tempered it with humor. I use the cynicism to oversee how I'm evaluating my input, but I don't want to turn into a cynical person. I couldn't live with that negativity.

Do you have any comment about what happened in San Antonio?

I made a comment several times at one point after the trial when I finally gave interviews. Not one person ever printed it—at least, I never saw it repeated. I said that it was inconceivable to me that anyone who had any information that someone was purposefully or routinely harming kids, that those individuals with that knowledge would not, somehow, go to the authorities. That was the basis for my believing what they told me, because I trusted in that. It never entered my mind that they would make a decision to *not* deal with the authorities over an issue like this. I knew politics existed, but I never knew that it could go that far. Never. And that's what one calls naiveté.

Is there anything that you regret?

I regret that I believed what I was told and made a decision based upon that information. I regret the decision I made to bring Genene here.

And I regret that Chelsea died.

EIGHTEEN

The truth is incontrovertible. Panic may resent it; ignorance may deride it; malice may distort it, but there it is.

Sir Winston Churchill

"WHEN I FIRST MET RON," THE INVESTIGATOR recalls, "that first day, I asked him, 'Do you mind if I just take off with this case?' And he said, 'Go ahead, you're on your own.' And it was great. I love those kind of people. It wasn't a question of him not caring; he gave me his confidence.

"Hill Country people are probably the greatest people in the world. They're like Cajun people in Louisiana. Once they accept you, or rather, once you allow yourself to be accepted, they're really good people. There's nothing cold or callous about them. They were friendly. They knew why I was there, plus, their butts were covered. They'd handled their situation very, very appropriately under the circumstances. They nearly cut it off at the pass. The incidents that happened in Kerrville were not attributable to any action or inaction on the part of the hospital. Exactly the opposite from down here in San Antonio. There was no one up there who wasn't cooperative. There was some apprehension; people still tend to look at people in law enforcement as somewhat of a . . . somewhat of a . . .

maybe a threat to them. There's a fearful element, a little bit of fear. But they're very down-home people, and for the most part easy to work with. The important factor, I think, in terms of their cooperativeness, was that they hadn't done anything that they felt they had to try to hide."

As the San Antonio investigation continued, the scandal surrounding the affair grew. Members of the county hospital's administration became increasingly unhappy. To counteract the negative publicity, both the school's and the hospital's public relations departments sent out regular press releases calling attention to "recent improvements, rising demands for service, new equipment, and fresh medical talent" at Medical Center.

Dr. William Thornton, board chairman of the Bexar County Hospital District, found himself cast as the unofficial spokesman for the affair and was often asked for official statements. He saw it as a responsibility of his office to respond, and he did.

In May he said: "The district became aware of the problems in the PICU in early 1982, but there was never any indication of criminal action by anyone." In August he would complain that the continuing investigation hung like a heavy, dark cloud over the hospital, crushing employee morale. "The innuendo and implication that things are not as they should be is beginning to take its toll on employees," Thornton said. "And finally, on a human level, it beats a person down and saps their energy. And we have enough significant problems ahead of us without having to devote energy and time toward this ongoing investigation." Because of federal cutbacks in Medicare and Medicaid programs, Thornton explained, the tax-supported hospital was faced with diminishing income and a rising number of patients from private hospitals. "We're getting more people and less money. We're running dog-close to 100 percent occupancy, and the largest increase has been by patients unable to pay their bills." He stressed over and over that Medical Center was a fine institution, and despite the negative publicity focused on the Center by the grand-jury investigation, the number of patients admitted to the hospital in recent months had actually increased.

"Concern exists," he continued, "as to the effects this investigation may have on the hospital's financial situation, in terms of its liability. This cloud of suspicion has got to be removed as quickly as possible so that when a family brings someone to our institution, they don't have to worry and wonder about the quality of care they're receiving." Thornton also expressed his concern over the fact that Moody's Investors Service of New York had suspended its rating on the district's $13 million in bonds sold in 1977. The suspension was to remain in effect pending the outcome of the grand-jury probe. Without the bonds, the hospital would find it very difficult to obtain the funds needed for expansion.

"We've never backed away from our problems," Thornton said, "and we've taken steps to solve them. We haven't been involved in any cover-up."

INVESTIGATOR'S LOG: 105th DAY, THURSDAY, 6-2-83:

Received telecon from Attorney Sharp who offered opinion that DA's case against Jones appears to be nonexistent. "I would prefer not to have anyone who may have intentionally harmed babies involved in society, open and free, but there appears to be no 'smoking gun' involved." Stated he has "done everything possible" to get doctors to talk with DA's office and has talked with everyone DA investigators have interviewed, but still sees no more than circumstantial data to link Jones to any harmful acts or deaths.

Sharp also advised that he is now representing *all* doctors and residents at MCH, and that as of this date, no investigator may talk to said docs unless he, Sharp, is present. Informed Sharp that these medics were not suspects, but rather witnesses, and that interviews were

merely to determine if they possessed any information
relative to the DA investigation. Sharp reiterated his
position, at which point writer told Sharp he would not
agree to this condition. Sharp then advised writer not to
bother showing up for the scheduled 0830 hrs. interview
with Dr. Filmore*, as he would not be there.

In the first week of June, Bonnie Gunderson informed
the Investigator that she would no longer be able to provide him with information about Jones, and she would not
be able to testify at any trial. She had received an anonymous phone call from a man who warned her: "If you
testify, you won't make it."

On June 14, an old high-school classmate of Jones contacted the DA's office to provide them with some positive
information about Genene and her past. Suzanne Hubert*
had known Genene since 1965 and remembered her as outgoing, gregarious, and fun loving.

Suzanne knew of only one dark incident from Genene's
past, an event that caused her friend great pain. When
Genene finished high school, she had volunteered her time
to Methodist Hospital, a private institution located near
Medical Center. Jones had told Hubert that she was at the
hospital on the day the ambulance brought her younger
brother in, dying from the explosion of his homemade
bomb.

After Genene came back from Tennessee, Suzanne and
her husband had socialized with Genene and her husband
for four or five years, then continued seeing Genene following her divorce. Though their contact grew more infrequent, Hubert kept up with her right through Genene's
employment in Medical Center's PICU. The only change
Suzanne noticed in her friend during that time was that
Genene appeared to be constantly tired, often bone weary.
"My knowledge of Genene is that she is a wonderful person. She had been a very good friend, and I cannot believe
she would, or even could, harm anyone."

INVESTIGATOR'S LOG: 130th DAY, MONDAY, 6-27-83:

Encountering considerable difficulty in retrieving statements rendered to numerous nurses some weeks prior. The term "harassment" is being applied to investigators' efforts at soliciting truthful explanations regarding various points concerning background knowledge of some PICU nurses. RN Hollenbeck* was emotional and shed tears twice during relatively brief interview in recent days. Apparently it is easier for her to avoid further questioning or contact with investigators if she claims "harassment."

Up north today, at the Kerr Co. bond hearing re Jones's bail, Sutton pulled the plug—revealed he had recently become aware that she intended to have him killed.

On the morning of June 27, Jones's attorney, William Chenault, made a motion to have his client's bail reduced from $225,000 to $45,000, so that he could get her out of the Kerrville County's jail where she had been for over a month. During the hearing before Judge Murray Jordan at the Kerrville courthouse, the low-key feuding between Sutton and Jones escalated to new levels.

Sutton had Genene on the stand. "What would you do if you got out of jail?"

"I'd get ready to fight you in court," Jones responded, her legs crossed, her fingers folded tightly in her lap.

"You wouldn't get a job?"

"No. I couldn't, thanks to you and all the publicity."

"So what you are really planning on doing is to do a full-time job on me, isn't that true."

"I don't know what you mean."

"You just said you wanted to get out of jail to fight me. Were you aware of arrangements being made by a Mr. Howard Lennon*—because of my prosecuting you for murder—to kill me?"

All eyes in the court looked to Genene. Accusations of murder plots were not often made in bail-bond hearings.

"No, sir," Genene replied, shocked. She turned to Judge Jordan, protesting, "That's incredible."

"Where were you the afternoon of May 25?" Sutton continued.

"Attending my husband's high-school graduation." Jones indicated Garron, a slight, young man with a sallow complexion, whose light blue suit complemented his red hair. He was seated prominently in the front row of the spectators.

"And the week before Garron's graduation," Sutton asked Genene, "were you not hiding, planning to disappear?"

"That's ridiculous. I wasn't hiding, I was honeymooning in Colorado with my husband."

"And Sally Benkert?" Sutton added.

"Yes, she came along."

"Cozy."

"Sally came along to check out the employment possibilities, same as I was."

"Isn't it a fact that you married Garron Turk so you could disappear into Colorado with a new name so no one would know who you really were?"

"No, sir."

"Isn't it true that before you read about Chelsea's exhumation, you were confidently telling friends nothing would ever come of this investigation?"

"No, sir," Jones said again, her lips tight.

Judge Jordan denied Chenault's motion. The next day, Genene's adoptive mother, Gladys, gave $10,000 and a lien against her home to Hill Country Bonding in Kerrville, which in turn posted the $225,000 bond required to free Genene.

Sutton was asked by reporters if he was worried about Jones's release. He responded, "The bondsman should be the one worried."

When the McClellans heard of Genene's release, Reid commented, "They won't find her now. She's gone."

On Wednesday, July 13, B. H. Corum appeared before

San Antonio's grand jury then in its sixth month of inquiry
into the Baby Deaths case. Corum testified that he first
became aware of the problems in the PICU on November
10, 1981. Dr. Franks had notified Corum at that time that
he was concerned about the number of deaths on the Unit
and about the fact that most of the deaths seemed to occur
during the 3–11 shift. Dr. Franks had told Corum that
Genene Jones's name appeared frequently in connection
with the PICU deaths. Corum advised the grand jury that
he had instructed his administrative assistant, John Guest,
to meet with Virginia Mousseau and Dr. Franks to determine just exactly what was going on.

John Guest also appeared before the grand jury that day
and confirmed the gist of Corum's testimony. Guest testified that Franks had reported back to him, in mid-De-
cember, that Franks had not been able to find any pattern
to the events in the PICU, nor any evidence of wrongdoing. Guest also told the grand jury that, during the January
25 meeting, after the Santos and Zavala incidents, he had
asked Attorney Paul Green several questions about
whether the hospital should take its information to the authorities. He reported that Green had concluded that there
was not enough there.

Dr. Franks ended the day's testimony, telling the grand
jury about a theory advanced by nursing personnel (which
investigators later traced back to Jones) to account for the
Santos incident. They speculated that a part-time agency
nurse must have confused a vial of heparin with a vial of
ampicillin and thereby accidentally administered the massive overdose. Franks conceded he had some difficulty accepting this explanation.

Near the end of July, the McClellans began to receive
disturbing phone calls from unknown individuals who
asked them prying and hostile questions. When Petti left
the relative sanctuary of her home, strangers approached
her, trying to start conversations that she felt were somehow threatening. The McClellans changed their phone
number, then changed it again. They obliterated their

name from their mailbox on the dirt road in front of their property, replaced it with a fake name painted in large black letters, and instructed the post office not to deliver any correspondence that did not have the "code" name attached.

Kathleen, too, was still receiving calls she felt were threatening, although their frequency had greatly diminished. At the beginning of August, one call in particular left her unsettled, fearful. A male voice on her answering machine angrily observed: "So, the bitch is still in town killing babies." The following evening, the headlights of Kathleen's car caught another message scrawled in the dust on the garage-door windows: "Hi there." She knew her feelings of unease over the innocuous message bordered on paranoia. Still, none of her friends had left it.

On August 7, Jones announced a press conference and told reporters she was "frightened but ready" to face her upcoming trial, at that point, just three weeks away. "The trial can't come too quick for me. I just want to get it over with. I'm tired of being a scapegoat. I'm tired of being called a murderess. I'm tired of the accusation that I'm trying to kill everybody in the world. It's just amazing to me that Ron Sutton thinks I'm that big a murderess. It's like he's obsessed with me."

Two days later, Genene called the Kerrville press to her home to complain publicly. "Five times this week vandals have broken into our home and have written obscenities and death threats on the walls and mirrors and doors and stolen documents I have compiled related to my trial. I just want the people who are breaking into our home to leave everybody alone. I want them to stop playing God and let the justice system take care of itself. Someone is going to get hurt, and there have been enough people hurt already. There doesn't need to be any more."

On August 9, Rothe was accosted by reporters at the airport upon his return from the East Coast and Toronto, where he had been interviewing members of the Conn review team. The next day's papers reported Nick Rothe's concerns over inconsistencies between statements made by Medical Center officials and information given him by members of the review team regarding the purpose of the review. The authors of the Conn report had all insisted they had been assembled to perform a quality-control evaluation and management study, nothing more: "Although we heard rumors about increased infant mortality," said Conn, "we were never instructed to look specifically into those allegations."

INVESTIGATOR'S LOG: 179th DAY, MONDAY, 8-15-83:

Case leading us around the world: Stuttgart last week tracking down the mechanic on the helicopter flight, and now we're off to Africa. RN Margie Peace now married and moved to the African bush with her husband; both now working for the CARE organization. Communication extremely difficult to initiate stateside. They are evidently "up river—in the bush" and must be located, then brought back to nearest American Embassy wireless.

Completed examination of Jones's hospitalization periods and ER visitations for various reasons during employment at MCH. Breakouts reflect Jones visited ER on ten occasions in an approximate six-month period (March thru early Sept. '81) for various ailments. Jones was also hospitalized for an assortment of ailments during an approximate nine-month period (March 10 thru Dec. 6, '81) for: (1) bronchitis (secondary to chronic cigarette smoking), (2) asthma, (3) acute asthma with acute sinusitis of the (R) maxillary sinus, (4) chronic constipation, and (5) small bowel obstruction.

Of particular interest is the fact that during these twenty-five days of hospitalization, no deaths occurred in the PICU.

Some nurses now fear testifying for the grand jury. They are afraid of media coverage, revelation of their identity, and the resultant publicity. More palpably, they say, repeatedly, they fear retaliation by Jones.

It's beginning to look as if we may just get an
indictment out of what happened to little Rolando Santos.

On September 12, the Honorable John Carter, judge of
the 227th judicial district north of Austin announced that
he, not Kerrville's Murray Jordan, would be handling the
Genene Jones trial. Judge Jordan had granted a motion by
the defense for a change of venue because of the rampant
publicity surrounding the case; the lawyers for both sides
had agreed that Jones probably could not get an impartial
jury from the citizenry of Kerr County. The trial had been
transferred 200 miles east to Georgetown—Judge Carter's
stomping grounds.

Carter made it clear to the press that he would continue
to enforce Judge Jordan's wide-ranging gag order, which
banned reporters from approaching principals in the case.
"The press will get reasonable access," he stated firmly,
"as long as you-all respect my wishes."

Also on September 12, Genene's new attorney,
Georgetown's Jim Bob Brookshire, a criminal- and fam-
ily-law attorney, announced he would be handling Genene's defense, taking over primary responsibilities from
William Chenault, who would continue on as cocounsel.
At the time, Brookshire was a forty-two-year-old former
marine with a full head of prematurely grey hair. Five-foot
seven, lean and compact, he would bring an aggressive
competitiveness to Genene's defense. "I agreed to take
this case because Judge Carter asked me to," Brookshire
explained to the curious press. "Also because it seems like
it'll be interesting, and because she's entitled to representation just like everybody else."

Virginia Mousseau appeared before San Antonio's
grand jury on September 19, 1983. She, like the other
administrators before her, told the jury that she first heard
reports of an allegedly excessive number of deaths on the
3–11 shift in the fall of 1981. She reported that, in response, she took measures to insure that the PICU nurses

followed proper policies and procedures in their treatment of patients.

When asked what specifically the nursing staff had done in response to the Santos incident, she again stated that she had made sure the nurses were following procedures. She could not, however, remember any measure taken to determine how or why Rolando's emergencies had come about.

INVESTIGATOR'S LOG: 221st DAY, MONDAY, 9-26-83:

Becoming quite familiar with medical charts, forms, reports, abbreviations, etc. Beginning to think like doctors and nurses.

LD telecon with Dr. Steve Fordek* in Houston, in response to recent letter requesting memory of events. Stated he recalls vividly how, as a first-year intern during the second half of 1980, senior residents cautioned him to "be careful" in his dealings with Jones; that he should "take with a grain of salt" what Jones said regarding both condition and treatment needed for patients in her care. Soon learned through personal contact with Jones (which was unavoidable in the PICU) that the warnings were merited. He described her (even as early as the latter half of 1980) as an overreactor, always complaining that the doctors did not care about their patients, insulting and degrading at times with certain doctors and other nurses; was often extremely critical of co-workers, and her emotions were usually sky high. She frequently shed tears and constantly and loudly expressed, for all to hear, her great concern for the patients. He felt she was often very disruptive in the Unit and was the principal cause of difficulty between docs and nurses. She wanted to be in charge and usually looked down on the younger interns, even senior residents if they did not immediately adhere to her requests—sometimes demands—concerning patient care. Recalls Jones constantly conveyed the impression her way was the only way to save a child from crashing.

Fordek's most vivid recollections are of her crying and emotional outbursts, her continuous complaints about docs and some nurses, and her constant vocalizing about how much she loved the patients.

"I guess it was about midway through this thing," Millsap recalled later, "a delegation of business leaders in this community paid me a visit. The basic thrust was, 'We have a shot at developing a first-class biotech center here in San Antonio—research initially, then development. Eventually it's going to be another Silicon Valley right here. And' they said, 'whether it happens or not hinges on whether the University of Texas system ends up being sullied as a result of your investigation.'

"They told me that if I continued to pursue this thing, it might cost the community as many as 15,000 jobs. And these were real heavy hitters in this city, including people who had been contributors to my campaign in 1982, you know? I threw them out of my office.

"It was one of those deals where you do it, and you know it's the right thing to do, but you put your head down on your desk after it's over and just, well, just sit there."

On September 26, Judge Carter denied a defense motion for a further postponement of the trial. It would begin October 17 as scheduled. After the hearing, Jones again spoke with reporters at length, much to the displeasure of her attorneys. "You just can't have your clients going around granting press conferences," Chenault complained, "but we really can't do anything about it."

"I haven't stopped crying for three days," Genene told the press. "I'm scared to death. I'm looking at a life sentence. At the very least, I'm looking at twenty years; by then my children will be grown, and they'll never know me. It's totally unfair. By October 17, Brookshire will have had only four weeks to prepare for the case; the state has had over a year. I almost got sick when I heard the news. I've come to learn that politics is frightening, and this is nothing but a prefabricated case. But I have to believe the truth will come out. That's the only thing that helps me keep my sanity. Being scared, I think, is a normal emotion.''

Brookshire renewed his motion for a continuance on October 11, arguing the state had failed to comply with the court's order to provide the defense with the methodology of the tests conducted in Holmstedt's laboratory. ''I need time,'' he told the judge. ''Thirty days is just not enough time.''

Perhaps because the court had just granted Chenault's motion to withdraw from the case, Judge Carter decided to relent. He granted Brookshire's request, delaying the trial until early January.

''The defense needs more time to prepare its case,'' was all the judge said. ''I want the woman to have a fair trial.''

''I appreciate the judge going out on a limb for us,'' Brookshire told reporters afterward. ''I simply need more time to study the methodology used in the state's tests. He gave me the time, and I thank him, but it really is only fair.''

''I was really disappointed at first,'' Sutton recalls, ''I felt like I was ready to go. But then I realized it would just give me *more* time to prepare, and that was fine.''

Jones appeared relieved by the delay. ''She's extremely happy,'' Brookshire reported, trying to take control of his client's public exposure. ''She was concerned about getting a fair trial, and she's happy to know that she'll be with her children this Christmas.''

In less than a week, however, Jones was back behind bars—Hill Country Bonding had revoked Glays's bond. Jones was rearrested without incident.

In mid-October, the Investigator undertook the task of scouting out and physically inspecting the locales in Kerr County that witnesses had mentioned during the investigation. He asked Kathleen to guide him to the hilltop Genene had often visited to ''talk with E.T.,'' or just stare at the stars and think. He checked the area for anything Jones might have left behind in her private place, but found nothing.

Locating the emergency landing site of the MAST helicopter that had transported Jimmy Pearson proved somewhat more difficult. The Investigator started with Sergeant Maywhort, who provided a map marked with possible grid coordinates. The Investigator then traveled north to visit the editor of the *Comfort News* on a tip that the paper had run an article about the emergency landing the previous year, identifying a specific ranch in the area. The editor had no information regarding the landing, but referred the Investigator to a local realtor who knew the surrounding ranches better than most. The realtor furnished the Investigator with a small-scale map that identified the tracts of land around Comfort, along with the individuals who owned them.

The Investigator was able to pinpoint the site with the help of two local ranchers. Both recalled seeing the army chopper on the ground the previous fall; neither had returned to the spot since. The Investigator checked the area carefully—noting the landmarks the military men had referred to in their statements. He searched the area thoroughly, but came away empty-handed. His inability to find any nonindigenous artifacts proved nothing for certain, but the Investigator himself was satisfied; if anything had fallen from the helicopter during its emergency landing, he would have found it.

During the last weeks of October and the early part of November, the television news show "20/20" taped a segment on the Texas Baby Deaths case. The segment featured clips from various interviews with Genene, who spoke calmly and persuasively on her own behalf.

In early November San Antonio DA Sam Millsap angrily announced that Dr. Marvin Dunn, dean of the medical school, would face a contempt charge levied by the grand jury for failing to probe deaths at Medical Center Hospital. The day before, Dr. Dunn had turned over a report—a copy of Dr. Conn's preliminary report—that

Dr. Dunn had failed to turn over in response to his original grand-jury subpoena, nine months earlier.

"The withholding of the documents," Millsap said, "cost this office thousands of dollars in wasted taxpayer money, because much of the investigation this past year has centered on uncovering information that is in the preliminary report."

"You've got to be kidding," said Toronto's Dr. Conn when told of the charges filed against Dr. Dunn. "We made rough notes of our own, but no preliminary report that I know of. I certainly can't remember anything like that being referred to anyone."

Dr. Conn's response was not as disingenuous as it seemed. The only difference between the preliminary and the final Conn reports was the single sentence identifying Genene Jones and Pat Alberti as the nurses who should be removed from the Unit. Conn may not have felt this detail was enough to merit the "preliminary" and "final" designations, or the importance the DA's office attached to it.

E. Don Walker, chancellor of the University of Texas system, stood behind his dean. Walker said it was the policy of the UT system to "cooperate fully with any inquiry by a law enforcement agency related to our institutions and personnel. I am satisfied this policy has been carried out, and that Dr. Dunn has acted in good faith throughout this investigation and has attempted, to the best of his ability under the circumstances, to put before the grand jury all information that has been available to him in this matter."

Dunn himself denied any wrongdoing. When asked, in a subsequent hearing, if he had ever intentionally withheld documents he believed the grand jury was entitled to, he replied: "No, sir. In fact, just the opposite." He explained that when he saw the articles in the papers concerning Rothe hinting darkly about "discrepancies," he contacted the university's attorneys and told them he wanted to appear before the jury and show them his handwritten notes—which the attorneys had, not he—to clarify the confusion.

In arguing for the contempt charge, Nick Rothe indi-

cated there was more than one document in question, and
that these documents "have one thing in common not
found in any other written evidence presented to the grand
jury: they name names. And the bottom line is, Dunn did
not comply with the original subpoena."

Dunn was found guilty by San Antonio judge David
Berchelman, who fined the dean $100. "I feel those items
were extremely important to the investigation," the judge
explained. "I really don't believe the investigation could
have proceeded any further without those documents."

In mid-November Dr. Murray Pollack, of Children's
Hospital in Washington, D.C., arrived to assist the investigation. He began by analyzing the medical histories
of the twenty to thirty children the district attorney's task
force had chosen to focus on. The Investigator was impressed by and grateful for the young man's tenacity and
dedication. After months of dealing with doctors and
nurses, some of whose codes of ethics, in the Investigator's opinion, left something to be desired, here at
last was a man who steadfastly embodied those ideals and
principles associated with the true physician.

On November 21, the San Antonio grand jury issued an
indictment against Genene Jones for the offense of injury
to a child, specifically, Rolando Santos. The Investigator
took the time to call Jesusa and Esubio Santos to inform
them of the indictment and to advise them to prepare
themselves for an invasion by members of the press.

**INVESTIGATOR'S LOG: 280th DAY, THURSDAY,
11-24-83:**

Chance encounter with Dr. Copeland during lunch at
MCH cafeteria. Copeland expressed strong personal
sentiments against the DA's handling of contempt charges
against Dr. Dunn. Claimed DA's office saw fit to try him
in the media. Labeled this "totally political." Copeland
alluded to a conference he and Dr. Dunn had with DA reps
in "late Feb. '83," when he listened to Dunn advising the
reps of details re the Pedi problems. Stated he thought

Dunn open and above board at the time, as was Copeland, who related details of events surrounding Rolando Santos. Copeland appeared bitter in his present attitude toward DA's office.

On November 28, San Antonio's grand jury, which had been convened expressly for the purpose of investigating the baby deaths at Medical Center Hospital, met for the last time. After some discussion, the citizens on the jury and the district attorney decided that except for the single indictment against Jones for the Rolando Santos incident, there were no other criminal charges to be issued. They did, however, prepare a statement recommending that the DA's office continue their inquiries. The Jones investigation, which began in Kerr County in October 1982, and continued in Bexar County for more than a year, at a cost of several hundred thousand dollars, was, for all practical purposes, ended.

In the last days of 1983, Rothe and the Investigator drove up to Kerrville to meet with Sutton, assistant district attorney Scott Monroe, and Sutton's administrative assistant, Janet Jones. Together they outlined their strategy for the upcoming Georgetown trial. Sutton had prepared a list of 73 possible witnesses, but expected to call only 43 to testify. He had also prepared a detailed schedule of witnesses and material facts in the order that he intended to follow in his presentation to the jury.

The prosecution team planned to meet in Georgetown on Sunday evening, January 15. Jury selection was set to begin on Monday and end on Tuesday. Opening arguments and the commencement of the state's case-in-chief was scheduled for Wednesday, January 19. Evidence regarding incidents involving children other than Chelsea McCellan, if Judge Carter ultimately decided to permit its presentation to the jury, was expected to begin on Thursday, January 27.

On Sunday, January 15, 1984, the day before the trial finally began, Judge Carter called a meeting of the press.

From a podium at the front of the press room that had been
set up in an auditorium at Southwestern University (a local
college just outside Georgetown proper, whose journalism
students were gaining some practical experience serving as
runners and aides to the dozens of reporters in attendance),
Judge Carter, in his congenial but dictatorial fashion, laid
down the law to those assembled. Reporters would not in
any manner attempt to question, photograph, or otherwise
harass the members of the jury. No one would be permitted to enter and exit his courtroom except during designated breaks. There would be no cameras or tape recorders
allowed in the courtroom or even on the second floor of
the courthouse, where the courtrooms were situated—
"Though all types of equipment will be allowed on the first
floor, and I will make sure that the defendant enters and
exits through the east door.

"If you-all want this lady to get a fair trial, like I do,
you'll cooperate with me. I've got a responsibility to do
everything in my power to keep this from becoming a big
circus. This is a cooperation talk, but it is also a court
order." Carter paused, letting his words penetrate. He had
only one more word of warning:

"The first violation will cause everyone to suffer. As
sure as the sun comes up in the morning, I'll put TV off
county property."

Genene Jones had undergone something of a transfor-
mation in the days before the trial. For months, she had
been appearing before reporters in jeans, a blouse, little or
no makeup, and short, straight hair. Patty Jones,
Brookshire's secretary and assistant, had done what she
could to make Genene more attractive. She had insisted
Genene allow Patty and a friend to give her a home permanent, so now Genene's short hair curled softly about her
face. Patty had also orchestrated a drive for donations of
clothing for Genene; a freshly cleaned tan and white polyester dress, an inexpensive gold brooch, and tan pumps
were laid out ready for the first day of trial.

Still recuperating from an attack by a fellow prisoner

two days before (child molesters generally are the most
reviled members of the prison population), Genene seemed
poised, if a little nervous, as she briefly spoke with favored reporters over the phone.

"I just have to keep believing that the truth will come
out. I have confidence in myself. My daddy always said if
you believe in yourself, you have no problem."

Genene's attorneys, Jim Brookshire and the more recently assigned Burt Carnes, a criminal lawyer from
nearby Taylor, had no prepared statements for the press.
They were still working as fast as they were able, drafting
the necessary motions, reviewing notes, preparing outlines
of questions, finalizing strategy. They had been running a
long-distance course at full speed ever since they became
involved in the case and now were dredging up reserves
they did not know they had for a final sprint to the finish.

Reid and Petti McClellan had been watching the slow
approach of the trial for months. They longed for it to
begin, and end, for it would be a kind of closure to their
long involvement with grief, pain, and frustration. Yet
they dreaded the coming days: Petti would be asked to
relive the death of her daughter on the stand for the jury;
from that assault, Reid could do nothing to protect his
wife.

The Investigator awaited the trial with some impatience
but with a resignation born of decades of experience. "As
far as Kerrville was concerned, my job was finished. I had
done all I could, turned over every rock I could find. At
that point, it was up to the lawyers."

Sutton was restless. He had been prepared since October; each succeeding week had meant only fine-tuning,
second-guessing, and polishing. A veteran of lengthy trials, he had installed a coffee maker and a well-stocked
refrigerator, complete with six-packs, in his motel room
(the state's command post) at the Georgetown Inn.

"I'm excited about finally getting started after fifteen
months," he told the press. "The only time I'm happy is
when I'm in the courtroom. Nothing gives me a bigger

thrill than working under pressure, and this is the most challenging case I've ever had." He grinned, his eyes disappearing, his teeth huge and white. "I'm ready. Open the gates and let me run."

Nick Rothe, more circumspect, nevertheless echoed Sutton's sentiments. "We really haven't turned up anything new in the past few weeks. We're just anxious to get started. We're ready to go."

Back in Kerrville, Kathleen was both welcoming and dreading the upcoming trial. Her life and her practice had continued to decline since her move to the Nixon Lane house back in May. For the month of April, she had grossed a pitiful $1,000. For the month of December, $250. In the days before the trial, her patient load was down to two or three per week. She was $150,000 in debt and was reduced to soldering pipes for Charleigh at $5.00 an hour.

Kathleen did her best not to think about the impending legal battle. She knew what was coming. Sutton had warned her. There would be days of testimony. She would be allowed to tell a portion of her story, but not all of it—this was Sutton's forum, not hers. On the stand, she would never really get the chance to explain why she had not been able to stop all this from happening. And, Sutton promised, Brookshire and Carnes were going to do their best to roast her. It was nothing personal, certainly, but in order to give their client a fighting chance, Sutton explained, Brookshire and Carnes were going to have to do their best to make it seem that, if there was a guilty party, that party was Kathleen Holland.

"You'll have to make them believe you, Kathy," Sutton told her. "You can't get angry, you can't get upset, you can't sweat. You just have to sit there and take it."

PART 4

The Judgment

NINETEEN

*Justice. To be ever ready to admit that an-
other person is something quite different
from what we read when he is there (or
when we think about him). Or rather, to
read in him that he is certainly something
different, perhaps something completely
different from what we read in him.*

Simone Weil,
Gravity and Grace

A TRIAL IS NOT, AS ONE MIGHT EXPECT, A
forum for revealing the truth; it is rather, a strange, un-
gainly ritual intended to conjure some approximation of
justice. Its principals—the lawyers, and the judge—engage in a three-party minuet, closing and parting, circling
and bowing to a tune only they can discern. This dance
gives shape to the story that gradually unfolds before those
who must exonerate or condemn. It is never the whole
story or even the true story; it is only those pieces that are
deemed necessary to the alchemy of judgment.

The trial of the *State of Texas* v. *Genene Jones* began on
Monday, January 16, 1984. Ron Sutton, Nick Rothe, and
Scott Monroe appeared for the state. J. B. Brookshire,
Burt Carnes, and Laura Little appeared for the defense.

On the first day of the trial, the court handled just two
matters outside the hearing of the prospective jurors. Having reviewed the juror questionnaires of the first thirty-two
members of the jury panel, the defense demanded that the
panel be reshuffled. Brookshire wanted to throw the dice
again and see if he could get a more favorable lineup.

The defense's second order of business was their motion to sequester the jury. In effect, Brookshire was asking the court to quarantine the jurors for the duration of the proceedings so they would not be contaminated by the massive news coverage surrounding the trial. He could not afford to have any of his jurors know about Jones's damning connection to the mysterious epidemic of death in San Antonio's Medical Center Hospital. He had already won a motion that prevented any mention of the San Antonio events during the trial, now he wanted to ensure that no one on the jury panel might accidentally learn of the San Antonio connection through a banner headline or a TV news teaser.

"We think that in order to make sure that the information doesn't get into the hands of the jury," he argued, "we just have to have them locked up. I would rather do anything than do this, but I don't know any way to get around it."

"I am of the opinion," Judge Carter replied, unable to stomach the idea of locking his jury away for over a month, "we can solve any problems we might have by numerous instructions to the jury as to publicity, as to not watching television, listening to radio broadcasts, reading newspaper or magazine articles, or discussing the matter with their family, friends, or anyone else. And I intend to give that warning at every break, every evening, every morning, and every opportunity that arises."

On Tuesday morning, January 17, Judge Carter cast a paternal eye on the potential jurors packed into his courtroom. "All right, ladies and gentlemen, we are now going to start the stage of the trial that we call *voir dire* in Texas. That's probably not the correct pronunciation; those of you who speak fluent French can correct that pronunciation, but I speak fluent Texan and that is the way it comes out when I say it. And it means, 'speak the truth,' and that is basically all we are asking you to do.

"Both the prosecution and defense lawyers are going to ask you questions to see if you have any predetermined knowledge or prejudices. The first thing you have got to understand is there are no right or wrong answers. The only answer you need to give is a completely truthful answer about what they ask you."

Judge Carter had initiated the process of judgment. Among the men and women who filled his courtroom sat the twelve who would bear the final burden of deciding another's guilt or innocence. The judge was intimately familiar with that burden. He knew how nervous these people must be. He proceeded to do his best to alleviate that anxiety.

When Judge Carter concluded his introductory remarks, the attorneys took over. Both sides were already acquainted with the men and women who sat before them. All 312 prospective jurors had been asked to complete lengthy questionnaires designed to reveal temperament and personality, containing questions about such things as church-going habits, favorite magazines and television shows, political and social affiliations, the size and composition of families, and the last book each had read. Armed with this information, the defense and prosecution teams already knew who among these men and women they wanted to sit on the jury; the trick was achieving that result.

Sutton had decided to go after conservative, well-educated mothers, fathers, and grandparents, "people who could use their common sense about kids." Brookshire had been advised by a psychologist that his best bet was to impanel as diverse a group of individuals as possible. "She told me that due to the emotional nature of the subject matter, I was just dreaming if I was hoped for an acquittal, because the *best* I was going to get was a hung jury. So, I was looking to mix different types, individuals with strong opinions who'd rather be stubborn than persuaded by the majority."

"Good morning, ladies and gentlemen," Sutton began formally, casually. "I will try to make this as orderly and

as quick as possible here today, but I can tell already that
it will probably be getting warm in this room in a minute,
so I want you to excuse me if I loosen my tie. I don't
particularly like ties.'' He smiled his friendliest.

"Now I'm sure you-all are familiar with Jim Brookshire
and Mr. Burt Carnes and Miss Laura Little here for the
defense, they're all local folks. But I guess you are probably wondering who some of the other people are here with
us.'' Sutton indicated the members of his team. They
stood briefly to be recognized. "Janet Jones works as my
legal secretary, and she came down here to help us orga-
nize the case and get witnesses here and whatnot. Clay
Barton, our deputy sheriff in Kerrville, is here to assist me
generally, as is Ranger Joe Davis. My assistant district
attorney, Scott Monroe, and of course, my colleague from
San Antonio, Mr. Nick Rothe. These are the people you'll
see walking around out here, coming and going.

"You know, I was very impressed with what the court
told you earlier about the responsibilities of citizens serving their country by serving on a jury. I would like to take
just a moment to emphasize that viewpoint.

"I believe it is a privilege to come forth and serve your
county, your state, and your nation in this way. Other than
in a time of war, I can think of no higher service one can
give to one's country than to serve as a juror and decide
questions of fact, because by so doing, you are protecting
your right to such a proceeding should the occasion ever
arise that you found yourself in a courtroom and needed a
jury to decide a disputed issue in which you were involved. It is a right we are all entitled to in our great
country, but a right we can only guarantee if good people
such as yourselves give their time and attention as you are
now. I know the monetary rewards of jury service aren't
that great, but I urge you to keep in mind that the rewards
of freedom are high.

"I want to talk to you now about what, if anything, you
may have already heard about this case. I assure you, I
have been here for the past several days, and I have read

certain things in the newspaper about it which are *not true;* they are *inaccurate* and *in error* from what I know about this case. And for that reason, to be a fair and impartial juror, one must be confident of one's ability to approach this case with an open mind. You must be able to sit and hear testimony from this witness stand and see the exhibits and evidence offered and base your opinion solely and only upon what you see and hear in this courtroom, what is admitted into evidence by His Honor, Judge Carter, and not to any degree whatsoever be influenced or form any part of an opinion on what you may have read in a newspaper, heard on the radio, seen on television, read in some magazine, or heard at the beauty parlor or barber shop, because all that is nothing more than hearsay. It is not *evidence*.

"Do you all think you can do that?" Sutton stood at the rail before the panel, nodding his encouragement.

None of the jurors indicated a problem. Sutton posed another question: "Any of you have any problems with favoring Mr. Brookshire or Mr. Carnes because of the fact they are local folks—members of your community, your churches, your clubs?" He smiled, confident that they would not.

"Now the question becomes, could you, in a case where you felt that the circumstances warranted it, assess in a murder case as much punishment as ninety-nine years or life? Is there anyone here who has any problems with that long a sentence?" No one had.

"Okay. Many of you, I am sure, remember a few years ago on television a show called 'Perry Mason.' It was one of my favorite shows, and I suppose that is where I first got interested in the law. On that show they were always talking about proving something 'beyond a shadow of a doubt.' But nowhere in our law books does it say anything about a 'shadow of a doubt.' It is not there. In our legal system, to take a person's life, liberty, or property away as a result of a criminal proceeding, what we prosecutors are required to do is prove our allegations beyond a '*reason-*

able doubt.' If, after you have heard all the evidence, something in your mind tells you, 'Well, this just isn't stacking up right; it is not reasonable; I don't believe it;' then that is a reasonable doubt, and you must vote 'Not Guilty,' because a defendant is considered legally innocent until proven—beyond a reasonable doubt—to be guilty.

"Now, what will your function be in this trial? What are your duties as a juror? First, you, as representatives of your community will decide what the facts are. That is the juror's primary role and responsibility. When selected, you will take an oath from His Honor, Judge Carter, that you 'will a fair verdict render according to the law and the facts, so help you God.' Now, where do you get these facts? From the witness stand and from the admitted exhibits—tangible things that we mark with a little number. Nowhere else.

"Many times jurors ask if they can take notes during the trial. I don't know what Judge Carter's policy is, but usually jurors are not allowed to take notes. The reason for this is that you might accidentally write something down wrong and then all of a sudden it becomes a fact in your mind when it isn't a fact at all. And rather than have that happen, the law would prefer for you to rely on your good memory to remember the testimony as it came in.

"What the lawyers say is not evidence. What I'm telling you here today is not evidence. What Mr. Brookshire will tell you later today or tomorrow is not evidence. Evidence is only what you get from the witness stand and or whatever exhibits are admitted by Judge Carter. Arranging that evidence logically will, in the end, make your decision easier.

"Another function of the juror, and one of the most important, is to determine the credibility of each witness. We do this on a day-to-day basis in our personal lives. You have heard the expression, I'm sure, 'Well, I can't put much stock in what so-and-so says.' That is judging a person's credibility. In a court of law we do it even more so. When a witness takes the witness stand, you have an opportunity to visually examine that person. The witness's demeanor is very important—how does he handle himself on the stand? Does he crouch down, you know, hiding behind his coat? What interest does he have in the outcome of the trial? What bias or prejudice does each witness bring in with him? What expertise does he possess? Then you assess in your mind, 'What weight am I going to give their testimony? How much stock am I going to put into what that person has got to say?' You may believe all of what a given witness says, you may believe only part, or you may not believe a thing he says.

"Now, I will read you what the indictment says and then show you what the state must prove. The indictment says, 'That on or about the 17th day of September 1982, Genene Jones did then and there with the intent to cause serious bodily injury to an individual, namely, Chelsea McClellan, did then and there intentionally and knowingly commit an act clearly dangerous to human life, to wit: The said Genene Jones did then and there intentionally and knowingly inject the said Chelsea McClellan with a drug, namely succinylcholine, thereby causing the death of said Chelsea McClellan. The state must prove first that it was the Defendant, Genene Jones; secondly, that it was on or about September 17, 1982; thirdly that it occurred in Kerr County; fourth, that there was an intent to cause serious bodily injury, that she intentionally and knowingly committed an act clearly dangerous to human life, and lastly, that she injected Chelsea McClellan with succinylcholine thereby causing the death of Chelsea McClellan.' That is what we must prove to you.

"As we go through the trial I want you to remember that there is no motive that the state has to prove in this case at all. It doesn't make any difference *why* anybody kills anybody. It is the fact that they kill them that we concern ourselves with. The why has nothing to do with it.

"Now, how are we going to get a jury out of this group here?" Sutton held his hands wide. "What we are going to do first is figure out who the first thirty-two people are who're otherwise qualified to be jurors—that is, thirty-two people who can be fair and impartial, and can deal with the concepts of law that are involved. Then what happens is, both sides in a felony case are entitled to what are known as peremptory challenges. They are also sometimes called strikes, because you strike a name from the list of thirty-two. Each side gets ten strikes. Twenty from thirty-two leaves twelve—the jury.

"I said I was going to be brief, and I am working up to being brief. It may take me 20 minutes to get there.

"This trial may take some time," Sutton apologized in closing, "although I assure you I want to get it over with as soon as possible. Mr. Brookshire wants to get it over with as soon as possible, and I'm sure the defendant wants to get it over with as soon as possible. But again, I would like to remind you of your duties and responsibilities should you be selected as one of the jurors in this case. If it takes a little of your time—which I know it is going to do—think of the experience as a privilege that we have as citizens living in a free society. Anything that is important and worthwhile is going to take a little time, and I believe that getting at the truth in this case is certainly worth twelve good people sitting here for however long it takes."

The morning was gone. Although Sutton had been talking for a long time, the consistently fair and gracious tenor of his remarks had made a good impression on his audience. And because he had done such a thorough job explaining the duties of a juror, Brookshire would not have an equal chance to create such a solid first impression. The opening and closing of a criminal trial is an advantage given to the state.

After the lunch break, Rothe took over from Sutton, explaining that he would like to make some very brief remarks. "I can see smiles on your faces like there is not a lawyer alive that can be brief about anything, but I am going to do my level best."

Rothe gave the jurors the agreed-upon explanation as to

why he, a Bexar County district attorney, was involved in
a Kerr County murder trial. "Because our office has almost 70 lawyers, we are therefore capable and willing to
assist adjoining rural areas." Neither side wanted the
jurors to start wondering about the connection between
San Antonio and Genene Jones.

Rothe spent the rest of that long day putting the same
litany of questions to one prospective juror after another.
Did the juror know Brookshire? Have you any precon-
ceived notions about the case? Could you award any sentence ranging from probation to 99 years? Some
individuals were excused by the court for health reasons—
it would be a long trial and a physical strain on those who
finally filled the jury box. Others were "challenged for
cause" when they admitted to the court that press accounts
they had heard or read had left them unable to render an
unbiased verdict. One gentleman was excused when he explained to the judge that he just did not feel capable of
passing judgment on a fellow human being. No peremptory challenges would be made by the attorneys until the
following day, after the defense completed its examination
of the selected panel.

On Wednesday, January 18, Jim Brookshire took the
floor. Like Sutton, he did his best to put the jurors at ease.
He quickly introduced the jury to the defense team, then
asked Genene to stand and face the jury. "This is Genene
Jones," he said, forcing the jury to see her as an individual, a fellow human being, worthy of their compassion.

He then spent a few minutes speaking in greater detail
about each member of the team assembled to defend the
accused. "My name is Jim Brookshire," he started, "or,
as Mr. Sutton has kindly referred to me, 'Jim Bob.' That
is really a dirty trick," he confided ruefully. "That is,
unfortunately, my name, but I try to avoid that. I am a
native of Texas from a town so small it no longer exists. A
town called Friendship that now lies at the bottom of Lake
Granger. I am a graduate of the University of Texas Law
School. I was a member of The United States Marine

Corps and served in Vietnam. I am married and have two children, ages three and six.

"Burt Carnes also claims to be a native Texan," Brookshire indicated his co-counsel with a smile, "though he was actually born in New York. Miss Laura Little is assisting us. She just recently graduated from law school, clerked for the court of criminal appeals for a year, and is planning to begin medical school in the spring, but wanted something interesting to do in the interim. We graciously allowed her to work with us for free."

Brookshire then took his turn at questioning the panel members. He focused initially on any knowledge that any juror might already have about the Jones case. The panel members were instructed to raise a hand if any had heard something about the case. Each individual with a raised hand was then called forward to explain quietly to the judge and attorneys exactly what he had heard. Both the defense team and Judge Carter wanted to take all possible precautions against contaminating the rest of the panel.

Brookshire then questioned each of the first 32 prospective jurors individually, getting a feel for them, asking them about their scientific and medical knowledge, asking them if they endorsed the concept of "innocent until proven guilty beyond a reasonable doubt," checking to see if any had ever served on a jury before.

At the end of the day, the two lawyers alternately used their ten strikes. When they finished, both sides were reasonably satisfied with the seven-woman, five-man jury, comprised of three managers, an engineer, three homemakers, a salesman, two secretaries, a state employee, and a microbiologist. Sutton had found twelve people with thirty-two children and grandchildren among them. From Brookshire's point of view, the panel had as much diversity as any he was likely to find.

The Honorable John Carter

I *volunteered* for the Genene Jones case.

Why did you do that?

Sometimes I wonder.

[THE JUDGE LAUGHED]

Well, the truth is, Jones's lawyers had come here asking for a change of venue to Williamson County, and our district attorney recommended that we allow it. I thought about it and decided I'd let 'em change venues and come here. Then (and this really was more or less an accident), in reading the newspaper, I saw that Judge Murray Jordan (from over in Kerrville, whose case this was) had commented that he had a five-county district. Now, I have only a one-county district court. ('Course, we have about the same population between us, as ours is a bigger county.) But he was complaining that the trial was going to put him way behind.

Well, we only have two courtrooms in this courthouse, and if they were going to tie up my courtroom for five or six weeks, he was going to put me way behind too, because then I would have no place to try any cases. We don't have any spare courtrooms here. So I got thinking about it and called him up and said, "Look, Murray, it doesn't make a whole lot of sense for us *both* to get behind. I might as well try this case." I said, "I don't know anything about it, but I'd just have to sit here at my desk and do paperwork for five weeks, and although I'm behind, I'm not *that* behind."

[THE JUDGE LAUGHED]

Murray said, "Well, that's great. It does make sense." So that's how I ended up volunteering. I'm not sure whether I would volunteer *again* . . . although it was a really good case, *really* good case. Best case I've tried since I've been on the bench.

The lawyers were excellent, just excellent. I have a court that has both criminal and civil jurisdiction, and so I see a wide variety of cases. I see excellent lawyers do real good jobs. I see some crummy ones too, sometimes, but not very often. But I've never seen any four attorneys do a better job than those four guys did on the Jones case.

How do you define a "good job" by a lawyer?

Well, first off, they have to know the law, and they have to be good at what they do in the courtroom. What I mean by that is there's a certain amount of "trial lawyer ability," which consists, I suppose, of a certain amount of drama, a certain amount of being able to think on your feet, and a certain amount of ability to express yourself well under pressure. Of course, the prosecution did one of the finest jobs you'll ever see. But you have to do all that within the framework of a good knowledge of the law. If you don't have a good knowledge of the law, you're just somebody up there talking.

Those four attorneys were first-rate. Both Sutton and Rothe were great prosecutors. And the defense was just amazing, both Jim Bob Brookshire and Burt Carnes. They each did an *amazing* job, in my opinion. Just to be able to digest the subject matter was extremely difficult, but then to go on and make a good defense based on some really tough stuff (stuff that, you know, we don't talk about every day on the street)—it was a good job. I was real proud of them. I really was.

How many cases do you try a year?

Oh God, I don't know. One or two major criminal cases a month. Then a whole slew of little civil cases, petty criminal cases. I tried the Genene Jones and the Henry Lucas cases, back to back. You know who Henry Lucas is? That case took six weeks to try. I've earned my pay this year.

They keep me pretty busy, but I like my job. I wouldn't give it up. I suppose I enjoy the nature of the combat in the courtroom. I enjoy orchestrating it. I like it.

What goes on inside the jury room after a case such as this?

Well, jurors always have some unanswered questions. Due to the nature of our laws, you just can't answer them while the case is going on. So we talk. Plus, I give them a little certificate saying, "Thanks for doing a good job." You know, it states the case they sat on, and it's just something they can stick on the wall, or throw away—whatever they want to do with it. I feel that if somebody comes up here and gives you five or six weeks of their time, it's the least we can do. See, we can only give these people ten dollars a day for being a juror; that doesn't even cover their meals, but that's all the state allots. It's six dollars a day until the jury's picked, and then ten dollars once they're on a jury. So, they're not getting rich up here, and they're doing their duty, so I just give them a little something for their efforts.

And then, the lawyers really like to be able to have a chance to talk to the jurors about what they screwed up on and what they didn't, you know, what they did good and what they did bad. And sometimes, the jurors *tell them*, they really do! They say, "We didn't like the way you did this," or "We didn't like the way you did that." But they didn't in the Jones case. I recall they praised the defense counsels quite highly.

And, if there's some tension (especially like there was in the Jones case), it helps break that tension. Somebody will say something a little humorous, and everybody'll laugh, and it'll break the tension, and everybody feels a little bit better before they go home.

There were a lot of interesting side things that went on during the Jones case, that made it a fun case (not fun—I mean different). For instance, we played musical courtrooms a lot, because there was a real crowd, I mean a *big* crowd in that courtroom. It was a packed house, every day. When we had a big day coming up, like the first day, and like when that guy from Sweden came in to testify, well, my courtroom just wouldn't accommodate everybody.

During that time, Judge Locke, whose courtroom is across from mine, had several jury trials going on also, and when he's got a jury trial, that's his courtroom. So, a lot of the time when we were over here, we had to have "Reserved Seating," with an area for the press. In fact, it got so bad, that we finally had to tell them to rotate in and out and share the information, 'cause we didn't have the room. There were three or four wire services and a *lot* of TV people here. There were three or four NBC affiliates and three or four CBS affiliates. The point is that if everyone from the press had been allowed in, that would've been it; nobody else would've been able to sit in the courtroom.

Now, our courtrooms are public courtrooms, and this was a case that was all over the national news, so a lot of the schoolchildren wanted to come and see it.

We had several high schools from around the county send their civics classes, to sit in for an hour's worth, or something like that, just to see the procedures and so forth. During that trial, I think we had a class from almost every town in the county, at one time or another. And, you know, I think that's part of the educational process; I think it's just fine for them to have come in and sat in on that trial. I wish that more of 'em would come down here and sit in. You can learn a lot about life in a courtroom.

And of course, we had a lot of people who were interested in the children involved and so there were several families who wanted to attend. Those that testified, of course, couldn't sit in the courtroom, but those who didn't testify, some of them sat in the courtroom.

You mean relatives couldn't sit in and watch the proceedings?

Well, in Texas, we have what's called "the rule." That's what we call it: "the rule." We swear in all the witnesses ahead of time here, and if someone asks for the rule to be invoked, then all the witnesses have to wait outside the courtroom until they're summoned, so they can't hear what anybody else has to say. The witnesses come in one at a time, as they're called, and while they're outside, they can't discuss the case with anybody except the lawyers involved. There's a bailiff who sits with them and keeps track of it all. And it's witness misconduct if they do talk. And they can get in trouble for it. But I've never had any problems with witnesses. All they need, sometimes, is a reminder.

Some humorous things happened too. The press was really overzealous the first day or two. There was a lot of press here for this trial, seems like they came in from *everywhere*, all over the *world*.

I held a meeting the Sunday before the trial, out at the university to set the guidelines as to what they

could and could not do, just so that there wouldn't be
any misunderstanding. I was trying something that
really's never been tried in this courthouse, and it
started off as a failure, but worked into a success, more
or less. Prior to this, it had been the policy that no
cameras were allowed in the courthouse, period. They
all had to be outside. Well, I've always had real good
relations with the press, and I guess I still do (I hope I
do), so I gave them a break. I told them I would allow
them to film in designated areas within the courthouse
on the first floor. Basically, I said they could film in the
center of the rotunda, which would give them a shot of
whoever they wanted. You can't get from the second
floor where the courtroom is except by the elevator or
by the stairs, and both of them come right down into
that rotunda area. So this would allow them to film
indoors and get "courthouse scenes" and so forth, but
they couldn't film in the courtroom itself, and they
couldn't film on the second floor at all. Now, we allowed any film crew that wanted to, to come in two
weeks before the trial and take some shots of the empty
courtroom, you know, just as filler (and a few of them
did), but other than that, they weren't allowed to film
inside, or on the second floor. Well, one of the more
ingenious ones—

[THE JUDGE LAUGHED]

It so happened, that at that particular time, we were
having trouble with the air-conditioning. We had re-
modeled the courthouse and installed a brand new air-
conditioning system, and it wasn't working. Texas is
very much like California, in that we sometimes have
hot weather in the winter time. You know, it doesn't
necessarily get real cold every year in the wintertime.
So, that first day, I think we called close to 300 jurors
in there, and with all those warm bodies and no air-
conditioning, it started getting warm. Now, we have
balconies outside of each one of our courtrooms and
we opened these balcony doors to let in some fresh air

and there was a guy from Austin KTBC who got very ingenious; he ran across the street and rented a room on the second floor of the newspaper office, which was directly opposite the open balcony doors.

Well, we were on a recess, and Genene Jones was sitting at her table. Remember, I had told them, "You cannot film in that courtroom." So, all of a sudden, Genene bolted up from the table and said, "There's a camera over there!"

I was up on the bench working on some paperwork (we were all on a ten-minute break of some kind). So I got down off the bench, walked over to the window (black robes and all), and looked out there, and there he was! With his camera pointed right at me!

So I yelled at the bailiff: "Marvin, go on over there and arrest that S.O.B.!" And they did, they went over there and got him.

This was the first day?

Yeah, the first day, Monday. And they brought him over here to me, and he came in and he said, "Oh, Judge," he says, "listen, hey, I'm sorry," you know, "I apologize."

And I said, "As far as I'm concerned, you violated the order of the court, and I guess I'm just going to have to put you in the Williamson County jail."

And he says, "Judge, listen Judge," he says, "the nature of these cameras in this bright sunlight is such that that darkened area of your courtroom just didn't come out. I got nothin'. I got no film of the courtroom at all. All I have is the window. And we really just wanted to show the open window and talk about the lack of air-conditioning. But I won't even show that if you just let me go."

He was really sweating bad, so I said okay.

It turned out that he really got to be my spokesman, as it were, because I got to know him from that deal, and he helped me. When the new people came in from out of town, he helped me explain to them, "Hey, don't do anything this judge doesn't want you to, because he'll put you in jail!"

Later, that same crew came out to San Angelo when we were out there trying the Lucas case. It was kind of interesting, being out there in San Angelo, because we were all in the same motel. Everybody involved with that trial was all in the same motel, just in different areas. It was one of these hollow-dome Holiday Inns where everything's inside a big bubble. It's an enclosed motel. You'll see a lot of them out in west Texas, if you get out there. They're almost like an Astrodome. They've got a bubble over the whole thing so you can swim year-round in there, and all that stuff. So, it's almost like being in the same building together, even though my rooms were way off on one side, and the defense counsel was off some place else, and the prosecutor was some place else. Anyway, in San Angelo, it turned out that the court reporter's room kind of got to be the central meeting place. After work, everybody would go over to the court reporter's room and sit around and talk and so forth. I don't remember quite when it was, but it was sometime during the trial, the guys from Austin's KTBC were up there, and I was over at the court reporter's room, and we all got to talking and laughing and joking, and the atmosphere got to be relaxed, when this cameraman says, "Judge, uh, has the statute of limitations run out on my offense that I pulled on the Jones case?"

And I said, "Oh, yeah, I guess so, I've forgiven you."

And he said, "Then I think you should know, I got it all.

[THE JUDGE LAUGHED]

"I even got what you said. You could read your lips when you pointed at me. But believe me, I wasn't *about* to put it on."

TWENTY

> *No terms except an unconditional and immediate surrender can be accepted. I intend to move immediately upon your works.*
>
> U.S. Grant

THE TRIAL PROPER BEGAN THURSDAY, JANUary 19, 1984. The courtroom was packed to capacity. Genene wore a maroon dress with lace at the collar; it hung to just below her knees and complimented her heavy frame.

The morning of the first day was taken up by motions discussed outside the presence of the jury. The lawyers were still jockeying for position, setting the parameters for the issues to be presented. The defense won its motions to prevent the use of or any reference to Genene's suicide note or failed polygraph test. Judge Carter then postponed making any decision regarding the defense's two remaining motions—the two most significant. The first asked the court to preclude any mention of the other children, besides Chelsea McClellan, who'd suffered emergencies in Dr. Holland's Clinic. The second argued that Judge Carter should keep Dr. Bo Holmstedt and his innovative test out of the trial completely. A victory on either motion would greatly enhance Brookshire's chance of persuading at least some of the jurors that a reasonable doubt as to guilt existed. The judge wanted to give more thought to both requests.

That afternoon, the jury was brought in and Ron Sutton delivered his opening remarks. "During the weeks to come, what I ask you folks to do is simply listen to the tragic story of the life and death of Chelsea McClellan as it unfolds here before you. As you watch and listen, I guarantee you, you're going to be wondering why—why would anyone do such a thing? How could something like this happen? That's perfectly natural, but as I said before, the state isn't required to prove a motive. We don't have to tell you *why* Genene Jones set out to cause serious bodily injury to Chelsea McClellan. We don't have to tell you *why* she injected succinlycholine into this little girl's thigh, causing her death. But I assure you, as these chapters chronicling the events of the summer of 1982 unfold and the testimony draws to a close, not only will you be absolutely convinced that Genene Jones murdered Chelsea McClellan, but the reason why will also be inescapably clear, without me ever having to tell you."

Sutton began with a subtle choice of witnesses. "The trick is the order; the structure behind the presentation," he later commented. "Whether you call five witnesses or thirty to forty like I thought I would here, you've got to tell those jurors an interesting story that first day. Pique their interest. I'd spent many, many days going over the witness list, organizing in my mind how I could best present the case—and prove it—to a jury. I went through it all four or five different ways before I decided upon the way we did it. I chose a way that I thought would maintain interest and be easy to follow. With something this big, it's real easy to get confused and to lose the ends of it.

"See, that first day what I wanted to do was convey to the jury something like when you turn on the TV and here comes an ambulance screaming into an Emergency Room at a hospital. This immediately grabs your attention. Something's happened. What's wrong? Who done it? And these questions are going to stay in the juror's minds all through the whole trial: 'Something's happened, what's wrong? Who done it?'"

Sutton's first witness, RN Sharon Keith, head nurse of Sid Peterson's Emergency Room, told the jury about Chelsea McClellan's Code Blue arrivals from Dr. Kathleen Holland's Clinic on August 24 and September 17, 1982. During her testimony Sutton propped up two large empty calendars. One represented the month of August 1982; the other, September. With a large red marking pen, Sutton would, throughout the trial, graphically document the events in Kathleen's Clinic as they were slowly revealed by his witnesses. His first two entries filled the squares for August 24 and September 17: "McClellan R/A," signifying Chelsea's two respiratory arrests.

A young physician specializing in emergency medicine, Dr. Richard Mason, took the stand next. He told the jury that, while in Sid Peterson's Emergency Room on September 17, he had assisted Dr. Holland in treating Chelsea. "When they first came into the ER, I didn't notice any movements in the child. They placed her on a table, and within a minute she began reaching up towards her endotracheal tube. She was lying on her back and moving her hands up about her head—" the doctor demonstrated for the jury "—raising her arms." At Sutton's prodding, Dr. Mason characterized Chelsea's actions as "gross motor movements." She was able to use the large muscles of her arms, he explained, but not the smaller muscles that controlled her wrists and fingers.

"From what you observed, Doctor, was her condition consistent with coming out from under the influence of the drug succinylcholine?"

"Yes, sir."

The jury now knew that on September 17, a little girl arrested, then exhibited strange movements as she recovered in the hospital's Emergency Room, movements which might have been caused by a drug called succinylcholine.

In response, on cross-examination, Brookshire compelled Dr. Mason to confirm that Chelsea's erratic movements might also have been the product of a postseizure, drowsy, semiconscious state. Throughout the trial, with almost every witness, the defense would return to this theme—there was another possible explanation, a *natural* explanation for Chelsea McClellan's medical problems.

When Brookshire finished with the witness, Sutton rose for redirect. He had one more tidbit—a curious anecdote—to put before the jury.

"Doctor Mason, would you tell us about a conversation you had with Genene on the seventeenth?"

"I was standing next to the examining table checking the little girl when, I recall, Genene Jones looked up at me and the people around, and said, 'They said there wouldn't be any excitement when we came to Kerrville.'"

"Thank you, Doctor."

Sutton now called his first expert witness to explain what the mysterious drug succinylcholine was. Dr. Roland Proust, a research pharmacist with the North Carolina–based pharmaceutical manufacturer Burroughs Wellcome, provided the jury with a detailed analysis of the specific type of injectionable succinylcholine Dr. Holland had purchased for her Clinic.

The largest pieces of the puzzle had been put in place. The District Attorney nailed them down. Sutton called Emergency Medical Technician Steven Brown, the driver of the ambulance for both of Chelsea's emergencies, to tell the jury the story of the little girl's death. In subdued tones, Brown spoke of Chelsea's unexpected cardiac arrest, the quick trip to Comfort, and thirty-five minutes later, Dr. Holland's order to discontinue CPR.

On cross-examination, Carnes closely questioned the medic about Chelsea's physical appearance on September 17, when they loaded Chelsea up for her trip south. "She looked great," he recalled. "Stable. Her color was back to normal. Seemed like everything was all right." The defense had a specific purpose for this line of questioning, which it would return to again and again. Brookshire wanted the jury to consider the possibility that Chelsea had recovered by the time she entered the ambulance, because if she had, then two corrolary propositions might also be true. First, anything Genene might or might not have done to Chelsea at the Clinic could not have caused the child's death, because she had recovered. Second, if Chelsea had indeed been injected with a drug that caused her death, it had to have been administered after she was loaded into the ambulance, and Brookshire would have more to say about that possibility later.

Sutton called two more witnesses—a nurse and the director of the local funeral home—to provide necessary information about the chain of custody over Chelsea's body prior to her autopsy. The first day's testimony ended with Chelsea's arrival at the funeral home.

"So we got the jury all the way through to the death," Sutton later explained. "In a short series of witnesses, we laid out the whole thing. We started with an exciting event—the emergency. We explained about the drug— what it is and what it does. Then we had the death and a funeral, leaving the question: 'Who done it?' And that was the first day."

On Friday, February 20, Judge Carter began by apologizing for his froggy voice; he was suffering from a bad head cold. He then instructed the prosecution to call its next witness, Dr. James Robert Fletes, the pathologist who performed Chelsea's autopsy. Dr. Fletes told the jury that his pathological and toxicological exams revealed no abnormality of the heart, no abnormality of the lungs, and no abnormality in any of the other organs.

On cross, Brookshire fleshed out his defense; he took Dr. Fletes through every bit of alarming information he knew about Chelsea's medical history. He also asked the doctor to describe a series of slides he had brought, slides that showed scarring in Chelsea's medulla—the part of the brain that controls cardiac and respiratory functions. Brookshire was painting a picture of a child who had suffered a long history of medical problems, with resultant or contributory scarring in her brain stem that *could* account for her death.

Dr. James Robert Galbreath, a former medical school professor and a member of a corporation of pathologists, took the stand next. Galbreath both corroborated and elaborated on Fletes's testimony—there was nothing physically wrong with Chelsea. Further, Galbreath testified, the scarring (gliosis) in the brain stem was "very subtle."

On cross, Brookshire took the witness in a different direction. With elaborate care, he again went over the child's medical history, reinforcing the picture of a very sick child. He asked very detailed questions about the reasons for, as well as evidence to support, the original autopsy verdict of Sudden Infant Death Syndrome. He was attempting to capitalize on the logic that had supported the original diagnosis—reached before Sutton had ever mentioned succinylcholine to Kagan-Hallet. The defense hoped that the confidence the doctors had once placed in their original SIDS verdict might create a reasonable doubt about the accuracy of their reevaluated verdict.

Brookshire slowly worked his way through to the concluding sentence of the autopsy's first verdict: "Probable labile autonomic nervous system secondary to prematurity." He asked the doctor to explain what that meant.

Galbreath complied. "The neurologist felt that, because of repeated bouts of hypoxia, or lack of oxygen, the autonomic nervous system, which controls respiration, heartbeat, and several other things, had been made extremely sensitive—labile—so that a number of conditions that might not adversely affect a normal individual could produce some ill effect in Chelsea."

Brookshire nodded, his point made: Chelsea was an extremely "sensitive" child, liable to experience problems when another, "normal" child would not. Sutton rose for redirect, and tried to turn the point around. His string of questions led Dr. Galbreath to agree that an injection of succinylcholine could very well be sufficient negative stimulus to kill a fifteen-month-old child who happened to have a sensitive area in her brain stem.

The next three witnesses provided information about Chelsea's exhumation; Detective Lonnie Agold had photographed the event; Gene Hutzler had returned the remains to the casket; and Stanley Zerkel, operator of the Garden of Memories Cemetery, assured the jury that the plot had not been disturbed prior to the exhumation.

At about 2:00 P.M., Sutton called Dr. Theodore Boyce, who, as Kerrville's health officer, had presided over the exhumation. Sutton used Boyce's testimony to establish that the tissue samples eventually provided to Drs. Reiders and Holmstedt did indeed come from the dead child and were not tampered with in any fashion.

Because Dr. Boyce, by chance, also happened to have cared for Chelsea shortly after she was delivered, the defense took advantage of this witness to delve into Chelsea's first day of life in more detail. Carnes focused on Chelsea's prematurity, the respiratory difficulties she had experienced, and the delay before Boyce had intubated her. Again the defense's message was plain: Chelsea was a sensitive child with a history of medical problems.

The final witness of the day, and Sutton's grand finale to the first week of testimony, was Dr. Vincent DiMaio, medical examiner of Bexar County, a forensic pathologist with nearly twenty years' experience. His expertise was unchallengeable: he had performed thousands of autopsies in his career, "closer to four than to three thousand," including hundreds on children. In his early forties, portly, slightly balding, bespectacled, with a rather noticeable tick to his left eye and shoulder, the doctor proved to be an impressive witness.

Brookshire later referred to DiMaio as "the smiling assassin from San Antonio." "You could tell," Brookshire explained, "that unlike those who had taken the stand before him, he had, on many occasions, testified to a jury. He would look at the person who was asking the question with a straight face, very attentive, and then, before answering, he would turn to the jury and this smile would come across his face as if someone had pushed the appropriate button. He was very self-assured, very knowledgeable, and very well respected."

Dr. DiMaio explained to the jury that pathology is the branch of medicine concerned with the study of diseases. "The *anatomical* pathologist examines tissue, generally removed in surgery to make a diagnosis of a disease. The *clinical* pathologist runs the laboratory. The *forensic* pathologist—that's what I am—is concerned with the application of the medical sciences to problems in the law. A forensic pathologist deals with the effects of trauma on the body. He deals with violent deaths, accidents, suicides, and homicides." In a case such as this, DiMaio made clear, the expert a juror ought to listen to was someone like himself.

Because DiMaio was from San Antonio, Nick Rothe, for the first time, handled the questioning for the prosecution. One of Rothe's first topics concerned the doctor's experiences with Sudden Infant Death Syndrome. "SIDS," DiMaio stated with confidence, "is not a single, isolated disease like tuberculosis or appendicitis. SIDS is essentially a wastepaper-basket diagnosis which includes deaths from many causes and in different manners that we, with our present medical knowledge, cannot differentiate among. Most SIDS deaths are probably natural; some are accidents, and some are actually homicides. Typically, SIDS children are babies who are put to bed, and when the parent goes to wake them up, they are dead. The age group that this occurs in is below one year of age. In fact, 91 percent of all cases classified as SIDS occur before the first six months of age. I myself will not sign any case out as SIDS if the child is over ten months.

"All forensic pathologists," the doctor continued, "know that a certain percentage of the cases that are signed out as SIDS are homicides. The percentage has been estimated at anywhere from 1 to 20 percent. Twenty percent is probably much too high, but we don't know for sure. Therefore, it's important to do a toxicological screen on any suspected SIDS case."

DiMaio maintained that if no toxicology screen is done, one cannot make a valid SIDS diagnosis. If a toxicological test indicates there is a drug in the body, then SIDS was not the cause of death. DiMaio further categorically stated that, because Chelsea was fifteen months old, she did not die of SIDS.

The prosecution then started to chip away at the defense's theory that Chelsea's death occurred naturally as a result of the flaws in her own system. "Doctor," Rothe asked, "has anyone ever conducted tests comparing possible SIDS cases involving brain-stem scarring with children who died in, say, car accidents, or as a result of gunshot, or in a fire, to determine if scarring existed in the control group any less than it did in those with SIDS?"

"Yes, sir," confirmed DiMaio. "And they found out that some of the children in the control group had *more* scarring than children who died of SIDS. The general consensus now is that this scarring is a very subjective thing: some children have more, some have less, and there is, at the present time, no evidence of any relationship between scarring and SIDS."

On cross, Brookshire contented himself with scoring three significant points against this formidable witness. "Doctor, are you a *neuro*pathologist?"

"No, sir."

"Have you examined the brain tissue in this case?"

"No, sir."

"Are you saying that it is impossible for brain scarring to affect body functions?"

"No, sir."

"Thank you. Nothing further, Your Honor." Brookshire knew that when a hostile witness is as persuasive as Dr. DiMaio, brevity is often preferable to providing the witness further opportunity to present his position.

The jury was dismissed early, at 3:55 P.M. following Judge Carter's triple-reinforced admonitions: "Remember: no newspapers, no magazines, no written materials of any form, no television broadcasts, and no radio broadcasts. I hope y'all have a nice weekend, and we will see you Monday morning at nine o'clock."

On Saturday, Sutton gave Kathleen a call to let her know that her turn was coming. Kathleen already suspected as much. She, like almost everyone else in Texas, had been closely following the trial's progress in the papers and on TV. Sutton also called Petti and asked her if she could possibly come to Georgetown the following evening and help him with some records. She should probably plan to stay over, he advised, as they could very well work late.

"When Petti arrived," Sutton recalls, "I brought her into the room, sat her down, and said, 'Petti, you've got to do something for me.' And she went white. 'What?' 'You've got to testify in the morning.' And she almost went limp—but she hadn't had two or three days to think about it and get even more worried and upset. So, all that night we talked. I sat in front of her and held her hands and Dr. Reiders and Dr. Holmstedt were there, and they sat on either side of her. We went over it all real easy, so there wouldn't be any surprises, but she was shaking and crying the whole time."

On Monday, January 23, Sutton began the second week of the trial by calling the mother of the dead child to the stand, out of order. Slowly and carefully, Ron walked Petti through her daughter's early medical history: her premature birth, her bout with pneumonia. Through Petti, Sutton helped the jury see a real little girl, just learning to walk, just learning to say her first words: "Mommy," "Daddy," "no," "bubba," "cookie." He and Petti recreated Chelsea's August 24 visit to Holland's Clinic and the ten days she spent thereafter in the hospital.

"How did Chelsea seem after that first emergency?"

Petti was firm in her answer: "She was fine. She didn't even stay in her bed very much; she was fine. She played and the nurses played with her and she walked up and down the halls."

Petti stated she never witnessed any breathing problems or any lack of coordination during that entire ten-day period; her little girl slept well, ate well, and seemed fine. Petti described her daughter's health after she was released as "fantastic."

Sutton then led Petti through the events of September 17. Slowly, her voice barely above a whisper, Petti recalled the details of her daughter's last day. She remembered that Chelsea was dressed in a "gingham red and white dress with lace on it, and a little red and white bonnet with lace on it to match." Petti publicly relived her daughter's death, recalling the strange, frightened look in Chelsea's eyes, the limpness that had invaded her body. "Raggedy Ann, that's just what she looked like: Raggedy Ann." Petti broke down and some members of the jury were also in tears as Sutton asked the court for a brief recess to give his witness a chance to collect herself before finishing her testimony.

When court reconvened, Sutton passed his witness to the defense. Burt Carnes handled the cross-examination very gently: "No one wants to pounce on a crying mother," he later pointed out. He, too, took Petti back through Chelsea's medical history, focusing on her many problems. Then he established one point firmly: after Dr. Holland had instructed her nurse to give Chelsea the immunization shots, Genene *did not go anywhere near* the medication refrigerator in the rear of the Clinic—she went straight to the examining room with the mother and child.

When Petti finished, Judge Carter called an early lunch break. In the afternoon, the jury was excused. The judge would now hear evidence relating to the defense's motion to prevent the state's use of Dr. Holmstedt's innovative test for the detection of succinylcholine. Brookshire's motion was predicated on a legal principle known in Texas as the Freye test: No new scientific procedure or test can qualify as evidence until it becomes generally accepted as valid within the scientific community. Brookshire elicited testimony from three witnesses, including Dr. Bo Holmstedt himself, to support the Defendant's contention that Holmstedt's test was *not* generally accepted, but was, rather, still an experimental procedure. Brookshire's argument turned principally on the fact that no one outside of Holmstedt's team of scientists had ever duplicated the Swede's gas chromatograph–mass spectrometer test for detecting succinylcholine. Further, even Holmstedt's team had only worked with rat tissue and human blood, never before with human tissue, and never before with the infinitesimal amounts of the drug measured in Chelsea's tissues. "What we are talking about here," he reminded the judge, "is *99 years*. The test ought to be accepted, reliable. It ought to be proven."

In response, Sutton offered testimony that the *procedure* used by Holmstedt and his team was identical to the procedures widely used since the early 1970s for finding acetylcholine, a close chemical analog to succinylcholine. There had simply never before been a need to apply that procedure to succinylcholine. Sutton showed that the only difference between acetylcholine and succinylcholine is that one is "an ester of choline and *acetic* acid," while the other is the "ester of choline and *succinic* acid." Since the gas chromatograph–mass spectrometer had been used for the detection of acetylcholine for many years and was a generally accepted procedure, the requirements of the Freye test had effectively been met.

"If there are any questions in the court's mind as to the duplicatability of the test, or how many times it's been published," Rothe concluded, "I think these issues go to the weight the jury gives the test and not to the question of whether it is admissible."

Within the hour, Judge Carter delivered his ruling: Dr. Holmstedt's test regarding the presence of succinylcholine

in the alleged victim's body would be admitted. The jury
would hear the testimony the following day.

Tuesday morning, before the jury was brought in, Judge
Carter began with an announcement. "After the hearing
yesterday morning, the jury reported to me that numerous
TV cameramen harassed them all over the square—followed them to their cars and stuck cameras in their cars—
in direct violation of this court's order. I didn't see it on
the news, but that wasn't the deal. The deal was there
would be no photographing the jurors. What they're doing
is tough enough. We are going to investigate, and I am
going to find out who did it. Those stations that I discover
photographed jurors yesterday will be placed off the
county property. If you cannot follow the court's order,
then you will suffer the consequences."

Never one to miss an opportunity, Brookshire rose from
his seat. "Your Honor, for the record, the defense will
move for a mistrial based upon the violation of the court's
order and the intrusion upon the jury by certain members
of the press and media." Brookshire knew there was little
hope the court would grant the motion; his sole objective
was to fill the record with protests establishing "the general unfairness of the proceedings."

"I was laying the groundwork for an appeal,"
Brookshire says, "in the event that should become necessary."

"Motion is denied," ruled Carter, as expected, then
turned to his bailiff. "All right, Marvin, bring the jury
in."

Sutton called Dr. Holmstedt to the stand. The lawyer
spent some time reviewing the doctor's background, im-
pressing the jury with his credentials. Holmstedt confirmed
that he was a professor of toxicology and a member of the
Royal Academy of Sciences, the body that each year
awards the Nobel prizes in chemistry and physics.
Brookshire remembers the doctor as "a fine old gen-

tleman, a grandfatherly looking old man, very quiet spoken, very pleasant, not haughty." A toxicological
researcher since 1948, Dr. Holmstedt had, years ago,
made two journeys into the Amazonian jungles to study
how the natives manufactured curare. He was one of the
scientists who helped develop the original synthetic form
of curare known as succinylcholine.

Sutton asked Dr. Holmstedt to explain for the jury the
drug's effects. "The nerve terminates in something called
the motor end plate," Holmstedt began in his lightly ac-
cented Queen's English, "which is in the muscle. Curare,
and also succinylcholine, blocks the transmission of the
action in the nerve onto the muscle at this point—
the motor end plate. The normal impulses that activate the
muscles don't reach them. For all the neuromuscular
blocking agents, including the unknown agent in the disease myasthenia gravis, the muscles are blocked in a certain order. The eye muscles and the muscles of the eyelids
are hit earliest; then the small muscles in the hands and
feet; then the leg muscles; then the muscles of the body,
particularly the ones in the back. The last muscle to be
blocked is the diaphragm. The muscles regain their activity in the reverse order as I have described."

"When it has its effect upon the respiratory muscle,"
Sutton asked, "what happens at that point?"

"You stop breathing."

Dr. Holmstedt informed the jury that, although succinylcholine results in a flaccid state of paralysis, it can
also cause, before total paralysis, something known as fasciculations—small twitchings of the muscles just under the
skin.

"What happens to the drug after it is introduced into the
body?"

"The drug is rapidly hydrolyzed—split into its constituent parts, succinic acid and choline—by an enzyme in the
blood called pseudocholinesterase, and thus very quickly
inactivated, so that its effects last only a short time."

Thereafter, for the better part of an hour, Sutton and

Holmstedt went over the intricacies of the gas chromatograph–mass spectrometer and the tiny unit of measurement it could identify: a nanogram, one one-billionth of a gram. Dr. Holmstedt explained to the jury that the GCMS, as he called it, was really a combination of two machines joined by a device that allowed test substances to pass from one to the other despite a potentially explosive difference in interior pressures and environments. The gas chromatograph separates the molecules of a test substance; the mass spectrometer then weighs the separated molecules.

On cross, Brookshire's task was to raise questions in the jurors' minds, to cast doubt on the whole process of GCMS testing. He insisted that a *theory*, however sound, does not adequately establish a technique's reliability. He did this by focusing on the apparent uncertainties built into the testing procedure. The first point raised, and the most weighty, was that the mass spectrometer does not measure entire molecules, but rather, only small pieces—specific ions—suspected to be included within the molecule in question.

Brookshire interrogated Holmstedt about the variables contained in the physical apparatus of the gas chromatograph–mass spectrometer that could affect the uniformity of results: Both the temperature and the atmosphere of the gas chromatograph's tubes are not constant, varying by fractions of degrees, or even several degrees, from test to test. Brookshire went on to challenge the standard against which Holmstedt assessed the readings made on the tissue samples from Chelsea. How can one compare, he asked, the reliability of test results obtained using tissues from a human child whose body was full of all kinds of chemicals with those obtained using tissues of white albino rats that had lived in sterile environs all their lives, and had even been fed special, chemically pure food? Chelsea had, after all, been through three emergencies during the last month of her life and had undergone numerous tests at the hospital. The tissue sample had been saturated with preservatives and were many months old by the time Holmstedt's tests were conducted. Wouldn't such variables, Brookshire argued, affect the reliability of the test results? Holmstedt acknowledged that that possibility did exist.

Brookshire had another question to raise for the jurors, providing them another possible ground for doubt. First he had asked Dr. Holmstedt to confirm the fact that succinic acid and choline—the constituent parts of succinylcholine—exist in the human body as naturally occurring elements. Then he asked: "Doctor, have you ever done any tests before, where you went below the 100-nanogram level to see if succinylcholine possibly exists as an endogenous [naturally occurring] compound?"

"I cannot rule out the possibility that this choline ester occurs in very minute amounts in the body, but not in an amount that causes paralysis."

"But it is conceivable then," Brookshire persisted, "that succinylcholine can and does exist in the body naturally at very low levels—say several nanograms worth?"

"I cannot say no, but it has not been proven."

On redirect, Sutton took pains to debunk Brookshire's rather novel theory that any succinylcholine found in Chelsea's tissue samples might have appeared there naturally. He needed the jury to feel certain that if succinylcholine had been found in Chelsea, then it had to have been placed there by an outside agency.

"Doctor, how do you make succinylcholine?"

"You react succinic acid with choline in a dry, water-free, chloroform solution."

"And that is what it takes to manufacture succinylcholine?" Sutton prodded.

"And heating," the doctor added.

"How much heating does it take?"

"Eighty degrees."

"Are you talking Celsius?"

"Of course," Holmstedt confirmed, affably. "Celsius was a Swede."

Because his jurors were Texan and not Swedish, Sutton needed the temperature spelled out in terms they could understand. "If we could convert eighty degrees Celsius to Mr. Fahrenheit's figure, what would we come up with?"

"I don't know. I refuse. Every civilized country in the world has converted to Celsius, a much more rational system."

Unwilling to debate the relative merits of Celsius versus Fahrenheit, he resignedly let the point pass; he would ask a different witness later. Sutton moved on to his crucial concluding question: "Doctor, do you have an opinion as to whether or not it is likely that succinylcholine could be formed postmortem in human tissue?"

"It is not known, however, I don't think it can."

Sutton's last witness for the day was Dr. Fredric Reiders, a small, round, balding man who habitually puffed on a Meerschaum pipe. Dr. Reiders, a native of Vienna, Austria, came to the United States as a teenager. After serving in World War II with the American forces, Reiders went on to study analytic chemistry and forensic toxicology, ultimately obtaining a doctorate degree in pharmacology.

Although Dr. Reiders was undisputably a brilliant toxicologist, he was only intermittently effective as a witness. Unlike the charismatic and always charming Dr. Holmstedt, Dr. Reiders betrayed a certain intellectual arrogance when he spoke, which delighted the defense and dismayed Ron Sutton.

Because the defense had, on several occasions, emphasized the impossibly small size of a nanogram, Sutton decided to give the jury another way to consider it. He began his examination of Dr. Reiders by asking him to describe how *large* a nanogram is. "It is one three-hundred-millionth of an ounce. Now that is normally thought of as a very small amount, but we measure such small quantities in the laboratory regularly for many, many things. Another way of thinking of a nanogram," Reiders suggested, "is by looking at how many molecules it takes to make one.

The number of molecules in one nanogram is about ten with fourteen zeros after it; so it is a very large number of molecules. And if you wanted to know how many electrons that is, then we would have to multiply *that* number by about 2,000. So size all depends on how you look at the thing.''

Sutton walked to the blackboard to write out for the jury the number of molecules Dr. Reiders had specified: 1,000,000,000,000,000. As he spun out the zeros, he smiled: ''Just tell me when to stop, Doctor.''

Brushing the chalk off his hands, Sutton drove home his point: ''Incidentally, Doctor, are you familiar with any substance that is lethal at one nanogram?''

''Many,'' Reiders confirmed. ''Tetanus toxin, for example. When you have tetanus, what makes you sick and kills you is the poison—the tetanus toxin. Diphtheria toxin also has a potential lethality in that amount. Some so-called bacterial toxins, and certain other toxins, are exquisitely toxic and are potentially lethal in nanogram quantities.''

Sutton and Dr. Reiders then launched into a lengthy discussion regarding just what the gas chromatograph–mass spectrometer test is, the procedure Dr. Reiders followed in the tests at issue, and the results he thereby obtained. Reiders explained that to find succinylcholine in tissue, one first takes a small quantity of tissue—in this case, ten grams—and in several steps, combines it with different chemical solutions. Each solution chemically bonds to specific matter in the tissue and allows that matter to be eliminated from the end product. After these initial ''washings,'' the technician is left with only ''quaternary ammonium compounds,'' including succinylcholine, if it is present, ''in a methyl-ethyl-ketone solution.'' This solution is then dried, and, by removing the methyl group—a carbon and three hydrogen atoms—a tertiary amine is formed, a compound that can be transformed into a gas. ''It is that tertiary amine,'' Dr. Reiders explained, ''that one can gas-chromatograph.''

Dr. Reiders compared the process of chromatography to dipping the edge of an ink-stained handkerchief into water. "The water is going to creep up into the handkerchief and is going to move the ink stain, spreading it." In the same way, in liquid chromatography, a liquid solution seeps into a spot of the test material, separating its components one from another. "Some of the components move faster, some of them move slower. What you end up with is a series of bands all the way up to where the solvent has stopped. Then you can use various means of visualizing the bands, of making the bands visible. Then you assess your results, and usually this is done by means of comparing your results to a standardized table." In gas chromatography, as opposed to liquid chromatography, the "ink spot" of the testable sample is injected into a heated hollow tube filled with a carrier gas that spreads the sample's molecules.

"The testable sample, in liquid form, is put in a syringe. The syringe goes through a septum at the top of the gas chromatograph, into a zone which is continuous with the rest of the column, but which is heated to a fairly high temperature. The heat causes the liquid to transform very quickly into a vapor. The column is filled with a carrier gas, usually nitrogen or helium, while the inside of the column is coated with a thick liquid medium. What happens is that this vaporized compound—the liquid you injected—is picked up by the carrier gas and carried through the column. As it is carried along through, the substances in it interact with the liquid coating on the wall, dissolving into the liquid, then, because of the heat, vaporizing back out into the carrier gas. Now, the different parts of the mixture dissolve to a different extent and at different speeds because they each have a different affinity to that liquid on the column's interior. The main thing that happens is that the different components, with their different affinities, will start separating from each other so that gradually the components start marching out at the far end of the tube in an orderly, separated fashion."

Sutton asked, "Is there a rate at which succinylcholine will traverse this tube?"

"Yes," said Reiders, definitively. "It moves along at a specific rate which is determined by the length of the tube, by the thickness of the liquid in it, by the kind of carrier gas used, by the rate at which the carrier gas is flowing, and by the temperature of the entire system."

The components that come out of the gas chromatograph then march into another instrument: the mass spectrometer. This second device cracks the molecule through chemical ionization, in the same way a jeweler cracks a fine stone along the line of cleavage: predictably. The mass spectrometer then takes the pieces; looks at them, and weighs each piece. Essentially, the mass spectrometer is a molecular weight scale.

"One of the beauties of this is that you can use, as an internal standard—a control—the same molecule that you're testing, but with a little bit different weight, obtained by replacing the hydrogen components of the molecule with deuterium, which makes the molecule heavier. The deuterium also makes it a little more fat soluble, so that you will actually get a certain amount of separation—usually a good deal—between the tested molecule and the control molecule in the gas chromatograph's retention times."

The explanation had been masterful, and Sutton was delighted. Not only had Reiders given the jury a palpable notion of how the almost magical processes of the gas chromatograph–mass spectrometer actually worked, he had established himself as a true expert—someone who could explain a complicated process in terms that a layman could grasp.

Sutton then led Dr. Reiders through the necessary details regarding Chelsea's exhumation, and asked the doctor to identify those portions of the body that were removed and personally taken by him to Sweden for testing: "A portion of the muscle from the front surface of each thigh, portions of kidneys, portions of liver, the gall bladder, and

the urinary bladder.'' Reiders had also taken a sample of
the embalming substance, a sample of the packing, and,
from Dr. Galbreath at Severance & Associates (the pathologist who had performed the original autopsy), samples from the formalin-preserved brain, kidney, liver,
lung, heart, and spleen.

Dr. Reiders then outlined the actual steps he took in
conducting the aforementioned tests, leading Sutton, at
long last, to the question everyone had been waiting for.

"Doctor, with regard to these samples, did you determine from any of them, after running your procedures,
that they reflected the presence of succinylcholine?''

Burt Carnes jumped up. "Excuse me, Doctor, before
you answer.'' He turned to Judge Carter. "For the record,
we would like to enter our objection, again, based on all
the reasons set forth in our motion and brief previously
filed with the court.''

Judge Carter nodded. "Objection is overruled.''

Sutton prompted his witness. "In your scientific opinion, Dr. Reiders.''

"Yes. In my opinion, I detected, identified, and measured succinylcholine in a number of the specimens I just
mentioned to you.''

With his bombshell for the day dropped, Sutton approached the bench. It was 4:45 P.M. After a short, whispered conference, Judge Carter wished everyone a pleasant
evening and recessed till morning.

On Wednesday, Sutton resumed his questioning of Dr.
Reiders. In greater detail, they examined the steps Reiders
took in testing Chelsea's tissues. The witness then
itemized the quantity of succinylcholine found in each
sample of tissue: 3.4 ng [nanograms] in the urinary bladder; 7.0 ng in the gall bladder; 3.6 ng in Dr. Galbreath's
formalin-fixed kidney sample; 0.3 ng in the kidney sample
taken at the exhumation; 1.3 ng in the formalin-fixed liver
sample; 0.8 ng in the liver sample taken at the exhumation; 1.8 ng in the left thigh muscle; and 6.7 ng in the right

thigh muscle. Dr. Reiders found no indication of succinylcholine in the brain or lung tissues.

After the morning break, and before the defense had its
chance to cross-examine Dr. Reiders, the prosecution requested permission from the court to examine another witness out of order. Ron Williamson, a pharmacist at Sid
Peterson's pharmacy, was feeling ill, and wanted to go
home.

Tactically, Williamson's illness was a lucky break for
Sutton. Immediately after Reiders's testimony, which had
indicated that there was succinylcholine in Chelsea Mc-
Clellan's tissues, the jury learned through two receipts,
identified by Williamson, that succinylcholine had been
purchased by Holland's Clinic on two separate occasions.
Clearly, the defendant had had access to the alleged
murder weapon.

The court excused Mr. Williamson and Dr. Reiders was
brought back in for Brookshire's cross-examination.
Again, the defense attorney's purpose was to expose any
possible weak links leading to Dr. Reiders's conclusions.

Brookshire pointed to the unprecedented nature of Dr.
Reiders's claimed results. Together the lawyer and witness
thoroughly reviewed all prior published articles on the
identification of succinylcholine and any prior tests conducted personally by Dr. Reiders. Nowhere had anyone
ever found succinylcholine in amounts smaller than 100
nanograms.

"This is the first time, then," Brookshire eventually
pinned the doctor down, "that you, or anyone, have used
the gas chromatograph on human tissues at these very low
levels?"

"Successfully, yes," Reiders admitted, "unsuc-
cessfully, at other times."

Brookshire next returned to the same line of questioning
he had pursued the day before with Dr. Holmstedt. "As I
understand your testimony, Doctor, even after the embalming process there is a great deal of, if you will, 'ac-

tivation' in the body tissues. Chemical activity continues, does it not, because chemicals are present.''

"Yes, sir," Dr. Reiders agreed. "And also, you do get microorganisms in, which are other living organisms.''

"Yes. So is it not possible, sir," Brookshire continued, "under some set of circumstances in the human body, under a given set of conditions, that the elements of succinic acid and choline—naturally present in the tissues—could reconstitute into the artificial product succinylcholine, at very low levels?''

"The probability cannot be denied," Reiders conceded, quickly adding: "The probability is extremely remote, however, and in my opinion, will not occur.''

Confident that the doctor could not document his off-the-cuff opinion, Brookshire pressed the point. "Have you done research into this area?''

Reiders was unwilling to be bullied. "Yes, sir, in a negative sense. All the work that I have done with clean, controlled tissues has never resulted in my detecting any amount of succinylcholine, and all of the work that I have ever reviewed that deals with the analysis of blank tissues of any sort, animal or human, did not reveal the presence of any succinylcholine, even though there is always choline and succinic acid present.''

Brookshire already regretted pushing this line of questioning, but felt compelled to carry it one step further. "Your research will not *preclude* this possibility, will it?''

"Nothing precludes it," Reiders responded, "but it makes it extremely unlikely.''

Brookshire turned his attention to the testing procedure and elicited the doctor's admission that in the testing Reiders was not actually looking for the molecule of succinylcholine itself, but only molecular pieces identified by their weight. "So," Brookshire summarized, "in this particular test, you're looking for three separate fragments of succinylcholine.''

"Right, sir," confirmed the doctor. "The fragments are

markers of the identity of what I am seeking, succinylcholine, and they are known markers. These markers, combined with other data from the testing procedure, enable me to formulate the reasonably certain opinion that, indeed, I've got succinylcholine.''

"Is there anything else that has the molecular weight of 58?" Brookshire asked, referring to the identifying weight Reiders gave for one of the three markers he had been referring to.

"Yes."

"Is there anything else that has the molecular weight of 71?" referring to the second marker of succinylcholine.

"I am sure there is."

"What about the molecular weight of 190?"—the weight of the third fragment.

"Many fluid things."

"So, many possible substances have these same molecular weights of 58, 71, and 190. Tell me, Doctor, when you've found fragments of these weights, what makes you think you've got succinylcholine? How are you able to eliminate all of the other possibilities?"

"You can never eliminate *all* of the possibilities," Reiders replied. "Scientists don't eliminate all of the possibilities any more than lawyers or doctors."

"Would it be fair to say, then," Brookshire continued, finally scoring a point, "that we are dealing with only a probability?"

"All of life is a probability," Reiders acknowledged, "but the probability is so high—" he paused a moment, then continued, "—is sufficiently high, in this case, that it leads me to the reasonably certain opinion that this is succinylcholine. And that is not just based," he added, "on these three numbers, but on the retention times, on the way they were extracted, on the way the specimens were prepared, and on the way the analysis behaved relative to an added known internal standard, the deuterated succinylcholine. In other words, I do not doubt that this is succinylcholine.''

Brookshire went on to ask Dr. Reiders why they did not find succinylcholine in either the lungs or the heart tissues, but never seemed to obtain any advantage from the line of questioning. He passed the witness at the afternoon break.

When court resumed at 3:10 P.M., Ron Sutton was determined to lay to rest, once and for all, Brookshire's misleading theories about the possibility of a dead body manufacturing succinylcholine.

"How does one make succinylcholine, Doctor Reiders?"

"You take succinic acid and choline, and you put these into chloroform—which is free of water—in an atmosphere of nitrogen that is very dry, and heat it to about 80 degrees centigrade for several hours, and then you would put in some dry hydrogen chloride gas to precipitate out succinylcholine chloride."

"Eighty degrees centigrade, Doctor, approximately what Fahrenheit range is that?"

"That is about 190 degrees Fahrenheit."

"190 degrees," Sutton repeated. "That's pretty hot, isn't it? For what period of time?"

"I think it is several hours that is required."

"Doctor, you testified earlier that you were present at the exhumation of Chelsea McClellan, did you not?"

"Yes, sir."

"Did you see anything upon her body or inside her casket that would indicate it had obtained a 190-degree temperature for several hours?"

"No. That would've cooked it."

Sutton could tell by the jurors' faces that he had won the point—it was virtually impossible for Chelsea's body to have spontaneously generated the trace amounts of succinylcholine that Reiders had found in the tissue samples. Sutton thanked Dr. Reiders, then Rothe stood to call the prosecution's last witness of the day.

"The state calls Dr. Kathleen Kagan-Hallet."

Both a pediatric- and neuropathologist, Dr. Kagan-Hal-

let was one of perhaps only 250 specialists of that kind in
the country at the time. She was the doctor who had performed the pathological examination of the brain tissue
samples from Chelsea McClellan. Because she had rendered the original verdict of atypical SIDS and then
changed her verdict, her credibility was in question. The
first point Rothe tried to establish, therefore, was the significance of the misleading information Kagan-Hallet had
received concerning Chelsea's medical history.

"Doctor, as a general proposition, is the history given
to a pathologist important in determining the cause of
death?"

"Yes, very important. You can be very easily misled by
either an erroneous or incomplete history to form the
wrong conclusions about the way an individual died or the
types of lesions or abnormalities that you're looking at
through the microscope."

"Is that something like the expression you hear people
use these days about computers, that the information that
comes out of a computer is only as good as the information that goes in?"

"Absolutely."

Rothe had raised the question—what had Kagan-Hallet
been told about Chelsea McClellan—but rather than pursue this point, Rothe chose to backtrack a bit first. He first
spent some time acquainting the jury with the somewhat
macabre procedures involved in a brain autopsy, further
engaging their sympathy and engendering an emotional reaction that would work to the state's advantage. He then
turned the discussion to the results of Kagan-Hallet's examination of Chelsea's brain tissue, focusing initially not
on what the doctor found, but on what she had *not* found.
As Rothe ticked off a series of complicated medical terms
with practiced ease, the neuropathologist confirmed that
she had found no signs of germinal mantel hemorrhage,
subarachnoid hemorrhage, hygroma, infarcts, or peri-
ventricular leukomalacic lesions, and that the cerebral ventricles were of normal size and the brain itself was

normally myelinated. Kagan-Hallet, at Rothe's prompting, explained that she had looked for those seven specific abnormalities because each was consistent with the history that had been given to her concerning Chelsea's prematurity, her hyaline membrane disease, the reported incidents of hypoxia, and her subsequent seizure disorders and respiratory arrests. The implication was clear—the condition of Chelsea's brain at death was not what Kagan-Hallet expected based upon Chelsea's reported medical history.

The only abnormality Kagan-Hallet *did* find was diffuse gliosis (or scattered scarring) in Chelsea's brain stem and cervical cord (the uppermost part of her spinal cord). The doctor concluded, "So, from the history that had been given me, and from my findings, I felt the cause of death was consistent with Sudden Infant Death Syndrome, aborted."

This diagnosis, Kagan-Hallet explained, refers to "a clinical and pathological condition by which children who are premature have repeated episodes where they stop breathing, but the parents are able to revive them, usually by shaking them. Children like that occasionally go ahead and die, and when they do, the findings in their bodies, particularly their brains, reflect damage from the multiple episodes of breathlessness. And the history I received made it sound like this might be the likely thing in Chelsea's case."

Now Rothe began the tricky process of justifying Kagan-Hallet's change in her death verdict by filling in the facts that were not available to the doctor when she entered her original verdict. "Would it not have been extremely important for you to know whether Chelsea McClellan received any emergency drugs prior to her death?"

"Yes, it would have been very important."

"Were you aware that Chelsea McClellan had, in August, been hospitalized for a period of time?"

"I was unaware of that. Knowing that hospitalization records existed and that people had observed her during the time she was in the hospital and that other laboratory studies had been done would have given me more of an idea what actual process was going on."

"Do you now know that the child went to Sid Peterson Hospital, Code Blue, and was treated and resuscitated?"

"Yes, I now know that."

"Are you now aware that a second trip in the ambulance came after that, at which time the child died?"

"Yes, I am aware of that now."

"Are the two episodes that you are now aware of, and the circumstances under which they came about, inconsistent with SIDS as the cause of death?"

"Yes, they are."

"I will ask you now, Dr. Kagan-Hallet, if, knowing what you now know—the facts you have learned over a period of months, and the studies you have done during that time—do all of these things change your conclusions as to Chelsea McClellan's cause of death?"

"Yes."

Finally Rothe reached the question the jury had been anticipating. "I will ask you now, Doctor, what is your opinion as to the cause of death of Chelsea McClellan?"

Dr. Kagan-Hallet turned to address the jury with as much authority as she could manage. "Well, in my opinion, the cause of death is respiratory arrest which then led to cardiac arrest and the death of the child due to injection of succinylcholine."

"Thank you, Doctor. Pass the witness."

Rothe had finished his examination at just after 4:00—a little too early. This day, for a change, the defense would have the last word.

Brookshire stood.

When an attorney faces a hostile witness (a witness testifying for the other side), he has a choice as to how he will approach the questioning. He can either try to put the witness at ease and solicit that witness's cooperation, or he can go on the attack. The choice the attorney makes partially depends upon the kind of information he wants. Because Brookshire had decided to try to provoke Kagan-Hallet into defending her original diagnosis of SIDS, he adopted an aggressive manner.

"Doctor, you have, have you not, gone over the various findings which culminated in your initial diagnosis of SIDS as the cause of death."

"Yes."

"Apparently, you were very positive of this diagnosis when you made it."

"Yes."

"You also attached an article proving that gliosis, such as you found, can and does cause death."

"It is associated with SIDS."

"So you had no doubt at that time?"

"That is right."

Brookshire now unsheathed his best weapon, his primary source of provocation: "Last week," he told the doctor, "Dr. DiMaio took you to task for finding this a SIDS death. It was his position that anyone is a *fool* for listing SIDS as the cause of death for a child over ten months of age."

Rothe popped up instantly. "Excuse me. I will object to Mr. Brookshire's remark. I don't believe Dr. DiMaio called anyone a fool, Your Honor."

"Objection sustained."

The lawyer persisted. "How do you respond to that opinion of Dr. DiMaio's?" Brookshire knew that every justification Kagan-Hallett now offered for originally reaching her "foolish" verdict of SIDS would enhance the defense's own theory that Chelsea McClellan might very well have died of natural causes.

"Well, I think that in the pediatric pathology literature," Kagan-Hallet began, "there is no absolute end or final time for SIDS, you know, it doesn't say you *can't* have SIDS if somebody's thirteen months old, or something like that. In fact, they stress that if someone is significantly premature, for example, they may have catching up to do, and they may get their SIDS attacks later than normal.''

"As I understand it," Brookshire encouraged her, "you are saying that contrary to Dr. DiMaio's opinion, SIDS deaths *do* occur, even up to age fifteen months."

"Surely."

"Are there any studies that substantiate that?"

"There is a textbook by Warren Gunteroth that came out last year, called *Crib Death (Sudden Infant Death Syndrome)*, and it makes these same observations. There are multiple articles by Maria Valdez-Dapeña that also support this."

Brookshire had what he wanted; not only did Kagan-Hallet disagree with DiMaio's absolute conviction that SIDS did not occur after one year of age, but two noted authorities and authors also disagreed. Brookshire had established that it was *possible* that Chelsea died of SIDS.

The defense lawyer had just two other points he wanted to establish before day's end. First, he discussed with the pathologist the kind of scarring Chelsea had suffered from—fibrulary gliosis in the brain stem or medulla oblongata. "What body functions does the medulla control, Doctor?''

"The medulla controls breathing, temperature regulation, blood-pressure regulation, and other, what we call autonomic functions—things that you don't have to think about."

"Heartbeat, and things like that?"

"Yes. Heartbeat."

"If there is scarring in that area, what could happen as far as your autonomic functions?"

"One of the things that could happen," Kagan-Hallet acknowledged, "is if someone stopped breathing, it might be difficult to start breathing again. Also, people might have irregularities in heartbeat, or little runs of abnormalities."

"Could the heart actually stop beating, or would it just slow down or speed up?"

"Potentially, I imagine, it could stop beating. It could stop."

Brookshire left the conclusion unstated—Chelsea's cardiac and respiratory arrest *might* have been caused by the gliosis. He merely nodded and moved on to his last major point of the day. He needed to establish that the scarring, which he was contending was a possible cause of Chelsea's death, could not be attributed to Genene's agency. "Doctor, could you tell how old those scars were?"

"No. Once they form, they could be three years or thirty. It doesn't matter."

"Well, let me ask you this: Were they a week to two weeks old?"

"No. You don't get scarring until— It takes at least three weeks to get scarring like that, of any kind, and so it is, you know, older than that, but how much older is hard to say."

Brookshire almost but did not quite score his point. Kagan-Hallett's answer established that although Chelsea's final respiratory arrest, on September 17, did not cause the scarring in her brain, it was possible that her first arrest on August 24 might have been the cause. If Genene had provoked that first arrest, then she may have created the very weakness—the gliosis—to which the defense attributed Chelsea's death. Yet Brookshire had given the jurors another basis for doubt.

The next morning, Thursday, January 26, Brookshire resumed his questioning of Dr. Kagan-Hallet. His goal: to illustrate for the jury that the pathologist had not changed her verdict from SIDS to murder because (as Sutton had insinuated) she had received any significant additional information regarding Chelsea's history. To this end, Brookshire went through Chelsea's entire medical history with Kagan-Hallet, asking her to identify any information she did not know at the time of her original verdict. The attorney repeatedly suggested the small amount of additional information thereby revealed was not sufficient to justify Kagan-Hallet's change in her verdict. Brookshire was contending that the pathologist changed her verdict *only* because Sutton had informed her Chelsea had been injected with succinylcholine, not because the SIDS verdict was in any way inconsistent with Chelsea's condition.

As Kagan-Hallet concluded her summary of the additional information, she unintentionally confirmed Brookshire's contention. "Finally," she testified, "I didn't know that Chelsea was at the doctor's on August 24 because of an upper respiratory tract infection, that she actually wasn't terribly ill, and that the convulsion did not occur as a spontaneous event."

"When you say this did not occur as a spontaneous event, Doctor, what do you mean?"

"I mean that the child was seen by a physician in an office and possibly given an injection, and the convulsion followed that."

Brookshire leaned across the podium, his voice patient. "Are you aware of any records, *anywhere,* which would suggest that Chelsea was injected with a substance which would cause a convulsion?"

The doctor acknowledged she was not. Delighted, Brookshire pointed out to the jury that Kagan-Hallet had to be basing her conclusion on something someone had *told* her, not, as she had earlier claimed, on additions to Chelsea's medical history.

Aware, now, of Brookshire's strategy, Kagan-Hallet objected, "Well, I think that the second admission to the Clinic was more telling, really, than the first."

"All right," said Brookshire, willing to accept that partial capitulation, "so up until the August 24 episode in Dr. Holland's office, your findings for the initial autopsy are still intact. You have nothing upon which to base a change in your verdict."

"That is right," Kagan-Hallet conceded.

"Then, let's take a closer look at the September 17 episode." Brookshire was reasonably pleased with his progress, for now the question had narrowed considerably: had Kagan-Hallet actually learned anything from the events of September 17 that could have caused her to alter her verdict of death? Again Brookshire began a point-by-point analysis of Chelsea's history. He was gratified and surprised to discover that the information Kagan-Hallet had about these events was not particularly accurate. She clearly had been laboring under certain misconceptions when she changed the verdict.

"You had access to the records, did you not, Doctor, reporting what happened on that trip?"

"Only in just descriptive detail. What exactly transpired, or whether she got cardio-aversion, or whatever, I don't know those things, no."

"Do you know what the cause of death was? The immediate cause of death?"

"The immediate cause of death," she responded, "was, I imagine, respiratory arrest. I assume it was. There are too many possibilities when you really get down to it."

"Are you saying then, that you don't really know what the cause of death was?"

Kagan-Hallet, realizing too late that she may have made some kind of tactical error, tried to sidestep, "I hate to get started on this kind of philosophical idea about what a *cause* of death is, and I think pinpointing the specific cause probably isn't possible in most cases, except gunshot wounds or poisonings, or something like that, but exactly why somebody who is ill expires when they do, and what they exactly expire of, specifically, is often kind of up for grabs. It is really kind of hard to say in some cases."

Satisfied with that ambiguous response and optimistic that the jury could see that the alleged changes in Chelsea's reported medical history really were not what had caused the doctor to change her death verdict, Brookshire pressed on. "Doctor, you have indicated that you received some information as to an injection of succinylcholine. Where did you gain that information?"

"The information was given to me by Mr. Sutton, that the child may have been injected with succinylcholine."

"And when did you gain that information?"

"In January of 1983."

"So," said Brookshire, adopting an accusatory tone, "you based a change in the clinical cause of death on something that Mr. Sutton *told* you?"

"Although the tests had been run by that time, I am sure."

"Doctor, I think you are assuming something. I think the evidence will show that the tests had *not* been run."

"Not in January," she conceded, "perhaps not."

"So, again, you changed your clinical cause of death based solely on what Mr. Sutton told you."

Kagan-Hallet would not give in. "I changed my clinical cause of death to not being Sudden Infant Death Syndrome, aborted," she insisted, "based on the additional history, yes."

"Tell me again, Doctor," Brookshire pursued her doggedly, "what was the cause of Chelsea's death?"

"My opinion is that the child died as the result of an injection of succinylcholine and had respiratory arrest leading to cardiac arrest because of the injection."

Brookshire nodded patiently. He knew, as Kagan-Hallet obviously did not, that Chelsea's initial respiratory arrest had preceded her cardiac arrest by more than *two hours*.

"Doctor, how did you become aware that Chelsea suffered a cardiac arrest?"

"I was given that information by Mr. Sutton."

Again the defense attorney nodded. "Are you aware, Doctor, of what precipitated the cardiac arrest?"

"No, I am not."

"Well, how is it possible, Doctor, if you don't know what precipitated this cardiac arrest, that you can make a diagnosis, as you have, that cardiac arrest was brought on by a respiratory arrest?"

"Because that is the usual modus of death in most people. You really don't have to—" the doctor faltered, at a loss. "You know, I think that probably everybody in this room will ultimately die from one of those two things: a cardiac arrest or a respiratory arrest. I think that's a safe statement."

"But how could a respiratory arrest occur if the patient was being properly bagged?" Brookshire was insistent. "What if the child were breathing on her own? Would that change your diagnosis at all?"

"It is hard to say, since I don't know if that were true or not."

"Well, assume for a moment it was true." (As, in fact, it was.)

"Well, at one point, she must not have, because she died."

"If she continued to breathe on her own," Brookshire repeated, "what would cause the cardiac arrest?"

"I don't know if I could even answer that because I don't know when the cardiac arrest occurred, or whatever. Since this wasn't witnessed, she must have—she *could* have had a respiratory arrest, probably did."

"You are making your diagnosis in a vacuum, Doctor," the lawyer observed. "You don't know if anyone was present, and you don't know what preceded the death."

"But the patient wasn't breathing on her own, was she?"

"Well, Doctor, how do you know that if you haven't *talked* to anybody?"

"Well," she said, confused, "I don't know if she was or wasn't."

Brookshire was completely satisfied. That was exactly the answer he had wanted. The witness—a young doctor who had never before testified in court—was tiring after more than two hours on the stand. Brookshire pressed her further. Under his skillful prompting, Kagan-Hallet admitted that with the kind of brain damage Chelsea had, other events, including a seizure, could cause a respiratory arrest. She also admitted that if an individual resumed breathing after a respiratory arrest and then stopped breathing again—as was the case with Chelsea—succinylcholine is not indicated. Finally, she admitted that the cause of death *might* have been due to succinylcholine, but it was also possible it *might not* have been.

When Brookshire finished his grueling cross-examination, Rothe rose to undertake the difficult task of rehabilitating Kagan-Hallet's credibility. First, in response to Brookshire's implication that Kagan-Hallet improperly revised her death verdict based upon Sutton's report that Chelsea had been injected with succinylcholine, Rothe established that the doctor's second death verdict was based on succinylcholine *as a hypothetical cause*. Second, Rothe reminded the jury that succinylcholine was in fact subsequently confirmed by means of Reiders's chemical assays—and at that point was no longer merely hypothetical. Third, Rothe built upon Brookshire's contention that Chelsea's resumption of breathing after her respiratory arrest did not indicate succinylcholine by making it clear that the recovery *also* contradicted a SIDS verdict.

Before Rothe allowed the doctor to step down, he had her reaffirm that in her opinion, whether the immediate precipitating event was a respiratory arrest or a cardiac arrest, the cause of death was an injection of succinylcholine. He also had her confirm that succinylcholine can sometimes stop the heart "if coupled with, perhaps, a problem of gliosis or a sensitive neural system." Finally, he called the jury's attention to a fact that Brookshire himself helped establish: in as little as three to three and one-half weeks, scarring will form in the medulla as a result of hypoxic episodes such as those caused by respiratory arrest.

Rothe gave the jury an alternative to the defense's theory that Chelsea's prematurity had caused a scarring in her brain that eventually resulted in seizures, respiratory failures, and death. It was also possible, Rothe made clear, that this allegedly deadly scarring had been caused by an hypoxic episode induced by an injection of succinylcholine on August 24.

*   *   *

The state's next witness was Dr. Sheila Schwartzman, a stately woman with impressive credentials, then director of cardiovascular anesthesiology at the University of Texas in San Antonio. "I called her to the stand to give just one particularly damning piece of evidence," Sutton recalls, "but I held off on that." It was still an hour before lunch break. Sutton wanted to drop this bomb right before the recess. Warming up slowly, he killed some time asking Dr. Schwartzman to describe for the jury the effects of succinylcholine.

"Shortly after its administration," she reported, "you may see generalized body movement, and the eyes moving from side to side. The eyelids may close, because all muscles are paralyzed, including the muscles of the eye, and the eye may be fixed. You may see some nystagmus, there could be some muscle twitching, or initial reflexing. This is usually seen if you give succinylcholine alone. You may not see it if another drug is given beforehand."

"Upon injection of succinylcholine," Sutton asked, watching the clock hands creep toward noon, "let's say intramuscular in sufficient dosage, how long would you normally expect the onslaught of symptoms to be, from the first visual symptom to complete flaccid muscle relaxation?"

"It may take a minute, maybe a minute and one-half in a healthy child."

For forty-five minutes, Sutton built upon the jury's knowledge of succinylcholine, helping them fit Chelsea's symptoms into the pattern of the drug's effects. When only minutes remained before noon, Sutton finally revealed the purpose of the doctor's presence. "Doctor, have you, during your teaching at the University of Texas medical school, ever had occasion to lecture to nurses?"

"Yes, sir."

"Did you have an occasion to give a lecture to the Pedi-ICU?"

"Yes, I did."

"What was the topic of that lecture?"

"Drugs used in pediatric anesthesia."

"Did that include, among other things, the use of the drug succinylcholine?"

"Yes, it did."

"Did you in your lecture also discuss the use of the drug atropine?"

"Yes, I did."

"Dr. Schwartzman, was Genene Jones present during that lecture?"

"Yes, she was."

"And who requested that you give this lecture to this particular nursing group?" Sutton turned to watch the jury's response to Dr. Schwartzman's answer.

"Genene Jones did." All eyes darted to the defendant, who glared fiercely at the doctor. Sutton nodded, smiled inwardly, and returned to his seat.

Since it was just a few minutes before noon, Judge Carter broke in. "Court will adjourn and reconvene at 1:30."

After the lunch break, Sutton continued his examination of Schwartzman, making one more point for later use before turning her over to the defense. "Is there any conjunctive use of the drugs atropine and succinylcholine?"

"One of the side effects of succinylcholine is that it may cause slowing of the heart rate, or bradycardia, particularly in children. So, many anesthesiologists will give a dose of atropine, which is a stimulant, prior to the use of succinylcholine to prevent the slowing of the heart."

Burt Carnes conducted the doctor's cross-examination, taking Schwartzman through a long, detailed analysis of the effects of succinylcholine, both as it is injected intramuscularly and intravascularly. The lawyer and doctor discussed the relative onset of symptoms (thirty seconds to two minutes), the length of time paralysis lasts (between five and ten minutes), and the movements a person might display coming out from under the effects of the drug (gross motor movements).

"And," Carnes clarified, "those movements would occur within the ten-minute period during which they are recovering from the injection, would they not, Doctor?"

"Yes, they would."

"What would the effects be if a larger-than-normal dosage were administered?"

"There are no different effects. Most patients will react in exactly the same way if you give them an extra amount."

"One final question, Doctor. You testified that Genene approached you about this lecture." Carnes eyed the jury, making sure they were listening. "Didn't she ask about the possibility of giving a lecture on pediatric anesthesia drugs *in general*?"

"Yes, sir."

"Pass the witness."

The state called Mary Mahoney, a dark-haired young woman in her late twenties who earned her living as a temporary nurse. When Genene was hospitalized for bleeding ulcers, from September 13 through September 16, 1982, Mary had filled in for her at the Clinic. She had been subpoenaed to tell the jury about an inventory she had conducted during that time.

Mary proved to be an excellent witness, testifying plainly, precisely, and firmly that she went through the entire office checking for supplies, including each of the treatment rooms, where she went through all the cabinets and all the drawers in the examining tables. Though the significance of her testimony was not yet clear, she stated unshakably that she had found no medications in any of the examination tables' drawers.

Shortly before 3:00 that afternoon, the state called Dr. Kathleen Mary Holland to the stand.

"Of course I was nervous," Kathleen recalls. "I had never been in a court before, except for my divorce, and

that's just, you know, a formality. Plus, I knew I was
supposed to appear to be *not* nervous—I was concerned
about appearing credible, because of what Ron Sutton and
Nick Rothe had said. So, I felt tense and was trying hard
to be natural, but I was drained before I even got started. I
didn't know quite what to expect.

"The first day, Ron Sutton tried to sneak me into the
courthouse, but the press spotted us and swarmed around,
asking questions. And that's a fairly frightening experience. You get this crazy feeling you're going to be
crushed. It's completely unreal.

"I remember one of the cameramen positioned himself
right in front of me, backing up with his TV camera
pointed at me. The path to the courthouse doors jogs
around this little medallion of shrubbery, but he didn't see
it because he was backing up. So all of a sudden he just
flops over backward into the little hedge. Right out of
frame—just gone. And I remember Sutton and I just kept
walking, trying not to smile because we didn't want to be
plastered all over the papers and the ten o'clock news with
great big grins on our faces."

Sutton warmed Kathleen up slowly. They began by discussing Kathleen's history, and because he knew the issue
would come up, the reason she happened to be living with
Genene at the Nixon Lane house. In just a few minutes,
the jurors were introduced to a reasonable, apparently normal woman, who—due to her obvious intelligence and her
training as a doctor—remembered events in remarkable
detail. Sutton then brought out a diagram of the Clinic's
floor plan and asked Kathleen to sketch in and describe the
contents of each room, giving the jury a concrete image of
the setting for a good portion of the trial's events.

For the first time, it seemed, Genene took real note of
the proceedings. Patty Jones, Brookshire's assistant, recalls that "Genene had told us all along that 'Kathy will
never say anything to hurt me. Kathy will never hurt
me.'"

Twenty minutes into Kathleen's testimony, Sutton introduced the first topic of real interest. He asked the doctor to identify a receipt for some of the medications that were part of the Clinic's initial inventory.

"Does this receipt bear anyone's name?"

"In the lower left-hand corner," Kathleen replied, "underscored with 'Customer Signature,' it bears the name 'G. Jones.'"

"Dr. Holland, would you please read out to the jury what drugs are reflected on that receipt."

"Five Chloromycetin ampules, 1 gram; three calcium gluconate inject; two Lanoxin, 2 milliliter inject; one 10-cc succinylcholine; 1 milliliter Neo-Synephrine, 1 percent; two aminophylline, 250 grams."

Sutton asked Kathleen why she had such a dangerous drug in her clinic. The doctor explained that she had been advised to stock it to be prepared for the slight possibility that she might have to intubate, on an emergency basis, a large, struggling child.

Sutton nodded to emphasize the reasonableness of that response, before asking Assistant DA Scott Monroe to add another entry to the big calendar, on August 18: 10 cc succinylcholine purchased.

Sutton then directed Kathleen's attention to August 24, 1982, and together they slowly reconstructed the events of that day. As she would throughout the trial, Kathleen demonstrated a truly uncanny memory, even recalling the substance of entire conversations. Sutton worried that the specificity of Kathleen's testimony might taint her credibility, but the details she offered were always sufficiently striking to be memorable, and she bore herself with such quiet dignity that her sincerity was unmistakable.

When Kathleen finished her account of Chelsea's subsequent ten-day stay in Sid Peterson's for observation and analysis, Sutton brought out a second invoice for the purchase of pharmaceuticals, dated September 7, 1982.

"Are you familiar with this, Dr. Holland?"

"Yes, this is a carbon copy of an invoice for which I have the original."

"And it is an invoice for what, Dr. Holland?"

"For succinylcholine, 20 milligrams per cc, 10 milli-liters. And atropine, 0.01 milligrams per milliliter."

"Did you authorize that order?"

"I recall indirectly authorizing the succinylcholine. At some point, approximately a week or so after we opened the office, Genene came to me and said, 'Such-and-such medication is missing.' And I was on the way out of the office as I recall, on the way to the hospital, and couldn't take the time to stop so I told her, 'Look for it. Look everywhere, in all the cabinets, and if you don't find it, log it as missing.' Before I walked out the door, she said, 'Wait a minute, do you want me to order a replacement?' and I said, 'Yes, go ahead, since we don't have any.'"

Again Sutton asked Monroe to log the purchase on the September calendar. Sutton then took Kathleen through what she recalled of the day Chelsea died. At the end of their discussion of the events at the Clinic, Sutton asked: "On that day, did Chelsea have any form of bradycardia, as she had on the twenty-fourth?"

"Yes, she did. And on the second occasion, it was more marked than on the first occasion."

"More marked?"

"Going slower. Her heart rate was getting slower than it had the first time this happened." Sutton nodded grimly, checking the jurors' responses. He hoped they were getting the idea that the little girl was weaker because of the previous assaults.

The lawyer pulled out Chelsea's medical records and directed Kathleen's attention to the temperature recorded: 100.6. "Doctor, was that the report given to you by Genene Jones when she orally told you what Chelsea's temperature was?"

"No. She told me the child was afebrile [without fever], that the temperature 'was only 100.'"

"Is there a significant difference between 100 and 100.6?"

"Yes. In a child, 100.4 is usually considered to be the

line of fever. Above that and you're febrile; below and you're afebrile. A temperature of 100.6 would make any pediatrician hesitate to give an immunization."

"If you had known that Chelsea had a 100.6 temperature, would you have directed Genene Jones to immunize her?"

"No."

"Why, Doctor?"

"I don't give immunizations to a child whose temperature is clearly within the fever zone."

Sutton and the doctor then focused on other notations Genene had made in Chelsea's chart that conflicted with Kathleen's memory of the events of September 17, ending with the trip to the hospital and the subsequent events in Comfort. He asked her if she had made any arrangements for an autopsy. Kathleen revealed that she had attempted to enlist the help of the Bexar County medical examiner's office in charge of investigating all suspicious deaths. "I described the full sequence of what happened to the best of my knowledge, including her early history as a neonate, her previous seizure in the office, the question of some dusky spells (whether they were breath-holding spells or not, I didn't know), as well as the events of that day, and the results of all the tests that I had run in the hospital, including her EEG. The physician I talked with told me, 'Gee, this is a very interesting case, but I don't think it's an ME's case.' And that's why I turned her over to Severance & Associates Laboratories. I wanted somebody to do a neuropathological examination."

"Okay, let's go down to September 20. On that morning, Doctor, did you have an occasion to be in the office?"

"Yes."

"Was Nurse Jones present that morning?"

"Yes."

"Do you recall any discussion with Nurse Jones as to the purchase of drugs or medications or supplies?"

"Yes. I recall that she came into my office and told me

that the crash room's medications needed to be restocked because of the emergencies we'd had. Several medications were mentioned. She said, 'We need more of this and this and this.'"

Sutton handed the doctor yet another receipt for a purchase of drugs. "The drug at the top of that list, Doctor, is what?"

"Succinylcholine."

"Succinylcholine? Did you authorize the purchase of another vial of succinylcholine?"

"No."

"Was your Clinic open that afternoon, Dr. Holland?"

"No. We closed that afternoon so that we could attend Chelsea's funeral."

"You attended Chelsea's funeral on the afternoon of the twentieth?" Sutton let a note of incredulity enter his voice.

"Yes."

"And on the morning of the twentieth, another bottle of succinylcholine was purchased?"

"Yes."

Sutton walked to the calendar and this time he personally wrote, in large red letters in the September 20 space: "10 cc's of succinylcholine." It was now nearing 5:00 P.M., and Sutton was determined to end the day dramatically. Quickly, he took Kathleen through the Friday, September 24, meeting before the Sid Peterson executive committee, the conversations she had had with Genene that weekend concerning the vial of succinylcholine, and her subsequent discovery of the vial with the puncture marks on Monday the twenty-seventh, leading finally to her confrontation with Genene.

"I asked her to look at the two vials," Kathleen remembered, "and her response was, 'Yeah?' I said, 'Genene, how did the holes get there?' She said, 'I don't know, there were a lot of people in that room.'"

"What was her emotional state?" asked Sutton.

"Kind of coolly defensive," replied Kathleen. "And I said, 'Genene, how am I going to explain these holes?'"

"And what was her response?"

"'I think we should just throw it out, and tell them we lost it.'"

Addressing the jury, Sutton repeated the key phrase: "Just throw it out."

Kathleen confirmed, "Just throw it out."

"Court was adjourned," the defense team's Patty Jones recalls, "and Genene was devastated. She was crying and carrying on, and I could hardly get her out of the courtroom. At first she refused to leave the courtroom at all, but I got her pulled together enough such that we could get out and face the cameras. On the way out, we were swarmed by newsmen, and I nearly had to drag her to the sheriff's car. She really hurt that day.

"At the office, we decided I ought to go down and talk with her that night. When they brought her to the tank, I don't think I've ever seen a more broken person. She wasn't angry, just extremely hurt. I think that may have been the first time she realized the prosecution was playing for keeps, and that this was not some game or some starring role for her. Reality hit home and I saw her as a vulnerable, frightened child. It was an awakening for me, too."

The next morning, Friday, January 27, the jury waited downstairs as the court and attorneys took care of technical matters related to the preservation of certain issues for appeal. At noon, before lunch, the jury was brought in to hear Sutton resume his direct examination of his star witness, Kathleen Holland.

The tone of Kathleen's testimony was now subtly different. The prior evening, Sutton and Rothe had given the doctor some gentle coaching. "You're doing a great job, Kathy, very clear, very sincere, very precise. But you're exerting so much control over what you're saying that you seem kind of like a machine with no emotions. You must be *feeling* something about what you're saying. Share it with the jury. Let them experience it with you.''

Kathleen recalls that when Sutton asked her to tell the jury what had transpired the day she called Sally to the Clinic to discuss the vial of succinylcholine, she did her best to do what Sutton had asked her to do the night before.

"I tried to remember not just what happened when, but how I felt that day—the confusion, the fear. It wasn't—it wasn't easy."

Kathleen spoke in long monologues, generally unimpeded by Sutton. Her normally strong, low voice grew softer and higher in pitch as she told the jury of Sally's account of her actions during Misty's emergency and how both Sally and Genene had denied any knowledge about the holes in the vial.

Kathleen then testified about her confrontation with Genene after Sally's departure. "At that point, I said, 'How am I going to explain these holes, Genene?' And Genene said: 'I don't think we should explain the holes. I think we should just throw it away.'"

Tears spilled down Kathleen's cheeks as she struggled with the memory. "I told her, 'I can't do that. Medically, legally, I can't do that. And for my own peace of mind, I just can't do that.'"

At Sutton's urging, Kathleen went on to speak of Genene's suicide attempt, of turning the vials over to the Sid Peterson administrators, and of having to fire Genene the following morning. One of the last questions Sutton asked before testimony concluded for the week was whether Genene ever had occasion after the day of Chelsea's funeral to again mention the child's death.

"Yes," Kathleen nodded. "As I recall, on September 23 or 24, we were walking out of the Intensive Care Unit at Sid Peterson Hospital and Genene paused outside the door where someone's portrait was hanging, and she said, 'Maybe some day this will be the Chelsea Ann McClellan Memorial Pediatric Intensive Care Unit.'"

"The Chelsea Ann McClellan Memorial Pediatric Intensive Care Unit," Sutton repeated.

"Yes."

"That was a difficult weekend for me," Kathleen remembers, "both because I was all over the news since I had just testified, and because I knew that Monday, I was going to have to face cross-examination. It wasn't so much that I was afraid of Brookshire and Carnes, although I certainly wasn't looking forward to facing them, I was afraid of blowing it by coming across too stubborn, or losing my temper."

That weekend, winter hit the Hill Country in earnest. "It was the coldest winter we ever had," Brookshire remembers. "It seemed like it anyway. Zero weather, *below*-zero weather, which we never have here. It was killing trees, and both Burt and I had the damn flu, and we were just dragging through this mess. It was horrible."

Burt Carnes was in charge of the defense's cross-examination of Kathleen and began Monday's proceedings by attending to tangential issues, clarifying almost insignificant details, quickly establishing a pattern of rapid-fire questioning that limited Kathleen to single-sentence answers. He thereby maintained control over the doctor's testimony, verbally pushing her into responses that enhanced Genene's credibility and detracted from her own. Kathleen soon became uncomfortable, obviously battling the constant impulse to be defensive.

"What was the title on Genene's badge again?" he asked her, referring back to earlier testimony that Sutton had elicited to demonstrate Genene's perpetual need to enhance her own importance.

"Genene Jones, Pediatric Clinician," which was a slightly inflated designation.

"And she wore this around the office?"

"Yes."

"She wore it as a regular practice?" he asked, and then

continued, almost incredulously, "and you *allowed* her to wear it?"

"Why not?" Kathleen retorted predictably, permitting Carnes to make his point.

"Doctor, I agree with you: why not?"

With Kathleen firmly on the defensive, Carnes then opened up his cross-examination, investigating with Kathleen the symptoms she and other doctors and nurses had noted in Chelsea's records. Carnes focused on specific symptoms such as apneic spells, staring spells, nystagmus, difficulty rousing from sleep, blue spells, mottled color, and twitching movements—anything indicating seizurelike activity, anything that raised serious questions about the health of this little girl. He brought up a drug that as yet had not been discussed in the trial, though it had been referred to several times, the anticonvulsant medication Dilantin, which had been administered to Chelsea daily after her respiratory arrest. "Doctor, what are the possible adverse reactions a person could have to Dilantin?"

"Arrhythmias and cardiac problems," Kathleen explained, "but those are extremely rare, and almost any medication under certain circumstances can cause such problems. The most common manifestations are what are called distonic movements, and they are just abnormal movements of arms, face, and mouth—tremulous kinds of movements. Nystagmus is possible, as is ataxia, which is uncoordinated movement—like staggering drunkenness. Also dysarthria (difficulty speaking) and respiratory arrest."

Carnes was content. Almost every symptom Kathleen had named could be found somewhere in Chelsea's medical records. He wanted the jury to consider the possibility that an inappropriate use of Dilantin may have caused some or all of Chelsea's medical problems.

Carnes then questioned Kathleen about medical records in general, about the standard practice of making such records at the time of, or shortly following, a medical event. He hoped the jurors would recognize that medical records by nature have a greater veracity and dependability than the memory of a witness testifying seventeen months after the event. A little past 11:00 A.M., after slightly more than two hours of cross-examination, Carnes finally turned his attention to the events of August 24, 1982.

As he and Kathleen now went through page after page of Chelsea's medical records, Carnes focused on every recorded symptom that supported the theory that Chelsea was in fact a very sick child who suffered from some kind of neurological problem. And as he had done with Kagan-Hallet before, he tried constantly to provoke Kathleen into defending her original diagnosis of some kind of seizure disorder. He questioned her aggressively, picking apart her answers, always searching for ways to reduce her credibility in the eyes of the jurors.

Kathleen provided the defense attorney with one such opportunity when she responded to his question about Chelsea's movements during her recovery from her first arrest.

"They appeared to be a couple of [clonic] beats."

"Doctor, I have problems with that phrase: 'appeared to be.' You were the medical doctor, you were there, you were the one watching, you were treating the child. *Were* they clonic movements?"

"'Clonic movement' is a term that is applied to definite seizure activity," Kathleen parried. "Chelsea's EEG never showed any seizure activity, so I have to say, from a physician's point of view, they appeared to be clonic movements."

"Doctor, we will get to the EEG in a little while."

"Okay."

"You were the doctor, you were there."

"Uh-huh."

"Not, 'did they *appear* to be?'" Carnes said, shaking his head. "*Were* they tonic-clonic seizure movements?"

"At that time, in the context of that moment of time," she said carefully, "I interpreted them as tonic-clonic movements."

"That is right," Carnes concluded, accepting the stalemate and moving on. He then focused aggressively on the fact that Kathleen seemed to be blaming her "misdiagnosis" of Chelsea on the false information received from Genene.

"I keep getting the impression from your testimony, Doctor, that everything after Chelsea's first respiratory arrest, everything that happened to her in the hospital, everything you attempted to do, all the tests you ran, were all based on what Genene told you. That is not right, is it? What was it exactly that Genene told you, that you relied on in making your original diagnosis of seizure activity?"

"I relied on her description of how the child had had the arrest."

"And what did she tell you? The child slumped over and went limp, right?"

"Uh-huh."

"And when you went in the room, you observed a limp child, right?"

"Uh-huh."

"So you observed everything that Genene Jones did, as far as the activity in that child, right?"

"No, sir. I did not see her go limp."

"The child goes limp sitting on a floor. Are you saying that *that* is the *key* to everything that happened for the next ten days—how the child slumped over on the floor?"

"No, Mr. Carnes, I didn't say that that was the key to everything."

"Doctor, the fact is, the child went limp and you were called into the room immediately, right?"

"That is true."

"I fail to see how you can then say that what happened for the next ten days is based on an accurate clinical description given you by your LVN, that the child went limp."

"Mr. Carnes, I never said that what happened in the next ten days was based solely on that."

"Was it based in *part* on that?"

"Yes."

"How much?" he continued.

"I don't attach numbers to it," she said, betraying a hint of temper, "but it was a very important piece of information given the child's history and the subsequent happenings in the hospital."

Carnes then directed Kathleen to read for the benefit of the jury certain portions of Chelsea's charts from her stay in Sid Peterson. On August 26, the nursing notes reported: "The total body is having shaking and jerking movements." On August 27, in Kathleen's own notes: "There was a question of seizure activity per mom." Also on the twenty-seventh, in the nursing notes: "Dark blood oozing from right nostril; injection, started crying and turned very cyanotic." And six hours later: "The grandmother reports some mild jerking of infant's lower extremities during sleep." On August 29, from Kathleen's progress notes: "Had two seizures yesterday P.M., lasting one to two minutes with postictal state following. Also thirty-second blue spell." On that same date, in the nurse's notes: "Little fingers twitch occasionally." A further entry late that night: "She had another episode, turned cyanotic when injection given." And again, on August 30: "The respirations stopped long enough for the apnea monitor light to go on two times, but the patient started breathing again." On August 31: "The grandmother also notes twitching in right foot and in fingers, and tremor noted down the back." And ten minutes later: "Small twitching movements noted in fingers and feet occurring every two to three minutes, while asleep." And on September 1, near the conclusion of Chelsea's hospital stay: "The sitter states right leg, hand, and fingers jerking irregularly." Taken all together, the number and frequency of observed seizurelike symptoms made it appear that Chelsea had indeed been a very sick child.

Carnes then questioned Kathleen about the day of Chelsea's death, again focusing on every detail in the medical records that tended to show that Chelsea suffered from a neurological disorder. With his last question, before he finally relinquished Kathleen to the prosecution for redirect, he had the doctor confirm that Petti and Reid Mc-Clellan were suing *her* as the party responsible for the death of their daughter.

When Sutton resumed his questioning, he made sure the jury understood that the probable reason Kathleen was being sued for Chelsea's death was because of her medical malpractice insurance, not because the McClellans necessarily believed Kathleen killed their little girl. He also had Kathleen testify that the day she fired Genene she discovered a second vial of medication—the drug atropine—was also missing. Addressing Carnes's avid interest in the many subtle seizure signs Chelsea exhibited, he had Kathleen testify, at length, to the fact that all of those signs can also be found in perfectly normal children.

Before Sutton yielded his witness back to the defense for recross, he took a moment to respond to an earlier question by Carnes regarding Kathleen's failure to spot any injection marks in Chelsea the day of her arrest. "Doctor, is there a place on the body where a child can be injected and the injections not be readily noticed?"

"Yes, there are a number of places."

"For example?"

"Under the tongue. Between the buttocks."

"Pass the witness."

On recross, Carnes returned to this possible shot between the buttocks. "Doctor," he asked, "did you hear Chelsea cry out or scream before Genene called you out of your office on the twenty-fourth?"

"I don't recall hearing anything."

"Would you expect a child who might get a shot under the tongue or between the buttocks to cry out?"

"I think that is a fair thing to expect."

When Carnes finished and sat down, Sutton rose for one last question on redirect: "Doctor, is there a way to prevent a child from crying if you do not want them to cry upon injection?"

"I guess you could put your hand over their mouth."

"Thank you, Doctor, that is all."

Kathleen had survived her first round of testimony. "I felt good. I felt it had gone well."

On Tuesday, January 31, the state called John R. McCutcheon, supervisor of the toxicology section at the Texas Department of Public Safety's crime laboratory in Austin. He testified that the vial with the holes in the stopper, which Kathleen had turned over to the authorities, was 80 percent dilute, probably with saline solution. Glenn Harrison, a chemist for the DPS, then appeared, corroborating McCutcheon's testimony.

In the late morning, Bardetta Kreiwitz, Chelsea's former babysitter, took the stand. Sutton needed Bardetta in order to contradict the defense's contention, based on notations in Chelsea's medical records, that Chelsea had suffered an impressive array of seizure symptoms during her stay in the hospital. Bardetta testified that she was the author of many of the notations in Chelsea's records—those attributed to the child's grandmother. "I was awake nearly all the time at night when I was watching Chelsea there at the hospital, because I was very concerned about her. And she would maybe move a finger or something, and I would write that down: the time it happened, how long it lasted, the whole thing. That was what Dr. Holland wanted done. And the only thing that I could see that she actually did was, at times, her little finger would move, or her toes, and that would be it."

"Did you see anything particularly unusual about those actions?"

"Well, I'm not a doctor, so I couldn't say," Bardetta answered cautiously, "but to me, it would just be like your muscles relaxing."

Bardetta also provided an explanation about the two occasions the apnea monitor went off. "All it was was she had rolled over and gotten off the monitor, see, so that is what caused it, the monitor, to go off."

Next Sutton called Bardetta's daughter, DeAnna Armour, who provided some testimony that proved to be an unplea-

sant surprise for the defense. She informed the jury that she
and her mother had been waiting in the hall outside Sid
Peterson's Emergency Room when Chelsea was wheeled out
for her final ambulance ride south. "Chelsea was flat on her
back," DeAnna recalled, "with her face turned over to the
side. She looked to me like she was asleep."

DeAnna followed Chelsea's gurney outside; just before
they loaded the child into the ambulance, she saw the defendant take a syringe from her black bag and give
Chelsea a shot.

"I asked her what she was giving her and she said she
was giving her a shot of Valium. I questioned her about it
because, you know, to me Chelsea seemed so out of it
anyway—but I'm not a physician, so I didn't know. She
said it was to ease the discomfort of the air tube during the
drive south."

"Looking back, I'd have to say that that was the most
damaging thing to our defense," Jim Brookshire later
speculated, "and we didn't even know it at the time. Most
of the medical testimony indicated that if the child had
sufficiently recovered from the arrest at the Clinic, death
after that time could not have been due to succinylcholine
unless there had been some later reintroduction of the
drug. And there DeAnna was, giving the jury the notion of
a second shot.

"I didn't pay much attention to it at the time. I mean,
she was a real country girl, very simple, and I just figured
the jury would see through her. I didn't find her testimony
credible. I guess I should have gone ahead and embarrassed her, but I didn't know I had to."

DeAnna finished her testimony at 11:00 A.M. Judge
Carter sent the jury home with instructions not to return
until 1:30 P.M., on the following day. The court then
heard evidence on the defense's most important motion,
their request that the court exclude any evidence regarding
the five *other* emergencies that had occurred at Kathleen's
Clinic.

That afternoon, outside the presence of the jury, Rothe

brought before the court a few of the witnesses—their three most impressive—whom the prosecution intended to call in connection with the so-called extraneous offenses: Sergeant First Class David Michael Maywhort, Specialist Five Gabriel Garcia, and Dr. Holland. The two MAST officers set the stage with their graphic and militarily precise testimony about Jimmy Pearson's emergency in their helicopter and Genene's peculiar behavior throughout. Kathleen then provided some of the details of the remaining four emergencies at her Clinic.

Sutton hoped to convince Judge Carter that these incidents were sufficiently like Chelsea's emergencies to constitute a "pattern of behavior," the single exception to the general rule prohibiting the admission of evidence regarding other criminal acts committed by a defendant. Sutton also had to persuade Judge Carter that these incidents' probative value (their usefulness as proof) outweighed their prejudicial effect (their capacity to sway the jury on emotional rather than rational grounds).

Carnes wanted to show that there simply was no continuing pattern or scheme. During his cross-examination of Sutton's witnesses, he pointed out that in each of these other emergencies, the child exhibited symptoms that differed markedly from Chelsea's. Each child's problems lasted for different lengths of time, and many of the reported symptoms were entirely inconsistent with the use of succinylcholine. The defense called no witnesses of their own.

The motion concluded with oral argument from both sides. Rothe spoke on behalf of the prosecution, reminding the court of the two circumstances in which this kind of evidence is admissible: "As proof of scienter or intent, and as evidence of motive." Rothe argued that the Clinic's other emergencies were admissible on both grounds.

"I recognize that testimony concerning extraneous offenses has a prejudicial effect," he concluded. "Nonetheless, our state courts recognize it is a question of what is more valuable to the jury—not to the court, not to the

defense, not to the state—but to the twelve people that
have to hear this case. The issue before the court is
whether evidence of the extraneous offenses will better enable the jury to make a valid decision on the ultimate issue
in this case—whether or not that lady sitting there," he
said, pointing to Jones, "intentionally committed an act
clearly dangerous to human life that resulted in a death.
Further, I think that our appellate courts hold that evidence
of a continuing plan or design is probative of the defendant's motive and therefore should be made accessible to
the jury.

"We submit that the state has shown such a continuing
plan or design in this case, and we think the value of that
evidence to this jury far outweighs any prejudicial effect it
might have."

When Rothe sat down, volunteer attorney Laura Little
had her first chance to speak for the defense, turning in a
sharp, well-reasoned argument. First, she contended, the
state had *not* shown a continuing plan or design in this
case because there was no testimony from any of the witnesses which showed that even *one* of these other children
had received succinylcholine. More important, Little argued, "it is our contention that the state has made no
showing that any other offense even occurred. We have
been told of sick children coming into a clinic, many in an
emergency situation, all receiving treatment by a nurse.
There has been no showing by the state that an offense
occurred in any of these other incidents. We have found
no precedent [no prior appellate decision] on the issue of
admissibility of extraneous offenses in which there was
any question whether a second offense had ever actually
occurred.

"In our opinion," Little concluded, "the state's introduction of extraneous offenses is only something used as a
smoke screen and has no probative value as to the material
issue in this case—whether Genene Jones did, indeed, inject succinylcholine into Chelsea McClellan. There can't
be any doubt as to the inflammatory potential of the admis-

sion of these extraneous offenses. It is therefore our contention, Your Honor, that they are not admissible in this trial.''

Judge Carter promised to render his decision after the noon break and adjourned for lunch.

"The court has decided that the evidence will be admitted," pronounced Carter upon return.

"In my opinion," Brookshire later commented, "this was one of the most serious blows to the defense. I felt we had a very good argument supporting their inadmissibility and that Judge Carter could have gone either way. Certainly, it was emotionally devastating evidence to put before the jury."

When the jury resumed their seats, Sutton began his presentation of the extraneous offenses with his most documented and most dramatic incident, Jimmy Pearson's arrest while in the care of the MAST medics. First he called Jimmy's mother, Mary Ellen, so that the jury could get to know Jimmy, both as a pathetic victim of severe birth defects and as a child loved by his mother. Then Sutton's most impressive witnesses—Sergeants Maywhort and Garcia, as well as Sergeant Torrongeau—gave the jury a detailed picture of Jimmy's emergency on the flight to San Antonio.

In his cross-examination of these men, Carnes focused on the small discrepancies in their stories and the inconsistencies between what they observed and what would be expected with a succinylcholine-induced arrest. Maywhort told Carnes that a couple of minutes passed after Genene's injection into the IV port before the onset of Jimmy's respiratory distress, which Carnes contrasted with earlier testimony that an intravascular injection of succinylcholine causes symptoms to appear within one minute. Maywhort also testified that he did not remember Jimmy ever experiencing a cardiac arrest, whereas Garcia remembered an increase in Jimmy's heart rate first, then a cardiac arrest, and

then signs of a respiratory arrest as the helicopter plunged
to the ground.

Carnes also focused on the fact that, at the time, no one
suspected that Genene might have deliberately injured the
child. "Sergeant," he said, addressing Maywhort, "I am
curious about just one thing: did you report this incident to
any civilian authorities afterwards?"

"I had no reason to."

On Thursday morning, Kathleen again took the witness
stand. Her testimony continued for more than two days.

Sutton's questioning was now directed toward completing the August and September calendars. Together lawyer
and doctor reviewed the events occurring at the Clinic day
by day, beginning before the Clinic even opened, with
Kathleen's initial purchase of pharmaceuticals. Scott
Monroe took position at the calendars, pen in hand. As
Kathleen testified, he made notes, slowly filling the calendars' squares with red ink. On August 17, he wrote: "Initial inventory: Twelve 250 vials of atropine."

Sutton and Kathleen skipped past August 23 and 24,
which already showed entries for the Clinic's opening and
Chelsea's first arrest, and moved on to August 27, the day
of Brandy Benites's emergency. With Brandy, as with
each of the succeeding children, Sutton carefully walked
Kathleen through the events of the emergency, focusing on
two objectives: to show the jury the remarkable similarities
between each of the Clinic's emergencies, and to highlight
examples of "guilty conduct" by Genene, particularly the
many instances Genene verbally represented symptoms to
Kathleen that differed from what was later found written in
the charts.

On August 27, Monroe wrote, "Benites, R/A." On
August 28 and August 29, Monroe wrote the word
"Closed." Sutton then moved on to August 30 and the
incident the jury was already familiar with: Jimmy Pearson's helicopter ride.

"What did Genene report to you about that incident?"

"She told me that the child, Chris Parker, the infant with stridor who accompanied Jimmy, had slept through the entire ride, and she said that Jimmy had been lying there, and that she had watched him very closely, and at some point in the ride, she had noted some abnormal eye movements."

"Abnormal eye movements. Did she put a term to that?"

"I recall her saying something about his eyes first, and then 'he began to seize again,' is the way she told it. And then she told me that she gave him some Valium because of his seizing and that he had arrested. She said they landed in a field and pulled Jimmy out of the helicopter. They tried to resuscitate him and to intubate him outside the helicopter but had some difficulty, so they put him back in the helicopter and quickly headed on to San Antonio."

"Did she say anything about the technical capabilities or qualifications of any of the MAST people?"

"She did make one comment about them not wanting to intubate Jimmy, not seeing the justification in it or thinking it was futile. I don't remember exactly what her words were, but something to the effect that they didn't see why they should bother."

"That is what she reported to you?"

"Yes. And she was upset about that."

"Did she discuss with you what happened to any of the medical equipment that she had taken with her?"

"She told me that on taking off from the pasture, the syringe that had the Valium in it, whatever was left, had fallen out of the helicopter and she was pretty sure that the laryngoscope had probably fallen out as well."

"But she stated that the syringe had fallen out *while* they were taking off."

"That is correct."

Sutton had one last point to make before moving on: "Doctor, is there any medication or combination of medications that upon injection through an IV line would in-

crease the heart rate and then subsequent thereto cause a
respiratory arrest?''

"Yes. That would be consistent with the combination of
atropine and succinylcholine.''

Sutton and Holland then moved on to September 3, discussing the events with the same kind of attention to detail. Scott Monroe wrote, "Misty Reichenau-R/A.'' On
the square for September 4 he drew a slash with "Closed''
below it to show that the Clinic was closed half that day.
The Sunday and Monday of Labor Day weekend, September 5 and 6, the Clinic was also "Closed.''

Sutton next introduced into evidence a pharmacy charge
slip from Sid Peterson showing the purchase of "10 cc's
of atropine, 10 cc's of succinylcholine'' on Tuesday, September 7. Nothing unusual occurred September 8 through
11, and on Sunday, September 12, the Clinic was again
"Closed.'' Across the squares for September 13, 14, 15,
and 16, Monroe wrote in the name "Mary Mahoney,''
Kathleen's substitute nurse.

Thursday, September 17, already contained a notation
for "McClellan-R/A.'' After another detailed discussion,
Monroe added Jacob Evans's name to the calendar below
Chelsea's on the seventeenth. Friday the eighteenth
showed a half-day closed, and on the nineteenth, the
Clinic was again closed all day. The twentieth already reflected the purchase of 10 cc's of succinylcholine and
Chelsea's funeral. Monroe added the information that another 6 one-milliliter dosages of atropine were also purchased that day.

Sutton and Holland moved on to the day of the Clinic's
last emergency, Rolinda Ruff. As Kathleen continued with
her recollections, Monroe continued filling in the calendar.
On the twenty-third, "Ruff-R/A.'' On the twenty-fourth,
"Hospital executive committee conference related to Genene Jones.'' On the twenty-sixth, "Conversation, Genene;
'bottle found; no holes'.'' The twenty-seventh, "Holland
finds holes; 'Throw it away'; Holland calls Hall, et al.;
Holland delivers vials.'' The calendar was now complete.

Sutton, however, was not yet finished. He had been working on a second piece of demonstrative evidence for weeks. He called it the "100 Percent Chart," and was confident that if he could get it before the jury, his case would be sewn up. The chart, on the left side, had a column of dates for each day Kathleen's Clinic had been open. Across the top there were four headings: (1) Children Under Two; (2) Injection; (3) Jones IV Used; and (4) Potentially Serious Illness. Sutton now intended to reveal the pattern behind the Clinic's emergencies.

When the prosecution pulled out the empty chart, however, Carnes leaped up. "Your Honor, I ask that he not be allowed to display this until its relevancy has been demonstrated."

Judge Carter asked Sutton: "How are you going to establish this chart's relevancy, Counsellor?"

"I assure the court that I will tie it in."

Sutton's earnest assurance was not enough for Carter. "Well, then, let's just put your chart together in front of the court first, until such time as its relevancy is shown."

The jury was moved out and Sutton began to construct his chart. For each day the Clinic was in business, he asked Kathleen whether she had had any patients under the age of two. If she had, he then asked her if any of those patients had received an injection, an IV, or shown symptoms of a potentially serious illness. As Kathleen supplied the information, Monroe filled in the chart.

DATE	UNDER 2	INJECTION	JONES IV USED	SERIOUS ILLNESS	[EMERGENCY]
8-23	1	Yes	No	No	
8-24	1	No	Yes	Yes	[Chelsea]
8-25	No patients				
8-26	No patients under two				
8-27	1	No	Yes	Yes	[Brandy]
8-28	Closed				
8-29	Closed				
8-30	2	No	No	No	
8-31	2	Yes—1	No	No	
9-1	3	No	No	No	

9-2	No patients under two				
9-3	1	No	Yes	Yes	[Misty]
9-4	No patients under two				
9-5	Closed				
9-6	Closed				
9-7	3	No	No	No	
9-8	1	No	No	No	
9-9	5	No	No	No	
9-10	No patients				
9-11	No patients under two				
9-12	Sunday— closed				
9-13	1	No	No	No	
9-14	1	No	No	No	
9-15	No patients under two				
9-16	1	No	No	No	
9-17	2	Yes	Yes—Both	Yes—Both	[Chelsea & Jacob]
9-18	2	Yes—1	Yes—but Kathleen prepped	Yes	
9-19	Sunday				
9-20	No patients				
9-21	5	No	No	No	
9-22	1	No	No	No	
9-23	1	No	Yes	Yes	[Rolinda]
9-24	2	No	No	No	
9-25	Closed				
9-26	Closed				
9-27	1	No	No	No	

According to Sutton, every single child under two who
came in with a potentially serious illness and for whom
Genene prepared an IV suffered a respiratory arrest. Sutton remembers that, after he completed the chart, "Judge
Carter looked so damn mad it was unreal. He was almost
livid. He looked at Genene and seemed ready to kill her
himself."

Carnes was angry too, but for different reasons. Instinc-
tively, he saw that the categories were subjective—open to

interpretation and ambiguity—but could not phrase his objections clearly enough for the judge.

"This is just another attempt to bolster their witness," Carnes protested. "They have already testified as to the extraneous offenses, put it out in big, bright red letters for everybody to see so that it would be in front of the jury the entire trial, and this is just another attempt to bolster that again. It raises irrelevant matters; they have chosen an arbitrary age division. And in addition to that, I object to the classification of 'Jones IV Used,' because that is not the fact. They were *Dr. Holland's* IVs. It's a very arbitrary thing. This is not statistical analysis, this is something the state has put together in a motel room, that's all in the world it is. Just trying to bolster what they've already got into evidence. We object on all those grounds."

Sutton handled the responsive argument with equanimity—he knew he already had Judge Carter's sympathies. "Your Honor, this chart is relevant on its face without question. This goes to show the motive and intent of Genene Jones. It shows that every time she got an opportunity with a child who had present symptomatology of a potentially serious health problem, that child went down. Every single one of them."

Judge Carter hardly hesitated at the end of the attorney's arguments: "The court finds it relevant. The court will admit it."

Sutton thereupon presented his 100 Percent Chart to the jury.

During Carnes's cross-examination of Kathleen, which began the morning of Friday, February 3, the lawyer followed the same strategy he had earlier used in relation to the McClellan emergencies. He pointed out to the jury the magnitude and quantity of alarming symptoms each child exhibited before he or she ever met Genene Jones, trying to establish doubt in the jurors' minds: were these children in fact poisoned, or was it possible that they were all sim-

ply terribly sick children? Whenever possible, he high-
lighted for the jury the inaccuracies and ambiguities he
could spot in Sutton's fancy, new 100 Percent Chart, and
he constantly deflected suspicion back toward Kathleen.
"As the state's star witness and Genene's chief accuser,"
Brookshire later explained, "if we could just get the jury
to doubt her motivations or veracity, the case against Genene weakened considerably."

Regarding Chelsea's emergency on August 24, Carnes
emphasized that Kathleen had heard no outcry and found
no needle mark and pointed out that Chelsea's arrest began
before her IV was started. Therefore, Carnes observed,
Sutton's inclusion of Chelsea in the "Jones IV Used" column on the 100 Percent Chart was "if not worthless, certainly misleading."

Carnes and Holland next discussed Brandy Benites's
emergency on August 27. Kathleen again confirmed that
with Brandy—as with Chelsea—the emergency began
before Genene started the IV, and Carnes again complained that the incident was improperly categorized on the
chart.

He asked the doctor to review her notes on Brandy's
emergency, pointing out to her, and to the jury, that nowhere did her notes describe the "limpness" that Kathleen
had repeatedly testified to. "Doctor, let's be practical
now," he coaxed, "after the twenty-seventh of September, it was clear in your mind, and everybody else's
mind, that in every case that you've testified to," the use
of succinylcholine was in question.

"I knew that it was being considered," Kathleen conceded.

"I mean, isn't that the point of your entire testimony,
Doctor? You're setting it up so that it could be succinylcholine, right?" Carnes no longer cared if Kathleen
was cooperative; he wanted to place these notions before
the jury.

"I'm not sure I understand what you mean by 'setting it
up,'" Kathleen replied.

"After September 27, you knew succinylcholine was going to be a major question in every one of these cases, right?"

"Subsequent to September 27, I had the occasion to reflect back at a time when I was still fairly close to the events and more carefully recollect what had happened, specifically, with those children."

Carnes continued on, knowingly, "And limpness is a very important observation when we are talking about the possible use of succinylcholine, is it not?"

"Limpness or lack of muscle tone is a major effect of succinylcholine, yes."

"I mean, even if you didn't think it was important on the twenty-seventh day of September, *after* the twenty-seventh, you knew it was extremely important, right?"

"I knew that it was something that in retrospect had to be considered."

"You knew it was extremely important," the tone of accusation was unmistakable, "and yet you did not mention it at all in your deposition of May 1983, when you were talking about Brandy Benites."

"I don't understand what your point is, Mr. Carnes."

"Forget the point, Doctor, just answer the questions."

Rothe at last jumped up with an objection, interrupting the attack on his witness. By the time Judge Carter overruled the objection, both the point and question were lost. Carnes moved on. He had established all that he needed already: before Brandy's emergency began, she had received no medications and no IV and no one had found any needle marks.

Carnes then peppered Kathleen with questions about Jimmy Pearson. "Who prepared Jimmy's IV?"

"Probably not Genene."

"Who prepared the shots you gave him in the ER?"

"Probably not Genene."

"Who prepared the syringe of Valium that she took with her on the helicopter?"

"One of the Sid Peterson nurses, I believe."

"What orders did you give Genene about when to administer the Valium?"

"If he began seizing as badly as he had in the ER, then she was to administer another dose."

Carnes picked up the *Physicians' Desk Reference*, asking Kathleen if she was familiar with what this text had to say about Valium: "'Extreme care must be used when administering injectable Valium,'" he read aloud, "'particularly by I.V. route . . . to very ill patients and to those with limited pulmonary reserve because of the possibility that apnea and/or cardiac arrest may occur.'" The implication was clear; Carnes was suggesting that it was the Valium prescribed by Kathleen that had caused Jimmy's arrest in the helicopter, not some mystery drug spirited aboard the helicopter by Genene.

Carnes had one last question for Kathleen concerning Jimmy Pearson. "Did it surprise you, Doctor, when you learned later that day that Jimmy had had an arrest during the helicopter ride into San Antonio?"

"No. When Genene reported to me that Jimmy had had a seizure and an arrest, I was not surprised."

Carnes turned his attention to Misty Reichenau. With Kathleen's help, he established the fact that the child *could* talk in short, simple sentences, contrary to Sutton's assumption that all children under the age of two were nonverbal. Carnes also established that, as with Chelsea, Kathleen did not remember any particular outcry from Misty that might have indicated the child had just been stuck with a needle, and that, as with Brandy, Kathleen made no mention of "limpness" in her records—Kathleen had only "remembered" it after the fact. Further, according to Kathleen's best recollection of the episode, the limpness lasted only about two minutes, with a second episode ten minutes after the first—hardly typical responses to an injection of succinylcholine.

In his review of the Jacob Evans episode, Carnes concentrated on reemphasizing the severity of Jacob's symptoms. "'A two-month history of screaming spells,'"

Kathleen summarized from the medical records, "'a bulging fontanelle, split sutures indicating intracranial pressure, slight sideways movement of the eyes, and blue and orange skin blotches.'" Kathleen remained adamant, however, that aside from Jacob's seizure, the child was well within the normal range of health and development.

Finally, Carnes began his examination of Rolinda Ruff's emergency. His review of that child's medical records with Kathleen established that Rolinda had been treated by another physician with Parepectolin for her diarrhea, and that one of the main ingredients of Parepectolin is the narcotic paregoric. His implication, clearly, was that the narcotic could have been one possible cause of the child's problems. And again Carnes raised the issue that Kathleen's notes on Rolinda did not reflect the word "limpness," nor did she use that word during her May 1983 deposition.

"You have testified that you are a highly trained medical doctor," Carnes said with mild sarcasm, "with seven years of training, trained to make clinical observations of people when they are experiencing a physical problem, yet in *every single one* of these cases, there is *no* indication in *any* record made at or near the time of the event, or in the May 1983 deposition, that any *one* of those children went limp for any period of time, is there?"

"That may be true, but that doesn't necessarily eliminate the existence of that."

"Now, Doctor," Carnes continued, all but ignoring Kathleen's response, "here today, in the courtroom, in retrospect, all of a sudden, in every single one of these cases, you have testified that there is this period of limpness. But you can't remember how long it lasted, you can't remember when it started or when it stopped, and it is always followed by what you, in your clinical observations, refer to as 'some' seizure activity. What is all this based on, Doctor?"

"It is based on a retrospective view," Kathleen repeated firmly, "that I undertook starting the week of September 27 when I was asked to look back and try to recall what, specifically, had happened."

"Doctor, you didn't recall it in May of 1983 when you gave your deposition. You are only now recalling it in the courtroom, sixteen or seventeen months later."

"Mr. Carnes, I don't recall the question ever having been asked in the deposition: 'Did, at any time, the children go limp.' I don't recall that question being asked."

"Come on, Doctor, you knew what they were looking for in this two-day deposition. They were trying to find out if there was any evidence of succinylcholine having been used, right?"

"All I know is they were trying to find out the facts, and that is what I was trying to give them."

Carnes again ignored the answer, driving home his point, "And they asked you, in every way possible, whether, in your clinical opinion, succinylcholine was involved in any of these other children, and you said 'no.'"

Carnes then raised two other issues regarding Rolinda Ruff. First, he pointed out that Rolinda's seizure activity—as recorded in her medical records—could not even have occurred if her respiratory arrest had in fact been caused by succinylcholine, because the respiratory muscles are the last to be affected and the seizure activity occurred *after* the arrest. Second, if Rolinda had, as Kathleen remembered, already started recovering from a dose of succinylcholine while at the Clinic (as evidenced by the muscle twitchings Kathleen reported), then Dr. Bradley could not have seen Rolinda "coming out from under" the drug a full ten minutes later at the hospital.

Carnes had done a masterful job of focusing on every single well-spring of doubt, every fact that called into question Kathleen's veracity, the relative health of the child, and the inconsistency of the child's symptoms with the presence of succinylcholine.

Although it was only 3:30 P.M. when Carnes concluded his cross-examination concerning Rolinda, he was ready for a break. Presumably, he wanted to finish his questioning of Kathleen on Monday, after he had had the weekend to gather his thoughts. Possibly he simply did not want to finish and again allow Ron Sutton the dramatic opportunity of asking the last questions of the week. The defense asked for an early recess.

"Dr. Holland hasn't been feeling well," the court informed the jury, "the lawyers on both sides have been feeling a little ill, and everybody kind of thinks we need to take a rest. So, we are going to stop at this point in time and take a rest until Monday morning at 9:00 A.M."

On Monday morning, Carnes rose to ask Kathleen the one question that had occurred to him over the weekend. "Of the additional children we talked about last week— Brandy Benites, Misty Reichenau, Jacob Evans, Rolinda Ruff, and Jimmy Pearson—how many of those sets of parents have filed lawsuits against you, Dr. Holland?"

"The parents of three of the five children have. The Reichenaus, the Evanses, and the Pearsons."

The defense had no further questions.

On redirect, Sutton did his best to rebuild Kathleen's credibility, though he kept his questions to a minimum. He asked her to describe again the occasion on which Genene made reference to the Chelsea Ann McClellan Memorial Pediatric Intensive Care Unit. He also asked her to describe the possible side effects of a less-than-recommended dosage of succinylcholine.

"My understanding is that low doses of succinylcholine can mimic seizure activity," Kathleen testified.

The district attorney then pulled out his copy of the *Physicians' Desk Reference* and asked Kathleen to read off and explain each of the listed possible side effects of the drug. "'A transient bradycardia,' or slowing of the heart rate," she began; "'hypotension,' which is a drop in blood pressure; 'arrhythmias,' which are disruptions in the normal rhythms of the heart; 'even a sinus arrest'—which is a cessation or disruption of the electrical impulses that cause the heart to contract—'may occur during endotracheal intubation.'"

Sutton's last request of his key witness was to identify the woman about whom she had been testifying, her former nurse and friend, Genene Jones. "Would you please point her out?"

"I looked her straight in the eye," Kathleen remembers.

She pointed her finger at the defendant, and spoke out plainly: "Sitting right there, in the striped dress."

The remaining dozen witnesses for the state appeared in quick succession; by the following afternoon, Sutton would complete the presentation of his case in chief and rest, turning control of the floor over to the defense.

This morning, Scott Monroe had the opportunity, for the first time, to conduct questioning for the state. His first witness, Nelda Benites, was called to provide additional details of the day her daughter arrested. It was difficult to tell who seemed more nervous, Nelda or the young attorney. Neither seemed to notice when Nelda responded with "Four or five months" to Monroe's question concerning the age difference between her two children.

Monroe's next two witnesses, Sarah Mauldin, the assistant director of respiratory at Sid Peterson, and EMT Phillip Kneese, told the jury of Brandy's second respiratory arrest in the ambulance on its way to San Antonio, at approximately the same location where Chelsea later arrested and died.

Kay Reichenau then testified about her daughter, Misty. On cross-examination, as Brookshire described the many symptoms, Kay objected to his reference to a stiff neck.

"Okay," responded Brookshire, "did she, or did she not have a stiff neck?"

Kay, a young woman of dark, delicate features, who displayed a remarkable amount of poise, spoke right up. "I didn't think she did, no, sir. I am not a doctor, but, I mean, they were taking the child's rectal temperature at the time that they did this—at the time they checked her neck. I think that is where the fight came from."

Jacob's mother, Lydia Evans, was called to tell what she remembered of her son's emergency, then her mother, Loretta Lardie, took the stand. She spoke of the night she visited Jacob at Sid Peterson when his IV had clotted with blood and needed to be changed.

"Genene happened to be there, so she took care of it. As she worked, Genene made the statement that she and Dr. Holland were hoping to, and I can't say definitely if the word was either 'prove,' or 'show' that the Kerrville hospital needed a Pediatric Intensive Care Unit," Lardie testified. "She said, 'Babies and young children cannot be adequately cared for in a regular ICU.'"

"She was hoping to prove a need for a PICU to the hospital?" Sutton asked.

"Yes," replied Lardie. "That's what she said."

Dr. Bradley, the Sid Peterson anesthesiologist who observed Rolinda Ruff's recovery in the ER, then described for the jury the gross motor movements he had witnessed in the baby. "This child exhibited the same type of phenomenon that we observe regularly when we give succinylcholine in the operating room to facilitate insertion of an endotracheal tube. When patients begin coming out from under the effect of it, they will reach up for the tube (it's very uncomfortable), but when they get their hand there, they can't do anything with it, because they don't have the finger control, just shoulder and elbow control."

Sutton asked the doctor to speculate on the difference between giving succinylcholine to an anesthetized patient and giving it to one who is awake. "I would anticipate," said Dr. Bradley, "that you would have some muscle jerking before the muscles became fully paralyzed—a fright type of response—but I have never given it to an awake patient."

Sutton then asked Dr. Bradley if, with a less-than-required dosage of succinylcholine, there would be any possible mimicking of seizure activity.

"Yes, you could get muscle-twitching—jerky, gross muscle movements. That is what I would expect, because if you gave it in less than optimal dose, then you would get less than optimal relaxation. They would still have some muscle control, and as they began to feel deficient in oxygen, then they would begin to jerk."

"What would be the onset of succinylcholine if it were given intravenously as opposed to intramuscularly?"

"Depending on the dose, size, and condition of the patient, the onset could vary anywhere from a half a minute up to a minute and a half, two minutes. It would depend upon how good the blood supply was in the area you injected the succinylcholine."

"Could it be as short as fifteen seconds in some cases?"

"It could, but you would have to put it in a very vascular area for the onset to be that short."

On cross-examination, Carnes also asked some questions about the effects of succinylcholine and solicited an unwelcome answer. Unlike the other experts who had gone before him, Bradley testified that the effects of succinylcholine last a variable amount of time depending upon the dose, the condition of the patient, and the ability of the patient to metabolize the drug. Carnes was surprised. "Well, Doctor, you aren't saying that a larger dose might lengthen the effects of the drug, are you?"

"Yes, I am."

"Is that through your own experience?" he challenged the doctor.

"Yes. It is through my own experience."

Carnes was incredulous: "The effects of the drug will continually get *longer*, the larger the dose?"

"I have given what I consider to be a slightly large dose for a person because I wanted to ensure no movement when I put the tube in. And I've found that succs *does* last longer if you use a larger dose."

Dr. Bradley repeatedly proved to be an intractable witness. At the conclusion of his cross-examination, Carnes pushed Bradley to admit that the motions he saw in

Rolinda Ruff could have been caused by something other than succinylcholine. Bradley, however, would not budge. "From my observation of the child," he said, "I know of no other drug that is in common use today that would cause effects like that."

"Forget drugs, Doctor," Carnes instructed. "Are you saying that there is absolutely no other explanation for those movements but coming out from under the effects of succinylcholine, or could it have been attributable to some other physical phenomenon?"

"Not a physical phenomenon that I am familiar with."

"So you are saying that that is what it was, and nothing else but?"

"In my opinion, I don't know of anything else that can mimic those symptoms in that short a period of time."

"Do you know that through studies you have done, or studies you have read, or is that—"

"Yes," replied Bradley, interrupting.

"Which?"

"Both."

Dr. Richard Mason then took the stand and testified that he too had witnessed Rolinda's recovery in the Sid Peterson ER, as well as Chelsea's and Jacob Evans's. He stated definitively that each of them had exhibited "gross motor movements."

Dr. Vincent DiMaio followed, taking the stand for the second time. His testimony raised no new information, but merely reinforced what had been said by others, until his cross-examination by Carnes. The defense attorney had decided to use DiMaio to establish one of their key points—that even if Genene had given Chelsea succinylcholine in the Clinic, it could not have caused her death over 90 minutes later during the ambulance ride to San Antonio. His line of questioning, however, produced an unwelcome response.

"Assuming, Doctor, that the alleged injection of succinylcholine was given at Dr. Holland's office, and assuming that the record will show that was one and a half to two hours prior to death, is it still your opinion that succinylcholine caused the death of that child?''

"It is possible," DiMaio replied. "It is more likely,
however, that another injection of succinylcholine was
given in the ambulance.''

"So your whole verdict on the cause of death is based
upon some presumed second injection of succinylcholine
in the ambulance?''

"No, sir," DiMaio replied, refusing to be forced into
the corner Carnes had chosen. "It is my opinion that this
is the most probable explanation, but it is also possible
that the electrolyte imbalance and the trauma set up by the
original injection, in the past, could have, in an infant,
caused an arrhythmia or death.'' The jury now had two
bases for a guilty verdict.

Ron Sutton ended his three-week presentation by returning to the issue of motive. The last witness to appear for
the state was LVN Mary Morris. Mary testified about her
conversation with Genene in which Jones talked about
opening up a Pediatric Intensive Care Unit at Sid Peterson,
and Mary had expressed her doubts about whether there
were enough patients to justify a PICU.

"What was it she said again?" Sutton asked.

"She said, 'Oh, they're out there. All you have to do is
go out and find them.'"

Shortly after 5:00 P.M., Sutton stood at the podium and
announced: "Your Honor, at this time, the state of Texas
rests its case.''

There was a day's break to give the defense a chance to
prepare. Then on Thursday, February 9, at 9:00 A.M.,
after counterpunching for fourteen days, the defense called
its first witness.

Ron Sutton

Why was Reid, in particular, barred from the courtroom in Georgetown?

Reid exhibited extreme emotional hostility. This was— I don't know, it's hard to explain the attachment that he had for that child. And— it was just extreme emotional hostility toward Jones and toward Holland. He would get Petti worked up through his emotionalism. So for that reason I tried to kind of keep them separated and not let him in the courtroom. I was concerned that if he got in there and saw Genene Jones or Dr. Holland or somebody, that he would jump up and make some emotional outburst in the courtroom which would result in our ending up in a mistrial in a case where we had a good shot at a conviction and after we'd spent umpteen thousands of dollars preparing.

Reid understood that. He didn't like it, but he understood it.

How did you feel when you finished your case in chief?

At that point in the trial I was hoping, really hoping, that Genene would take the stand, testify in her own defense. I had a list of questions two pages long. I planned to confront her with all the lies she'd told. We'd talk about the holes in the vial, her name being on the receipt, in her handwriting, and the notes—the nursing notes—where she verbally represented one thing to Dr. Holland or a mother, yet wrote down something else. Then there was a series of misstatements between what she told the Kerrville and the San Antonio grand juries as to what happened to all these kids. I had a whole long list. I was ready for her.

Sounds like you plan everything out in detail, ahead of time.

Well, not in all that much detail. Generally we plan what we're going to do, and what points we're looking for, but you don't want it to look rehearsed, 'cause you'll lose the jury. It's all got to be spontaneous. And then there's all those other little tricks you can do while the defense is presenting its case.

Like when they had Dr. Holmstedt on for a day and a half. See, I like to play with things. 'Cause a jury, if they will get tired of what's going on, will watch you play with something. I'll play with a book or—or in this case, I had these syringes, about four, of different sizes. I'd be sitting there, and the jury was *right there*, right next to me. And I set these syringes up on the counsel table like little missiles. And the jury can't help but look at these things during the course of the trial. Set 'em up every day, all these little missiles.

One time, I had my father's pocket watch, and things were draggin' on, I think they were hammering on Dr. Holland. So I took out this pocket watch, and I took it apart, and cleaned it, and what-not. And I looked up, and the jury—all of them—were watching me clean my watch.

You seem to relish your work.

I do. I like to keep busy.

Janet, what was it they were sayin' about me and this case? That I was possessed, or something?

(JANET) Yeah, possessed. The press said that quite a few times.

(SUTTON) They said I was possessed. I guess I was. But these things just get under my skin. And this case just came together so nicely at trial. See, the biggest problem the defense had was that they really didn't have a case, other than doubt. Well, normally handling that is not all that difficult, but this case was so multi-faceted, so complicated, that something like doubt is a little hard to keep control over, so I did my best to keep things concrete.

And sure the logistics for all those witnesses was a pain, sure the flu was going around, sure it was terrible getting by on two or three hours sleep a night, for weeks, but we still won all the motions, still presented all the evidence we thought we should. I'd have to say it was one of the most satisfying experiences of my life.

TWENTY-ONE

*Through his questions, he must destroy the
evidence amassed against his client— he
must diminish it, limit it, explain it away.
As the prosecutor tries to build, the defense counsel tries to tear down.*

F. Lee Bailey,
The Defense Never Rests

BURT CARNES CONDUCTED THE EXAMINATION
of the defense's first witness, Suzie Bateman, an emergency medical technician from Kerrville. Bateman had
been one of the two medics who assisted with Misty
Reichenau's emergency transport—the one involving Sally
Benkert and the never-used vial of succinylcholine. Carnes
pointed out, throughout his thorough examination of
Bateman, that Kathleen's seemingly very clear memories
of this incident did not really jibe with the memories of
another credible, and disinterested, eyewitness.

Bateman testified that when she came into the Clinic's
examination room, "they were still attempting to intubate
Misty, and she was having seizurelike movements." Kathleen had earlier told the jury that by the time the EMTs
arrived, Misty had already received her Dilantin, was intubated and motionless. In addition, contrary to the compact
sequence of events Kathleen had related, Bateman's EMT
log established that the entire emergency had taken approximately thirty minutes. Bateman also testified that she
witnessed the injection of Dilantin "about halfway

through" the thirty-minute period she was present at the Clinic.

The EMT testified for less than an hour, then the defense called Sally Benkert. Laura Little rose to conduct the long and gentle examination.

Sally had done her best to make a good impression. She wore a dark, tailored suit and carefully applied makeup and had been meticulous with her hair. Throughout her testimony, however, she appeared uncomfortable with the large crowd of newsmen and onlookers. She made an effort to phrase herself formally; her speech was halting, almost stiff. She had never grown used to the attention her friendship with Genene had generated.

Sally had been called to bolster the defense's version of events, to throw doubt on Kathleen's and to establish that the clinic's first vial of succinylcholine was pristine and untampered with on the day of Misty Reichenau's emergency, subsequent to the alleged succinylcholine-induced crises of Chelsea, Brandy Benites, and Jimmy Pearson. Little began by asking Sally to tell the jury how Misty Reichenau appeared on the day of her emergency.

"The child was slightly cyanotic in the face," she said quickly almost automatically. "She was very stiff, trembling. Her hands were clenched, turned in toward the body, and her extremities were trembling, shaking all over."

"What was the state of her face?"

"Her teeth were clenched. Her eyes were rolling back up in her head."

Little then walked Sally through the emergency, permitting Sally to show the jury that she remembered Misty's crisis in every bit as much detail as Kathleen, perhaps more.

"When I walked in the room, Genene was trying to start an IV in the patient's hand. She was having some difficulty locating a vein, because Misty's peripheral circulation had shut down. Dr. Holland was trying to hold the child down for Genene and also maintain an airway. She, too, was having a great amount of difficulty."

"What did you do, Sally?"

"I turned to evaluate whoever else was in the room. The mother was up against the wall at that time, and she looked like she was getting ready to be very hysterical, so I asked Ms. Johnston to escort her out before we had another patient on our hands. And at that time, I guess I stomped all over their feet to get around the table to help Dr. Holland and the child."

"So, what did you do then?"

"I leaned over and picked up the O_2 mask and took over holding the child. Dr. Holland was attempting to put a stationary tube down the child so she would have an airway, but the child's teeth were clamped, and we could not use a laryngoscope to see, so Dr. Holland was attempting a blind intubation through the nose. We had one tube taped down when she started throwing up and the tape came loose and the tube came out. So, we were trying another blind intubation, and about that time Dr. Holland asked for succinylcholine."

"Do you specifically recall Dr. Holland making that request?"

Sally nicely tied her recollection down to a specific, "Yes, because I looked up at her. She asked for succinylcholine, and I asked back where it was kept. And at that moment Genene looked up and said it was kept in the icebox. And Dr. Holland agreed, so I left to go get it."

"Did you observe anything else as you were leaving the room?"

"I heard Miss Jones ask Dr. Holland if they could try Dilantin first."

Laura asked Sally if she popped the cap on the vial, but Sally could not remember clearly. She did not think she did, however, since she was only preparing to draw it up. "Usually," Sally explained, demonstrating with her hands, "when you get prepared, you have your syringe and needle prepared to draw up the solution, and you hold your bottle prepared to pop the cap off and open the syringe at the same time, as the doctor gives you a dosage.''

"Would you describe this as an automatic reflex?''

"Yes.''

Little moved on, questioning Sally about the day Kathleen summoned the nurse to the Clinic. "Did you ever have occasion to discuss that vial with Dr. Holland?''

"Yes. She called me up one morning, I guess over a week later, I'm not exactly sure [when it was] because I was working quite a bit at that time.''

"Do you have any estimate as to when that might have been?''

"If I remember right, it would be the first day after Genene had gotten out of the hospital,'' Sally said, again tying her memory to a specific, and contradicting Kathleen's version of the events by more than a week. "She had been in the hospital for a bleeding ulcer, and it was right after she had gotten out of the hospital.''

"What makes you think that that is when this occurred?''

"Because I had been working, and Bonnie Gunderson had woken me up saying that Dr. Holland wanted to talk to me, and I was really surprised that Genene wanted to go to work that day.''

"I'm sorry?'' asked Little, not understanding this confused response.

"I was really surprised Genene wanted to go to work that day, because I felt like she should have stayed home.''

"Could this have occurred any time after the weekend of the twenty-fifth?''

"No. It was before the weekend of the twenty-fifth.''

"Is there any reason why you would be pretty sure of that?''

"I don't remember seeing Dr. Holland the weekend of the twenty-fifth because I think she was with her husband that weekend, and on that Monday, I only saw Dr. Holland once, and I never saw her again after that.''

Little asked her last question of the witness casually, knowing that its importance would be made clear much later in the defense's closing arguments. "The day you got that vial out of the refrigerator and returned to the front treatment room, was there a cap on the vial?"

"Yes, there was."

When Sutton rose to cross-examine Benkert he was after three things. First, he wanted to show the kind of friendship that Genene and Sally had shared for years. Second, he wanted to establish the depth of Sally's loyalty to Genene. And, third, he wanted the jury to know that months before Kathleen even opened the Clinic, Genene and Sally had researched the effects of succinylcholine.

Very quickly, Sutton set a definite rhythm to his interrogation. His questions were short, slyly phrased. He changed topics often. Like a young, quick prizefighter jabbing at an older, slower opponent, he kept Sally off balance, but he always kept his questioning gentle. He did not want to alienate the jury by appearing to bully this simple, stolid woman. Above all else, he did not want this witness to have the jury's sympathy.

"Do you know whether or not Genene ever had an active LVN license while she was in Kerrville?"

"Yes, she did have an active LVN license."

"Are you sure about that?"

"Yes, because I got her the money for it."

"Do you know whether or not she ever sent the money in?"

"I believe her and I—wait a minute. Yes. We went to Austin to go hand it straight to them."

"But she was in fact not relicensed until November of 1982. And her license had expired in July, isn't that correct, Ms. Benkert?"

"I don't know when. I did not ask her when her license expired, but I did make sure that the money was there for her to renew it."

"You provided a lot of money to Genene Jones, didn't you?"

"We both worked together."

"But you paid most of the bills, didn't you?"

"Well, both of us worked together to pay the bills."

"And you are a very, very close friend of Genene Jones, are you not?"

"Yes, I am."

As evidence of the kind of friend Sally was for Genene, Sutton proceeded to question her about an incident in May 1983, when Sally refused to inform law enforcement officers where Genene was, referring them instead to Genene's lawyer.

As Sutton progressed through his interrogation, he also embraced every opportunity to use Sally to reveal some of the more aggressive aspects of Genene's personality. Sally's passing reference to "Genene and other RNs in the Unit" provoked Sutton to cut in.

"You don't mean to imply that Genene is an RN do you?"

"No."

"In fact, she didn't like RNs, isn't that correct."

"No, she liked RNs," Sally shrugged, branding the comment ridiculous.

"She did?" countered Sutton, his disbelief plain.

"She has some very special friends who are RNs."

"She had a lot of *un*-special friends who are RNs too, didn't she?"

"She had a few, yes."

When Sutton finally turned his attention to Misty Reichenau's emergency, the incident Laura Little had questioned Sally about so carefully, he had already been interrogating Sally for more than forty-five minutes. He asked the witness, again, to describe the movement she saw in Misty when she first entered the room to assist. As he had hoped, almost word for word, she provided the same description she had earlier supplied Laura Little. "She was cyanotic. Her extremities were stiff, trembling. She had her hands in a clenched fist, turned toward the body. Her teeth were clenched, her eyes were rolling back up into her head.'' It had an unmistakably rehearsed quality.

Sutton posed one more question of significance concerning Misty's arrest. Sally had earlier testified that the child was struggling and seizing when she arrived, but Sutton's witnesses—the emergency medical technicians called to the scene—had testified the child was out cold. Knowing full well which of the witnesses the jury would believe, he asked her, ''If the EMTs described the child as being unconscious, would they be wrong?''

Sally sensed the trap and shied away from a direct answer, but after several exchanges, Sutton pinned her down: ''Would they be wrong?''

''On Misty Reichenau,'' Sally said firmly, ''yes.''

''They would be wrong.''

''Yes.''

Before he released the witness, Sutton pointed out to Sally that, on the day of Misty's emergency, it was *Genene* and *not* Kathleen who actually knew how big a dose of succinylcholine to give Misty. All had agreed that Dr. Holland wasn't sure, and Sally herself had testified she had no idea what the proper amount would be. ''But Genene did,'' Sutton pressed her, implicitly asking ''why.''

''Maybe she read up on it more than I,'' Sally offered.

''Maybe so.''

After lunch, the defense called EMT Tommy James, one of the two medics in Chelsea's ambulance the day of her death. He was there to establish just one fact. ''If Genene Jones had injected anything into Chelsea, or Chelsea's IV, would you have seen her?''

''Yes, I would have.''

''Mr. James, during that ride south to San Antonio, did you ever see Genene Jones inject anything into the line leading into Chelsea's body?''

''According to my recollection, no.''

''Did you ever see Genene Jones inject anything into the body of Chelsea McClellan, period?''

"According to my recollection, no."

On cross, Sutton did his best to dislodge Tommy's rock-hard certainty, but the medic refused to budge. Throughout, he maintained that, seated where he had been and keeping the kind of vigilance that he had, he would have noticed if Genene had given the child any injection. "He was retired military," recalled Brookshire, "an ex-marine. Very credible. He described Genene as very professional, very confident, and very self-assured, and held her in high regard. He was, in fact, one of the few witnesses we had who actually considered her a friend."

The fourth witness to testify on behalf of the defense was Dr. Angela Clark, a professor of nursing and a recognized expert at reading and interpreting medical records. She assisted Carnes in preparing a piece of demonstrative evidence that could compete with the large, dramatic chart the prosecution had propped up before the jury since the first day of trial. The defense had supplied Dr. Clark with Chelsea's medical records and asked her to draw from them a summary of "significant medical facts." For more than three hours, Carnes and Clark sifted through Chelsea's history, beginning with a prenatal notation of Chelsea's slow heartbeat just prior to the caesarean section, and ending with her death on September 17. Any notation Clark deemed significant was added to the chart. The defense intended to send along a graphic summary of Chelsea's many medical problems when the jury adjourned to commence their deliberations.

Although Sutton ultimately consented to the admission of Carnes's chart into evidence, during his cross-examination of Dr. Clark, he attacked its credibility on three grounds: First, the chart only included negative symptomatology, no positive; second, certain medical records containing favorable reviews of Chelsea's health had not been submitted to Dr. Clark for her consideration; and third, no effort was made to identify the author of the negative symptoms noted in Chelsea's chart—whether doctor, nurse, EMT, or the defendant herself. For these reasons, Sutton argued persuasively, the chart was not a fair representation of Chelsea's true medical history.

Brookshire next called Dr. Eric Comstock, the founder and president of the American Academy of Clinical Toxicology and a member of its board of examiners, which grants certification to clinical toxicologists. Comstock had spent the previous thirty years specializing in the treatment of poisonings and had been called to testify in detail about the effects of succinylcholine. The one significant additional piece of information Dr. Comstock added to the jurors' knowledge about the drug was that a suboptimal dose will only depress the activity of the muscles that move the arms, legs, and fingers, and will "leave the muscles of respiration essentially functional, or with varying degrees of weakness or impairment of breathing activity. You would not," he stated, "expect to find convulsive or seizurelike activity as a result of a suboptimal dose."

On cross-examination, Sutton posed a hypothetical question to the defense's expert witness: "Now assume, Doctor, that a child goes into a Clinic, gets an injection in each leg, and within a short period of time goes limp and has a respiratory arrest. The child later dies and through an autopsy and exhumation procedure, succinylcholine is found in the body tissue. Would that be consistent with an injection of succinylcholine?"

"You are stipulating that, in fact, succinylcholine was there?"

"Yes."

"If you tell me that, and I must accept that they have got succinylcholine in the body, then it had to come from somewhere."

"We will pass the witness."

On Monday, February 13, the defense called its star witness, Dr. Joseph Balkon, a forensic toxicologist from New York. Brookshire had chosen his expert carefully. Dr. Balkon was a young, likable, and very believable witness, the kind of man who, when talking about his academic and professional background, twice mentioned his wife fondly.

Brookshire said of him: "He was a very knowledgeable witness. I think probably as knowledgeable as Dr. Holmstedt. He was certainly a much better witness, I thought, a more knowledgeable witness, than Dr. Reiders. He was very professional and to the point. I think it was his youth that hurt us." One of the first points Dr. Balkon made to the jury was that he was a forensic and not a clinical toxicologist, emphasizing that his interests were oriented toward providing evidence for the prosecution in criminal trials. He knew what kinds of tests and what kinds of results constituted "proof" in criminal proceedings, and his clear implication was that Dr. Holmstedt and Dr. Reiders—both *clinical* toxicologists—did not. He was there to criticize, even contest, the results obtained in the Swedish tests, explaining to the jury that truly clean, definitive results were never obtained.

Dr. Balkon's testimony was based entirely on his analysis of the measurements Dr. Reiders had made with his gas chromatograph–mass spectrometer. The GCMS's measurements take the form of a jagged series of peaks on a graph similar to those from an EKG, EEG, or seismograph. The distance between peaks indicates the order in which the fragments of tested matter emerged from the gas chromatograph's tube. The height of each peak indicates the fragment's molecular weight. "What we want to see," Dr. Balkon explained, "is a sharp, well-resolved, well-defined peak in the graph, clearly paired with the control sample, the deuterated succinylcholine. When a succinylcholine molecule emerges from the gas chromatograph, the mass spectrometer cracks the succinylcholine molecule into three ions with the molecular weights of 58, 71, and 190. The deuterated succinylcholine molecule is broken into the same three ions, except these have molecular weights of 62, 75, and 194. The heavier of each pair is always recorded first, followed closely by the lighter, natural ion."

Dr. Balkon then took Dr. Reiders's measurements from each test run and analyzed them in front of the jury.

"There are five different tracings here for the right thigh muscle," Balkon reported, sorting through the small stack of papers. "On the top tracing, the ions monitored are the 58 ion paired with the 62 deuterated ion. In tracing number one, there is a 62 peak which is about 143.5 millimeters in height and is a nice, cleanly separated, and well-resolved peak. The peak for the 58 ion, however, is rather diffuse, indicating multiple ions being measured. However, the peak seems to have the right shape, so to speak, and coincides with the 62, so we would characterize that as being, you know, a pretty good indication that we should look further for whether we can confirm this indication of possible succinylcholine.

"Tracing number two is the same kind of thing. We have a 62 ion at 144 millimeters exactly, a peak we can tell something about, in terms of its shape. So we might say, in terms of the right muscle, that tracing number one and tracing number two look okay. They give us an indication that we should go further in this investigation.

"On tracing number three, we have a peak that simply does not match the criteria we originally established. It is a very fat peak, and it appears by looking at the diagram that there were extensive attempts to determine where exactly the peak resides. If I had this particular tracing alone, and didn't have the other two, I would have to say, 'Well, now, there is no succinylcholine in this particular case. The peak shape just does not match.' So we might say that we have two indications of an okay situation, but tracing number three really gives us some kind of hesitation.

"On tracing number four, there is a recording of the ions of 71 and 75. The 75 peak is a nice, large peak, but then there are really two fat peaks that occur in the vicinity of that 75. They are off in terms of where they occur, and they are certainly off in terms of the shape of the peak."

"What's that really mean," Brookshire interjected, "'the shape of the peak'?"

"The shape tells you something about the chemical character of the compound. A broad-shaped peak means that there are extra oxygens or extra nitrogens involved in the fragment. We also see that the peak labeled 'sample' [the 71 peak], is actually coming out *before* the internal standard—the deuterated 75 peak. But the deuterium internal standard *always* comes out before the actual succinylcholine sample that it's paired with. So we are seeing this material that is labeled succinylcholine coming out in a place where it's not supposed to be coming out. So, in regards to tracing number four, the 71/75 tracing, we would have to say that it, too, does not confirm the original hypothesis.

"In tracing number five, we are dealing with the ions 190 and 194. Now, there are a lot of peaks on the page, and there is really nothing wrong with that. The 194 ion appears as a fairly well resolved peak, but then where the 190 peak should be, we have this strange mix of material. In this particular case, it is hard to tell which peak, exactly, that we are interested in. They are not well resolved from each other, and because of this lack of resolution, we can't be sure whether we are measuring something that is specific for succinylcholine or just a lot of garbage in the background. So, we would have to say, about the 190 peak in tracing number five, that this did not confirm our original hypothesis either."

"All right, sir," said Brookshire, "let me ask you this: based upon the facts which you have developed from these tracings, can you say that succinylcholine was found in the right ventral thigh muscle?"

"No, I cannot."

"And why not?"

"Because it simply has not met the criteria of a positive identification."

"Doctor, is there anything unique about a 58 molecular weight so far as a chemical analysis goes?"

"No, there is not. Fifty-eight is a very common fragment. Particularly with drug materials that are alkaloid. In fact, a prominent researcher has identified at least two contaminants that are found in blood that give a 58 and also a 71. There are even materials that can get into the tissue samples from their containers that can contain 58s and 71s."

Dr. Balkon then reviewed the tracings Dr. Reiders prepared for the left ventral thigh muscle. Again, Balkon found them inadequate for a positive identification. His review of the tracings for the preserved kidney sample was slightly more favorable. "I think we have one trace here," he concluded, "which provides us with some sort of indication—an okay indication—and the rest of those traces are really not indicative. Based upon these findings, I could not ascribe the presence of succinylcholine."

Nor could Dr. Balkon support the presence of succinylcholine in the gall bladder tissue. He was even harsher in his criticism of the tracings from the formalin-fixed liver sample, finding that two of the three tracings did not indicate succinylcholine at all. By the time Brookshire passed his witness, Dr. Balkon had raised some serious doubts.

In a duel between competing expert witnesses, the lawyer's job is to make his expert look more expert than the other guy's. To this end, Sutton began his cross-examination by asking Dr. Balkon to read from one of his own articles: "'A recent report contributed a significant advance in the detection of this substance, vis-à-vis succinylcholine, employing selective extraction techniques in a highly specific capillary gas chromatographic–mass spectral detection scheme.'" The quoted material referred to was an article prepared by Drs. Forney, Carol, Nordgren, and Holmstedt concerning the possibility of detecting succinylcholine.

Sutton asked Dr. Balkon: "So you are complimenting Dr. Forney, Dr. Carol, Dr. Nordgren, and Dr. Holmstedt on their testing procedures."

"That is correct."

"And you said their research was somewhat a basis for your own article, is that right?"

"Absolutely." Balkon had no reluctance to give credit to Holmstedt and his associates. Nevertheless, Sutton was satisfied he had established who was the primary and who was the secondary authority.

For the benefit of any juror still inclined to accept Dr. Balkon's testimony that the tests were only an indication and not proof of succinylcholine, Sutton now began to build an alternative basis for finding that succinylcholine was present. He suggested over and over again, through different and seemingly innocuous, almost unrelated questions, that even if what Dr. Balkon said was true—the tracings were somewhat ambiguous—there was copious circumstantial evidence in this case to confirm the test results that succinylcholine had indeed been administered to these children.

Sutton then returned to his attack on the young man's expertise, as compared to that of the prosecution's two experts.

"Doctor, you are not saying that succinylcholine is *not* present in those samples, are you?"

"I am saying," Balkon answered, "that on the basis of the scientific investigation conducted, succinylcholine was not demonstrated to be present."

"So you don't agree with Dr. Reiders."

"No, I don't."

"What qualifications do you have to quarrel with Dr. Reiders's test, if you, as you have admitted, have never attempted to run the test in that low a range, less than ten nanograms?"

"The reasons why I have the 'guts,' so to speak, to challenge this," answered Balkon, slightly flustered, "are based upon solid scientific criteria—it is based upon his supporting information and the fact that he has not met those criteria one iota.''

"As a matter of fact, Doctor, right now you and Dr. Reiders also disagree on test findings in a horse case, don't you?''

"That is correct.''

"So you disagree with him on that, and you disagree with him on this.''

"I—certainly, if given the opportunity—*will* disagree with him on that, yes. Because his criteria proven in that case are even worse than in this.''

"You haven't been granted any Nobel Laureate awards, have you, sir?'' Sutton asked, falsely insinuating that either or both of his experts had.

"No, sir.'' Sutton nodded and relinquished the witness to the defense.

Brookshire aimed his redirect examination at just a couple of points. "When Dr. Reiders was down here testifying, as I recall, he made a point that interpretation of these tracings is an art. Would you describe this procedure as an art, Dr. Balkon?''

"As an *art*?'' repeated the doctor, taking a moment to consider his response. "That implies there is a lot of subjective evaluation of the information supplied by these tests. In my opinion, the subjective component is a much smaller component and the objective component is much larger. I mean, either the test material chromatographs the way it should, or it doesn't. Either the 71 or the 190 piece is there at the right place, or it isn't. What I mean to say is, the test results are not grey. They are black and white.''

"So basically what you are saying is, the test is interpreted by means of established criteria.''

"That is correct. Drs. Forney, Carol, Nordgren, and Holmstedt make a particular point in their article to set criteria for the identification of succinylcholine—it was identified by retention time and by mass spectra in the electron impact mode.''

"Would you explain what that means?"

"That means that Dr. Forney and company set as a criterion for the identification of succinylcholine the establishment of a full mass spectra."

"And has Dr. Reiders met this criterion for a full mass spectra in the tissue analysis which you have commented upon?"

"No."

The defense next called Dr. William Goldie, a respected pediatric neurologist whose main areas of interest were epilepsy, the specifics of the development of sensory pathways through the brain stems, and disorders of the brain stem that can occur in infants. Together with Brookshire, Dr. Goldie focused more closely on the many troubling aspects of Chelsea's medical history. He started by commenting upon the drug that had been used to treat Chelsea's cyanosis following birth. "Theophylline," he explained, "is a stimulant for breathing which has been found to be very effective if the child is not breathing adequately because something is wrong with the brain drive."

"And what," Brookshire asked, "would the use of this drug that stimulated the brain centers suggest to you about Chelsea McClellan?"

"Well, it suggests that somewhere along the line someone was concerned about this child's central drive for breathing, meaning that there wasn't adequate brain drive for adequate respirations."

"Were you able to study the nurses' notes regarding Chelsea's behavior while in the hospital?"

"Yes. I was impressed that the child slept a great deal and was not described as being very active. And, of course, that is always a little bit worrisome."

"Why is that worrisome?"

"Well, you usually expect a child to go through specific sleep states, and during active sleep states (and, of course, wakefulness) you expect to see a good deal of activity— moving around, sucking behavior, grimacing, movement of the hands and legs and so on. When it is absent, the concern is that the child is not neurologically normal.''

"You made, as I understand, some notation as to head circumference also?"

"Yes. I was impressed that upon her arrival in San Antonio, I believe, the initial head circumference was described as 32 centimeters. And at the time of discharge, when the child was about nineteen or twenty days of age, the head circumference was described as 31.5 centimeters—or a loss of one-half a centimeter.''

"What does the loss of one-half a centimeter tell a physician?"

"Well, as a pediatric neurologist, I depend on the head circumference as an indicator of the growth of the brain, the good health of the brain. When there is not adequate head growth, that bothers me. It makes me think there may be something wrong with the quality of the child's initial development.''

Dr. Goldie also explained that the normal EEG reading for Chelsea meant relatively little. "I tend to specialize in pediatric EEG, and I realize its limits. I have seen seizures in children who tested normal; I have seen children with rather significant neurological problems test normal. I recall one very unfortunate child—initially described as a breath-holder and who also tested normal EEG—who developed rather severe seizures and actually had to be maintained in the hospital for over a year because of repetitive seizures. He subsequently died and even after meticulous examination during the autopsy, we were unable to find a specific cause of death.''

Brookshire referred Dr. Goldie to some selected notes and charts from Chelsea's medical history that had earlier been supplied to him. Dr. Goldie had found in the notes a diagnosis of autonomic instability recorded by a Dr. Rutlan, a consulting pediatric neurologist. "That implies," Dr. Goldie explained, "that in the absence of other signs of nervous system disorder, if the autonomic nervous system is somehow selectively dysfunctional, then you can have rather serious consequences.''

"Such as what?"

"Apnea, lack of respirations, and instability of heart rate.''

"Okay," responded Brookshire, "during the course of the August 24 visit to Dr. Holland's Clinic the medical records reflect that the child suffered an apneic spell, followed by a respiratory arrest. The child was then described as limp, followed by a tonoclonic seizure. Would this description of a child's behavior pattern alarm you in any manner?"

"It is very worrisome. I would consider the possibility that this child is, indeed, in high risk for neurologic disease, including epilepsy, or some form of brain-stem dysfunction.''

Brookshire and Dr. Goldie then went through the available notes chronicling Chelsea's stay in Sid Peterson following the August 24 emergency. Brookshire directed the doctor's attention to the notation for August 27, which stated, "After receiving injection, the child became cyanotic.''

"Did you attach any significance to that, Doctor?"

"Well, I think it certainly fits into the picture of this child as being very, let's say unstable—a child who seems to have unusual reactions to stress. It suggests a child who is unstable in the automatic control of respirations and heart rate.''

"You will note," Brookshire directed, "that on August 29 there is, in addition to a small finger twitch, an indication that 'two seizures occurred last P.M., child was postictal followed by a blue spell.' Again, would these continuing patterns, even after the Dilantin dosage had been increased, cause you concern?"

"Well, in our institution, this child would be in an Intensive Care Unit with constant EEG monitoring.''

Brookshire continued: "Again at two o'clock on the

twenty-ninth, two days after the first time the child had received an injection, the nurse notes a second injection: 'The child became cyanotic, and sleeps soundly after each episode.' Again, is this indicative of the child's sensitive autonomic system?''

"I think this whole picture is quite consistent with that, yes.''

Brookshire turned their discussion to September 17. "Assuming that there had been no observation of any movement in that child, in other words, the child was not breathing and was totally limp, is there any medical explanation as to why a dose of 80 milligrams Dilantin IV push would have been administered?''

"Well, again, assuming that the physician was well trained and well experienced, I cannot understand why there would be any reason to administer Dilantin other than to treat ongoing seizure activity.''

"So should we, then, be able to safely assume there *was* seizure activity in order for a dose of that magnitude to be given?''

"Yes.''

Summing up the September 17 incident, Brookshire posed a hypothetical question to Dr. Goldie regarding the effects of succinylcholine. "Doctor, assuming a child was fifteen months old and weighed approximately twenty pounds, received an injection or injections of succinylcholine at approximately 10:30, 11:00, was taken to the hospital emergency room where her color was good, was intubated, breathing on her own, and—at least according to her medical records—was stable enough to be transferred to another hospital out of town, I ask you, could the administration of succinylcholine one and a half to two hours earlier bring about cardiac arrest?''

"No.''

"And when you say it cannot, would you please explain why it cannot?''

"Given intravenously, the effects last about five to ten minutes. Given intramuscularly—which I am not familiar with—it is a little more erratic and may last up to twenty minutes, maybe a half an hour at most. Certainly with the intervening well-documented history of a stable child at the emergency room, the effects of succinylcholine would have been gone.''

In reviewing the autopsy records, Dr. Goldie told the jury that Dr. Kagan-Hallet's description of fibrillary gliosis and nerve cell loss was significant. ''It is a real, true finding which has been associated in the literature as being found in children who die from sudden death—children who have suffered rather prolonged hypoxia or severe hypoxic injury in the perinatal period [immediately following birth], like Chelsea. It is not a trivial finding.''

''Can such scarring as was found in the brain tissues of Chelsea McClellan be said to have caused the death?''

''I feel that given the entire picture, including the perinatal history, the associated risk factors of the birth, the past history of respiratory instability, the diagnosis of autonomic instability, and the unusual reactivity this child had, I would have to, in my own judgment, assume that these pathological findings played a major role in this child's death.''

Brookshire wrapped up his case in chief with one last question: ''Could succinylcholine have been the cause of this child's death?''

Dr. Goldie answered carefully: ''The medical records which were available to me—Dr. Holland's notes, the emergency room notes, the ambulance staff's notes, et cetera—do not describe any instance of prolonged hypoxia, and the autopsy specifically denies any findings of hypoxia as would be seen in the neurons of the hippocampus of the cerebellum. The story, as I see it, is not at all compatible with death caused by an injection of succinylcholine.''

''I will pass the witness.''

Sutton began his cross-examination cautiously, ''Doctor, you are not saying that this death was *not* caused by succinylcholine, you are just saying *in your opinion* it was not, based on the history given to you by Mr. Brookshire, right?''

''I can only offer my opinion.''

''Yes, sir, but your opinion is based upon the story as told to you by Mr. Brookshire and the records he made available to you, correct?''

''Specifically, upon review of the records that were available, yes.''

''Doctor, I will show you state's exhibit number 6 [the photo of Chelsea], and ask if that appears to be a healthy child. It does, does it not?''

''It looks like a nice, healthy child, as do many children with neurologic disease.''

''Well, you are assuming neurologic disease, aren't you, Doctor?''

''I am adding that as a possibility.''

''You never saw this child in your life, did you?''

''No, I did not.''

''You never examined this child in your life.''

''That is correct.''

''And you are making all these assumptions on the basis of some medical reports that you don't have any idea whether or not they are true or false, isn't that correct?''

''When I consult on a case, I rely predominantly on the history and records, and then add to that my own examination.''

''If there were false records in here, false reports of seizures, then your conclusions go right out the window, don't they, Doctor?''

''Yes.''

Sutton then offered his own hypothetical question to Goldie, a long question that lasted almost ten minutes, progressing through three objections by Carnes. In this hypothetical case, Sutton provided Goldie with an anonymous but rather detailed summary of each of the other five emergencies in Kathleen's Clinic. At the end, he asked: ''Now, Doctor, from what I have described, you being an expert in the field of pediatrics who operates his own clinic, from what I have described, is this consistent with somebody in that office using succinylcholine in such a way that it caused respiratory arrest in these different children?''

Carnes objected yet again—the question was too general. The court instructed Sutton to narrow his scope.

''I think I can do it this way, Your Honor,'' he said, turning back to the witness. ''If the same situation were to occur in your clinic, Doctor, would you be concerned about it?''

''Well, the only way I can respond to that is to state that, obviously, the picture is worrisome and deserves investigation.''

''Okay, Doctor, I think that is a very fair answer. If such were indeed the facts here, Doctor, would that cause you to possibly reevaluate your opinions as to the death of Chelsea McClellan?''

''My opinions on the death of Chelsea McClellan are based on the facts which were provided to me, which I read, made notes on, absorbed in great detail, and made my conclusions from.''

''Would it surprise you, Doctor, to learn that some of the 'facts' you reviewed were absolutely false history?''

''Well, I think, that, you know, what we have to go on here is the history that is available.''

''Have you ever had occasion, Doctor, where people giving you history just outright lied to you?''

''Yes.''

''And it sure messes up the thought processes in trying to arrive at the truth, does it not, Doctor?''

''I always try to figure out whether there is a particular reason. That is oftentimes very revealing, but obviously it interferes with the attainment of the truth. The facts have to be specific.''

''And truthful and accurate. Isn't that correct, Doctor?''

''Well, obviously that clouds the entire issue.''

''Yes. I appreciate that very much. Thank you, sir.''

* * *

On the morning of Tuesday, February 14, outside the presence of the jury, Genene Jones herself took the stand, but only to confirm that she had knowingly and intelligently waived her right to testify.

"There'll always be some question as to whether or not Genene should have gotten up and testified," Brookshire later reflected. "I still feel comfortable, and Burt Carnes agrees in this, that the right decision was made in that regard. Early on we discussed it quite frankly with Genene, on many occasions. It was our feeling that, in the end, Genene couldn't really add anything. All the testimony was in, and the only thing she could do was make a personal appearance before the jury—and we didn't think that would increase her chances.

"Quite frankly, Genene's temperament is such that she just can't control herself. She and Sutton literally despised each other. I knew if we put her up there, he would play on this and bully her to the point where she would lose control. We didn't think she had the emotional capacity to stand up there and slug it out with Ron. Genene herself made the decision not to testify. I think she recognized that Ron Sutton had the capacity to get her goat whenever he wanted to. She used to say, 'Ron Sutton is the most evil human alive. He's the devil.'"

Before Genene resumed her seat, she stated for the record that she was satisfied with the services of Brookshire, Carnes, and Little. At that point, the jury was brought back in, and Brookshire rested his case.

Counsel for both sides then presented rebuttal testimony, evidence intended to contradict and disprove the points made by the opposition. Through a rather bizarre procedure, the prosecuting attorneys read testimony taken nearly two weeks earlier, out of the presence of the jury, from Dr. Holmstedt and Dr. Reiders while they were still in town. Rothe played the parts of Holmstedt and Reiders, while Sutton read the questions he had previously put to the two witnesses. The testimony thus presented concerned a second series of tests that Dr. Holmstedt's assistant, Dr. Ingrid Nordgren, had run on Chelsea's tissue samples. The results confirmed Dr. Reiders's earlier tests.

Brookshire's cross-examination of the witness, also read from a transcription of earlier testimony, focused the jury's attention on the possibility that succinylcholine might be manufactured in the body through an enzymatic reaction among the constituent elements of succinylcholine—all found naturally occurring in the body. "Not enough succinylcholine to paralyze someone," Brookshire clarified, "but enough to measure in trace amounts." Perhaps even as much as several nanograms.

Brookshire, with "Dr. Holmstedt's" assistance, brought one other interesting fact to the jury's attention with this reenacted testimony. The reason, in Holmstedt's opinion, that the greatest quantity of succinylcholine was found in Chelsea's right thigh muscle was probably because the injection introducing the succinylcholine had been given to her intramuscularly in the right thigh. The testimony compelled the conclusion that if Genene indeed had injected Chelsea with succinylcholine, she had done it at the Clinic, under the guise of an inoculation. Since Chelsea had thereafter recovered from the drug during her hour-long stay in Sid Peterson's ER and resumed normal breathing, presumably it was not the succinylcholine that killed her, but the natural weaknesses in her neural system.

The state then called Dr. James Garriott, chief forensic toxicologist for the Bexar County medical examiner's office in San Antonio and medical professor for the University of Texas's Health Science Center in San Antonio. At the ME's office, he and his staff of five toxicologists performed "just about every kind of forensic laboratory testing, other than ballistics." They made constant use of the gas chromatograph–mass spectrometer, running ten to twenty tests per day, so Garriott was very familiar with the kinds of results the gas chromatograph–mass spectrometer produced.

Sutton called Dr. Garriott to refute Dr. Balkon's testimony that Dr. Reiders's test results did not meet the criteria necessary for a finding of succinycholine. Dr. Garriott explained why the test results did not present the nice clean peaks Dr. Balkon evidently was accustomed to.

"The mass spectrometer has, for most compounds, a detection limit in the low-nanogram range. When you get below the detection limit, or if you are pushing it to its sensitivity limit, you get into the noise ratio of the instrument. So if you are looking for very, very small peaks on your ion chromatograms, you are going to have some variability. By that I mean you may have a very slight shift in your retention time, or you might have a broad peak rather than a sharp peak. But at these low levels, the important thing is to take everything, all the characteristics, into consideration."

"And having reviewed all these charts, in your opinion," Sutton asked, "is it conclusive as to the presence of succinylcholine?"

"In my opinion it is conclusive, yes."

"Is that a reasonable scientific certainty?"

"Yes, it is."

On cross, Carnes raised the possibility that the finite amounts of succinylcholine found in Chelsea's tissues may have been deposited there during an earlier medical episode, or even prenatally, due to an administration of the drug to Petti McClellan. He induced Dr. Garriott to confirm that, although succinylcholine disappears from the blood in six to ten minutes, it may be retained in the tissues and organs for much longer, perhaps even months.

Brookshire called only one witness in rebuttal, again putting Dr. Balkon on the stand, albeit in the same ghostly form as Drs. Holmstedt and Reiders earlier. The court reporter played both parts this time, reading from his machine-made shorthand hieroglyphics, since a transcription of the testimony had not yet been prepared. Through the reporter, Balkon reviewed and criticized Dr. Nordgren's test results, just as he earlier had Dr. Reiders's, tracing by tracing. Each time the defense asked the question: "Does this tracing demonstrate the presence of succinylcholine?" Each time, the witness answered: "No." Before the defense relinquished its paper witness to the state, the court reporter offered the jury Balkon's somewhat startling observation: "I might also add one more point in regard to this, and that is in terms of the review of the other tracings that were supplied by Dr. Reiders. There are tracings in that package of material [from Dr. Reiders] which are *exactly* the same as these traces here [from Dr. Nordgren]."

Sutton's cross-examination of Dr. Balkon was also read in flat tones by the court reporter. Even so, it was clear that Sutton was outraged by Dr. Balkon's concluding observation.

"Okay, Doctor, you say these tracings are exactly the same. What do you mean by that?"

"I don't have all the material here present, but if we spread these out and spread out the tracings from Dr. Reiders, we could match them identically, peak for peak; a trace from this package [Dr. Nordgren's] to a trace from the package that Dr. Reiders provided."

"Are you saying Dr. Nordgren just xeroxed Dr. Reiders's work?"

"I am not saying anything of the sort. All I am doing is making the observation."

"That is your opinion, that she copied his work."

"I don't know why they are that way."

"That is the implication you are making."

"All I am making is the observation, Counsellor."

"That is the implication, isn't it—that she copied Dr. Reiders's work, just xeroxed it?"

"Your implication, Counsellor."

"That is what you are saying: 'They are exactly the same.'"

"All I am making is the observation."

"You haven't done any measurements on those?"

"Which kind of measurements?"

"Measuring the peaks."

"Have I gotten a ruler out and measured them line for line?"

"Yes, Doctor."

"No. What I have done is I have taken this tracing, placed the other tracing behind it, held it up to the light, and the lines matched identically."

"And you can distinguish between a point of one-hundredth of a nanogram by holding it up to the light?"

"Maybe the answer to this criteria, Counsellor," Dr. Balkon suggested, "is to take two and simply do that."

"I am sorry?"

"Taking this and superimposing the other chromatographic tracing one to one—it has virtually all the same features all the way down the line, and indicates that they are, possibly, the same."

"But you didn't do any measuring."

"No, I did not."

"And you can't detect by holding them up and looking at them a hundredth of a degree of a nanogram difference in the reading."

"I could not do that."

"As a matter of fact, Doctor, if they were *not* consistent, that could be more of a concern than if they *were* consistent."

"Possibly, yes."

On that exchange, the prosecution and defense both closed. Judge Carter took over.

"Ladies and gentlemen of the jury, we have now concluded the evidentiary stage of this trial. Tomorrow we will conclude another stage. At nine o'clock in the morning, we are going to have final arguments in this case and each side will have their opportunity to sum up. After that, we will go into the stage of the trial where the case is in your hands."

Jim Brookshire

I'm a firm believer that that jury didn't listen to a damn thing we came up with. I think we were literally turned off because of those damn big calendars they had set up and, uh, Genene didn't help.

She sat there and she'd mess around writing letters and glaring at people, and, oh, eating candy, just generally being a jackass. And the jury got mad at her. They didn't like her. She didn't act at all sorry, or even too concerned. Most of the time she just looked . . . kind of bored.

She did stare at Holland, as I recall. She just couldn't believe Holland would turn around. I don't know what she thought Holland was going to say, but Genene— See, Genene has a very intense personality, by that I mean her will, her drive, her determination is very strong, very powerful. She was ripped apart by Holland testifying against her the way she did.

But ol' Genene, she's a lot like a cockroach I guess, 'cause the next morning she came in and just sat there straight-faced.

How is it that you got involved?

Well, the last few years I've been doing more criminal work because I enjoy it more. It affords me a freedom that I find civil work and office practice doesn't. I just can't stand to sit in an office. There's nothing fun about it. But criminal work, I don't know, I guess maybe it has to do with the excitement of being in a damn courtroom, you know? I mean, while you're in it, you cuss yourself out and you cut it down and you say it's miserable and "I'll never do it again" and "God, I hate this stuff," but you really don't. It's just such a huge challenge that when you come out ahead, it's worth it. It's an accomplishment. See, for a defense attorney, in criminal law at least, the wins are very few. Very few. You measure your wins by maybe saving a guy twenty years off a forty-year sentence, or something like that. The state's got it all going for them—no matter what anybody says about all our rules, you know, about protecting the defense. Bull. A prosecutor knows, *going in,* what his case is worth, and if it's not worth a damn, he's gonna offer you a plea bargain. If you don't take it, you're not doing your client a good service. So, most times you plead out. On those cases he's got you nailed to the wall, he's not going to offer a deal, he's going to trial, chalk up another win for himself. Usually you're left just sitting there while he nails you. So, you know, in criminal defense, we do what we can.

What were some of the worst days in this case?

I really can't recall, specifically. I remember there were a couple, but I just can't tell you which they were. The worst thing about it all, I mean generally, the worst aspect, was just sitting there for two solid weeks listening to them day after day stuffing it down our throats. Person after person. They just hammered us. And then, you know, we'd score a couple of points on cross-examination, and we'd be up. Then they'd crush us back down with the next witness—you never know just what they're going to say. And so we were down and had to work our way back up again. And, of course, that kind of spilled over into our life outside the courtroom. Sutton lost his wife because of this thing. Cases like Genene's, they're marriage destroyers, no doubt about it. If you're scoring on a good case, you're up, but I can remember days that were so goddamned low, I mean lower than whale shit. It was horrible. Sick as we were, we were down there every morning at 6:00 A.M., fixing her hair, and we bought her dresses so she could look nice. She'd had a pair of blue jeans when she came here, that's it. We got her six or seven dresses—a couple of our secretaries donated some—and we rotated cleaning service on them. Patty put her makeup on.

Patty, what's your impression of her?

(PATTY) Well . . . I visited Genene every day—almost every day. They let me be in the tank with her and I'd sit there and visit for a couple of hours, maybe ten minutes, maybe most of the day, depending on her mood. I'd say, looking back, that Genene was her own biggest enemy. She had this wonderful fountain pen and loved to write. And loved to grant interviews, and loved to have people listen to her talk. It seemed that from the start, when we first got involved, her face was on the front page of all the newspapers and on every newscast. She constantly put herself in front of the public. That's what she wanted, but it wasn't what was good for her, and that was hard to deal with. When Jim says we worked twenty-five hours a day, he means it. We did. Seven days a week. Every day. I looked at a calendar one day and I realized I had worked something like 28 days in a row. No time off. We were tired. We were trying to save her life, and it was almost as if she really didn't care.

(BROOKSHIRE) I remember every once in a while she'd put on a goddamned show, some number, like one day she was gonna faint because of a sinus attack. Another time, and this was near the start of the trial, she had to be rushed to the hospital 'cause, well, because she had told somebody right before we were to start that she thought she was pregnant. When we got her to the hospital, it turned out she was constipated. Genene hurt herself as much as anything. She hurt herself.

What do you think? Did she do it?

I will never know until my dying day whether or not she killed those babies. Burt and I are of the same mind, and I think Patty and Laura are too. She tells a legitimate enough story that . . . except for . . . had it not been for that bottle of succinylcholine, the one from the Clinic, the one Holland turned in, I could believe her right on down the line. But for me, that vial is a real problem. What happened to it? It wasn't even supposed to be open, yet it was all but gone. Diluted. Why?

But, still, even with that, I'll still never know. Somebody diluted it, certainly; but who? Because the other thing is, we've had doctors tell us: "She may have killed these kids, but she damn sure didn't kill 'em with succinylcholine. Impossible."

Questions.

Yes. Always will be, I guess.

TWENTY-TWO

So ends the bloody business of the day.

Homer

WEDNESDAY, FEBRUARY 15, 1984, "THE rule" was suspended and anyone who wished to and who could fit into the crowded courtroom could attend the final Act of the trial. And everyone was there. Space had been reserved for the parents and relatives of the children who had been the subject of testimony, and most had sent representatives, as had newspapers and TV stations from across the country.

"Ladies and gentlemen," Judge Carter began the day's proceedings by addressing the jury, "good morning. We are now at the stage of the trial in which I am going to read to you the charge of the court. After I have read the charge, I am going to give the lawyers an opportunity to make their final arguments. They may split up those arguments, or one person may argue for the entire side. They decide.

"After the final arguments are concluded, you will take the charge with you to the jury room and will begin your deliberations."

Judge Carter slipped on a pair of reading glasses and cleared his throat, then read: "'Cause No. 83-297-K, the

State of Texas v. *Genene Jones*. The law that applies to this case is as follows:

"'A person commits the offense of murder if she intends to cause serious bodily injury and intentionally or knowingly commits an act clearly dangerous to human life that causes the death of an individual. A person is criminally responsible for an act if the result would not have occurred but for her conduct, operating with her alone or concurrently with another cause, unless the concurrent cause was clearly sufficient to produce the result and the conduct of the actor clearly insufficient.

"'Unless you find from the evidence beyond a reasonable doubt that the death of Chelsea McClellan was caused by an injection of succinylcholine administered by the defendant, Genene Jones, you will say by your verdict "Not Guilty;" if you have a reasonable doubt thereof, you will say by your verdict, "Not Guilty."

"'Our law provides that a defendant may testify in her own behalf if she elects to do so. This, however, is a privilege accorded the defendant and in the event she elects to not testify, that fact must not be taken as a circumstance against her. In this case, the defendant has so elected, and you are instructed that you cannot and must not refer to or allude to that fact throughout your deliberations or take it into consideration for any purpose whatsoever as a circumstance against her.

"'You are instructed that if there is any testimony before you in this case regarding the defendant's having committed offenses other than the offense alleged against her in the indictment, you cannot consider said testimony for any purpose unless you find and believe that it has been proven beyond a reasonable doubt that the defendant committed such other offenses, and even then you may only consider the same in determining motive, intent, design, or scheme of the defendant, if any, in connection with the offense alleged against her in the indictment in this case, and for no other purpose.

"'You are the exclusive judges of the facts proved, of the credibility of the witnesses, and of the weight to be given to their testimony, but you are also bound to receive the law from the court, which is herein given to you, and you are governed thereby.

"'In all criminal cases, the burden of proof is on the state and the defendant is presumed to be innocent until the defendant's guilt is established by legal evidence beyond a reasonable doubt; and, in this case if you find you have a reasonable doubt as to the defendant's guilt, you will acquit the defendant and say by your verdict "Not Guilty."'

"Ladies and gentlemen of the jury, that is the charge of the court." Carter then handed the charge to the bailiff and turned to the lawyers. "Are we ready to proceed?"

"Yes, Your Honor," replied Sutton, "the state is ready to proceed."

"All right, I have 9:20. Go ahead."

Scott Monroe stepped to the podium for the state. He began by again thanking the jury for their time and attention, then explained to them just what the legal system expected of them in the coming hours.

"The charge of the court will be handed to you when you retire [so that] you can read and refer to [it] from time to time as you might [see fit]. If you remember back to the first and second days that you all were here, each of you took an oath that you would follow the law as given to you, and that you would render your verdict according to that oath. Each of us here is now holding you to that oath.

"You may have heard someone mention that today (really, the past month) has been Genene Jones's day in court, and in a lot of respects, that is true; but I submit to you, ladies and gentlemen, that this is a lot of other people's day in court, too. It is Kerr County's day in court. It is the state of Texas's day in court. It is a day in court for the United States." Here he gestured to the assembled audience, "and it is a day in court for a lot of families sitting out here too. One in particular.

"There is a lot more at stake here than just the defendant's day in court, and you twelve people—I am sure you are aware, the judge has instructed you every day about the media coverage—you know the importance of this trial. Your decision is going to be scrutinized by many, many, many people, looked over dozens of times. In many ways, you enjoy a certain privilege because you are on this jury. You are setting the course for a lot of events to come. And you are making a decision that a lot of other people would love to make.

"You know, weeks ago Mr. Sutton told you, and Mr. Brookshire told you, that as a juror you have to do one thing that some people find very difficult to do: to sit in judgment of their peers and to weigh their credibility. That means you have to decide who you believe and who you don't believe. You may have to reflect back to several instances in this trial when there has been a conflict in testimony, and you will have to decide who it is you are going to believe. That is sometimes difficult to do, but you told us [in the beginning] that you would be able to do that when the time came, and today we are asking you to reach down inside yourself and do just that. Now is the time. And remember, the decision that you make will not long be forgotten.

"I want, also, to remind you all of one thing: Each of the attorneys, Mr. Sutton, Mr. Rothe, and Mr. Carnes, will presently remind you of the facts as they remember them, but bear in mind that it is how *you* remember the facts that is important, how you interpret them, and which facts you choose to hold on to and which facts you choose to disregard. I can assure you, you will hear more than one version of the facts today, as there are two sides to every story, but as we told you in *voir dire,* the state is responsible for proving certain facts. We had to prove them—each and every one— that 'Genene Jones, in Kerr County, Texas, on or about September 17, 1982, did then and there, with intent to cause serious bodily injury to an individual, namely, Chelsea Mc-Clellan, intentionally and knowingly commit an act clearly dangerous to human life by injecting Chelsea McClellan with succinylcholine, thereby causing her death.'

"Ladies and gentlemen, I submit to you that after you have heard all the arguments and you retire to deliberate, you will be compelled—not just inclined, but *compelled*— by whatever spirit that moves you, your conscience, your

God, or whatever, to find the defendant, Genene Jones, guilty of the offense. Thank you very much.''

"You used ten minutes, Counsellor. Mr. Rothe.''

"Thank you, Your Honor,'' began Rothe, moving to the podium. He checked his watch and the clock on the wall; he had just under an hour to speak his piece. "You know, as time goes by in my career—and each time I look, it seems to go by faster—I've stood before many juries, delivering many closing arguments for many different reasons, but I really can't say that ever in my life have I stood in front of a jury who was being asked to judge a set of facts such as you have heard here in Georgetown. I have never seen anything like this, and I hope I never do again.

"It is, I think, important to remember that when you were summoned here as jurors, you were summoned as citizens, as people who live here, who have jobs, who do whatever it is you do every day. You weren't asked to come here in some unique capacity. You were simply asked to come here—and I think you all have—as honest, tax-paying citizens of this county, and as human beings as well. And one thing that we all have—or should have—is common sense. Unfortunately,'' he said, turning to the defendant, "common sense is something that some people *don't* have.

"What you folks have to do in looking at this situation— and it is a complex situation, I might even say it is bizarre, totally bizarre. Why? Because of its setting. What we are dealing with here is a setting in which a murder took place, but in a setting in which that is the *antithesis,* the *opposite,* of what is supposed to happen. In this case, we have a murder that took place in the context of a medical environment. The Hippocratic oath, and all those things we hold near and dear in terms of physicians, tells us that the ultimate responsibility of anyone in the medical field is to *preserve* life. And that is why this case is so bizarre, so unique, and so horrifying—a murder in a medical environment. And beyond that, we are talking about babies, babies as victims, and that is unique. And because this case is so unique, what we ask you to focus on is the whole picture, not any little narrow portion of it, but the whole picture. As Mr. Sutton said in the beginning, if you remember, he said it would be like building a pyramid with blocks until you get to the top, and when you top it off, then it's a structure. It is complete. This case is such a structure.

"When you get back in the jury room, you'll take these exhibits with you, the calendars. Look at them. You'll also be taking in what you remember of the trial: the witnesses, what they said, their credibility. What we want you to do is think back and remember it all with the best of your ability. We think that if you do that, you'll come to the right decision.

"One thing that I think can happen when you have fifty-plus witnesses like we've had here, maybe you lose sight of what it's all about. It's easy to think: *'There are so many details!'* And maybe feel a little bit overwhelmed. There were big fights here, arguments, lengthy, contradictory testimony about extremely complex, sophisticated, state-of-the-art electronic equipment, state-of-the-art pharmacology, toxicology, expert doctors discussing EEGs and things like that for hours and days and weeks! And sometimes you can lose sight of something. And so I'd like to remind you now about what this case is all about. What you are going to be deciding about. It's about two things." Rothe picked up Chelsea's photo from the exhibit table and crossed to the jury box. "It's about a dead little girl." The photo showed a small blond child in a blue dress with white lace trim and blue bonnet to match. The little girl in the picture is laughing, probably at her mother standing somewhere behind the photographer's right shoulder. Rothe gave the front row a good look, then turned to Genene, whipping the photo from view. "And it's about a nurse. A self-proclaimed 'pediatric clinician,'" and now he turned back to the jury, "which she is *not*. That is what this is all about."

After weeks of facts, someone was finally talking about something else, something emotional, and everyone was listening. Rothe now held the photo up for the second row of jurors who had not yet clearly taken another look—he had not forgotten them. "And what this is all about is:

how did *that* nurse affect *this* baby so that we are all sitting here today? And that is what we need to talk about." Rothe moved to the state's table.

"How did Chelsea McClellan, a fourteen-month-old with the sniffles, end up moments later at the Sid Peterson emergency room because she couldn't breathe? How did that happen? It happened because that nurse," he pointed at Genene, "was alone with this baby," holding up the picture, "because the mother," and now he gestured toward a section of the audience where Petti and Reid sat listening, "was talking with the doctor.

"So, that child is alone with the nurse, and what happens? Down she goes." Rothe carefully set Chelsea's photo on the exhibit table and crossed to the podium. "With what? 'Seizures.'

"I've heard that an awful lot lately. It kind of seems like there must have been almost an epidemic of seizures running through the Texas Hill Country, there in Kerrville, if we are to understand the defense. Strangely enough, all these seizures only occurred in the immediate vicinity of one nurse, not anywhere else. And, I might add, not before, and not since."

Rothe commanded his audience's complete attention. He took them through the beginning of the final emergency, telling each of them the facts of the case as he remembered them, constantly insinuating that the only reason they were all sitting there was because Chelsea had had the terrible misfortune to cross paths with the defendant.

"She went there because her brother had a problem of some sort, but it was determined that she ought to get her immunization shots.

"All right, now the doctor, again—interestingly enough, at that point in time—is not in the room. The *nurse* is, and so was Chelsea and so was Chelsea's mother. And the interesting thing is that here, at this point, the sheer, audacious bravado of this nurse becomes very clear. Some egotistical thing of some sort. The baby is sitting in its mother's lap to get her immunization shots.

So she gets a shot in the thigh, Chelsea McClellan, who didn't go there to be treated, and what happens?''

He gestured toward Petti again. ''What did the mother tell you? Petti McClellan'' he pointed at the witness chair, ''who sat right there—a very, very difficult thing for anyone. Can you imagine?

''So the child starts to tremble and shake, okay? And the mother said: 'There is something wrong with her.'

''And what does the nurse say? 'Oh, she is just mad. She is just a mad kid. Doesn't like the shots.'

'''She's shaking. Something is wrong.'

'''She is just mad.''' Rothe looked into the eyes of the jurors, shaking his head at the unbelievability of it. ''Can you imagine?

''So the child gets a *second* needle. Wham. Then what happens? Can't tell if she is mad anymore, because she is looking her mother right dead in the eye and she *can't move!*

''And what did the mother say? 'I have never seen anything like that.'

''Now you all have seen scared kids. I have. I have been scared myself. Every one of us has. Again, let's look at this with some common sense. What does your common sense tell you? When you look into someone's eyes when they are scared, you know. You can tell that they're scared. And there may be,'' he said, looking at Genene, ''somebody in this courtroom that may be afraid of me, but can you imagine,'' he said, turning back to the jury, ''what a child . . .'' And now, for the first time, Rothe was momentarily at a loss for words, struggling with a thought he had difficulty expressing. ''Can you imagine? A child, who can't defend itself, who can't yet even talk, is looking into its mother's eyes and can't move and can't breathe, and the mother doesn't know what is wrong and says to the nurse, 'Do something.'

'''She is just mad,''' he repeated, letting the words sink in.

''As the scenario continues to unfold, the child is what? Limp as a rag doll, she just drops. And that isn't the first time it'd happened. You can go back through the calendar,'' striding over to the charts, he directed the jury's attention to the red ink, "and add the names up. There are rag dolls all over these calendars because they are all the same, except one, which we will talk about in a little bit.

"So the doctor comes in. What do we hear again? 'She had a seizure.' So seizure is set up. And anybody who is not there has to rely on what they are told and treat accordingly. They don't know any different, except the nurse who knows, but she isn't talking.

"On the way to Sid Peterson, what happens? Code Blue. Heart stops. The respiration has already stopped. In the ER, Dr. Mason is there. Being an emergency room physician, what does he say in retrospect after having seen a couple more? He says, 'This child appeared to me to be coming out from under the effects of succinylcholine.'

"'Succinylcholine.' That we have heard a lot about too. One thing I think everybody can agree on is that it is one of the deadliest drugs known to mankind. You give somebody a shot of that stuff and they sit back there and look out at you horrified, *and can do nothing.* Imagine what that must be like, to be looking out at somebody, and you want to say help, but you . . . just . . . *can't.* You are thinking, 'My God'—because the stuff doesn't stop your brain—but you can't *do* anything!

"So, they load the baby into the ambulance because they are going to go to San Antonio. And as they are getting into the ambulance, we have a witness who came in here and testified, a little gal by the name of DeAnna Armour: 'Jones shoots the child in the leg.'"

And now Rothe again enacted the conversation, playing both parts. First DeAnna: "'What is that?'

And then Genene: 'Valium.'

"But," he reminded his listeners, "the kid has just had Valium."

"They get in the ambulance, they start on their way to San Antonio, and what happens? The nurse screams out—keep in mind the nurse has a little bag of goodies with her—'Stop this son of a bitch. Pull this car over.'

"'What is the matter?' Dr. Holland jumps back in there,

and the kid is not breathing. They run to Comfort, and Chelsea McClellan is dead on September 17. She is *dead*. And that was the end of it at this point. The end of that little girl.

"You heard Drs. Galbreath and Fletes tell you that they found absolutely nothing wrong with that baby, *nothing* to account for its death. So they sent slides of the brain to Dr. Kagan-Hallet who, as the defense witness Dr. Goldie told you, is a respected pediatric neuropathologist. She looks at the slides and comes up with 'subtle gliosis.' She doesn't know anything else, you see, because she hasn't heard the whole history. She hears a history of what? Of seizures. So that is what Kagan-Hallet is looking for. She finds gliosis in the brain, probably as a result of Chelsea's premature birth fifteen months earlier, which she survived nicely and had grown up, caught up, and was doing great. Until she met this nurse, twice.

"Kagan-Hallet calls it atypical SIDS, but she doesn't really know. So she's asked, 'Take a look again. Go back and look at the slides of this baby's brain one more time and give some thought to succinylcholine being stuck in her by somebody, for whatever reason.'

"And she does. And what did she tell you, under oath, right here? She said, 'In my opinion, today, now that I know what really happened, now that I see the whole picture,' she said, 'the cause of that baby's death was succinylcholine.' She went further than that. She said that the gliosis had nothing to do with it. She even went further than that and said if it wasn't for that injection of succinylcholine, this little girl would be here today. There is your cause of death.

"Then you hear from Vincent DiMaio, a forensic pathologist, a man who deals in legal matters. He deals in murder. That is what he does every day as the head of the San Antonio medical examiner's office. What does he say? Death in this case was caused by succinylcholine, and the gliosis had nothing to do with it. Again, that baby would be walking around today except for succinylcholine.

"Now, Dr. Goldie testified for the defense. Remember

him? One of the things we mentioned to you that you were going to have to do when you listen to a witness is look at them and note their reaction to things. Remember how Goldie came in and testified about all those seizure things, but not having been told the whole picture—which you have—and which he only heard on the witness stand. Remember the rather dumbfounded look on his face when he said, 'I didn't know that. I didn't know about all those things.'

"And then, when asked, 'Well, what do you think now, Doctor, now that you've got the whole picture?'

"'My opinion goes out the window.'" Rothe paused, nodding. "'This whole situation needs to be investigated.'

"All right. Here we are. It's *been* investigated.

"Dr. Bo Holmstedt you heard. The world's most renowned specialist in the field of these choline esters, succinylcholine being one of them. And he said that in his opinion succinylcholine is in the tissues of Chelsea McClellan. So does Dr. Reiders; so does Dr. Garriott.

"The defense called Dr. Joseph Balkon to dispute Dr. Holmstedt, a young man who has written an article based primarily on Dr. Holmstedt's work, but who takes issue with the test.

"Garriott, who reads those test results every day says, 'You can't look at one peak, you've got to look at all of them. Consider *all* the facts.'

"Remember, Dr. Balkon wouldn't say, if you noticed, that succinylcholine was not there, he said, 'I am not saying it is not there. I just don't see it in these reports.'

"Now," Rothe continued, taking a deep breath, moving back to the calendars, "I want you to shift your thoughts back to the Clinic again. On the seventh," pointing to the red notation, "the nurse reports to the doctor, 'We are missing a vial. Do you want to reorder or not?'

"'Yes, go ahead, reorder.'

"Now, during a period of time from the thirteenth of September, 1982, through the sixteenth, while Jones was hospitalized for her ulcers, a substitute nurse named Mary Mahoney worked at Dr. Holland's Clinic. And what did she do? She inventoried that entire Clinic for drugs. Any drug. Every drug. She even looked in the bottom drawer of the examination table, and she didn't find any drugs. She even took the paper out," Rothe misremembered. "No drugs in there.

"Mary Mahoney is there for four days. Now, again, use your common sense. Kids are being treated, they are coming through the front door, and they are going right back out through the front door. No rag dolls. But the day Mary Mahoney leaves, the day the other nurse comes back, Thursday, September 17, what happens? Chelsea McClellan. Down she goes. Dead.

"And then, one of the most horrifying parts of it all, the same day," he stabbed the chart with his finger, "the nurse takes the baby to the morgue, then goes back to the Clinic, and two hours later that same day, down goes another one, Jacob Evans. Use your common sense, okay? Think about it.

"And then what happens? As time goes on in the Hill Country, another one, another baby, down she goes. In the meantime, look at this—" Rothe picked up the receipts from the evidence table and waved them in the air, "—succinylcholine, succinylcholine, succinylcholine. Thirty cc's," he tossed the slips back on the table, "and it has never been used in the Clinic says the doctor. You bet. Never by her. And who is ordering the stuff? The nurse. Thirty cc's of succinylcholine.

"At this point in time, common sense tells the people at Sid Peterson Hospital there is something really bizarre going on, so they call a meeting. 'What is going on? Never have had anything like this in Kerrville. What is going on here?'" Rothe moved back to the calendars.

"They call the doctor in. They want to talk about office procedures, and then what do they ask her? 'What about succinylcholine, Doctor?' They asked her that, and nobody had mentioned it before.

"A few days later, the nurse says, 'Oh, by the way, I found the missing vial.'

"'What vial?'

"'Of succinylcholine.'

"The doctor says, 'We didn't use it.'

"'Sure we did. We had it out when Misty seized.'

"'But we didn't use it.'

"'Don't worry about it. It is all there. There are no holes in it.'

"'Where did you find it?'

"'In the drawer of the examination table.'

"And about that time, I think, Dr. Holland begins to see the light. 'My God, what is going on here?'

"She checks the office, the doctor does, and finds two vials. She looks at them. One doesn't have a cap on it and it doesn't look quite full. So the next time she runs into the nurse who happens to be coming back from the grave of this child, with a ribbon in her hand that she got from that grave, the doctor confronts her with it. Holland hands her the bottle and says, 'What about this? How did the holes get there?'

"'Remember Misty, we argued about the dosage.'"

Rothe broke from his re-creation of the conversation for a moment. "Remember too, by the way, that the only person who had the exact dose was the nurse. She had it right."

He resumed the dialogue. "'How did the holes get there?'

"The nurse says, 'A lot of people were in there that day. I don't know.'

"'Well, how am I going to explain these holes to the executive committee?'

"'Well, don't explain it, okay? Just throw it away. After all, we did really lose it.'

"*Use your common sense,*" Rothe pleaded with the jurors.

"The doctor then called Sally Benkert who was there with Misty. She says, 'Oh, yes, I got it out, but I never opened it. It was never opened, and I put it up on the counter. That was the last I saw of it, and it was unopened.'

"Then, very shortly thereafter, the defendant nurse tells the doctor, 'I did a stupid thing. I took some pills. Doxepin.' So she gets hospitalized this time by Dr. Holland for an overdose of doxepin.

"The doctor calls Drs. Bradley, Hall, and Vinas over at

the hospital, they come over and take possession of these vials in question. They subsequently send them off to the lab. When they get to the lab, what happens? Sure enough, one of them hasn't been opened. The other one has, and it's got two holes in the top and five-sixths of it is not succinylcholine, but saline.

"Dr. Proust from Burroughs Welcome comes down and tells you that succinylcholine is extremely stable, and yet it is five-sixths diluted. Your common sense tells you somebody used the succinylcholine and then squirted it back full with saline. Somebody did it. The question is, who?"

And now, again, he turned to Genene. "The nurse."

Rothe glanced at the clock before turning back to the jurors, satisfied that he had plenty of time.

"I want to talk to you now very briefly about one other case. One little boy, Jimmy Pearson. If you look at Mr. Sutton's 100 Percent Chart, you'll notice that, at first, Jimmy Pearson doesn't quite seem to fit; but by golly, he *does* fit if you think about it.

"What are the tests for fitting that chart? One, you can't be a talker. Two, you have got to be under two years old. Three, you've got to be at the Clinic. Four, he's got to be treated by the same nurse. Okay, you've got that one. But, now, let's look at what happened.

"Jimmy was seven and a half because he'd stayed alive that long. A miracle. Simply a miracle this kid was alive that long. Everything that fate can throw in your face to have go wrong with a baby went wrong with him. It is sad. It is horrible." Again Rothe seduced the jury with emotion. "But what is even worse is to think that somebody would deliberately hurt him.

"He had little bitty arms, he weighed just eighteen or twenty pounds, he couldn't see; he had cataracts. When he was born, his feet were against his shins so he spent the better part of his first months of life in full-leg casts. He couldn't really move, he couldn't walk, he couldn't crawl. And what else? *He fits this chart.* He was a nontalker.

Seven and a half years old, but Jimmy couldn't tell any-body what'd happened to him.

"And he had real honest-to-God seizures, all right. He really did. It is not surprising, he had everything else wrong with him. This little boy should not have been seven and a half years old. He shouldn't have made it that long, but what did his mother tell you? 'He was a fighter.' He was a fighter all right; he had handled every misfortune that can be thrown at an infant and he was able to fight off everything, all of these things, and stay alive.

"But he met the biggest threat of his life when he had the misfortune to get a blue spell one day and have a seizure and meet this nurse." And again Rothe indicated Jones.

"He was stabilized at Sid Peterson. They call MAST. You heard those military men. Sharp people. By the num-bers. They don't move somebody unless they are stable, and they put him in the chopper. Who else is in the chop-per? The nurse is in there with her bag of goodies. Neo-Synephrine, and Valium, and God knows what else.

"He is stable. Everything is fine. These guys know what they are doing. They tell her, 'Hey, by the way, Ms. Pedi-atric Clinician'—who theoretically knows something about MAST helicopters—'don't try to use a stethoscope because you can't hear in a helicopter.' The man from Vietnam told you that. He knows you can't hear. Maywhort knows it and Garcia knows it, but the nurse doesn't know it.

"Ten minutes out, she puts her stethoscope on and sticks it on the little boy's chest. Why? She is setting the scene for what is going to happen. Just like clockwork, every time.

"She says, 'He's seizing.' Garcia looks at the monitor. He turns around and says, 'There is no problem. He is all right.'

"What happens? Maywhort sees Jones, who he now doesn't trust because she lied to him—anybody that says 'I can hear' is a liar, and he knows it, and he smells a rat. He says, 'Stop her. Stop her.' And what happens? Drug goes into the port, and the nurse backs off. As he said, 'I couldn't stop her in time.'

"Very shortly thereafter, down goes Jimmy Pearson. While the nurse is hyperventilating in the corner of the air ambulance, Sergeant Maywhort is breathing into this baby's mouth, and Garcia is punching on his chest trying to keep him alive.

"Then what does she say she gave him? She tells the medic, 'I gave him Neo-Synephrine.' But she tells the mother and Dr. Holland, 'I gave him Valium.' I suggest to you she gave him succinylcholine. Why not? Got a pattern of doing it.

"Why give that boy a shot?" Rothe asked, resting his hands on the jury box railing. "That is the ultimate question. Why do it?" And he turned on Jones again, pointing his finger. "Because this devious nurse, to enrich her own impoverished ego, *needed* to have critically ill kids, so that at Kerrville, Texas, she could have a Pediatric ICU, where she would be in charge.

"This whole thing is frightening. It is bizarre. It is terrible that some human being would do that to a baby, but worse, to bab*ies*. Over and over. And by the way, the nurse is right there," he said, again pointing. "That nurse that killed that baby is right there, and her name is Genene Jones." Rothe knew that the jury was going to need courage to send this woman to prison, and he was doing his best to give it to them.

"Why?" he repeated, heading back toward the podium. "Because she wants to cause serious bodily injury, and by definition, when you do that and somebody dies, you have committed murder."

Rothe ended his argument with a quotation from the most persuasive authority he could offer these twelve men and women from the heart of Texas. "Jesus said, 'But who so shall offend one of these little ones which believe in me, it were better for him that a millstone were hanged about his neck and he would drown in the depths of the sea.'

"Ladies and gentlemen of the jury, justice is what we are here for, and justice is ofttimes harsh. I would ask you, by your verdict, to tie a millstone, if you will, of justice around this woman's neck, and say by your verdict, guilty of the offense of murder of Chelsea McClellan.''

When Rothe resumed his seat, silence hung over the courtroom. In the fifth row of the audience, an awed reporter involuntarily summed up what everyone was thinking: ''Adios, motherfucker.''

If Judge Carter heard the comment, he showed no sign of it as he called a one-hour break. When the court reconvened, Carnes would take the podium to deliver the defense's final argument.

At 10:45, Carnes stepped to the podium and addressed the jury. He knew he was going to have a fight even to persuade the jury to listen to him, and he did not have the kind of gut-wrenching, emotional arguments Rothe had used so effectively. All he had were the facts and the dozens of small holes that the state had not been able to fill, the questions Sutton and Rothe had not been able to answer.

Like Monroe, Carnes began by thanking the jury. ''I have got to tell you, I think it is incredible how much attention each and every one of you has paid to the facts as they have been presented to you in this courtroom over these past four and a half arduous weeks of trial. And that is exactly what the defense in this case is counting on.

''Don't expect drama from me. Don't expect courtroom theatrics,'' he said, cocking his head toward Rothe. ''What I want to do is get your focus back to what this entire trial is about, and that is the charge in this case.

''Hasn't it struck you as strange that the state spent more than half the time in the courtroom talking about other things, other instances? Has that ever worried you even a little bit, that so little time was spent by the state on the actual facts surrounding the death of Chelsea McClellan? Well, we are going to show you why.

''The reason why is that whenever you get down and focus on the facts that have been presented to you from the witness stand and the facts in the medical records, you understand exactly why the state has avoided that like the plague.

"Instead, they are relying on this—" Carnes gestured dismissively toward the state's demonstrative evidence, the calendars and the chart "—all the red. One time wasn't enough. They did it twice for you. I would be willing to bet a little bit of money it will be done one more time for you before this day is through.

"And that is all right. That is their prerogative. They can throw out every smoke screen in the world if they want to, but the defense is relying on the twelve of you to both use your common sense and follow the law in the state of Texas, and put the state to the burden of proof just as each and every one of you promised you could do four and a half weeks ago when you took an oath to serve as a juror in this case. You have known from day one the defense does not have to prove one single thing. The defense has no burden of proof.

"The elements of the offense," he said, announcing the next topic. "Seven of them." As he spoke, he counted each element by raising a finger. "Kerr County, Texas," one finger is raised up, "September 17, 1982," a second finger is raised, "Genene Jones," the third, "with intent to cause serious bodily injury to Chelsea McClellan," the fourth, "did intentionally or knowingly commit an act clearly dangerous to human life," the fifth, "by intentionally or knowingly injecting Chelsea McClellan with succinylcholine," the sixth, "thereby causing the death of Chelsea McClellan," the seventh.

"The state has to prove every single one of those elements to each one of you beyond a reasonable doubt or this woman is innocent. That doesn't mean maybe. That doesn't mean possibly. That doesn't mean probably. They've got to *prove* it.

"Ladies and gentlemen, if you get back there and review the facts, and there is any question in your mind on any one of those elements—'I don't know, you know, something worries me about that'—*that is a doubt,* and the law requires you at that point to vote 'Not Guilty.'

"And that is what we are relying on, ladies and gentlemen, because this entire case is fraught through with doubt. That is why they have continually tried to get the focus onto their calendars and away from these seven elements.

"Do you remember way back—it was very slyly done, I have to admit—where they started setting you up? 'We have got all these witnesses, but we might not call all of them because some of it is going to be repetitive stuff, and we don't want to waste your time here.'

"Do you remember that? Think back. Think about some of the witnesses they chose not to call. Who knows about all the other witnesses they chose not to call?

"He," Carnes indicated Sutton, "is going to get up and say, 'Well, the defense could call those witnesses.' Wrong.

"We aren't going to start putting up witnesses that won't talk to us ahead of time, at whoever's direction. That will be the day when I, as a lawyer, start throwing people in the courtroom just to see what they might or might not have to say.

"I want to get in just one more general comment. I respect these three gentlemen highly as attorneys, but I am deathly afraid that what we have seen is what can happen when a prosecutor becomes obsessed with a case, and I think that is exactly what has happened in this instance." Carnes concluded this assessment gravely, looking directly at Sutton and Rothe, then turned back to the podium and his notes.

"Succinylcholine," he said, focusing the jury. "They have to *prove* an injection of succinylcholine, and they have to prove succinylcholine *caused* the death of Chelsea McClellan.

"What do we know about succinylcholine? You probably know more than most third-year medical students by this time, but let's look at it once more.

"We are dealing with a drug that has a very, very short active period in the body, four to six minutes normally, maximum of ten minutes in an IV injection, right? Effects as you are going under: muscle fasciculations, twitches; the eyes might be the first thing to twitch a little bit. Now, all this testimony about the eyes, think about that. It sounds real good until the doctors get up and say, 'Well, what happens is, they are paralyzed and they tend to droop shut.' We didn't hear about that from any of the witnesses about the eyes being shut, but we know now that is what should have been happening had it been succinylcholine.

"Dr. Comstock testified that in somewhat less than a third of the patients you might notice muscle twitches. These aren't full-scale jerky movements. Dr. Comstock made it clear we are talking about just individual muscle twitches, things that we probably all have experienced at one time. Dr. Comstock basically said you would have to be an idiot to confuse that with seizure activity.

"What about coming out from under the effects of succinylcholine? We know that the diaphragm starts moving first, and then the chest muscles and then it spreads on out to the outer muscles and the hands last. Think about that, and think about Dr. Holland's testimony.

"When the state realized that Holland's testimony didn't look so hot once it got her in here, in the courtroom, under cross-examination, all of a sudden we hear: 'Maybe it was an underdosage'—since these periods of limpness she testified to were so undefined and momentary, and she couldn't give us any idea how long it may or may not have lasted. Sounds good, doesn't it?"

Carnes picked up a pad and read from his notes: "Dr. Comstock on an underdosage: 'You may get some weakness in more sensitive muscles and some varying degrees of impairment.'

"Question: 'Can it cause convulsive activity?'

"'No.'" The lawyer looked up at the jury. "No hesitation, no ifs, ands, or buts; just plain and simple: 'No.'

"The issue of *over*dosage was also raised by the state. More smoke to confuse the issues. What about an overdosage?" Carnes returned to his notes. "Dr. Schwartzman, the state's own witness, told us: 'There are no different effects from a larger than normal dose. Most patients can metabolize the drug and will react in exactly the same way as if you gave the normal amount.'

"Is it possible to have seizure activity while you are under the effects of succinylcholine?

"Dr. Comstock said no. Every witness that you could finally pin down on the point said no, absolutely impossible. And you know it. You have heard what the muscle relaxant does. The seizure activity may be going on in your brain, firing off all the neurons, but it is not getting to your muscles. It is blocked.

"What about the dangerousness of the drug? Well, every witness, Dr. Schwartzman included, testified it is used in every hospital in the United States, daily, untold numbers of times. Not one witness—not even Dr. DiMaio, the professional witness—not one witness testified that they knew of one recorded case where succinylcholine caused cardiac arrest. Said the drug had very, very little effect on the heart. If anything, it may cause a short period of bradycardia.

"The *PDR* says that the bradycardia is actually caused because you have to intubate when you use the drug, and when you intubate, you get the stimulation of the vagal nerve in the throat and *that* is the cause of the bradycardia, not the drug itself. Every witness that knew what they were talking about testified if you are properly ventilated, the drug is very safe.

"What about Dilantin? Dilantin is the drug that they," he indicated the prosecution, "have ignored so far. Dilantin, you remember, is the drug that was used quite a bit, used in both of Chelsea's visits, right?

"What is Dilantin? It is an anticonvulsant drug used only to control seizure activity. I asked Dr. Comstock about a possible overdose of Dilantin." Again Carnes read from his notes. "He said: 'You can have impairment of coordination, difficulty in walking, slurred speech, nystagmus, disorientation, and depression of brain activity; if given enough, coma and death.'

"One other piece of groundwork—postictal state. That is the state following seizure activity when you are dazed and semiconscious. You may have some muscle movement and you would react to trauma, such as when being intubated.

"Extraneous offenses. What does the charge tell you about extraneous offenses? You are instructed that '. . . you cannot consider testimony regarding extraneous offenses for *any* purpose unless you find and believe that it has been proven beyond a reasonable doubt that the defendant committed such other offenses, and even then you may only consider them in determining the motive, intent, design, or scheme of the defendant.'

"Any testimony regarding extraneous offenses is supposed to be used for a very limited purpose. Use your common sense. You know exactly why it's been used. To try to worry you so much about those red letters on that calendar that you feel like, 'Golly, I don't think they really proved it to me, but there is so much smoke, there has got to be fire.' That is what they are relying on for a conviction in this case. Carnes was moving freely about the room, now, trying to keep the attention of the jury constantly engaged.

"They aren't relying on the facts as they came to you from the stand. Maybe as Mr. Rothe told them to you this morning, but that was an awfully well edited version. They have been trying to stampede you; from the time Mr. Monroe got up and talked about how the state's eyes are on you, to try to put pressure on you. From the time Mr. Rothe gave such a wonderful, dramatic talk about some of the tragedies surrounding these events. They don't want to deal with the facts of this case. They have been *avoiding* the facts of this case.

"Let's look at some of their extraneous offenses. Brandy Benites, August 27. Had been sitting down in the hospital for a couple of hours. They couldn't see her because she didn't have any money, so they referred her to the new physician in town. Two months premature, one month of age at that time—a very tiny infant. She is dehydrated. She has had diarrhea for days. Little children don't have much body fluid to begin with, and it doesn't take much of a loss for them to be in serious trouble.

"Dr. Holland makes the decision to hospitalize the child, and Dr. Holland has this unheard-of standing procedure." For the rest of his argument, Carnes would say Kathleen's name with the same inflection of accusation he had just used. He would waste no opportunity to question her motives and her competence, to throw suspicion her way. "Dr. Holland starts an IV and draws blood in her office. Now, surely you have heard enough testimony to understand that that is a traumatic event for a small child.

"You notice how Holland sets this all up in her testimony? For every one of these children, she gets out of the room just long enough to give Genene the opportunity to do the deed. Right? And then she slides back in and, of course, it has already been done.

"Holland testified that she called EMS for transfer at 11:37. The EMS arrived at 11:39. That is two minutes' time. In between, she returned to the treatment room. Brandy was being bagged with O_2. She looked lethargic, and all of a sudden went limp. Pooped out, went limp.

"The EMS report states specifically that spontaneous respirations were resumed shortly after arrival. Remember, we are dealing with two minutes' time. If succinylcholine had been administered, you know from everything you have heard in here, it would be absolutely impossible for spontaneous respirations to resume that quickly. That alone tells you that there was no succinylcholine involved in this case at all. When the EMS attendants moved the child from the stretcher, she quit breathing again. If you are under succinylcholine, you do not resume breathing and then quit breathing again within that small a time frame. You don't resume breathing at all.

"Dr. Holland testified, 'I believe she did recover before we took her to the hospital.' Of course," Carnes added with heavy sarcasm, "Holland testified just about any ol' way.

She just kind of laid it out there and left it open for everybody to make their own interpretation from what she was saying.

"Now, does it strike you at all curious that they didn't bring those two EMTs in to testify? Other than Dr. Holland and Genene, they were the first people to see this baby. They didn't bring them in. Why not? Does that bother you? It bothers me.

"At the ER room, they decide to take the child to Santa Rosa. We now have Sarah Mauldin in the back of the ambulance and Phillip Kneese. The prosecution brought *those* two witnesses in. They said, 'We are not going to bring in repetitive testimony,' yet they brought in those two people to say the same thing. Does that kind of lead you to the conclusion that maybe whenever the repetitive testimony was supportive of their position or good for their position they didn't mind running them in here?

"Ten or fifteen minutes out on the highway, the child started having problems. Sarah Mauldin testified she could tell the child wasn't breathing. Sarah also testified that at that point no new IV had been started, no syringes, no injections, no nothing.

"They pulled off to the side of the road; they got the child's heartbeat going again. Then, on the way, Genene Jones started another IV. The state tried to make a point about that, poked her with another needle. What do you do whenever a little baby is dehydrated? You get fluid in them. She was trying to get fluids into this child. It is that simple. There is absolutely no evidence of anything else going on.

"They had to continue bagging her all the way to San Antonio, another forty-five minutes. That is not consistent with succinylcholine. The child was in trouble.

"Everything about Brandy Benites indicates a young child who was dehydrated, had problems, and got sufficient fluids to bring her back out of those problems, but what was it that Sarah Mauldin and Phillip Kneese said about Genene that was really probably more important in this case?

"She was aggressive, and she seemed to step on people's toes. She was bossy. If she felt like something had to be done, she didn't mind telling anybody to do it. That was the impression they got from her, and they didn't like it, especially didn't like it when they realized she was nothing but a lowly old LVN."

Carnes was beginning to get his audience involved, as Rothe had before him, but without the same kind of freedom Rothe had enjoyed. Carnes was in a defensive posture and had certain points he knew he had to touch upon, to explain, because Genene had not taken the stand. Carnes stood at the podium a moment, organizing in his mind the points he had not yet covered.

"Jimmy Pearson," he said finally. "I really think it is shameful that Jimmy Pearson's case was ever even brought before you. I really do. You have got a seven-year-old child with a horrible medical history whose mother brought him to the hospital. He'd had a Tet seizure that day because he had five holes in the walls of his heart. In addition, for the first time in his life, he was seizing through his seizure control medicine. Everybody testified, from Dr. Holland to Maywhort to Garcia: one syringe." He held up a finger. "There was only one syringe, loaded at the hospital by one of the nursing personnel there and *given* to Genene Jones to take.

"Dr. Holland said she gave her Valium. Maywhort and Garcia testified that she told them it was Neo-Synephrine. One or the other of them is mistaken. That sure isn't anything to lie about," and Carnes made it sound reasonable. "Either way, it was medication given to her by Dr. Holland with the instructions to use it at her discretion, and that's exactly what happened.

"Whatever Maywhort and Garcia thought, Genene Jones had been given specific authority by Dr. Holland to administer that medication when she saw fit, and that is all in the world the state has proven that she did. She administered the medication drawn at Dr. Holland's order.

"After that point, I believe, Jimmy went into respiratory arrest or started having heart problems. Whichever, they ended up landing out in the middle of a field somewhere trying to intubate the boy.

"And one thing struck me because I was sitting there waiting for it, and I never heard it: 'Limp.' They never said: 'He went perfectly limp.'

"They got him south and Jimmy was hospitalized from that point till seven weeks later when everything finally was too much for him and the young man died. And I am really incredulous that Nick Rothe would get up here and imply, *imply*," his voice rose in disbelief, "that the incident in the helicopter had anything to do with that, because he knows better. The young man was in and out of the hospital all of his life, and he had finally reached that point where it was all just getting too much for him physically.

"And inside the medical records there is something that I avoided bringing out, but it is there. When he was brought back to Sid Peterson on the twentieth, three weeks later, the decision was made not to intubate him any further or resuscitate him anymore and to let nature take its course. And I think it is absolutely *shameful*," Carnes paused for effect, "that they would come into this courtroom and imply that the events that took place in the helicopter have anything to do with this child's death.

"Again, they managed to run in all three army people who told close to the same story. They didn't have any qualms about running in repetitive testimony on that point, did they?

"Misty Reichenau, September 3, 1982, came to the office with four days' fever and mouth sores and a history of high-pitched screams. Went in the treatment room with her mom, the neck was stiff," he tilted his head back, "extreme dorsiflection position. Dr. Holland made the decision to hospitalize. The EMTs were called at 2:32 and arrived at 2:34. At that point there had been absolutely no evidence or indication of any injection.

"Dr. Holland testified that Misty was crying after they started an IV, stopped crying, and stopped breathing. Then the EMTs arrived, and the mom was shuffled out the door. We know that had to be less than two minutes after the supposed injection because of the time of the call and the time they arrived.

"Now, here is where Holland really starts walking the fence." Carnes resumed his attack. "She says: 'Then, seizurelike activity occurred.' We know that in the deposition taken in May of 1983, she said, 'The child suffered a breath-holding spell followed *within 15 to 30 seconds* by tonoclonic movements and extensory tonic seizure.' This wasn't something Genene had told her, this was what the doctor had observed and written in her notes herself, and it's absolutely, *totally* inconsistent with the injection of succinylcholine.

"They didn't bother bringing Susie Bateman in, did they? Thank goodness there are a few people left that are willing to stand up and speak out and say what is right, and Susie Bateman is one of them. She was one of the EMT personnel that day.

"She testified that whenever they got there—and this, again, had to be within two minutes after the IV injection—that child was seizing, and that child continued seizing until they finally got another IV started, pushing Dilantin in her.

"You heard the experts testify there is absolutely no reason to give Dilantin after the seizure is over because its only purpose is to control the seizure activity. Holland gave it. She had to be observing that seizure activity.

"They didn't call Sally Benkert. Sally testified that she held the O_2 mask while Dr. Holland tried to intubate Misty but couldn't because the child's jaws were clenched so tight and she was seizing so hard. Sally also testified that *Dr. Holland* ordered the succinylcholine out of the refrigerator—not Genene Jones, as Dr. Holland testified. And what did she tell you about the vials?" Carnes again read from his notes.

"'Sally, did the succinylcholine bottle the day you were in there, September 3, 1982, did it still have a cap on it?'

"'Yes, sir.'

"She was absolutely positive it was in position on that bottle of succinylcholine when she got it out of the refrigerator. That is uncontradicted.'' Carnes let the jury wait a moment for the point. ''On September 3, that little cap was on the bottle of succinylcholine purchased on the twenty-eighth of August.'' He pointed now to the red notation on Sutton's calendars. ''The replacement vial was purchased on the seventh,'' he said, tapping the date. ''Misty Reichenau, September 3,'' again tapping the date. ''The one vial of succinylcholine on the premises at that time was in the refrigerator with the cap on. That means it had not been used at all. Therefore, the state has itself proved that succinylcholine was not involved in these first four extraneous offenses.'' Carnes indicated Chelsea on August 24, Brandy on August 27, Jimmy on August 30, and Misty on September 3. ''There is absolutely no way,'' he insisted, ''that bottle of succinylcholine had been used, because *it had the cap on it*.'' He stood regarding the jury, compelling them to face this challenge. ''Think about that.

''Jacob Evans,'' he announced, moving on. ''The office notes show that the child appeared with eyes that 'were large with nystagmus, extremities tremoring. He was pale, jittery, hyperactive, in good spirits, fontanelle bulging, sutures spread'—that is to say, the bones of the skull were actually spread apart from the pressure. 'Right pupil sluggish to light.' Jacob had been crying unconsolably, and his young mother brought him there because she was at wits' end.

''Dr. Holland was still at the hospital dealing with Chelsea McClellan.'' With heavy sarcasm, he commented, ''This is awfully worrisome. Just think a moment about what we know so far: we have got an aggressive nurse who is willing to take charge and do whatever she thinks is necessary. I believe young Jacob's mother testified that Genene said Dr. Holland had authorized, over the phone, an IV and the administering of the Dilantin to control the seizure activity. The medical record itself says that the Dilantin was given as ordered. The state would have you believe that that is supposed to mean as ordered by Dr. Webb, and it doesn't say that. It says '*as ordered.*' What about Dr. Holland?

''See, she has got the bases covered. I have to give it to

her. She got up there and testified that she called the office, but it was to tell that young mother to bring that baby straight down to the hospital. By the time Dr. Webb arrives, the IV is started, the Dilantin has already been administered, and Jacob is 'limp.' I would think that would be a part of what you would expect whenever you have just injected the initial large loading dose of Dilantin, plus the child is possibly in a postical state on top of it.

"Rolinda Ruff, the last of the extraneous offenses, showed up with a history of thirteen days of diarrhea. Dehydrated. Again, Dr. Holland made the decision to hospitalize the child. Again, she went out in the hall to talk it over with the mom and give Genene the opportunity.

"You notice there has never been any testimony that Genene walked back to the refrigerator where the succinylcholine was kept. That could only mean," his tone conveyed his disbelief, "that Genene had it hidden away somewhere, just waiting for that next available child.

"Holland says whenever she went back in the room, shortly after that, the child stopped crying, stopped breathing, and went limp. Again, 'limp.' You look through Rolinda Ruff's medical records, you won't find the word 'limp' in there. It wasn't mentioned in that deposition Holland gave in May of 1983, either. She came into the courtroom, sailed in here, and laid it out for the first time, 'Yes, that child went limp.'

"Again, I refer you to the record, the emergency room record (thank goodness the emergency room made Dr. Holland fill out those records, or we might not have any written record of what really went on). Dr. Holland stated that as the IV was being started by the MD, the child had a breath-holding spell, turned dusky, and had a tonic seizure lasting two minutes.

"Again, *absolutely, totally inconsistent* with the administration of succinylcholine.

"Dr. Bradley testified that he saw the child at the ER, and to him it appeared that child was coming out from under the effects of succinylcholine. It was ten minutes, according to the EMS records, from the time they got to the Clinic until the time they got down to the hospital. Ten minutes is the absolute outside time limit of the effects of suc- cinylcholine.'' Carnes shrugged slightly and shook his head. ''I don't know what Dr. Bradley observed. I do know he observed it from thirty feet away, and he never got his hands on the child. The postictal state testified to by the experts could easily explain the movements he saw, especially once Dr. Holland started trying to intubate the child. And the other doctor they chose to bring in to bolster what Dr. Bradley had to say admitted he had never seen a patient actually coming out from under the effects of succinylcholine.''

And now Carnes paused. He stood before the jury and spoke as frankly and sincerely as he was able.

''Ladies and gentlemen, I don't know what to tell you about the extraneous offenses. I am not sure what hap- pened, but I have got some ideas. I think there is a high possibility that we are dealing with a young doctor who is in her first clinic situation, just out of a residency, a resi- dency served in a hospital where she was used to seeing children in very serious trouble, a young doctor who had a tendency to push the panic button and maybe overreacted and possibly overtreated. Maybe it wasn't necessary to start all those IVs. And whenever they had a little breath- holding spell after the IV, maybe it wasn't necessary to start jamming those tubes down their throat.

''Maybe it is total incompetence on Dr. Holland's part. Maybe she was doing something that was just flat wrong that caused the problems. I don't know, but I submit to you the state hasn't proven Genene Jones did anything to any of those children, not beyond a reasonable doubt.

''They want to bring Holland in and tell you to believe her today and forget what she wrote at the time. I submit to you the more believable is that which was written at the time of the event in the medical records, and those medical records prove absolutely that succinylcholine could not have been used in these cases.

''In addition, you now know that the one vial of succinylcholine hadn't been opened in the first four cases. Beyond any doubt whatsoever, it could not have been succinylcholine. It is all a smoke screen, ladies and gentlemen," he said, trying to force them to listen. "That is all it is there for.

"The great motive," he said, stating the next topic. "We were promised a motive, and by God, they came up with one," his voice again filled with sarcasm. "Genene Jones was going to make sure there was a Pediatric ICU in Kerrville, Texas. And I guess whenever it was she took that course from Dr. Schwartzman, she had already started her plans. The whole idea I find so absurd, so ridiculous, it is really hard to deal with. You are going to go out and harm these children to guarantee that they are going to get a Pediatric ICU? That is just really incredible!

"I have no doubt that the idea was bantered about. Sally Benkert herself testified that Dr. Holland and Genene had talked about it with the nurses down at the hospital. I can believe that an aggressive person such as Genene Jones might think that, by talking it up enough, she could get some action. She sure didn't mind telling somebody if she thought they were doing something wrong or needed to do something different. I have no doubt that she stepped on toes in doing that, but as a motive for injecting succinylcholine into children, it is just ridiculous."

Carnes moved on to his next point. "Dr. Holland testified about certain conversations, and this was what was most incredible to me about Dr. Holland's testimony. She was as vague as a person can be on all the extraneous offenses. I spent a lot of time trying to nail her down and get specifics from her. What I got were these nonspecific images of an emergency situation. But, boy, she had those conversations on the twenty-sixth and twenty-seventh down pat. You could ask her fifteen times, and it would come out the same each time. 'Genene was coolly defensive,'" he repeated, mimicking Kathleen, "'I nodded. Genene kept talking.'" Carnes snapped his fingers. "Just like turning on a tape recorder.

"We know that by the twenty-fourth of September the

heat was on Dr. Holland. On the twenty-seventh, after Genene has come and reported to her that she found the missing vial, what does she do? She goes to the hospital in the morning, but she doesn't mention this to anybody. She gets back to the Clinic at noon and all of a sudden discovers these holes and confronts Genene, confronts Sally. And she has that whole conversation down pat.

"What does she do then? She waits until 9:00 P.M. that night to turn it over to anybody. And the next morning, on the twenty-eighth, the first thing she does is fire Genene Jones on the advice of her attorney.

"If you will remember, Sally Benkert testified that the conversation about the vial of succinylcholine occurred sometime after Genene got out of the hospital, which was on the sixteenth of September. That means that Dr. Holland knew in the middle of that week sometime that that vial of succinylcholine had been found.

"I have thought about that. I have *worried* about that.

"By the week of the twentieth, Dr. Holland had to have been feeling the heat. It was immediately after Chelsea McClellan died. It was immediately after Dr. Holland ordered DT and MMR shots to a child with fever, which is absolutely wrong, especially for a child who has a history of seizure activity.

"To me it is a possibility that at that point Dr. Holland made the decision it was time to cover herself." And now Carnes was deadly serious. "It is a possibility that third vial of succinylcholine was Dr. Holland's vial, and *she* punctured it, *she* withdrew the succinylcholine, *she* filled it back up with saline. I suggest it is a distinct possibility that Dr. Holland *planted* that vial and waited for Genene to do her next weekly inventory and all of a sudden find it.

"The one thing you have got to understand is, if Genene Jones had been using that vial of succinylcholine to harm children or to inject children, why in God's name would she turn it in to anybody? If she were half as devious and half as smart as the state has painted her to be, what do you think she would have done with that vial of succinylcholine?" He stood before the jury, demanding they find an answer.

"If it were you, would you go turn it in? As Mr. Rothe said, use your common sense. It is like somebody shooting somebody, then turning in a smoking pistol with two cartridges burned out of it. It is totally absurd. It does not make any sense."

Carnes returned to the podium and his notes. "I promised you I was going to get back to the focus in this case, and I have spent the majority of my time following down the state's rabbit trails, but I [felt it was] important to look at that so you can understand what they have been telling you.

"Let's get back to Chelsea McClellan. These are the medical records of Chelsea McClellan," he said, holding up a fistful. "They are all in evidence. You take them back and you read them. Chelsea McClellan had problems from the time she was born. The child was cyanotic twenty minutes after her birth. At 1:00 P.M. she had an X ray showing possible hyaline membrane disease. The child was acidotic. At 2:30 P.M., an hour and a half later, the child was finally intubated by the good Dr. Boyce.

"Ladies and gentlemen, there is absolutely no excuse for leaving that child under an oxyhood for that long a period of time, premature, when she is already having problems breathing. Dr. Boyce took ten minutes attempting to intubate her and finally got another doctor to do it for him. At some point, for God knows what reason, he withdrew the tube and reintubated her fifteen minutes later when she again became cyanotic because she wasn't getting enough oxygen.

"Dr. Goldie told you that was crucial. The state even now has to admit that the brain-stem scarring could easily have begun at that point. They say, 'Well, that is all right, she recovered. She did well.'" Carnes nodded knowingly. "After twenty days in the hospital she was doing pretty well, but you look through those birth records. You will see throughout those records that she was having ventila-

tion problems most of her stay. They were having to constantly adjust the ventilator.'' He checked his notes.

"The next hospitalization was when Chelsea was ten
months old. She was presented with a history of having
turned blue and stopped breathing, according to the
mother. She'd had two spells the day before, where she
stopped breathing and turned blue. She was hospitalized
for six days. One of the doctors stated that the child may
be suspect for having a tendency to SIDS.

"Chelsea was then presented in Dr. Holland's office on
August 24, 1982. You see a sequence here? There are increasingly short periods of time between Chelsea's problems.

"Holland's initial observation of the child out in the
waiting room—remember that?—was mild perioral cyanosis. She was blue around the mouth. In her ER report, Dr.
Holland states that the child was presented with a history
of erratic breathing. Now, that is not based on anything
Genene Jones told her. That is based on something only
one person could have told her—Chelsea's mother.

"The state has made a major point out of saying that there
was something Genene Jones told Dr. Holland that led to the
hospitalization on the twenty-fourth and to all of this bad
history, which ultimately led Dr. Kagan-Hallet to make the
wrong findings in her autopsy report. Stop and think about it.
Don't be buffaloed. Don't be panicked into something. Just
stop, think, and look at the record. What does it tell you?

"Dr. Holland saw this period of limpness herself. And I
want to point out to you right now that this is the only time in
any of these medical records of Chelsea McClellan or any of
the other children involved that the word 'flaccid' is used, or
'limp,' in association with the description of the seizure
activity. That was the only time that term was used because it
was the only time it was observed, on August 24, with
Chelsea McClellan. And then Dr. Holland reports the child
began ten minutes of tonoclonic seizure activity.'' Carnes
shook his head emphatically. "Not while you are under the
effects of succinylcholine. It is absolutely impossible.

"Does it make any sense that trained medical personnel would keep the child hospitalized for eight days because an LVN said 'seizure,' especially when you know the doctor observed everything the LVN observed from that period of limpness through the tonoclonic seizure activity and everything after that?

"One point, one telling point about this incident. The cool, reserved, competent Dr. Holland," he allowed his contempt to creep in once again, "what did she testify she did whenever she walked in there? Genene was putting the child on the table and getting ready to bag her and try to get her some oxygen.

"Did she take charge and send the LVN out to get help, to get an ambulance? No, she blew right out the door, ran out in the hallway somewhere, and hollered at two carpenters to get help, and then came back in. That might give you some insight as to the competence of Dr. Holland in these emergency situations and what might have been going wrong with some of the children.

"Review Chelsea's medical records for her hospitalization in August of 1982. Time after time it refers to her body having shaky and jerky movements, 'question of seizure activity per mom last P.M.,' 'cyanotic when given injections,' and 'little finger twitch.'

"The child was discharged, then brought in on the seventh of September for a follow-up visit. Again, a report of seizures, two seizures, the longest was for four minutes with cyanosis.

"What is really important about this hospitalization is that Dr. Holland knew there was something here. She knew a child doesn't have this ongoing problem that seems to be becoming more frequent all the time without there being a problem. She ran test after test after test looking for it, thought maybe it was a metabolic disorder, couldn't find anything.

"That brings us to the date of September 17. Dr. Holland and Mrs. McClellan both testified that Chelsea was there by happenstance. But we know now that is not exactly right. If you will remember, on cross-examination Dr. Holland testified that, indeed, Chelsea McClellan had an appointment at 10:00, according to the appointment book, and Cameron had an appointment for 10:15. The initial complaint written by Judith Johnston on the seventeenth was for a bluish tint to the face.

"The temperature. Why would Genene Jones report a temperature of a hundred and then write in the record that it is 100.6? If she were going to lie to the doctor about whether that child had a fever or not, surely she wouldn't prove she were lying by writing it in the record.

"I think it is a reasonable deduction from the evidence that that story has changed because Dr. Holland now realizes that what she did was absolutely wrong. You do not give immunizations to a child with fever. It can be extremely dangerous." Carnes checked the clock and again referred to his notes.

"Petti McClellan testified that one shot was given through the thigh. For a couple of minutes Chelsea was breathing funny. The second shot given in the second thigh, and like 'that,'" again Carnes snapped his fingers, "she went limp. But that is not what the written record shows us, ladies and gentlemen.

"Dr. Holland testified that the defendant came and got her and said Chelsea had gotten mad, started breathing shallowly, and that she had given her oxygen by mask. Holland went to the treatment room, Mom was holding her and bouncing her. Her color looked good, and her respirations were shallow. Holland said, 'Put her on the table.' At that point the child went momentarily limp. Dr. Holland testified that there was then one seizure contraction of the arms and the tone decreased. The ER report also says the child turned cyanotic and began seizing. It doesn't mention any period of limpness or flaccidity or anything else." Carnes had picked up the pace of his delivery.

"The EMTs were called at 10:57 A.M. Holland testified under cross-examination that the child was transported after resuming spontaneous respirations. The child was taken to the ER room. Sharon Keith testified that when they brought her in, her color was good, she was respirating, and she was moving. The first thing Sharon noticed were the two injection sites.

"Assume with me for the moment that succinylcholine *had* been administered at the office. The effects by this time had obviously totally worn off and could not have resulted in the death of Chelsea McClellan." He stopped and repeated that. "Absolutely could not have.

"The state began to see that trap coming so they started laying groundwork to try to tell you that there must have been a *second* injection in that ambulance. But Tommy James came in here and testified that he saw no injection of any sort during that entire trip. Thank goodness we have got people like Tommy James who are still willing to come in and tell their side of the story," Carnes said, reminding them of Tommy's credibility. "No injection, whatsoever.

"DeAnna Armour, a friend of the family, came in and testified, remember? I think that probably the state's attorneys were more surprised than anyone when she claimed to have seen Genene Jones inject the child in the thigh again and tell her it was Valium." Carnes was now working to do what should have been done on cross—attack the credibility of this witness who had turned out to be such an important cornerstone to the state's case. "And, you remember, that supposedly happened in the presence of all these doctors and nurses that were around there. It *didn't happen*, ladies and gentlemen. You *know* it didn't happen. It is totally absurd. It is absolutely clear that there was not and could not have been any second injection at all. And that becomes really crucial whenever you get back to these elements and try to determine what is the cause of death.

"Mr. Rothe argued that the child went into respiratory arrest. That is not what any witness has testified to. The child had a *cardiac* arrest. Rothe said they got a heartbeat back. That is not right. Tommy James testified they never did get a heartbeat."

Carnes stood before the jury, put his hands on the rail, and tried his best to reach each of the twelve men and women. "Ladies and gentlemen, it is a sad fact that a pretty fifteen-month-old child passed away on September 17, 1982. And it is a shame, but there is not a thing in the world that you or I or anybody else can do to bring that child back. And it doesn't justify trying to railroad somebody on the kind of evidence the state has brought to you today, or I should say, over the past four weeks. It doesn't justify it in any way.

"The record shows a history of subtle seizure activity, as reported mostly by the mother. What did the mother say? Remember when Tommy James testified about when Genene Jones handed the child over?" The lawyer's sadness was palpable, "'That is all right. She will wake up. She has done this before.'" Again Carnes paused for emphasis, crossing back to the podium.

"Let's look briefly at the cause of death. What we have here is a specific recorded cause of death by Dr. Kagan-Hallet. Brain-stem damage, neuronal loss resulting in respiratory problems, and cardiac problems. Then we find that the state has gone to Dr. Kagan-Hallet and said, 'Doctor, succinylcholine was used. Does that change your opinion?'

"Stop and think a minute," the lawyer begged the jury. "That is five months before Dr. Reiders even ran his test. The prosecutors didn't say it *might* have been used. They said it *was* used 'We need a new report from you. We need a new cause of death.'

"And Dr. Kagan-Hallet gives them a new cause of death. She says, 'It is because of all the new history they brought me.' But if you remember in her examination, it turns out she didn't even know or have any information about the first six hours of the child's life. She didn't know about the mother being hospitalized for twenty-eight hours. She testified she never talked to Tommy James, she never talked to Dr. Holland, she never talked to Genene Jones, she never talked to the doctor at Comfort Hospital. She never talked to one single person that was involved in the medical treatment of

Chelsea McClellan on the day of death. She was relying on the story as told to her by the state's attorneys.

"Under cross-examination she finally admitted that, yes, absent succinylcholine, *any* interference in that child's breathing mechanism could have resulted in her death. And that is exactly what happened."

"Five minutes, Mr. Carnes," the court interjected.

"Thank you, Your Honor." Carnes hurried on, trying to hit all his remaining points, all his remaining questions. His voice got a touch higher, tighter.

"Even Dr. DiMaio, under cross-examination, admitted that if you had one injection of succinylcholine and a person lived for almost two hours and had completely resumed spontaneous respirations, you have got to have a second injection of succinylcholine before you can even say it is the cause of death. And, again, that did not happen in this case.

"The last area, for which I haven't left myself much time at all, deals with the tests. Dr. Balkon testified he reviewed those test run sheets, and labeled the attempts made at 71 and 190 inconclusive. Showing the positive results for the 58 ion only suggests the possibility, the *possibility* that succinylcholine was present, but possibility hasn't ever been enough in a criminal case to prove guilt beyond a reasonable doubt.

"Dr. Balkon testified that based on his review of all those records, succinylcholine had not been proved to be present. They come back with, 'Dr. Holmstedt ran those confirmatory tests.' Wrong." Carnes shook his head emphatically. "Holmstedt didn't run them. His associates ran them. *Holmstedt* didn't do *any* hands-on work in this case *at all*.

"Dr. Balkon referred to the fact that some of these runs seem to be the same as the runs that were presented into evidence. And I am going to tell you, I am not going to go through them one by one, but each one of these seems to have an individual computer-assigned number at the top. Each one of them is totally individual. You look at this number at the top of these. For every one of these four confirmatory tests, you can find a run with that very same number in Dr. Reiders's tests. Hold them up to the light and compare yourself to see if they don't look similar.

"I am not saying anything was going on. I am sure not saying Dr. Holmstedt had anything to do with it because he didn't run the test." Carnes did not want to attack the state's beaming, brilliant expert—he knew the jury liked Holmstedt. "His associate, Dr. Nordgren, did. But Dr. Nordgren wasn't brought into court so we could cross-examine her."

Again, Judge Carter interjected, "One minute, Mr. Carnes."

Now Carnes talked even faster. "Ladies and gentlemen, you have got to look at motives. I want you to consider Dr. Holland, because in the bottom line of this whole case, the final analysis, all their equipment, all the IV bags, all the syringes they had laying around on the table for four and a half weeks, all of it doesn't mean anything if you don't believe Dr. Holland. She was the one there observing ongoing seizure activity.

"If anybody has got a motive for misrepresenting the truth," Carnes finally stated flat out the defense's nomination for the guilty party, "it is *Dr. Kathy Holland*. I think it is clear to you she is trying to cover her tracks. She is hanging Genene Jones out there to dry and letting her try to face the heat that is due to the doctor's own incompetence or possible intentional wrongdoing." In the audience, Kathleen could feel the weight of the attention suddenly directed her way.

"We talked about presumption of innocence," Carnes continued. "Mr. Sutton promised you he was going to chip away at that presumption of innocence until there wasn't anything left and you reached the inescapable conclusion that Genene Jones is guilty. I am going to tell you they spent four and a half weeks trying *to cover it up*. They have thrown *blankets* at it. They have put up *smoke screens all around it*. They have done everything in their power to direct your attention *away* from the *facts* of this case surrounding the death of Chelsea McClellan. All that red lettering on the calendar is an attempt to hide the truth from you and confuse you and panic you and bully you into returning a verdict of 'Guilty.'

"Ladies and gentlemen, that presumption of innocence remains inviolate. It is still there. They have not dented it."

Judge Carter advised Carnes, "Time."

"May I conclude briefly, Your Honor?"

"Yes, you may."

"Ladies and gentlemen, I simply ask that you take your time," and Carnes was pleading. "Don't be totally influenced by emotion. Sit down and reasonably go through the evidence brought before you, and you will see the presumption of innocence remains. They have not met their burden of proof. They have not come close to meeting their burden of proof. And therefore, the law requires a verdict of 'Not Guilty.'

"Thank you."

There was a ten-minute break, from 12:45 to 12:55; then the jury was brought back in.

"All right, Mr. Sutton," began Judge Carter, "are you ready to proceed?"

"Yes, Your Honor, I am ready to proceed."

"I have two minutes to 1:00."

Sutton had saved the last, and dirtiest, job for himself—rebutting the points and answering the questions raised by the defense in their closing argument. His remarks would not be as eloquent or as moving as Nick Rothe's, Sutton had not rehearsed this; he was flying by the seat of his pants. It was the kind of work the country lawyer loved most. He moved to the podium, where he bowed slightly toward the judge and then toward the defense's table. "May it please the court, counsel." He then turned to his audience of twelve. He had 55 minutes. "Ladies and gentlemen of the jury, I will try to be as brief as possible in addressing myself to the remarks of Mr. Carnes. You know, when we started this trial, I told you that it was a privilege and an honor to sit on a jury, and it certainly is. As you will notice, the jury box is elevated above the floor, as is His Honor's bench, to signify that you occupy and sit in a position of honor, respect, and trust.

"Now," Sutton spoke confidentially, Texan to Texan, "it seems that this case is not any different from any other from a defense lawyer's viewpoint, in that what he attempts to do is to put everyone else on trial except the defendant, and that, exactly, is the nature and thrust of Mr. Carnes's argument.

"He seems to have implied to you that either myself or Mr. Rothe, or a combination of the two of us, have enough prestige and power that we can go out and bring in forty-some-odd witnesses from across Texas, the United States, and even go over to Sweden and bring them into this courtroom, and in some form of conspiracy, have them commit a series of aggravated perjuries. That is exactly what his argument implies. Exactly what it implies.

"What Mr. Carnes has laid out for you is a prescription for a perfect crime, because if you can find a way to kill someone with an injection of succinylcholine and then, by creating a 'smoke screen,' say that the state has not proved its case beyond a reasonable doubt, the defendant goes free. And I tell you, the only thing the defense has not suggested in this case as a hypothesis for Chelsea's death is that she committed suicide."

Sutton then responded to Carnes's very potent observation that the vial of succinylcholine purchased in the Clinic's initial pharmaceutical order remained unopened after the first four emergencies. He suggested to the jury that before Genene came to Kerrville, she had indeed already formulated the intent to commit these crimes. He asked the jurors to recall Dr. Schwartzman's testimony regarding the lecture she gave about succinylcholine. Jones had known about this stuff for years. Perhaps, Sutton hypothesized, Genene, or even Sally Benkert, had brought some succinylcholine up from San Antonio. "I suggest to you that Genene's 'motive, intent, scheme, plan, and design' started before Chelsea's first emergency. I suggest that when Genene Jones first arrived in Kerrville, she carried her own little bag of tricks with her.

"Now, as to the elements of the offense," Sutton went on, "the evidence is undisputed that it occurred in Kerr County on September 17, 1982, and that Genene Jones was the nurse."

He read from the charge the fourth and fifth elements the state had to prove: "'With intent to cause serious bodily injury.' It goes without saying," Sutton tried to gloss over this troublesome point, "as the witnesses have described, when you give someone succinylcholine, and they stop breathing, that is a very serious bodily injury." Sutton ignored the defense's vigorous dispute on this point—succinylcholine, Brookshire and Carnes had reminded the jury over and over, is not in and of itself dangerous if competent artificial respiration is maintained.

"'Committing an act clearly dangerous to human life,'" Sutton read the sixth element. Again he skipped past a point subject to contention. "By what?" he asked. "By injection with succinylcholine. Not by an anesthesiologist, not even an RN, but by an unsupervised, untrained LVN. An act," Sutton concluded with the seventh element, "which resulted in Chelsea McClellan's death.

"As the pathologist told you, the gliosis that she discovered in the child's brain stem made Chelsea McClellan particularly vulnerable to hypoxic episodes. You recall what an hypoxic episode is; that is when the breathing stops. Chelsea was particularly vulnerable.

"And I think it is reasonable to conclude from the evidence—from DeAnna Armour's testimony—that when no one else was standing around, right before Chelsea was loaded on the ambulance, she observed Genene Jones give Chelsea another shot. Having been previously a nurse's aide," Sutton slyly slipped in this helpful bit of information even though it had not been part of DeAnna's testimony, "she inquired of Genene: 'What is that?'

"'Valium.'

"But the child had already had Valium. The RN in the ER had already given the child Valium through the IV line. There was no cause or need to give the child more Valium.

"And then what happened? Immediately thereafter, the child was loaded on the ambulance, and when they got started towards San Antonio, they had to bag the child all the way.

"As to witnesses who are called and not called," Sutton explained, "we have tried to present you with almost every conceivable witness who could add something, without being repetitious. And, you'll notice," Sutton went on the attack, "the defense didn't call any witnesses who ran tests. Why? Were they afraid they would find the same result we found? Because it is pretty easy for Dr. Balkon to come in here, not ever having run a succinylcholine test below the 200-nanogram range, and criticize someone else's work. That is easy to do, especially at $150 an hour"—the standard fee for expert witnesses; Sutton's own witnesses had been paid at least as much, but the jury did not know that.

"What about Dr. Comstock?" Sutton continued his attack. "Who is Dr. Comstock? Operates a drug-abuse center in Houston. He doesn't have any overdose cases of succinylcholine. He is such a professional, that to become board certified, you recall, he set up his own board. How do you compare the credibility of a witness like Dr. Comstock with that of Dr. Bradley, who uses succinylcholine on a daily basis, and during the course of his career has used it some 200 to 300 times on children, and who testified that less than the therapeutic dose could and does mimic symptoms of some types of seizure?

"I also want you to notice there is nowhere in any of these records that any child had more than the general therapeutic dose of Dilantin," Sutton tried to deflate another of Carnes's alternative theories. "It is just not there.

"These extraneous offenses," he continued, changing

subjects as he crossed to the calendars, ''are certainly not to panic anyone, but to lay out the story, the whole scenario of events that occurred, and what Genene Jones had in her mind when she arrived in Kerrville, Texas, and what she did after she arrived there, and what happened when she got caught in her madness.

''Brandy Benites.'' He tapped the calendar. August 27. ''Let's talk about Brandy for a minute. I notice Mr. Carnes didn't mention to you that Brandy, from Sid Peterson Hospital on the way to San Antonio, had a cardiac arrest at almost the same location as Chelsea.

''He didn't mention to you that this whole time, Sarah Mauldin was bagging little Brandy Benites. She could not tell if Brandy's breathing was voluntary or involuntary. Neither could Genene Jones. That is why, a moment after the second IV, Genene picks up the little baby's leg and watches it fall to see whether or not succinylcholine has taken effect. And what does she scream out? 'Bag like hell. Let's get to San Antonio.' Once they got there, Dr. Ratner could find no reason for that child to have had any form of respiratory arrest.

''Jimmy Pearson.'' August 30. ''What was it that Genene said in her clairvoyant kind of way as the medics took little Jimmy out to the Veterans Hospital to load on the helicopter?'' Sutton was referring to an incident Sergeant Garcia had related. ''She said, 'I think he is going to go sour before we get to San Antonio.' *She knew what she was going to do before they ever loaded little Jimmy on that helicopter*.

''If the incident with Jimmy Pearson was all so innocent, why lie? Why tell the MAST people you gave Neo-Synephrine? Why then tell the mother and the doctor that it was Valium? Why lie about it? Why make up a story about the syringe and tracings falling out the door of the helicopter as they were lifting off the ground?'' Sutton lifted his eyebrows and cocked his head slightly, indicating the answer was obvious.

''Misty Reichenau,'' he said, tapping September 3.

"No seizures before or since. What happened? About her stiff neck," Sutton adopted Kay Reichenau's theory, "I would suggest to you that this little girl didn't like it very much having a rectal thermometer at the time.

"Shortly after insertion of the IV, little Misty went limp, as did the others. And in San Antonio, the doctors found no reason for respiratory arrest, and, as I said, she's had none since.

"Now, dear Sally Benkert. Long-time friend of Genene Jones; roommate in Kerrville, and then in San Angelo. I was not at all surprised at anything that Sally Benkert had to say. After all, you recall, she is the one who testified that she voluntarily kept Genene Jones from the grand-jury process, on her own. If anybody would go to that much trouble for a friend, I would certainly hold their testimony open to suspicion.

"Jacob Evans." The name in the same square as Chelsea. September 17. "Why the big lie about Jacob's history? You heard the mother and the grandmother. And yet when you read the medical record, as written in Genene Jones's own handwriting, it sounds like a completely different child. 'Obvious nystagmus,' and all the other fanciful little terms that Genene is so eloquent with.

"Jacob Evans, likewise, went to San Antonio for a neurological follow-up. No reason found for seizure activity, and has had none since."

He tapped the last square, September 23. "Rolinda Ruff. Code Blue into the hospital. All the doctors come rushing over. It just so happens that this day Dr. Bradley, the anesthesiologist, is there. He observes this child and immediately, from his experiences, determines in his own mind that this child is coming out from under succinylcholine. He sees gross, purposeful motor movements, not flailing movements, as you would expect in a seizure.

"Mr. Carnes has gone to great lengths to try to put Dr. Holland on trial here. Dr. Holland had just finished her residency, probably hadn't had all that much experience in pediatrics because of the way they have to rotate through

the hospital. They catch a month here and a month there. I
would imagine that Dr. Holland relied quite extensively
upon a nurse who had several years' experience in an Intensive Care Unit in San Antonio to be able to document
accurate medical histories. She, in good faith, relied upon
Genene Jones to assist her, to help her get her Clinic
started. But, as with these kids, the faith was misplaced.

"I think Mr. Carnes said earlier that our motive theory
is ridiculous. Is it? We didn't develop this motive," the
lawyer protested, inverting Carnes's logic, "the defendant
did. It is her ridiculous motive, not mine.

"Do you recall the conversation that Genene Jones had
with Ginger Morris [Sutton misremembered Mary's first
name], the nurse who was working at Sid Peterson on
weekends—about the sick children? Ginger Morris had
been there a good while. She knew what the frequency of
sick children through the hospital was, and she commented
to Genene—after Genene told her that they were going to
create a PICU with an all-LVN staff—you recall she said,
'Well, Genene, there just aren't that many sick kids.'

"'Oh, yes there are. All you have got to do is go out
and find them.'" And Sutton paused to let that sink in.
"Go out and find them.

"Do you also recall the conversation that Genene had
with Dr. Holland sometime after little Chelsea's death,
and they were coming out of the hospital? She remarked
that 'Maybe one day this will be the Chelsea Ann Mc-
Clellan Memorial Pediatric Intensive Care Unit.' Remember that? Why would she say that?

"And do you also recall Petti McClellan's testimony as
they were walking out of the emergency room to go over
to the Clinic to get their purses and Genene's little bag of
tricks? As they walked out that door, Genene shielded
Petti's eyes, and Petti looked and saw there was a hearse
there. A hearse. Petti commented to Genene, 'What are
you doing that for? Chelsea is not going to die.'

"I suggest to you that Genene Jones was going to *make
sure* that Chelsea died, because the previous emergencies

hadn't done anything yet, hadn't brought about any plans for an Intensive Care Unit. The child had to die because Genene wasn't getting anywhere by sending the kids to San Antonio.

"So Chelsea had to die. And Genene was so distraught about it that she does it again that afternoon: Jacob Evans. And then, on the day of little Chelsea's funeral, she buys *another* bottle of succinylcholine.

"As to why Genene turned in the vial, well, you know, nobody has ever accused Genene Jones of being a genius, but she had to have a vial. She had to come up with one because of the conversations in the executive board meeting. She had to come up with another vial somewhere because that was going to get pretty suspicious, a lost and missing vial. It was just a matter of time before Dr. Holland began to put it together in her own mind, anyway. So to forestall that possibility and maybe elude detection, she came up with the vial. A diluted vial.

"Now, these medical records that Mr. Carnes says they have outlined," Sutton gestured dismissively at the defense's chart, "neither of Mr. Carnes's witnesses were aware of, or apparently saw, the fact that after the child had been born premature, the child recovered normally and was a healthy child."

Judge Carter announced: "Thirty minutes, Counsellor."

Sutton went right on; he was just about where he wanted to be. "They didn't suggest to the witnesses, apparently, that Dr. Ted Boyce saw little Chelsea at age four months for some routine matter, and Dr. Ted Boyce described the child as an average, healthy, four-month-old child.

"Moreover, the medical records are replete with certain misinformation, and I would suggest to you that the evidence in this case shows rather dramatically that most of that misinformation came from Genene Jones.

"The mother and grandmother stayed with Chelsea during the hospital stay, no problems up there, but they were asked to make notations every time the child moved, so in all precaution, they did. Every time the child moved its hand or little foot or something, they made a notation of it.

I think most of you have children, grandchildren, or nieces and nephews. When little children sleep, they just jump around all the time.'' Sutton allowed himself a small smile. ''You would especially know that is true if you've ever had to sleep with a little one.''

''I believe I mentioned earlier that Dr. Bradley's testimony was that in some instances, with doses of a certain level of succinylcholine, it very well could, and does, mimic seizure activity.

''And don't forget about that second shot, ladies and gentlemen, observed by DeAnna Armour. Was it Valium or was it succinylcholine? Intramuscular, how long would it take? Intramuscular injection right before she was loaded. The evidence suggests that the child was loaded, doors were shut. As Tommy James testified, bagging began.'' Sutton was postulating that they would not even have noticed the onset of the arrest because of the bagging.

He jumped to another subject. ''Dr. Kagan-Hallet was working in the dark, as was the defense doctor, Dr. Goldie, who testified that if you have a false history in the records, his conclusions go right out the window.

''Dr. Kagan-Hallet was very exact in the cause of death, that little Chelsea had a very sensitive brain because of these hypoxic episodes, having had one at birth with hyaline membrane disease, and another one on August 24. She says the damage to the brain is instantaneous, although it may take some time for the scar to form. I suggest that this little child's heart and brain couldn't take it anymore, ladies and gentlemen. Just couldn't take it anymore.

''Dr. Holmstedt, Dr. Reiders, and the test,'' he said, moving on to his next topic. ''We talked a whole lot here about number 58 and its significance in looking for succinylcholine. Now, I think we kind of got all wrapped up in the different procedures and kind of skipped over something that I want to go over with you briefly.

''Do you recall in preparing the tissue for the test, Dr. Reiders and Dr. Holmstedt discussed that they put it in a wash?

They put it in certain solutions of certain chemicals, ran it through a centrifuge, with first one wash and then another.

"And since they were going after suspected succinylcholine, they added certain chemicals to this wash to pull out other, extraneous compounds. They try to leave only choline ester compounds so that when they run the test, if they find a compound at number 58, it must be succinylcholine. So, the wash is very important—it washes out all the other compounds which may have the number 58. You recall that the other esters have different retention times as they pass through the tube. So, when you run a tissue through and get a 58, and the retention time is right, properly paired with the deuterated control, you have got a confirmed test. Dr. Holmstedt and Dr. Reiders testified that to their knowledge, there is no other molecule with weight 58 and the same retention time as succinylcholine. And I would surmise that from Dr. Bo Holmstedt's experience, who is an authority in the field, if there were such, he would be one of the first to know about it."

Sutton had covered all of his points in forty-eight minutes. He had only one more task left, to give the twelve men and women before him the kind of hardened resolve they needed in order to convict Genene Jones of murder.

"In this day and time," he began, "we hear a whole lot about, you know, 'When is somebody going to do something? When is somebody going to get out there and stop what is going on?' For sixteen months now, this investigation has been going on. It went all over the country, into Philadelphia, to California, even over to Sweden. For sixteen months, there has been somebody on it every day— sometimes many people, but every day, *somebody* was doing something on it.

"And now, ladies and gentlemen, when we ask, 'When are they going to do something,' the 'they' becomes you. You are the jury.

"You know, since I have been here in Georgetown, I have been very impressed with the beautiful lady that adorns the top of your courthouse. The statue of Justice is such a beautiful sight, on such a beautiful building. What more fitting symbol can you have on the top of a courthouse, standing there with a sword, the representation of justice being swift and sure.

"And that is what I think this case deserves, ladies and gentlemen. If Genene Jones is allowed to walk out of this courtroom acquitted, on the basis of the testimony and the evidence that you have had before you, I would suggest that we go up here on the top of this courthouse and remove that sword from the statue of Justice and insert a syringe.

"Ladies and gentlemen, as we sit here today, in this most respected of rooms in any community, the hall of justice, I think that if we are real quiet for just a minute, we will hear the echo of the gates of hell slamming shut on Genene Jones's condemned soul for what she did to Chelsea McClellan. And I am sure that after due deliberations, you will reach the same conclusions.

"And I do thank you so very much. You have been most kind and attentive." And with that said, Sutton sat, his case concluded.

The jury was excused at 1:50 P.M. Deliberations began following lunch. The first polling showed ten jurors in favor of conviction. By 6:10 P.M., the holdouts were persuaded. Jury foreman Ed Edwards informed Judge Carter they had reached a unanimous verdict.

Ed Edwards

This whole thing has been an odd chapter in my life. I did not ask to be a jury member. In fact, I tried to get out of it. I did everything I could, legally, morally, and ethically, to get off the jury.

And you ended up foreman.

Yes. And I tried to get someone else to be the foreman. But the others handed it to me. The jury chose me.

How does that work? There was a vote?

That's right. We were together there for about five weeks, and we got to know one another pretty well. I know them well enough that if I were accused of some crime and I were *innocent,* I might like those people on my jury, but if I were guilty, I'd want people who were . . . less ethical.

I was surprised that they allowed anyone with an education on that jury. I thought that the defense would, normally, kick off anyone that had any kind of education. As I recall, there were five college degrees on that jury.

I'm an electrical engineer, a registered professional engineer in the state of Arizona. There was a microbiologist there, she was what I'd call a young whippersnapper. She was the youngest member of the jury; she'd just turned thirty. There was also a mechanical engineer, and there were a couple of retired military men.

What are the duties of a jury foreman?

Well, legally, I'm the one that has to accept all of the paperwork from the judge, and I'm the one that has to sign the piece of paper if I want to talk to the bailiff, in order to get additional information, and I'm the one that has to sign the verdict. The foreman has to sign everything.

During the deliberations, I have to direct them. I'm in charge. And I made sure that they considered the charges, and only the charges that were presented. It's very easy to get off onto a tangent. Very easy.

Had you heard anything about the case before the trial?

No, I knew nothing about it at all. In fact, I think I'll read the newspapers more regularly so I won't be put on one like it again.

[THE SPEAKER LAUGHS]

When I received word that I had indeed been chosen to sit on the jury, I told my supervisor at Motorola. He said, "Well, then, Ed, your assignment for the duration of the trial is to do the best job you possibly can. Your salary will be paid, and your work will be here waiting for you when you get back." And by gosh if the work *wasn't* waiting for me.

[THE SPEAKER LAUGHS]

I did not ask for it, I would not ask for it again. If I had it to live over—if I had it to face again—I just might drum up a *real good* excuse.

[THE SPEAKER LAUGHS]

But we tried to make it bearable. In fact, we went to great lengths to try and get a little bit of levity into it, because it was, sometimes, quite depressing. I made some friends on the jury. I enjoyed the camaraderie that we developed. All of them have a great degree of civic responsibility, and I guess I respect them. I felt that I could, in front of all of them, say what I wanted to say, and mean it, and I don't think any of them would misconstrue my meaning. And conversely, whatever they had to say, I think I would, after this experience, listen to them. Some of them had very strong opinions, like I did. I got the impression from a couple of them that they were kind of hoping they could find some way to keep her from being guilty.

They were trying to find some way to explain it away?

But there was no way they could do it. They couldn't.

Did you find it an unpleasant experience?

I found it, uh, I found it pleasant, I found it unpleasant. I found it horrifying. I found it depressing. I also feel as though I contributed as a member of the jury, and also as a member of the community. I don't think it's really changed my life, though it has made me a bit more aware of man's inhumanity to man, and of the fact that everyone (anyone, even so-called educated people) has the potential of being quite inhumane.

See, she's not crazy, she's sharp. She's intelligent. She's very capable. She's a very forceful woman, very domineering, and was, apparently, a very good nurse. But she misused her capabilities. I think what she did was— I think she had something planned which I don't fully understand. She's not crazy, but she has a warped sense of duty, somehow. I can't account for it, but I've got granddaughters Chelsea's age, and I don't want her walking the streets. It's not safe.

Did you have any trouble with the evidence?

You mean like the tests' accuracy? None whatever. The technical presentation of the information pertaining to the residual traces of succinylcholine, explained by Dr. Holmstedt (his credentials, of course, were impeccable) and laid out by the computer printouts, was, to my mind, conclusive. It's like your five fingerprints. It only takes one to identify a person, and that's all it took here. There should have been *none* in the body. So it's just like a fingerprint of mine showing up on a glass, it only takes one to show that the glass was in my hand. And that's all there was to it.

And you folks were convinced.
Absolutely.
Why do you think she did it?

I really feel that she became— that she did it to make herself into a hero, and this happened time and time again down in San Antonio. Now, this came out subsequent to our trial, but what was shown here was that she apparently tried to immobilize all of these babies so she could come in and use those heroic, lifesaving techniques, which she was very capable of doing. But it got out of hand with this little girl, the first time she tried it, because she had brain-stem problems. And I think she saw it getting out of hand the last time, that's my opinion, and I think that's when she decided to really kill that little baby.

And she always did it to babies who could not talk. Well, one of them (and I couldn't tell you which) was seven years old, but he couldn't talk either and weighed only, something like, twenty pounds. He hadn't been given the same large quantity, but here again, to effect that torture upon that kid after all that he'd been through? Talk about inhumane!

And there's no doubt about what she did. It's too well documented, even though she tried to cover it up. She was a real con artist. We searched for the most time-consuming penalty we could find, the harshest punishment we felt would stand up to an appeal court's scrutiny. If we could have made it 199 or 299, even 499 years, something like that, I think we would have done it. But, in the back of my mind it kept comin' up: "Make sure you don't do something that the defense can later say was unreasonable or would not stand up under some kind of judicial review." So I backed away and we went with the 99—the maximum the judge would let us go for. However, had we had the option of 499 years, we would have chosen that. Even the grandmothers agreed. There were an awful lot of grandmothers on our jury, and they knew a lot more about babies and what doctors talk about and nurses talk about when somebody takes a baby in for treatment, than any of the rest of us.

Me, I understood all the measurements in the trial, because I deal with microseconds and nanoseconds and stuff like that in my work daily. And I'd had enough college chemistry to see what they were doing and how they were doing it and why they were doing it. We do the same things in electronics daily, and even I've pushed the frontier forward a bit myself. So all that was duck soup for me, it was no problem at all. But the rest of it . . . I could get a *sense* of it, but it was those grandmothers and mothers that really explained, "Wait, that's not right, what she said, because that's not the way babies react."

Whereas *I* couldn't fully understand what was going on in this area of the testimony, boy, those grandmothers did. I tell you, they knew just exactly what they were talking about. So they played a very, very important part. They may not have had a degree in microbiology, but by golly, they knew little babies. So I really appreciated that, I really did. That would have gone by me. When we finally got around to a vote, we all had a real consensus, with no problem.

It was a quick decision. How many votes did you take?

Really only one vote. There were two really on the fence. So, we discussed it all a little more. I think the biggest concern, with both of 'em, was the fact that they just *couldn't believe* that this woman, who was a mother herself, would hurt a little baby, for *any* reason. That was the only concern I could see, with either one of them.

They didn't have any specific problems with any of the facts?

No, the facts show it, and they could see that. So, we just got to talking about it and went right down the evidence. Was it one of these so-called crib deaths, or— what is it they call it? There's another word for it. SIDS disease, that's it. SIDS is just a term doctors use to label a death they can't explain. Somebody probably got a federal grant to call it that.

But we went right down the charge, *every step*, all the way. When we got down to the last point, we said, "Yes, this child died a death other than a natural death, and it was at the hands of someone else."

A couple of the jury members seemed to think that Dr. Holland should also bear some blame for what happened. They felt she was the responsible person in that Clinic—it was under her direction when all this took place. I can't see that. I think she was also a victim. Whether she likes to admit it or not, she was also a victim of that nurse. Genene took advantage of her inexperience. Because the only experience that she did have (before she set up this office) was in an Intensive Care Unit, where this kind of emergency was an everyday occurrence.

When the final arguments were completed, we retired to the jury room, and we were instructed to select a foreman. That's the first thing we did. Then, like I said, we just went right down through it all. I sat down and I said, "All right, let's do it this way, because remember, the prime point is, number one: whatever we do, it has to stand up in the face of any appeal and any judicial review. And number two: we have to be unanimous with it." Whatever decision we came up with, each one of us, individually and collectively, has to be able to live with it for the rest of our lives. I did not want another set of twelve people to have to go through what we twelve had to go through. So whatever we were going to do, I wanted to make sure it was within the law, and the statutes as they existed at that time.

After finding her guilty—which really didn't take very long—they locked us up in the Georgetown Inn. We went over and had supper, then the next day we got into the punishment phase. I guess it was early in the morning when they presented the arguments for assessing the penalty. Then, I think it was in the early afternoon that we went through that decision. And that was the worst part of it all.

A lot of us had spent a sleepless night, knowing what was coming up the next day. We'd judged this woman, now we had to decide what to do with her. Also, that night, we really didn't know what guidelines we would be given. As it turned out, a lot of our apprehensions were undue, because we were only given about four, maybe five choices. But then, listening to the arguments, knowing she was guilty, beyond any doubt that any of us could come up with, it still wasn't easy.

I think I approached this stint on the jury like the rest of them did—I considered her not guilty until *proven* guilty. To the best of my knowledge, we all started with that in our minds; everyone that I talked to did. But then, the scene changed when we had to assess the penalty.

It boiled down to the fact that for what she did, there was no suitable penalty available to us. So we picked the penalty that would keep her as far away from society for as long as possible. That's the reasoning that was behind it, that's the reasoning we used. As I said, had we had the opportunity to assess 199 years, or 299 years, I'm sure that would have been our choice. And I say that as the one who had to sign the order, as the one she directed her venom at when she was found guilty.

What did she do?

Do you know what utter *hatred* is?
[THE SPEAKER PAUSED]
She thought she had gotten away with it.

PART 5

The Lie

TWENTY-THREE

It is good to see in another's evil,
the things that we should flee from.

Publis Syrus
Sententiae No. 57

TWENTY-FIVE MILES NORTH OF AUSTIN, HIGH-
way 36 splits off from Interstate 35 and cuts through the
heart of the state toward Abilene. The roadway was built
just after World War II by the men stationed at Fort Gates,
the army's Texas 36th Division, hence its designation. The
fort's main gates open onto its highway just two miles
southwest of the incorporated municipality of Gatesville,
population 6,260.

Gatesville typifies most small towns of central Texas:
the citizens are reasonably happy, reasonably well off; the
municipal buildings are a mix of turn-of-the-century brick
and granite and post-war functional. Signs outside town
boast the fact that Gatesville sits on the Brazos Trail, one
of the main arteries north to the railroads during the days
of the cattle drives. Today, Gatesville's distinguishing features are the several military posts that surround it, all coordinated through nearby Fort Hood, and the women's
penitentiary that sits in a pleasant valley on the north side
of town. No one has ever escaped from these facilities.
There's nowhere to go.

The Mountain View Unit of Gatesville's prison is a roughly square but irregular forty-two acres of land defined by twin fences of heavy-gauge metal. The fences extend into the earth below and stand over twenty feet high, the top edge capped with razor wire.

The compound's buildings are 100 feet inside the nearest fence and look more like a grade school than a prison, perhaps because the facility was originally constructed as a school in the sixties, then purchased and converted by the state in the early seventies. Each building is lined with flower beds free of leaves and weeds. The lawns are kept tidy.

In addition to the dormitories, the compound's maze of single-story buildings includes a sizable greenhouse, a rec room, a full gym, a baseball diamond, a track, an interior volleyball court, and a school offering college and computer courses.

Inside the building nearest the visitor's gate, down a narrow hallway, through a heavy wooden door, and down the building's wide central corridor, what once might have been a very small classroom (about twenty by forty feet) now serves as a visiting room. On the southern wall, two windows let in sunlight. A small table between the windows holds mugs, plastic spoons, a Coffeemate jar, an open package of sugar cubes, a coffee maker, and an array of cookies and donuts. A blackboard hangs on the northern, interior wall, covered with chalk notes detailing inmates' work assignments. A large rectangular metal table sits in the center of the room, with four chairs on each long side, another at either end. The floor tiles are grey, the cement-block walls white. The room is oppressive in its unadorned utility. It is a long way to the other side of the second fence.

At 9:25 A.M., on December 7, 1984, Genene Jones— who will be incarcerated in the Mountain View Unit until at least 2009, the date of her first parole hearing—entered the reception room. Under a too-large green jacket, she wore a loose, two-piece white cotton uniform that hung like pajamas. Her shoulders hunched forward a bit. Her gait was smooth and steady—with no trace of bounce. Her hair was short, parted in the middle, and carefully brushed back in two layers. Her eyes are what catch the attention: slightly bulging, stretching the eyelids, revealing more of the pupils and the surrounding white than normal. Though her eyes are not set unusually far apart, her face is so narrow that they seem to wrap around her head—an Egyptian wall painting come to life. Nineteenth-century mesmerists must have had eyes like these. They search for you, find you, and then lock in on you.

She smiled and extended her hand, only to quickly withdraw it, asking the guard, "Is it all right?" Her grasp was delicate.

"Just what is it you intend to write about me?" she asked.

"Well, we're not quite sure, yet. We heard about you, your situation, from a friend in the DA's office who worked on the case."

"Who was that?"

"One of the attorneys."

"What did she tell you?"

"She said we ought to look into this case. She thought it was a helluva story. We said, 'Well, what's it all about? We haven't heard the first thing about it. What happened?'"

"You mean they don't know about me out in California?"

"I'm afraid not. We've got our own breed of bizarre goings-on."

She smiled, then turned to the guard. "Would it be all right if I had a cup of coffee?"

"One or two sugars, Genene?" asked the guard.

"Two. Thank you, Helen." She turned back and the eyes focused in again, reestablishing contact.

"We came here today, Genene, because we'd like to hear your version of everything that's happened. We've heard what the DA thinks you've done, and we've talked with a number of people who've told us you're a killer. But we have a hard time with that. We don't understand. We don't know if you're guilty or not.''

''I'm not.''

''Fine. If you ever want your side of the story told clearly and completely, this is the time to speak up.''

''Well, let's hold off a minute. I want to get some things clear first. This book— what are you going to write? I mean, what we say here today—before you print anything, I want to approve it.'' She turned to the guard, ''Is smoking permitted?'' She tapped a cigarette out of a crumpled package.

''Well, we have a problem with that.'' The eyes came back. ''Everybody involved in these events has their own personal point of view about what's happened. If we agreed to this with everyone, (and we'd have to if we did with anyone) we wouldn't be able to write anything. We'd end up with a book of blank pages. So, I'm sorry, but we can't agree to that. We have to have the final say. We're the ones who'll be telling the story; we'll be writing the book.''

She pushed back her chair. ''Then I guess we have nothing to discuss.''

''If that's the way you want it, it was a pleasure meeting you. But we want you to know, we *are* going to write this book.''

Her eyes were level, assessing.

''We'll go this far: after we type up our notes from to-day's meeting, we'll send you a copy. You can check it over, and before we include any information you give us today in our book, you can correct, clarify, or expand any section.''

A second guard then appeared and presented a press release for Genene's signature. She balked. ''We haven't quite gotten our ground rules worked out yet.''

''If you don't sign the form immediately, your guest will be asked to leave immediately.''

It was up to her.

''What'll it be, Genene?''

Genene sighed, snatched up the pen, and scrawled her name. She then sat back, focused in again, and took her first drag on her first cigarette of the day.

"We understand you're missing breakfast to talk with us. Thank you."

"Well, one of the reasons I agreed to see you was because I don't get many visitors. Not even my lawyers come much anymore. Have you read the transcripts from the trial yet?"

"No. They won't be available for another eight months or so."

She nodded. We didn't know much.

"You gotta understand, right up front," she said, "I didn't kill anybody. I know for a fact that I have done nothing wrong; that I have caused the death of no one. I shouldn't be in here. But, I am, so I try to make the best of it. I've accepted it, you know? I'm a born-again Christian and—"

"Really. How long have you been a Christian?"

"About nine years now. —And I believe that God has put me in here for a reason. It's not a whole lot of fun; it's rough. But He's not going to give me anything I can't take."

"But twelve people found you guilty. How could that—"

"I'm *not* a *murderer*. Chelsea was a sick child, had been since birth, and Petti was insanely prejudiced against me. I couldn't believe what she said on the stand. She had simply decided—after certain people got to her and convinced her of it—that Chelsea had been murdered and that *I* had murdered her. But she didn't think that at first. She and Reid took an ad out in the paper—did you see that?— thanking Kathy and me for what we did. We tried to save her, but . . . she had problems. Some people do, some don't. Chelsea'd had at least two arrests at home—Petti'd had to give her CPR. But at the trial, the prosecution made it seem as if it never happened.

"A lot of the prosecution's witnesses just lied—*just lied*—on the stand. I don't know why.

"For example, the night I went to Sid Peterson, I was

unconscious. My nose was broken, I had a nasogastric tube, and because I'd been in so much pain, they had to knock me out. But Sutton had a nurse on the stand testify that I'd said some ridiculous thing about starting a PICU in Kerrville.

"A PICU in Kerrville was never *my* idea, that was Kathy, not me. Kathy was going to be head of the Neonatal Intensive Care Unit. That was her plan from the very beginning. I couldn't believe it when she blamed me just to protect herself from malpractice suits and from losing her medical license.

"The whole trial was unfair. It was all a fake show, a well-rehearsed movie. It wasn't the truth. Take that Dr. Holmstedt. Very cute man, but isn't it kind of strange that there's only one doctor in the whole world who can do this test? It isn't *accurate*. Not to the degree he says it is. It's a numbers game. There's an easy way to misinterpret his test, and it happened all through the trial. Just take a ruler and put it against the graphs, and you can see the test is invalid. Any child could disprove it. There was no succinylcholine in any of those tissues. Ask the Hogedas if I'm a murderer. I stayed with them for a while after Kerrville. Ask them what they think of me."

She stubbed out her cigarette. "I was, originally, going to take the stand, but I think I made the right decision. I would have, in all honesty with myself, probably have lost it with Ron Sutton. How I feel about that man is hard to put into words. He has not only destroyed my life, he's destroyed the lives of my children. My mama's aged ten years. He's just ruined my family's lives over a *lie*. When I heard the verdict, I just simply could not believe it. I remember sort of breaking apart.

"I was just amazed the jury hadn't seen the truth, hadn't seen the snow job. There's just one thing I still regret about that trial—about not testifying—and that's that I'll never be able to convince Reid and Petti that I did not harm their baby. There's just no way I can ever convince them now; thanks to Ron Sutton. No way in the world. But I'd like them to know, straight from the horse's mouth, that I *did not* kill her.

"Chelsea was a blond-haired, blue-eyed darling, but she was sick. She could look at you with those little blue eyes and just make you melt. A beautiful baby. I cried for almost a week over that child."

She chatted then about prison food ("The inmates, they call it ambrosia") and prison life ("lonely"). We spoke of the car she'd owned ("a gold '81 Chevette"), the places she'd been ("not many places really, Tennessee, Florida, well, lots of places on the Gulf. New York once. I'm just a southern girl at heart"), and what life had been like before the night she was arrested.

"I guess the happiest times I can remember were when I was a girl. When Daddy and I would go driving around town fixing his billboards. He used to let me drive the truck down the dirt roads. That was when I was just a kid. I'm not sure how old. As soon as I could reach the pedals and see over the dash. San Antonio was a much smaller town back then." Her eyes dropped to the table. She took out another cigarette. She leaned forward. Her eyes came up.

"If you haven't read the transcripts, how do you know . . . about what's happened?"

"We've read about 700 newspaper articles and have been talking to a few people. Not many yet. A few."

"Newspapers and magazines aren't very accurate, you know. They make a lot of stuff up."

"So we understand."

"Did you know that, originally, the autopsist, Dr. Galbreath, said that Chelsea had received brain damage at birth and that *that* was what caused her SIDS?"

"No. We heard that Dr. Kagan-Hallet—"

"Right, but the DAs *told* Kagan-Hallet to change her diagnosis. It wasn't voluntary. You didn't see that in the newspapers? She admitted it on the stand."

"What are you doing with yourself these days?"

"They've got me making dolls. S.P. Ragg dolls. It's a

Christmas project. There's a pile of them in front of the counter in reception. You must have seen them on the way in. I enjoy it, it's entertaining. Every day we each do a different thing on the dolls. Right now I'm doing the eyes. They sell them for about $25 or $30 to officers in the system. The kids like them.'' She talked a while then about her own children, how much she missed them. But she made it clear she did not want them to be part of the book. "Please, they're not part of this. Not at all. Please, they could be in danger.''

"From whom?''

"I'd really rather just keep them completely out of all this, okay?''

"All right. Let's talk about San Antonio.''

"I'm their scapegoat. I did *nothing* to those children. What got me in trouble, I guess, why I was singled out by physicians and got to the top of the DA's hit parade, is because of my big mouth. Mouthy, I guess. I tend to be abrasive. But if I felt something was wrong, I said something, I told someone about it. Doctors don't like to be told when they've done something wrong.

"In early 1981, I— See, the ideal way to operate an intensive care unit is with a medical *team,* and in 1981, I started to see that there was a real lack of communication developing between the doctors and nurses in the PICU. Our team was falling apart. No nurse's judgment was being respected, and so we started to complain about it.

"The problems stemmed, I think, from doctors who were too busy to check on the patients, and interns who could not yet handle emergencies. But that's just the way it was in that place at that time. It's no one's 'fault,' really. See, when an intern faces his first respiratory arrest, he can either fake it or let his ego and his pride down and say: 'What do I do?' But there's a mystique about physicians, even interns, and they say, 'I am the doctor. I am the physician. I am in charge.' It's degrading for them to say, 'I don't know what to do. Tell me. Tell me what to do.' So, they bluff their way through; they fake it. And meanwhile, the kid's dying. But really, the nurses usually do know more about what's immediately best for a patient. You get to know them pretty well. So, compared to the doctors, well, we really were more experienced. And we tried to bring that to people's attention.

"See, I think that I stepped on so many toes, that I had been so vocal against the people I worked with there in that Unit, in that PICU, that I was framed. Don't kid yourself, it happens. They didn't like me, so they blamed me to save themselves. Every one of them. They're liars." She dropped her head. Then, as if it took great effort, she repeated: "The problems in the Unit—the deaths, the incidents—I blame that on the substandard care given by the inexperienced doctors and nurses I had to work with. You do understand that Medical Center Hospital was a teaching hospital, right? Three of the worst were Houghuis, Bezecny, and Yee.[1] They were the most incompetent doctors in the Unit, although a few others weren't far behind. I had a patient, a little girl, and a doctor came in to examine her after bowel surgery without washing his hands. I mentioned it to him, and he told me he didn't have time. Well, that child infected and died. And that kind of thing happened all the time.

"During June and July of '81, there was a large changeover of doctors and nurses—a lot of 'em graduated, left, moved on. As replacements, I got onto the 3—11 with me, two LVNs, and five new graduate nurses—people who're fine on medical theory but who have no experience. Sally and I were taking care of the critical patients at that time because we had the most experience. We helped the GNs treat the less seriously ill kids when we could, but it could get real hectic in there. If you've got three kids

---

1. Every other individual who expressed an opinion about these three doctors described them as excellent, even exceptional physicians. The authors have included Ms. Jones's comments about them and other individuals, because we feel the comments reveal Jones's character and defensive patterns, not because the authors endorse or in any way share Jones's opinions or vision of reality.

already—'cause somebody's on a break, let's say—and a kid Codes, well, it's hectic.

"At one point, Dr. Robotham asked me to train these GNs and take charge of the Unit, but I didn't feel I had the appropriate title. And, there was going to be a lot of red tape involved, and I just didn't feel right about it. I didn't want to get into any trouble with the nursing board. I don't really have the credentials to teach. I said no thanks. We'd gotten along okay up to that point, but after that, well, let's say it cooled, and stopped getting better.

"I can remember when the Unit had a lot of camaraderie, a lot of mutual respect among the personnel—before Robotham came. I know that's a long time ago, but I was there; I saw it happen. When he came, he started putting wedges between the nurses. See, Robotham was a pediatric intensivist, and the staff wasn't used to it. It's no secret he came there to make a name for himself and for the Unit. Well, he instituted a number of new policies to reach that end—all of which made for more work—and most of the nurses didn't like it. I wasn't the only one.

"Here's an example," she said, lighting another Marlboro. "At one point he said that every patient admitted to the Unit was supposed to get a Swan-Ganz catheter inserted. A Swan-Ganz is a very sensitive device that gets inserted down the artery of the neck into the patient's heart and measures the amount of blood the heart is pumping—which is a good thing to know, sure, but there are easier ways to check it. Inserting a Swan-Ganz is a difficult procedure. And it's no fun for the child. So that increased the tension, and that's just one example of how his creating more work contributed to the overall problematic atmosphere.

"Another thing about Robotham was that he liked to administer a lot of drugs to his patients. So, naturally, there were a lot of IVs inserted. I'd say close to 15,000 during the time I was there. I got to be pretty good at it, I guess, and Robotham began to ask me to do it a lot, you know, demonstrate how I did it. He had me do a lot of special things for him. I babysat his kids a couple of times. Anyway, as things progressed, I felt very much in the middle because I was getting a lot of extra attention; he's a brilliant guy and he was teaching me things I could never have learned anywhere else. Also, though, I wanted what was best for the Unit, so I went to Belko and told her the problem as I saw it. She wrote a memo the next day which specifically outlined the different duties to be performed by various-level nurses. It was very specific. But even after this, one morning, during rounds, Robotham asked me to demonstrate some specific procedure for the interns. Well, I was busy with my own sick patient. It just infuriated me. I spoke to him privately and put a stop to it.

"That's when J. R. stopped singling me out, but he still made me responsible for all the sickest patients in the Unit; he knew I was one of the better nurses there, and they were mine, my responsibility. Whenever anything went wrong with them, I was called in—twenty-four hours a day. I lived just about five minutes away. This went on for almost eight months until one day my son mentioned to me that he never saw me, and I realized he was right. I told Robotham it had to stop. Two days later, on my day off, Robotham called me to come in to take a look at 'my' patient who didn't look so good. I told him no. Our relationship deteriorated markedly after that.

"I don't want to sound like I'm picking on Robotham or his handling of the Unit, but while he was there, it was a lot like 'musical beds' at times, which was another strain. Pretty soon after he got there, he made it policy to accept *any* child who needed treatment, so we had beds everywhere—out in the hallway sometimes. Sometimes when this happened, to make room, we'd discharge patients before we really should have.

"You should understand, too, the way the Unit worked. During any twenty-four-hour period there was just one resident available, one or two interns floating about, and a few medical students. These student doctors—well, yeah, technically they're doctors, but they've still got a lot to learn—they were scheduled by Brunell, Franks, and Mangos and were responsible for both the Unit and the general Pediatrics Ward; not one of the doctors worked just the ICU. They were always busy, and they didn't like being paged into the PICU for an emergency. Most of 'em would just freak out. Did you know that Robotham had started the practice of morning rounds with his interns?''

"Yes. That was one of his attempts at improving both patient care and cooperation between departments, wasn't it?''

"Right. At first this seemed like a good idea, but then he started really putting his residents on the spot. He'd ask a question, and if the intern didn't know the answer, Robotham would humiliate him. Now this kind of 'on-the-spot-testing' can have two effects: one, it can get the interns more on their toes and knowledgeable, or two, it can urge them to be ready to cover for themselves, and *that's* what happened. Because Robotham would lay into them so hard whenever they blew it, the interns and residents got defensive. They started questioning the nurses just like Robotham had questioned them.

"Also, though—and this was really irritating—they began to report to Robotham things that they had done for the patients which they in fact had left for us nurses to do. They did this to impress J. R., I think, but it was unfortunate because they were often reporting incorrectly, and it could be very embarrassing. You could be standing right there, and the resident would say he'd just done a certain procedure, when *you'd* just gotten through with it—not him—five minutes before.

"We started telling the residents to do their own work and insisted that they correctly report the help they were receiving from the nursing staff. See, you have to stay two steps ahead of those kids, and it's not easy. You've got to give them all your attention, watch for any little change. A sick baby can be smiling and happy one minute, and dead the next—and vice versa. And when you're standing there waiting for some scared graduate doctor to tell you what to do to save this kid's life— See, as a nurse, on our own, we're only supposed to keep a child alive—pump their heart and lungs and that's about it. We're trained to never take responsibility for injecting anything without specific instructions. Well, for me at least, it became unbearably frustrating. The interns were always too busy somewhere else.

"After about four or five months of this, the nurses got together and went to Robotham about it. We said: '(a) the kids are suffering; (b) the doctors and nurses are defensive and uncomfortable in one another's presence; (c) the PICU is not functioning as a *unit;* and (d) these are not good working/healing conditions, so we want improvements.' Nothing happened.

"So, I went to both Brunell and Corum, personally, to try and get things corrected. They told me that the doctors were having fun and to lay off. 'Leave them alone'— meaning the doctors—they told me. After I went through a whole list of incidents that concerned me, giving him admission numbers and dates, Corum just patted me on the shoulder and said, 'We'll take care of it.' Four nights later, my son called me at the Unit and told me to get home fast." Stubbing out her cigarette, she explained: "Someone had ransacked our apartment.

"It was at about that time that the administration's message was becoming clear to me: 'Whatever your complaint may be, keep out of where you don't belong.'[1] By this time, J.R. and I weren't talking anymore. He was pissed because I had gone over his head reporting problems in 'his' Unit. Except for Belko and Benkert and a couple of others, towards the end it was real icy for me there.

"I want to say that I think Dr. Larry Houghuis was probably the worst offender as far as making any real effort to take care of the kids is concerned. He really

---

1. The authors do not believe or intend to imply that anyone at Medical Center Hospital or the University of Texas was responsible for the reported damage to Jones's apartment.

slacked off sometimes. He was hard to get a hold of. And I wasn't the only one who disliked him. As for the so-called incident with him, the reverse is more like the truth. Houghuis was treating this little boy baby and having some trouble inserting an IV line. For some reason—I forget now just what it was—he orders straight heparin, and I was stunned. The kid didn't need heparin and certainly not *straight* heparin. Houghuis's sidekick, Dr. Yee,[2] drew up 3 cc's of heparin and placed the syringe on the bedside table. Houghuis instructed me to inject it, and I refused. He had a real attitude problem. He thought he was God or something. So he picked up the syringe himself and over the next three minutes, injected all 3 cc's of straight heparin into the poor kid.

"So I reported this all to Belko, our supervisor, and the next morning she really cut down Houghuis bad during rounds. In front of everyone, she accused him of lying, then told everybody what really happened." She shook her head faintly. The eyes dropped again, disengaging. A fifth cigarette flared. "I'm looking forward to seeing my kids over Christmas."

We talked about the Clinic then, its layout, its atmosphere. She sketched the floor plan, drawing in a room she labeled "my office." Two years later, Kathleen described that space as "a little alcove" between the front and second treatment rooms with enough room for a cot and a built-in table at one end.

"Tell us about the vials."

"Let's see," she hardly hesitated, "we had one vial to start with. Kathleen had wanted it for emergency purposes—in case some older child went into grand mal seizure or something. We ordered another, a second vial, on the seventh, because the vial Sally had fetched for Misty had gotten itself misplaced. Now, I was in the hospital for

---

2. Again, the authors do not share or endorse Jones's comments about Drs. Houghuis or Yee, nor have they found that Jones's comments are in any way supported by the facts. Both doctors are, by all accounts, exceptional physicians.

a week with my ulcers and when I returned, on September 17, I started an inventory. While I was doing the inventory, I saw that there were two vials in the refrigerator. I told Kathleen immediately, but just then, the McClellans arrived and we got sidetracked. After Chelsea was dealt with, Dr. Holland called some independent doctors and gave them the two vials for analysis.''

"How do you suppose they got to be different concentrations?"

"I don't know. I have no explanation."

"What about the Clinic's third vial?"

"I don't know anything about that either. The handwriting expert never identified the order as having been written by me. He simply identified it as 'writing.' That's the kind of evidence they used against me. Can you imagine? What would you be doing if you were in here?"

"I have no idea. What were you thinking about when you said, 'Why are so many babies dying on my shift?'"

"That was in San Antonio, and I was just sick and tired of seeing kids die. I mean, at that point in time, when I made that statement, I had *a lot* of pressures on me, and I was just sick of the pressures and sick of sick kids and sick of people dying on me. I was just really tired of it."

"How does it make you feel, knowing that at least some people think you are a murderer, a baby killer?"

"How does it make me *feel*?" She paused, a moment, thinking. "I wish I could put it into words. Anger. A lot of anger."

"Did you really hold your patients and rock them and talk to them after they died?"

"I would sing to them, certainly. It wasn't a broadcast. It was a private thing between the child and me. It was my tribute to them. My helping them die with dignity."

"But, presumably, their souls had already passed on."

"I don't know that. I'm not God. I don't know when someone's soul has passed on. I *do* know that if I had a child and that child was dead and someone treated that body as a 'dead body,' I would be very upset. And this is what really bothers me, I mean really, how would *you* feel? Is that why I'm locked up, because I sang for the kids who died on me? Where is the *proof* that I'm responsible for *any* crime whatsoever? The toxicology reports on all the kids are not, to my knowledge, indicative of my having done anything unlawful or unconscionable. And yet, here I am, in jail.''

Prison visits are never very long. There are counts to be made, schedules to keep. Unfortunately, there would be no more interviews; Genene rarely speaks to anyone more than once.

"Are you sure about everything you've told us today? Are you sure about the dates and numbers you've mentioned? Much of what you've told us is substantially different from what we've read and heard from other people, and we'll be checking into it.''

"Well, now, I'm not positive about some of the specific *dates*. I mean, I could be off here and there, but as to what happened, yeah, those are the facts.''

"And if someone else gives another version, then they're lying?''

"That's right. Or remembering it wrong.''

"Did you do it?''

"All I can do is sit here and tell you I'm not guilty of anything except loving kids and trying to take care of 'em. I will plead guilty to that.''

"Thank you for seeing us. We'll never forget it.''

"Before you go, I want to emphasize, that this—well, I guess it was an interview, wasn't it?—this was important to me. I haven't granted any interviews for a long time. I used to, but my words got so twisted, and, I always seemed to say what I thought the writer wanted me to say, instead of what I actually meant—or even, sometimes, what was true. But now, I'd like the facts to come out.

"I am not a murderer,'' she said. The eyes were wide and clear. "I loved those kids.''

The Investigator

As to *who* she *is*, obviously I can't give you a positive, I-know-this-for-a-fact answer, but I think that Genene's need to be the hero superseded everything else. I don't accept—I don't have any evidence—I see not one iota of evidence that she was not intelligent enough, knowledgeable enough (especially being a nurse), to know, or at least consider, the pain that she was inflicting upon these kids. And yet she did it over and over again. But, y'see, who was going to complain? I think Genene Jones's need to become the hero coupled, at least to some degree, with her passionate, not dislike, but *hatred* for select doctors, was probably why she did what she did in case after case after case.

And you can't view this (or, I should say, it should not be viewed) as only Bexar County or only Kerrville. You have to mesh them, you have to connect the sequences and consider the whole. In Bexar County you had a maze of people around. Theoretically, anybody could have done it. Theoretically. And don't think we didn't consider even the cleaning person, because we did. Kerrville kind of brings it into perspective. If anyone doubts her responsibility for nursing misadventure in Bexar County, in spite of the log book, in spite of the known dead, the lab reports, the CDC's statistics, in spite of the direct testimony, and everything that later became proven, you just have to go on to Kerrville.

There we had a situation which, except for it being medical in nature, was far different from Bexar County. An isolated unit—a clinic—with a limited number of people involved. She's pushing all the drugs (save in one instance when she gives the filled syringe to Kathy Holland), and all the kids suffer or sustain the consequences, in the same way. All the kids recovered except one. She too recovered, once, then succumbed later on. Chelsea McClellan just couldn't take it. Realistically I have to say that overall, looking at the whole nine yards, I still see the need to be a hero. I still see hero.

Some of the quotes and demeanor attributed to Genene Jones, even by her friends, is quite revealing. She was the kind of person who liked to tell nasty jokes. She had colorful, salty language. She was abrasive, she was brash, she was rude. She had a lengthy list of write-ups in her file. She came in intoxicated once; evidently made quite a scene. In the fall of '81, one of the nurses was having a party—a bachelorette party, I think—and a number of the nurses got together (six or eight of 'em, something like that), and went to this male strip place out on the north side. They evidently did that three or four times that year and they liked to do that. They all had a good time. Anyway, one of these nights, Genene invited the lead dancer and some of his friends to come home with the ladies and she'd pay. Although it didn't happen, she was, evidently, serious. I think that says something about her, the way she thought about other people. In Kerrville, there's the events in the MAST helicopter—when they had that emergency landing in the cow pasture out there—that's also interesting. They got that kid off the top level so that they could try and intubate him. (You know the bunks are stacked. It's cramped.) They had problems trying to intubate him because, well, he was deformed. They had to get him down and hold him in a certain way; they had to get that head tilted way back to get that tube down there. Meanwhile, she was getting hyper in the chopper 'cause when they drop, they *drop*, you know? They landed in that cow pasture, and there are guys out there on horses wondering what the hell's going on, 'cause when that crew chief yells "Mayday! Mayday!" the pilot doesn't ask questions, he just looks for the first place to land safely.

Upon touchdown, they jump out, and Genene's just sitting there, she's gone bananas, she doesn't know what the hell to do. The medics just took over. "Nurse be damned," you know? The patient is their responsibility while it's in the chopper. They got that kid out, intubated him, and he spit it out. They couldn't do it that way, so they had to give him mouth-to-mouth and the kid is barfing, and the army medics really had to go to work on him. They saved his life. Hey, those guys are great, man. I'll tell you, if you ever need medics, army MAST are the best. If it wasn't for those MAST guys, I wouldn't be here today.

After Genene got back to Kerrville, she called Tony Torres, I think it was Tony, anyway, it was one of the nurses, and the nurse asks, "Hey, how are you doing?"

Genene says, "Oh, I just had a helicopter ride!" It was a big deal, you know? "Man, you should have been there. I really took care of that kid. We had to land in a field. We got that kid out and really took care of him. He was ready to die, but he's okay now. Boy, it was one of the most exciting days of my life."

So she took credit for it? And enjoyed the excitement of it?

Right. According to her, *she'd* saved the kid's life.

And oh, she got tremendous rush out of it. I think that was part of it. I think that was a big part of it.

We wondered if you thought any of it might have been mercy killings?

No. I see nothing of that. Nothing of that.

We heard that Genene said to the parents of the Sawyer boy, for example, that if he survived, he would probably be brain damaged.

Yeah, she did say that of the Sawyer boy, that's right. But man, I just can't see mercy killings. I can't see her having done it. The possibility . . . yeah, I guess it's possible, but I can't see it. It doesn't fit. I see hatred, and I see the need to play the heroine role, but I don't see mercy, in spite of that Sawyer thing. A couple of these other ones, too, might be looked at that way; Jimmy Pearson is a good example. He was a grossly deformed kid. I mean he had problem after problem; some say he should have died at birth, that he should have died before age one, and before age one and a half, before age three, and here the kid was seven and one-half years old and still around. He couldn't do a thing for himself, he didn't have the physical ability to suck his own thumb, but he had loving parents. I could see where somebody would feel sorry for a kid like that, "He's going to die anyhow," but that kid had to be a fighter. Something in there had to be pushing that kid on. *Somebody*, some power, beyond us earthlings wanted that kid alive, because he *was* alive.

I guess the mercy aspect could have been another part of it, but I don't think so. I don't see mercy killings. There's too much selfishness in Genene Jones to allow even the suggestion of mercy killing, no.

If she said that to me and allowed herself to be pinned down and explained it in rational terms that I could understand, I might give it some heavy consideration, but she'd have to give me ABCs, which I'm not hopeful of receiving from her. I'd like nothing more than to talk with Genene. I've never talked to her in my life.

Oh, no?

Well, I held her hand one time when we took her out of the courtroom after her guilty verdict and the press was everywhere. I helped the deputies up there (after the verdict, when we cleared the Georgetown courtroom), because it was a situation where they seemed immobile. They just stood there and asked, "How do we get out of here and into the car?"

I jumped in. I said, you know, "Get two guys up front and the crowd'll move." And that's essentially what happened. We just literally picked her up and carried her out by the arms. She was just— For the first time I really felt—I felt *sorry* for her. As we were taking her out, she was terrified of the converging mob of media and mikes. You really have to walk that gauntlet sometime to understand what it's like. One misstep and "squish," they're on you like a mob scene.

We got her in the car, and that's the only time I talked to her. I said, "Everything'll be okay." She needed to hear that. She was a wreck. Just totally caved in on herself— like somebody had pole-axed a steer, you know? I never had the opportunity to talk to her in any official capacity. By the time I got involved, they'd already talked to her at the grand jury, and she already had her attorney.

Another important aspect to this case is that Genene went through what we're pretty certain were psychosomatic problems. She was evaluated, rather cursorily, about 1980, by a doctor at Medical Center Hospital. I think he was one of the professors at the UT Health Science Center. The bottom line of his report suggests "Psychosomatic: there's nothing we can ascertain to be wrong with her. She's got aches and pains, muscular pain, stomach pain, but I can't find anything physically wrong with her." Her intelligence was not questioned, her mental faculties were really not questioned. So, what was causing it? Well, we really don't know. There was no follow-up done on it, but she *did* have various aches and pains—real or imagined—and she was hospitalized a few times. During short periods of time, she had a couple of surgeries for abdominal obstructions. Through information we picked up through various sources, she implied that she had a heart problem, yet there's no record of a heart problem. There are rather strong reports, from people who were close to her, that she was on heart medication. Well, why take heart medication if you don't have a heart problem? For the stimulation? There's no proof known to the investigators that she has a heart problem, there's no proof she ever had any real physical/health problem at all—save for the abdominal obstructions, because there was surgery performed for that.

In fact, the timing of that is very, very important. In November of '81, as you can see on the chart—
[THE INVESTIGATOR POINTS TO THE CHART REFLECTING PICU DEATHS]

The "untoward events" really picked up momentum in the late summer, early fall of '81. Now, in November of '81, there are two deaths, yet neither one of them connected with Genene Jones. She was undergoing surgery and was out much of this month. Then in December, when she's back from the surgery we've got, well, let's see, we've got . . . In total, there were seven children who succumbed in the Pedi-ICU that first month she was back. Four of them in Jones's direct care.

She worked on December 10, when Bobby Souza died, but she didn't have that kid assigned to her like all the others. The only one from the chart of deaths where she wasn't at least present when the kid died was on Dec. 19. That death occurred on the 7–3 shift. For that one death we can't determine any link. But December was a heavy month. It slowed down some in January, but in

January of '82, she was very, very busy for several days with Rolando Santos. He took up a lot of her time.

Are you suggesting that her psychosomatic illnesses were somehow connected with her psychological aberration?

I don't know. I don't know. All I know is I think she does have psychological aberrations. There's documentation that there are some psychosomatic problems. Her physical ailments, even if they were real—based on the abdominal structure—that was supposedly corrected by surgery, and it wasn't a significant enough procedure or problem to hospitalize her for more than a few days, so it couldn't have been that severe. I saw nothing in her physical situation that might in some way just completely drive her over the edge.

And yet, on the chart, twenty-two out of forty-three deaths in the Unit were kids under her direct care. More than half. The Center for Disease Control examined numerous other facts and figures in an extensive study into other areas of concern, namely the unexplained codes: the bleed-outs, the arrests, the need for resuscitation, the need for resuscitation when resuscitation did not seem to apply to the kids' illnesses to begin with, or the arrests were not compatible to the kid's condition an hour before Genene took it. This happened repeatedly with some of her infant patients.

I have to assume that anyone who would hurt an infant for *any* reason, even to cause it intentional discomfort, would have to be, well, I don't know the proper medical term for it, but this is the term I apply to it: a complete psychological wacko.

TWENTY-FOUR

Results are what you expect,
Consequences are what you get.

Anonymous

FOLLOWING GENENE'S TRIAL, DISTRICT AT-
torney Ron Sutton spent months attending to other matters
that necessarily had been delayed. He also immediately
began to shift his attention and energies to a second bizarre
murder trial.

"A land-rich/money-poor family over here in Kimball
County had been kidnapping hitchhikers and forcing them
to work their farm. Some of the prisoners were tortured,
and one of them died. We've got some teeth and bone
fragments." He would later obtain convictions against the
father and the son on state organized crime charges. The
son received a fifteen-year sentence; the father, probation.
Sutton would be reelected for his third four-year term in
1986.

When asked why, in his opinion, Jones committed these
crimes, Sutton says, "For me, the evidence we presented
in Genene's trial explains why. She's a very domineering,
calculating, cold sort of person. Very goal oriented and
abrasive. But, she can also turn around and appear to be
the nicest, sweetest person you ever met. I think it was in

October 1982 that she went to New York (ABC flew her and her husband, Garron, out for a few days for that '20/20' interview). Their top man, Tom Jarrel, did this long interview with her, but they didn't release it until the week after the trial. The producer, Peter Kunhardt, was in town at one point, and he told us that the people in the room with her—filming the interview—took a poll afterwards. The majority felt that she wasn't guilty. See, she'd just mastered the situation. She's got that type of personality. She can control a situation.

"Looking at her background, you can see that she always wanted to be in control. She's like the fireman who goes out and sets a fire, then goes and turns on the fire alarm, then goes and puts out the fire. But she was creating *medical* emergencies. Since she created them, she would know immediately what to do. So she looked like the Super Nurse. She liked the attention. But she got to playing around with this succinylcholine, and it got her into trouble. Of course, she should never have done it to start with, but she wanted to draw attention to their new Clinic. In a rural area, you know, the word gets out. All of a sudden it's: 'We've got the greatest doctor and nurse in the world. My kid would have been dead had it not been for the actions of this nurse and doctor.'

"She also seemed to get some kind of thrill from it. One of the air medics described her—after she had given the Pearson boy the shot—as behaving like someone who was experiencing an orgasm. She appeared to be in some kind of euphoric state.

"Another thing that addresses that point but which I really didn't develop during the trial (because it would've brought in what'd happened while she was down in Bexar County, and we weren't supposed to do that) is this: All right, now the scenario is that she's already been let go by Bexar County Hospital, even though they had evidence linking her with suspicious deaths. When these kids started popping out in Kerrville, they went to different hospitals for additional treatment. But Chelsea, on the day she died,

Holland sent her to Medical Center Hospital. Now, Genene couldn't have that happen. If the people down there
were to become aware of her association with 'bad' kids in
Kerrville, she'd get them thinking about her again. And
she didn't want that. I think she had to kill that kid. When
she found out that baby was going to Medical Center, she
had to do it.''

Sam Millsap ran again in 1986 for the office of district
attorney of Bexar County. He was defeated. He is now in
private practice in San Antonio. Millsap's successor did
not ask the Investigator to stay on board. "You know how
that is," the Investigator explains, "they just take a big
broom and sweep everybody out. They have favors to pay
and their own people to take care of. It doesn't matter
whether you've done a good job or a bad job. I think it
should matter, but it doesn't.''

Millsap's chief deputy, Nick Rothe, terminated his association with the San Antonio district attorney's office after
he won a second conviction against Genene on October
23, 1984. The Honorable Pat Priest found Genene guilty
of felony injury to a child—for the incidents involving
Rolando Santos. The next weekend, Rothe arranged to be
alone for a few days to recuperate at his ranch south of the
city. "These long, complicated trials take a lot out of you
if you do them right," he says. "And I like to do things
right." The Saturday following the verdict, Nick got up at
5:15 A.M. and fished all day. "At sundown I was cleaning
the fish—they were beauts too—and I stopped, looked
around, and just stood there for a minute. I hadn't thought
about Genene Jones, or the case—not at all, not once—all
day. And I realized then just how long it'd been since she
hadn't been a part of my life. I was glad to be free of her.
But you know, I still think about her a lot.''

Nick rejoined his partner, John Hrtnr, at their downtown
firm and found that his clientele had changed. "It's a little
different now, which I like. It's a lower-volume, higher-
fee (as opposed to a low-fee, big-volume) business. I did

that for years, and it can drive you wacko. I don't know what happened while I was gone those fifteen months. I guess it had something to do with the exposure.''

Hrtnr, Rothe's partner, joining in a conversation with Rothe, volunteered that he had always thought Genene was doing it, "for whatever strange reason, not to kill kids, but to improve her own self-worth.''

"In some way, yeah,'' Rothe agreed, "to call attention to herself. She's got a tremendous inferiority complex. And when she injected those drugs, I think she said to herself: 'Okay, you dumb-ass doctors, see if you're smart enough to figure *this* one out. Sure, you think it's DIC. But see, ha, it's not. It's heparin!' If the kid died, then she'd just turn it around and think: 'See, you don't know how to treat DIC, you bunch of dumb shits.'

"Her hope in Kerrville (and I really believe this) was to produce a number of critically ill children so as to get a Critical-Care Unit up there, where she'd be the big chief in charge. I really believe that. That's why she had to create critical situations—but not let 'em die! Dead kids aren't any good. You don't need a Critical-Care Unit for dead ones; you've got to save 'em.''

"But a couple of 'em, she couldn't save,'' offered Hrtnr. "You think they just got away from her?''

"Yeah. With little Chelsea, she just overdid it. Played the game too long. Down here in San Antonio, I don't think that was her motivation at all. I think, early on at least, it was to show up the other nurses, to show that the RNs weren't as smart as she was.

"Assume for the moment (as I think we must, based on the two convictions) that she did everything that she's accused of doing. What kind of a mentality does that? I defy you, as an at least somewhat rational person, to figure it out. I don't think a rational mind *can* figure it out because it defies rationality. See, that's the point. She's insane. Got to be. Totally insane.

"Well,'' said Hrtnr, "not criminally insane.''

"That's true. Someone who is legally insane is a psychopath—someone who does not know the difference between right and wrong and cannot aid their lawyer in their defense. She doesn't fit that definition, and yet she did do these things. Now, explain. Go for it. Take your best shot. I'm listening. Hell, I've heard nine million theories. I've got a couple of my own. And I don't buy either one of them either.''

Of the half-dozen administrators who attended the January 25 meeting after Rolando's crisis and Patrick Zavala's death, most are no longer with the hospital. Only John Guest (B. H. Corum's former assistant) remains, elevated to the position of acting executive director of Medical Center Hospital upon Corum's departure. He has since been given the position permanently.

Pat Alberti no longer likes to talk about the Jones affair. ''I'm afraid for my job, you know? This isn't such a big town. Most people just thought of me as a troublemaker. It was real hard for me for a while there, but things have finally more or less settled down.'' Pat now works the Night Shift for another hospital in San Antonio.

Her friend, Suzanna Maldonado continued to work at Medical Center, in a different department. She firmly declined to be interviewed. Her father said on her behalf, ''Why don't you people just leave her alone?''

Rolando, Jesusa, and Esubio Santos continue their lives in Pearsall. Rolando is now a handsome little boy with a shy, mischievous grin. He appears to have suffered no long-term ill effects from his encounter with Genene Jones. Esubio and Jesusa eventually hired a lawyer to file suit against Medical Center Hospital, but all they want, Jesusa says, is to be relieved of the still outstanding $18,000 hospital bill for Rolando's care.

Garron Turk, the young man who married Genene shortly before her arrest, contacted Jim Brookshire just after the Georgetown guilty verdict. He wanted to notify Genene that he had filed the necessary papers to begin divorce proceedings.

Reid and Petti McClellan continue to live in Ingram; Petti has since obtained her credentials and is a licensed vocational nurse. The McClellans still blame Kathleen for the loss of their child, although their lawsuit against Kathleen was later amended to name as additional defendants Genene Jones and Medical Center Hospital. When they attempted to obtain documents relating to their allegations that Medical Center was in part to blame for Chelsea's death, they were repeatedly frustrated. Their lawyer moved the court to compel the production of these documents, and that motion went all the way up to the Texas Supreme Court. The Court ruled that the hospital should turn over most of the requested information. The McClellans' attorney, Jim Mac Perdue of Houston, Texas, offers the opinion that he hopes eventually to be able to establish tortious liability on the part of the hospital for the death of Chelsea Ann McClellan. He does not, however, expect to come out ahead. "We'll probably end up making about $5.00 an hour on this case. But there are some you just do, because it's right."

In early 1988, the Hill Country papers carried the news that Reid and Petti had finally succeeded in adopting a little girl. Petti was quoted as commenting, "She doesn't *replace* Chelsea, but she sure fills a lot of holes."

Two years after moving out of her Clinic at 320 Water Street, Kathleen Holland reestablished her Kerrville practice in a yellow cottage three blocks south of Main Street. To the kids, it's Dr. Kathy's, a pleasant, homey place to go and get fixed up when they feel bad. Her relationship with Charleigh continued to deteriorate, until it ended some two years after their official "divorce."

"We never really recovered," Kathleen says. In 1985, she remarried another Kerrville doctor. The administrators at Sid Peterson Hospital have repeatedly declined to reestablish her privileges; in 1986, Kathleen sued to force them to reverse this decision or to at least provide an ade-

quate justification for it. In her complaint, she sum-
marizes:

ON SEPTEMBER 28, 1982, THE EXECUTIVE COMMITTEE
OF SID PETERSON MEMORIAL HOSPITAL VOTED TO
"TEMPORARILY SUSPEND" MY STAFF PRIVILEGES. MY
UNDERSTANDING, AT THAT TIME, WAS THAT IT WAS
BECAUSE OF THE GRAND-JURY INVESTIGATION INTO THE
EVENTS SURROUNDING SIX EMERGENCIES IN MY OFFICE. I
WAS, HOWEVER, NEVER OFFICIALLY NOTIFIED AS SUCH.
APPROXIMATELY ONE MONTH LATER (THEN AGAIN ONE
YEAR LATER), I SPOKE WITH REPRESENTATIVES OF SID
PETERSON HOSPITAL REGARDING A REQUEST FOR
REINSTATEMENT. BOTH TIMES I WAS TOLD TO WAIT UNTIL
THE INVESTIGATION WAS COMPLETE. CONSEQUENTLY,
AFTER APPEARING AS THE CHIEF WITNESS FOR THE
PROSECUTION AT THE TRIAL OF GENENE JONES IN
GEORGETOWN IN EARLY 1984, I YET AGAIN REQUESTED
REINSTATEMENT OF MY PRIVILEGES. I WAS GRANTED A
HEARING BEFORE THE EXECUTIVE COMMITTEE, AT WHICH
TIME SEVERAL ISSUES WERE RAISED. MY REQUEST WAS
DENIED. IN JUNE 1985, I SUBMITTED A NEW APPLICATION
FOR STAFF PRIVILEGES, WHICH WAS ALSO DENIED. I THEN
EXERCISED MY RIGHTS UNDER THE HOSPITAL'S BYLAWS AND
REQUESTED AN APPEAL OF THAT DENIAL, WHICH AFFIRMED
THE DENIAL. WHEN WRITTEN CHARGES HAVE BEEN
PROVIDED, THEY HAVE BEEN VAGUE AND THUS IMPOSSIBLE
TO RESPOND TO. WHEN VERBAL CHARGES HAVE BEEN MADE
DURING THE HEARINGS, HOWEVER, THEY HAVE BEEN QUITE
SPECIFIC AND NOT CONSISTENT WITH THE WRITTEN
ALLEGATIONS.

"I look back on it all now," says Kathleen, "and
think— Well, I don't know, I think there's a tendency,
to— There have been a lot of things that I've learned
about myself and about the world because of what happened. I learned a lot about my own strengths and my own
weaknesses, and that I can gather myself together and
stand up against things that I don't understand or that I'm
afraid of. I think when you end up coming through some-

thing like this, it makes you feel as if maybe you know yourself a little bit better—even if you did all along. You know what I mean? You sort of get some reinforcement through experience.

"It has also changed my outlook on other people. I guess I'm somewhat saddened by all of this, in the sense that this experience has left a lot of us pediatricians feeling that we have to be more suspicious of any changes with patients. I'm saddened by that really, because— Well, I guess that's part of my naiveté still coming through. The hardest realization for me, right from the start, was to think that someone who was trained to help children could actually do this. I don't think I'll ever be able to accept that. I find it— I don't know, I just— it's still kind of hard to deal with. I gave up a long time ago trying to figure out why. As far as I'm concerned, it doesn't matter what the 'why' is. There is no 'why' worth it. There is no 'why' that can justify it."

"Not too long ago, a friend of Kathleen's nominated her for admission to one of the local women's charitable societies," the Investigator reports. "The nominees were supposed to attend a luncheon where they would be officially voted into the organization by a poll of the members. The vote was largely ceremonial, I mean, no nominee had ever been rejected. But, you know, Kathleen had to go in there and put herself at their mercy.

"She showed up late and kind of sat at the back. When it came time to announce the nominees, each stood up, and the ladies applauded. Then they called Kathleen's name, and she stood up to dead silence. A few moments went by, then someone started clapping and they all jumped in, and it was, you know, just thunderous applause.

"Maybe they were embarrassed and overcompensating, but I figure most people realize Kathy was one of Genene's victims, too."

When we encounter goodness in people, we may marvel, we may even be surprised, but we rarely ever ask "why?" When we encounter individuals like Genene Jones—those who engage in recognizably evil acts—the question wells up almost involuntarily, demanding an answer.

Why did she do it?

We ask the question as if we expect there is some way to explain it, some chain of causation, some convoluted set of circumstances in the killer's past that compelled her to acts we cannot imagine having a desire to commit. Feeling helpless to comprehend it, we call her insane, and turn our thoughts to something else. Yet it is possible to understand why Genene did it. The clues are there.

Many people spoke of Genene's excitement during a Code, her almost orgasmic reaction to it. This reaction, though extreme, is not anomalous. A Code Blue is an extraordinary experience. Time seems to expand; awareness telescopes toward infinity. It is a life-or-death challenge for which a medic must summon all his courage and skills. It is a rush, a high, a frightening thrill, like skydiving or shooting the rapids, except someone else is taking all the risk. Genene loved this thrill.

She also enjoyed the Code's aftermath. If the child survived, she was a vital part of that victory, a hero in her own and others' eyes. If the child died, then she immersed herself in grief, visibly luxuriating in the depth of her compassion, empathy, and ability to love. That she actually *lacked* compassion, empathy, and love only made this hollow experience of grief all the more necessary. It served as concrete behavior that validated her image of herself as a caring, heroic woman.

Witnesses described Genene as a very controlling person—pushy, domineering, aggressive. During our meeting with Genene at Gatesville's prison we, too, felt Genene's hunger for control, in her efforts to set the ground rules of our conversation and in her skillful mixture of truth and lies, but even more, in the force of personality that she projected. We experienced the intensity behind her lies as a palpable influence, an attempt to control the reality we perceived. We *believed* her, if only for a while. The ultimate expression of this demand for control was the act of murder, through which Genene exerted a godlike dominion over her patients' lives.

The possibility that Genene herself had been a victim of child abuse (as she once confided to a friend) may also contribute to an explanation of the "why" behind her actions. The child who grows up with no concept of her own value as a human being can have no real concept of another's value. Perhaps this lack enabled Genene to engage in conduct that would be repugnant to anyone with a normal fellow-feeling for humanity. Perhaps each child she victimized was, in some way, a symbol of her infant self and she the parent figure who both abused and then consoled. Perhaps, over and over again, Genene reenacted the drama of her childhood, hurting and rescuing, expressing the obverse sides of a perverted love.

We can, if we choose, understand the satisfaction Genene derived from the act of inducing emergencies, but to explain why the act gratified her does not explain why she did it. To understand the appetite is not, finally, to explain the act. We must also understand how she could indulge her appetite in the face of the enormity of it, the overwhelming and unmistakable *wrongness* of it. For Genene knew that what she was doing was wrong.

Genene clearly acted in a premeditated manner. She planned her crimes. She waited for the opportunity presented by a child whose symptoms were troublesome, whose sudden descent into a Code or death would not be surprising. Hours or even days in advance, she would lay a foundation of bogus medical problems in her victims' charts—setting up their demise. The crimes smack of calculation and intention, not irresistible impulse.

She also clearly knew the nature of her acts. She recognized and participated in the table of values that prohibits murder. She professed to be a Christian, said grace at meals, and wept over the sentimentality of *E.T.* She displayed grief for her dead patients, compassion for their parents, charity toward the troubled teenager she took in as a live-in babysitter. She felt well able to direct moral criticism at others: the MAST medics who allegedly said "Let the kid die," the D.A. whom she called the very personification of the devil, the young doctors whom she accuses of criminal arrogance and ignorance. Genene knew the moral code that we all share; she simply chose not to follow it.

The question, therefore, is not why she did it; the question is how could she do it even though she knew it was wrong?

M. Scott Peck, in his book, *People of the Lie*, suggests that the "essential component of evil" is the individual's unwillingness to tolerate a sense of his own imperfection, to acknowledge the need for change. "At one and the same time," he writes, "the evil are aware of their own evil and desperately trying to avoid that awareness." As long as the evil can evade self-knowledge through the lies they tell themselves, they—we—do not have to change.

Genene, rather than change—leave her job, deny her appetites, or choose *any* other path—tried to deceive herself and everyone else. She tried to shift the blame. She rationalized. She hid behind half-truths and a mask of compassion. She continues to refuse, to this day, to admit that she ever did anything wrong. Rather than responsibility, Genene chose a lie, and to a lesser degree, so did the administrators, doctors, and nurses who suspected the truth about Genene Jones but allowed her to go somewhere else.

The "why" behind Genene's perverse appetites is the sum of her circumstances, but her circumstances do not explain or excuse her actions. Though circumstances dictate the options an individual faces, he is responsible for the choices he makes. And the possibility of choice always remains.

ACKNOWLEDGMENTS

Without the assistance (monetary, literary, and legal), guidance, and faith of the following individuals, this book would not exist. We want to thank those who have helped—just enough, at just the right time.

Pat Alberti, L.V.N., Linda Anderson, Esq., Charleigh Appling, Robert Asahina, copy editor Linda Venator, Margo Beotticher, Mark Brown and our friends at Kinsella, Boesch, Fujikawa & Towle, Janet Boudreau, Jim Brookshire, Joe Cabaza, Donald Cameron, Patricia Cameron, the Honorable John Carter, Texas Ranger Joe Davis, Vincent DiMaio, M.D., Ed Edwards, our attorney/agent Don Farber, Esq., Tom Filer, Sandy Fox, Esq., Jay Goodwin, Royal Griffin, Esq., Van Hilley, Esq., Kathleen Holland, M.D., Janet Jones, Patty Jones, Reid and Petti McClellan, former District Attorney Sam Millsap, Cmdr. Lundi Moore, U.S.N. Ret., Lore Moore, brothers Chris, Casey, Shane, Ryan, and Maryanne Moore, Genevieve Mynster, Linda Norton, M.D., Kirk Passich, Esq., Murray Pollack, M.D., Tom and Maureen Reed, Kathleen Louisa Campbell Richards, former Assistant District Attorney Nick Rothe, Anthony Russo, Esq., Jesusa Santos, her daughter Anna, and her youngest son Rolando, Ed Shaughnessey, Esq., Jim Shields, Tom Stolhandske, Esq., Paul Slevin, Esq., District Attorney Ronald Sutton, Roy Toburen, Lisa Vischer, R.N., David Weiner, Esq., Pamela Woods, Esq., Mel Zerman, who persuaded his old friend, Joan Kahn, to take a chance on us, and the many kind individuals who prefer to remain anonymous: thank you.

GLOSSARY

ABCs: Military acronym for airway, breathing, circulation (or CPR).

ABGs: Acronym for arterial blood gases, a test run to determine how oxygenated the blood is—how well the lungs are working.

Acetylcholine: A chemical compound known as an ester, formed by bonding the alcohol choline and acetic acid, an organic acid. (Compare succinylcholine.)

Acidosis: A condition characterized by an abnormal accumulation of an acid or the loss of a base.

Acute: When symptoms of a disease begin abruptly, with marked intensity and sharpness. (Compare chronic.)

Afebrile: Without fever. An indication that one's metabolism is functioning normally.

Ampicillin: A form of penicillin—an antibiotic.

Anoxia: An abnormal condition characterized by a lack of oxygen.

Apnea: The absence of spontaneous respirations—the absence of breathing.

Arrhythmias: A deviation from the normal pattern of heartbeat.

Arterial line: A catheter inserted into an artery as opposed to a vein.

Asystole: The absence of heartbeat precipitated by a brief period of accelerated heart rate; electric activity persists but contraction ceases.

Atropine: Normally used for gastro-intestinal problems, although sometimes used to steady heart rhythms. The more serious adverse reactions include an abnormal increase in heart rate (tachycardia), chest pain (angina), nausea, diarrhea, blurred vision, eye pain, loss of taste, and skin rash.

Attending: A senior physician responsible for patients in a specific Ward or Unit during a given period of time. In a university setting (such as MCH), an attending physician often also has teaching responsibilities and holds a faculty appointment.

Bilateral: Involving both sides of the body.

Bleed-out: Term used to describe an incident wherein a patient suffers an unexpected, prolonged episode of excessive bleeding.

Blind intubation: Intubation without the use of a laryngoscope.

Blood pressure: The pressure exerted by the circulating volume of blood on the walls of the arteries, the veins, and the chambers of the heart.

Bolus: A premeasured dose of medication meant to be injected intravenously all at once.

Book: A double-paged statistical log in which patients' admission date and time, age, weight, temperature, height, the initial symptoms, problem areas and diagnosis, each of their assigned nurses, and the date and time of discharge, reassignment, or death are recorded.

Bradycardia: An abnormal circulatory condition in which cardiac output is decreased, causing faintness, dizziness, chest pain, and eventually circulatory collapse.

Brain stem: The lower portion of the brain, which controls motor, sensory, and reflex functions.

Bronchi: The two main air passages that branch from the trachea; one leads to the left lung, the other to the right lung.

Bronchials: The main air passages that stem from the bronchi.

Bronchitis: Inflammation of the bronchi; acute symptoms include a productive cough, fever, a swelling of the mucus membranes, and back pain.

Caesarean section: Surgical procedure in which the abdomen and uterus are incised and a baby is delivered transabdominally.

Calcium chloride: A concentrated solution of the chloride salt calcium used to replenish calcium in the blood.

Cannula: A flexible tube inserted into a body cavity, used for either suctioning fluids out or blowing gases in.

Cardiac arrest: A form of heart attack; the sudden cessation of cardiac output and effective circulation (usually precipitated by ventricular fibrillation or ventricular asystole).

Cardiopulmonary resuscitation: A basic procedure for life support, consisting of artificial respiration and manual external cardiac massage to establish effective circulation and ventilation in order to prevent irreversible brain damage resulting from anoxia.

Cardiotonic: Of or pertaining to a substance that tends to increase the efficiency of contractions of the heart muscle.

Case in Chief: The direct examination of one's own witnesses.

CAT: Acronym for computerized axial tomography.

CAT scan: A painless, noninvasive procedure in which a computerized, narrow-beam X-ray scanner provides a series of detailed visualizations of tissues, usually the brain, at any depth desired. The organ is scanned at two planes simultaneously at various angles. The computer calculates tissue absorption, and produces a visualization that demonstrates the densities of the internal structures.

Cataracts: An abnormal progressive condition of the lens of the eye, characterized by a grey-white opacity that contributes to a loss of transparency.

cc: An increment of measure. One cubic centimeter, or $1/1000$ of a liter.

Centrifuge: Device for separating components of different densities contained in a liquid by spinning the liquid at high speeds. The resulting centrifugal force pushes the heavier components to the outside.

Cerebellum: The part of the brain located behind the brain stem, concerned with coordinating muscular activity.

Cervical: Pertaining to the region of the neck.

Cheyne-Stokes respiration pattern: The breathing pattern commonly exhibited by dying patients gasping after their last breaths.

Child abuse: The physical, sexual, or emotional maltreatment of a child. The abuse may be overt or covert and often results in permanent physical or psychiatric injury, mental impairment or, sometimes, death. Child abuse occurs predominantly in children under three years of age and seems to be the result of multiple and complex factors compounded by various stressful environmental circumstances, such as poor socioeconomic conditions, inadequate physical and emotional support within the family, and any major life changes or crises, especially those arising from marital strife. Adults at high risk for abuse are characterized as having unsatisfied needs, difficulty in forming adequate interpersonal relationships, unrealistic expectations of the child, and a lack of nurturing experiences, often involving neglect or abuse in their own childhood—current studies indicate that over 90 percent of all child abusers were, as children, abused themselves. In Texas, as in many other states, it is legally required to report suspected child abuse to authorities.

Chloramphenicol: Trade name for an antibacterial and antirickettsial agent.

Chloroform: The first inhalation anesthetic to be discovered.

Chromatogram: The record produced by the separation of gaseous substances or dissolved chemical substances moving through a column of absorbent material that filters out various absorbates in different layers.

Chromatography: Any of several processes for separating and analyzing various gaseous or dissolved chemical materials according to differences in their absorbency with respect to a specific substance and according to different pigments.

Chronic: Referring to a symptom that continues over a long period of time.

Clinic: An office staffed and equipped such that medical care can be given to patients not requiring hospitalization. (Within this book, when Clinic is capitalized, this refers to Dr. Holland's Pediatric Clinic in Kerrville.)

Clinical: Pertaining to bedside medical care.

Clonic: A condition characterized by muscle spasms.

Code Blue: An emergency wherein a patient is suffering from a respiratory or cardiac arrest and needs immediate treatment.

Code Team: Doctors and nurses working on a patient suffering a Code Blue.

Coma: A profound state of unconsciousness, characterized by the absence of spontaneous eye movements, vocalization, or response to painful stimuli. The person cannot be aroused.

Congenital: Present at birth.

Consciousness: The term generally applies to a person who is awake, alert, aware of his or her external environment, and capable of responding to sensory stimuli.

Constipation: Difficulty in passing stools or an incomplete or infrequent passage of hard stools.

Convulsion: A sudden, violent involuntary contraction of a group of muscles that may be tonic, clonic, focal, unilateral, or bilateral. (Also called a *seizure*.)

CPR: *See* cardiopulmonary resuscitation.

Crash cart: A metal cabinet that contains all the medications and tools doctors may need in an emergency situation.

Critical Care Unit: *See* Intensive Care Unit.

Curare: Derived from a tropical plant, curare is a potent muscle relaxant that prevents the transmission of neural impulses. Large doses can cause complete paralysis. As with other neuromuscular blocking agents, its use requires respiratory assistance by a qualified anesthesiologist.

Cut down: A minor surgical procedure where the physician cuts through the skin, locates a vein, inserts a catheter into the vein, then stitches the wound, pinning the catheter in place. The result is a temporarily permanent IV.

Cyanosis: A bluish discoloration of the skin and mucous membranes, caused by an excess of deoxygenated blood reaching the area.

Decadron: Trade name for an anti-inflammatory agent. Commonly referred to as "steroids," drugs of this kind promote the release of amino acids from the muscles, mobilize fatty acids from fat stores, and increase the ability of skeletal muscles to maintain contractions and avoid fatigue.

Defib: *See* defibrillation.

Defibrillation: The termination of ventricular fibrillation by delivering a direct electric countershock.

Defibrillator: A machine that delivers an electric shock to the body in hopes of counteracting ventricular defibrillation.

Detoxify: Any procedure performed on a patient (or by a patient's own organs) designed to diminish or remove the toxic effects of chemical substances.

Deuterated succinylcholine: Succinylcholine that has been made heavier chemically by bonding it with the radioactive isotope deuterium. This synthetic substance becomes the control, the identifiable substance in the procedure.

Deuterium: A radioactive isotope of the hydrogen atom used as a tracer. Also called heavy hydrogen.

D5W: An electrolyte solution of 5 percent dextrose (sugar).

Diarrhea: The frequent passage of loose, watery stools, sometimes accompanied by abdominal cramps, and general weakness. Untreated, diarrhea may lead to rapid dehydration and electrolyte imbalance.

DIC: *See* disseminated intravascular coagulopathy.

Digitalis: A cardiac stimulant.

Digoxin (or digitoxin): A heart stimulant that, in too-large quantities, can cause heart failure.

Dilantin: Trade name for a commonly used anticonvulsant.

Diphtheria: An acute, contagious disease characterized by the production of a toxin that circulates throughout the body, but is most damaging to the heart and the central nervous system. A thick, false membrane is produced that coats the throat, interfering with eating, drinking, and breathing. Untreated, the disease is usually fatal.

Disseminated intravascular coagulopathy: A grave condition resulting from the overstimulation of the body's clotting and anticlotting processes in response to disease, injury, low blood pressure, poisonous bites, severe trauma, or extensive surgery resulting in severe hemorrhaging.

Distal: Away from or being the farthest from a point of reference, usually the midline of the body.

Distonic movements: Abnormal, tremulous movements of the arms, face, and mouth.

Diuresis: An episode of increased formation and secretion of urine.

Diuretic: A substance that increases the formation and secretion of urine.

Dopamine: A naturally occurring compound that stimulates the heart, general metabolic actions, and the central nervous system. Used to treat shock, low blood pressure, and low cardiac output.

Down's syndrome: A congenital condition characterized by varying degrees of mental retardation and multiple structural defects, the more serious of which are bowel disorders, heart disease, visual problems, abnormal tooth development, and susceptibility to chronic respiratory infections and leukemia.

Doxepin: An antidepressant that comes in pill form. Possible adverse effects are gastrointestinal, cardiovascular, and neurologic disturbances, sedation, and dry mouth.

DPT: The Diphtheria, Pertussis, Tetanus vaccination.

Dyspnea: A shortness of breath or difficulty in breathing.

EEG: *See* electroencephalogram.

EKG: *See* electrocardiogram.

Electrocardiogram: A graphic record of the heart's electric activity, as detected by electrodes placed on the chest.

Electroencephalogram: A graphic chart on which the electric potential produced by the brain cells, as detected by electrodes placed on the scalp, is traced.

Electrolyte: An element or compound that, when melted or dissolved, breaks into ions and conducts electricity. In the body, electrolytes affect the movement of substances between cells. Proper quantities of principal electrolytes, and balance among them, are critical for normal bodily functions.

Endogenous: Growing within the body. A naturally occurring condition.

Endoscope: An illuminated optic instrument for viewing the interior of a body cavity or organ.

Endotracheal tube: A plastic catheter inserted through the mouth or nose through the larynx into the trachea to a point above the juncture of the bronchials. The tube is usually tipped with an inflatable cuff to maintain a closed system with the ventilator in order to prevent aspiration of material from the digestive tract in the unconscious or paralyzed patient. The tube permits suctioning of trachial and bronchial secretions, or administering of positive-pressure ventilation that cannot be given effectively by mask.

"Epidemic Period": Term applied to the ten-month period from June of 1981 to March of 1982, when deaths in MCH's PICU rose dramatically.

Epilepsy: A group of neurological disorders characterized by recurrent episodes of convulsive seizures, sensory disturbances, abnormal behavior, loss of consciousness, or all of these.

Epinephrine: Refers to a natural hormone or a synthetic stimulant for muscles of the autonomic nervous system. Among the more serious adverse reactions to the synthetic form are arrhythmias and increased blood pressure.

Esophagus: The muscular canal extending from the throat to the stomach.

Ester: A class of chemical compounds formed by the bonding of an alcohol and one or more organic acids.

Expert witness: A witness who, based on his knowledge of a subject, is allowed to offer opinions and conclusions.

Extension: A movement that increases the angle between two adjoining bones.

Exudate: Fluid, cells, or other substances that have been slowly discharged from cells or blood vessels through small pores or breaks in the cells' membranes. Perspiration and pus are exudates.

Fasciculations: Small twitchings of the muscles just under the skin.

Fibrilary gliosis: Scarring of the fibrils, small filamentous structures in cells.

Fibrillation: Involuntary recurrent contraction of the muscles of the chambers of the heart, resulting in inefficient, random contraction.

Flat-line: Referring to the straight or flat line on a heart monitor when the heart has ceased beating.

Flexion: A movement allowed by certain joints of the skeleton that decreases the angle between two adjoining bones, as in bending the elbow. (*See* extension.)

Focal seizure: A transitory disturbance in motor, sensory, or autonomic functions resulting from abnormal neuronal discharges in a localized portion of the brain. Typically, the seizures begin as spasmodic movements in the hand, face, or foot, then spread progressively to other muscles, ending in a generalized convulsion.

Fontanelle: The spaces between the bones of an infant's skull covered by tough membranes. Increased intracranial pressure may cause these areas to become tense or to bulge. If the child is dehydrated, these areas may be soft and depressed.

Forensic medicine: The branch of medicine that deals with the legal aspects of health care.

Formalin: A clear solution of formaldehyde (a toxic gas) in water. A 37 percent solution is used for preserving biologic specimens.

Gas–chromatograph–mass spectrometer: Actually two devices in one, designed first to separate the molecules of a test substance (the gas chromatograph's function), then weigh them (the mass spectrometer's function) in an attempt to identify just what compounds are in the substance.

GCMS: *See* gas chromatograph–mass spectrometer.

Gentamycin: Trade name for an antibiotic.

Gliosis: A kind of neural scar tissue.

Graduate Nurse (GN): A newly licensed nurse with little clinical experience.

Gross motor movement: Refers to the ability to use one's larger muscles, but not the smaller muscles that control the wrists and fingers.

Gynecology: A branch of medicine concerned with the health care of women, including their sexual and reproductive functions and the diseases of their reproductive organs; almost always studied in conjunction with obstetrics.

Heart attack: The sudden cessation of cardiac output and effective circulation (usually precipitated by ventricular fibrillation or ventricular asystole)—the result of loss of local blood flow to the cardiac muscle.

Hematology: Scientific medical study of blood and blood-forming tissues.

Hemoglobin: A complex protein-iron compound in the blood that carries oxygen to the cells from the lungs and carbon dioxide away from the cells to the lungs.

Hemophiliac: A person who suffers from one of a group of hereditary bleeding disorders in which there is a deficiency in one or more of the factors necessary for coagulation of the blood.

Hemorrhage: A loss of a large amount of blood in a short period of time, either externally or internally.

Heparin: A commonly used blood-thinning agent to prevent intravascular clotting. (Its effects are neutralized by protamine sulfate.)

Hepatitis: A serious, infectious, inflammatory condition of the liver, characterized by jaundice, hepatomegaly (enlargement of the liver), anorexia (lack or loss of appetite, resulting in the inability to eat), abdominal and gastric discomfort, abnormal liver function, clay-colored stools, and dark urine.

Hippocampus: Part of the lateral ventricle of the brain.

Hyaline Membrane Disease: A respiratory emergency characterized by respiratory insufficiency. Symptoms include shortness of breath, rapid breathing, inadequate oxygenation of arterial blood, and an increase in arterial CO_2. (Also called *acute respiratory distress syndrome*.)

Hydrocephalus: An abnormal accumulation of cerebrospinal fluid, usually under increased pressure, in the space between the skull and the brain. An 80 percent survival rate when treated. Survival depends on the cause of the condition.

Hypertension: Increased blood pressure.

Hyperventilate: To breathe at a rate greater than metabolically necessary for the exchange of respiratory gases.

Hypotension: An abnormal condition in which the blood pressure is not adequate for normal profusion and oxygenation of the tissues.

Hypovolemia: An abnormally low circulating blood volume that, if uncorrected, will lead to a state of physical collapse caused by circulatory dysfunction and inadequate tissue profusion.

Hypoxia: An inadequate, or reduced, supply of oxygen in the cells characterized by cyanosis, tachycardia, hypertension, peripheral vasoconstriction, dizziness, and mental confusion.

Immunization: A process (usually injection) by which resistance to an infectious disease is induced or augmented.

Incubator: An apparatus used to provide a controlled temperature, level of light oxygen and moistness or dryness.

Infarct: A localized area of dead tissue resulting from a lack of oxygen caused by an interruption of the blood supply to the area.

Infection: The invasion of the body by microorganisms that reproduce, multiply, and cause disease by injuring local cells, secreting a toxin, or by disrupting the host's immune system.

Influenza: Highly contagious infection of the respiratory tract transmitted through airborne droplet infection. Symptoms include sore throat, cough, fever, muscular pains, and weakness.

Inoculation: A substance meant to induce immunity or to reduce the effects of an infectious disease administered by injection, or by placing a drop of the substance on the skin, then either making multiple scratches in the skin or puncturing the skin with an instrument that has multiple short tines.

Inspiration: The act of drawing air into the lungs in order to exchange oxygen for carbon dioxide, the end product of tissue metabolism.

Intensive Care Unit: A hospital unit equipped with sophisticated technical equipment where patients requiring close monitoring and intensive care are treated by specially trained doctors and nurses.

Intracranial bolt: A device that measures the pressure within the cranium.

Intravenous: Pertains to the inside of a vein. In *Deadly Medicine*, this usually refers to an "intravenous infusion," which is the process of administering a solution into a patient's vein—normally by means of a simple injection, or, over a longer period of time, by means of a plastic or glass vacuum bottle or bag containing the solution hung above the level of the heart and connected (by a plastic catheter) to a needle inserted into one of the patient's veins.

Intubation: The passage of a tube into a body aperture, specifically the insertion of a breathing tube through the mouth or nose (or directly into the trachea by means of a tracheotomy) to ensure an airway through which the patient can breathe.

IV: *See* intravenous.

Labile: Unstable, sensitive or having a tendency to change.

Laryngoscope: An endoscope for examining the larynx, usually used prior to intubation to help ensure safe placement of the endotracheal tube.

Larynx: The organ of voice that is part of the air passage in the throat at the Adam's apple.

Lesion: An abnormal change in the structure of tissue due to injury or disease.

Lethargy: The state or quality of being indifferent, apathetic, or sluggish.

Licensed Vocational Nurse (LVN): A person trained in basic nursing techniques and direct patient care, who is normally expected to practice under the supervision of a Registered Nurse. The course of training usually lasts one year.

Lidocaine: A local anesthetic with antiarrhythmic qualities.

Life-Pack 5: A small, eight-pound portable heart monitor specifically designed for use in environments where there are apt to be strong electromagnetic fields, such as inside a helicopter.

Measles: An acute, highly contagious disease involving the respiratory tract and characterized by a spreading blotchy red rash, fever, malaise, and lymph node enlargement.

Medical Center Hospital: The University of Texas's teaching hospital, associated by means of an Affiliation Agreement with Bexar County. (Sometimes referred to as Bexar County's Medical Center Hospital or Bexar County Hospital.)

Medulla: The mid-brain, center of the autonomic nervous system that regulates involuntary vital functions, such as heart beat, breathing, gland activity, digestion, and blood pressure.

Meniscus: The interface between a liquid and air. When measuring a liquid in a transparent container, the meniscus appears as "the dip in the fluid."

Metabolic rate: The amount of energy liberated or expended by the body during a given period of time.

Metabolism: The aggregate of all the chemical processes that take place in an organism and result in growth, generation of energy, elimination of wastes, and all other bodily functions relative to the distribution of nutrients in the blood after digestion.

Microbiology: The branch of biology concerned with the study of microorganisms.

MMR: Mumps, Measles, Rubella vaccination.

Morbidity: An illness or an abnormal condition or quality.

Mortality: The condition of being subject to death, or the rate of death in a given segment of the population.

Mumps: An acute viral disease involving the central nervous system.

Myelin: A substance composed largely of fat that constitutes the sheaths of various nerve fibers throughout the body.

Narcotic: A substance derived from opium or produced synthetically that alters one's perception of pain, induces euphoria, mood changes, mental clouding, and deep sleep.

Naso-gastric tube: Any tube passed through the nose into the stomach for such purposes as to relieve gastric distension by removing gas, gastric secretions, or food; to instill medication, food or fluids; or to obtain a specimen for analysis.

Neonatal: Referring to the period of time covering the first twenty-eight days after birth.

Neo-Synephrine: Trade name for a vasoconstrictor.

Neurology: The field of medicine that deals with the nervous system and its disorders.

Neuron: The basic nerve cell of the nervous system containing a nucleus within a cell body and extending one or more processes.

Neuropathologist: A pathologist who specializes in the study of diseases of the nerves.

Neurosurgery: Any surgery involving the brain, spinal cord, or peripheral nerves.

Nuclear medicine: A branch of radiology concerned with imaging radioactive materials infused into body organs.

Nystagmus: An involuntary, rhythmic twitching of the eyes.

Obstetrics: The branch of medicine concerned with pregnancy and childbirth, including the study of the function of the female reproductive tract and the care of the mother and fetus throughout pregnancy, childbirth, and the period immediately following. (*See* Gynecology.)

Oral airway: A curved, tubular piece of rubber, plastic, or metal placed in the mouth and down the throat to maintain a free air passage and keep the tongue from falling back and obstructing the trachea.

Orthopedic: Refers to the body's skeletal system: the bones, joints, muscles, and associated structures.

Oscilloscope: An instrument that displays a representation of electric variations on a fluorescent screen. (Also called an oscillator.)

Paregoric: A derivative of opium, normally prescribed for the treatment of diarrhea.

Parepectolin: Trade name for a paregoric.

Pathologist: A physician who specializes in the study of disease.
> *Anatomical pathologist:* One who examines tissues, generally removed during surgery, to make a diagnosis of disease.
> *Clinical pathologist:* One who runs a laboratory.
> *Forensic pathologist:* One who is concerned with the application of the medical sciences to problems in the law. He deals with the effects of trauma (violent deaths, accidents, suicides, homicides) upon the body.

Pathology: The study of the characteristics, causes, and effects of disease, as observed in the structure and function of the body.

Pediatric clinic: An office staffed and equipped for children who do not require hospitalization.

Pediatric clinician: A title normally referring to an RN working in a hospital.

Pediatrics: A branch of medicine concerned with the development and care of children.

Perinatal period: The period immediately following birth.

Perioral: Around the mouth.

Peritonitis: An inflammation of the peritoneum, the membrane that surrounds and links each of the organs of the abdomen; the outermost layer of each organ is part of the visceral layer of the abdominal cavity (the peritoneum itself), but between each organ there is a small space filled with fluid, allowing the organs to slide freely. The inflammation might be produced by either an invading living organism (a bacterium) or some irritating substance introduced into the abdominal cavity by way of a penetrating wound or a perforation of the GI or reproductive tracts.

Pertussis: An acute, highly contagious respiratory disease characterized by fits of coughing that end in a loud, whooping inspiration, hence it is commonly known as whooping cough.

Pharmacology: The study of the preparation, properties, uses, and actions of drugs.

Phenobarbital: An anticonvulsant, sedative-hypnotic that can be addicting. Used to treat various seizure disorders and as a long-acting sedative. It depresses respirations, blood pressure, temperature, and the central nervous system.

Phenylephrine: Prescribed to maintain blood pressure and to constrict the blood vessels of the nose or eyes. Side effects can include arrhythmias and an excessive rise in blood pressure.

Physiology: The study of the processes and functions of the human body and the physical and chemical processes involved in the functioning of all living organisms.

Placenta: A highly vascular fetal organ through which the fetus absorbs oxygen, nutrients, and other substances and excretes carbon dioxide and other wastes.

Plasma: The watery, fluid portion of the lymph and blood in which the cells of the blood are suspended. Essential to circulation, plasma contains no cells and is made up of water, electrolytes, proteins, glucose, fats, and gases.

Plasmanate: Trade name for a kind of synthetic plasma.

Pneumonia: An acute inflammation of the lungs wherein the alveoli and the bronchi become plugged with a thick, fibrous exudate. Symptoms include severe chills, high fever, headache, cough, and chest pain. Respiration becomes painful, shallow, and rapid. Heartbeat often climbs to 120 or more BPMs. Treatment includes rest, fluids, antibiotics, and oxygen.

Postictal state: The rather drowsy level of consciousness that follows a seizure.

Preemie: Physician slang for a premature infant.

Premature infant: Any baby born before thirty-seven weeks of gestation. Weight is a significant criterion for identifying these high-risk infants who are born with underdeveloped organ systems.

Prenatal: Prior to birth. Something that occurs or exists before birth, referring to the care of the woman during pregnancy and the growth and development of the fetus.

Protamine sulfate: Heparin's specific antagonist—used to diminish or reverse the anticoagulant effects of heparin. Protamine's more serious adverse effects are low blood pressure (hypotension), lowered heart rate (bradycardia), and difficulty in breathing (dyspnea). Dosages larger than needed to neutralize the heparin present can be toxic.

Prothrombin time: A one-step test for detecting plasma coagulation. An elevated prothrombin (PT) time indicates a deficiency in one of the coagulation factors.

Proximal: Nearer the point of reference, usually the trunk of the body.

Pseudocholinesterase: An enzyme in the body that splits succinylcholine into its constituent parts, succinic acid and choline, thus inactivating the drug.

Psychosomatic medicine: The branch of medicine concerned with the interrelationships between mental and emotional reactions and the human body, in particular, the manner in which intrapsychic conflicts influence physical symptoms. Practitioners of psychosomatic medicine maintain that the body and mind are one inseparable entity, and that both physiologic and psychologic techniques should be applied to the study and treatment of illness.

PT time: *See* Prothrombin time.

Radio-immuno assay: A technique in radiology used to determine the blood concentration of an amino acid, antigen, antibody, or other protein.

Radiology: The branch of medicine concerned with radioactive substances and using various techniques of visualization, with the diagnosis and treatment of disease using any of the various sources of radiant energy.

Registered Nurse (RN): A professional nurse who has completed a course of study at a state-approved school of nursing and has passed the National Council Licensing Examination.

Respiration: Part of the breathing process—the molecular exchange of oxygen and carbon dioxide within the body's tissues. (Compare ventilation.)

Respirator: An apparatus used to modify air for inspiration or to improve breathing by means of positive pressure. (Also called a ventilator)

Respiratory arrest: The cessation of breathing.

Resuscitation: The process of sustaining the vital functions of a person in respiratory or cardiac failure while reviving him or her through artificial respiration and cardiac massage, correcting acid-base imbalances, and treating the cause of the failure.

Rubella: A rather mild contagious disease, most dangerous if a woman acquires the disease while pregnant—birth defects result. Symptoms are similar to but less intense than measles, and include fever, malaise, mild upper-respiratory-tract infection, lymph-node enlargement, and a diffuse skin rash.

Sedative: A substance or procedure which has a calming effect.

Seizure: An electrical discharge within the brain that exceeds the normal paths of conductivity, spreading to adjacent areas of the brain. Such abnormal activity can be manifested through various levels of convulsion, staring, lip smacking, or complete limpness.

Sepsis: The uncontrollable spread of poisons from a localized infection.

SIDS: *See* Sudden Infant Death Syndrome.

Sinusitis: An inflammation of one or more of the nasal sinuses, causing pressure, pain, headache, fever, and local tenderness.

Sinus rhythm: There is an area in the heart tissue that generates the cardiac electric impulse in response to signals generated in the medulla, the center of the autonomic nervous system; the pace or rhythm of these impulses determine the BPMs. A "normal sinus rhythm" is between 60 BPMs (below which is bradycardia) and 100 BPMs (above which is tachycardia).

Sodium bicarbonate: An antacid and electrolyte.

Spontaneous: Occurring naturally (as in spontaneous respirations) or without apparent cause (as in spontaneous remission).

STAT: Acronym for Shortest Turn Around Time.

Straight-line: Referring to the flat or straight line on a heart monitor when the heart has ceased beating.

Stridor: An abnormal, high-pitched, musical, respiratory sound (usually heard during inspiration) caused by an obstruction in the trachea or larynx.

Succinylcholine: A chemical compound known as an ester, formed by bonding the alcohol choline and succinic acid—an organic acid. Also known as synthetic curare, succinylcholine is a neuromuscular blocking agent that prevents any nerve impulses from reaching the muscles by interfering with the chemical processes at the motor end plate. Its use results in a flaccid state of paralysis, most useful during surgical procedures to relax and paralyze every muscle in the body completely, including the diaphragm and, when used in large quantities, the heart. It does not, however, affect consciousness. (*See* curare, compare acetylcholine.)

Succs: Slang for succinylcholine.

Sudden Infant Death Syndrome (SIDS): The unexpected and sudden death (usually during sleep) of an apparently normal and healthy infant, leaving no physical or autopsic evidence of disease. The origin of SIDS is unknown even though it is the most common cause of death to infants between two weeks and one year old. The babies at highest risk seem to be the premature offspring of smoking mothers who have recently had a minor illness, such as an upper respiratory infection.

Swan-Ganz catheter: A long, thin cardiac catheter, with a tiny balloon on its tip, which measures the pressure and function of the left ventricle.

Symptom: A subjective indication of a disease or a change in condition as perceived by the patient. (Compare sign.)

Systemic: Referring to the whole body rather than a localized area or portion.

Tachycardia: An abnormal condition in which the heart contracts regularly, but at a rate greater than 100 beats per minute.

Tetanus: Infection with this toxin, one of the most lethal toxins known, is an acute, potentially fatal infection of the central nervous system, which, if unchecked, eventually puts all the muscles of the body into spasm.

Theophylline: A bronchodilator that has been found to be an especially useful stimulant if a child is not breathing adequately, because impulses from the midbrain are impaired.

Tonic: Reflecting a condition in which there is muscle contraction or tonus.

Tonic-clonic: Reflecting a condition in which there are muscle spasms.

Tonoclonic: Reflecting a condition in which there are muscle spasms.

Toxicological screen: A series of tests performed in the laboratory to detect the presence of poisons in blood and tissue samples.

Toxicology: The scientific study of poisons, their detection, their effects, and the best methods of treating the conditions the poisons produce.

Trachea: A nearly cylindrical tube in the neck composed of cartilage and membrane; normally about 11 centimeters long and 2 centimeters wide, it extends from the larynx down to the bronchi of the lungs.

Tracheotomy: An incision made into the trachea through the neck below the larynx to gain access to the airway below a blockage.

Trache-tube: *See* endotracheal tube.

Transducer dome: The part of a heart monitor that converts the heart's contractions into electronic signals that the device can then visualize.

Trauma: Either a physical injury caused by violent or disruptive action (or by the introduction into the body of a toxic substance), or a psychic injury resulting from a severe emotional shock.

Traumatic nursing: One trained in such techniques who can effectively treat injuries resulting from trauma.

Tubal ligation: One of several sterilization procedures in which the fallopian tubes are irreversibly blocked to prevent pregnancy.

Tuberculosis: A chronic infection (usually in the lungs) resulting in listlessness, a vague chest pain, loss of appetite, weight loss, fever, and night sweats.

Ulcer: A circumscribed, craterlike lesion of the skin or mucous membrane resulting from an inflammatory, infectious, or malignant process.

Unconsciousness: A state of complete or partial lack of awareness and the inability to respond to sensory stimuli.

Unilateral: Involving just one side of the body.

Vaccination: Any injection administered to induce immunity, or to reduce the effects of an infectious disease.

Vagal stimulation: Refers to stimulation of the vagus nerve—either of the two cranial nerves essential for speech and swallowing as well as the sensibilities and functions of many parts of the body. The vagus nerves communicate through thirteen main branches that connect to four separate areas of the brain.

Valium: Trade name for an antianxiety agent.

Vasodilation: Widening or distension of the blood vessels, particularly arteries, usually caused by nerve impulses or drugs that relax the smooth muscle which composes the blood vessel's walls.

Ventilation: The process by which gases are moved into and out of the lungs. (Compare respiration.)

Ventilator: An apparatus used to modify air for inspiration or to improve breathing by means of positive pressure. (Also called a *respirator*.)

Ventricle: A small cavity, such as the right or left ventricles of the heart, or one of the cavities in the brain filled with cerebrospinal fluid.

Ventricular arrhythmia: An abnormal condition characterized by a deviation in the normal, rhythmical pattern of heartbeat.

Ventricular asystole: The total lack of heartbeat.

Ventricular fibrillation: A cardiac arrhythmia marked by a complete lack of organized electric impulses and ventricular contraction. Blood pressure falls to zero, resulting in unconsciousness. Defibrillation and ventilation must be initiated immediately or death may result in as little as four minutes.

Virus: A parasitic microorganism, much smaller than a bacterium, that has no independent metabolic activity. To replicate, it uses the energy and raw materials in a cell of a living plant or animal host. More than 200 viruses have been identified as capable of causing disease in humans.

Vital signs: The measurement (and evaluation) of pulse rate, respiration rate, body temperature, and usually, blood pressure.

Whooping cough: *See* pertussis.